M000096489

ONE
TRIBE

M. EVELINA GALANG

New Issues

 WESTERN MICHIGAN UNIVERSITY

ACKNOWLEDGMENTS

I want to thank my tribe—my generous, diverse, opinionated, wise, and very often loud and hungry tribe. Thank you for your contributions to this work—you may not have known it, but you have helped me through this great process.

For every time I ran through the neighborhood yelling, "MIKEMANNYMYRNAMARCMARCEL! TIME TO EAT!" You are my first experience in tribalism. I love you guys.

To my 1996 FASA Crew at ODU—for your openness, your stories, your good humor and your dedication to honoring our presence in American history. You got me started on this tale.

To Sara Kristina San Juan. Thank you for your honesty and your courage.

To my current crews at UM—FSA and Screaming Monkeys—thanks for being such a light in the midst of all this writing. Let your spoken words be heard—and honored.

And to my friends and colleagues—for your amazing support, your careful readings and your challenges, gentle and otherwise. Thank you, Tara Agtarap, Cyd Apellido, Lisa Boyle, Karen Campion, Julia Carino, Gaytana Carrino, Daniel Chacón (four times!), Jane Davis, Oliver de La Paz, Denise Duhamel, Liam Durnan, Anida Yoeu Esguerra, Marlon Unas Esguerra, José Grave de Peralta, Kay Gustin, Tassie Gwilliam, Barbara Haas, Luba Halicki, Hugh Haller, Maxine Hong-Kingston, Jesse Lee Kercheval, Geeta Kothari, Dayna Lee, Don Lee, R. Zamora Linmark, Manuela Mourão, Renee Oleander, Judith Ortiz-Cofer, Ranen Omer-Sherman, Janet Peery, Karen Piconi, Bino A.

Realuyo, Luis Rodriguez, Mariana Romo-Carmona, Maureen Seaton, Ali Selim, Heather Sellers, Andrea Slane, Mihoko Suzuki, Eileen Tabios, Pearl Ubungen, Anthony Vigil, Marie Villanueva, Helena Viramontes, and to my crew at Yoga Grove.

To Nick Carbó, for every time you asked, "Evelina, is it done yet?"

To Ninotchka Rosca, for inspiring. Yes, I am wearing bangles. Yes, my suitcase has wheels. And yes, I am saying yes to the universe. Thanks.

To the Lannan Foundation, the Ragdale Foundation, the Illinois Arts Council, the Iowa State Faculty Summer Grant Program, the University of Miami, and to the Dominador and Loreto Galang Kingston New York Summer Retreat—for granting me time, space, and money to write six drafts.

To every grad student at Goddard College, The School of the Art Institute, Iowa State University and the University of Miami who has taken my seminar on The Shape and Substance of the Book. Thank you for your intellectual discourse, your resistance, and your tenacity. Sorry if I scared you with the suitcase of drafts.

To my peers at Colorado State University who read the seeds of this work in workshop and said, "This is not a short story—it's more like the outline for a novel."

To Gizelle Galang Jacobs, for helping me get it together.

To Laura Kina and her vision. Thank you for the artwork. Talagang, WOW!

For the face of Claire Martinez—Talagang, wow na wow! And the doodles of Gayle Mendoza.

To Rigoberto Gonzales and Elizabeth McCracken for choosing *One Tribe*—thank you.

To The Association of Writers & Writing Programs and New Issues Poetry & Prose, thank you.

And to Miguel and Gloria Galang, for everything.

Maraming salamat po!

for Miguel, Manuel, Myrna, Marcial, and Marcelino—
members of my Original Tribe

ONE

On the seventh day of her new job, Isabel Manalo created the world.

"Quietly," she whispered to her first grade class. They sat cross-legged in perfect rows, little cabbages planted on a brown area rug. Some sat on their heels and rocked to their own internal clock. Boys to the left. Girls to the right. They kept their hands to themselves. She held out her arms. "Let's get into a circle."

No one moved. She crawled on the floor and looked into their faces. She was used to the Midwest, where Germans and Poles and Swiss had settled and everyone was a shade of beige and every head was a variation of blond—dishwater, strawberry, yellow flaxen and gold. But today she didn't see her students sitting in front of her; she saw versions of herself—brown children with apple cheeks, black moons for eyes, and wide smiles.

"No, really," she whispered. "Get up off those butts. I'm the teacher. It's okay."

The children rose to their feet, stretching as if waking from a long nap. When she danced around them, they stared at her, a little startled. "Come on," she said, tugging at their sleeves, "we're going to make a play." She started them off jumping like kangaroos, stomping wildly like dragons, crawling like caterpillars, then falling like snowflakes, like stardust, like rain. This was the warm-up. At first the jumping kangaroos were more like walking dead. The stomping dragons tiptoed silently until she ran after them, yelling, "Fee-Fi-Fo-Fum!"

"That's a giant!" someone shouted. "Not a dragon!" Then they all screamed together, "Fee-Fi-Fo-Fum!" The children walked with their feet spread wide apart, and they growled and stormed their way off the carpet and onto the gymnasium floor.

She had them whisper like wind and then she had them shout like thunder. "Spin!" she commanded, raising her hands. "Spin like twenty-two hurricanes!" She spun her own body in circles and watched the lights hanging from the ceiling blur. She let her body move with the momentum, swung her arms around her torso. She could feel the first graders turning too, bumping into her legs and finally understanding the game. "Twenty-two hurricanes swooping down Virginia Beach!"

She closed her eyes and continued spinning, the room and the children circling her. They were laughing now. Their shadows chased across the gymnasium walls. Shoes squeaked and burned on polished wood. Their reflections dappled the bricks, shimmering like water. "Faster!" she called out. "Faster!"

Then suddenly a door slammed shut. A whistle blew. Harsh and angry hands clapped. "Children. Stop. Where is your teacher?"

The children froze in their places. She felt the weight of several children who had fallen on top of her. She peered from under her sleeve and saw Andrea Calhoun standing with her arms crossed, her old neck bent forward, scanning all of them. "Where did your teacher go?"

"I'm right here," Isabel said. "It's okay."

Andrea Calhoun wrinkled her brows. Squinted. "Ms. Manalo?"

"It's all part of the drama," Isabel told her. "Everything's fine."

"Right. I didn't see you," said Calhoun. "I thought . . . well, they seemed . . . Right. Don't let me interrupt."

Isabel felt her face go red. Breathing hard, she crawled out from under a pile of children and escorted Calhoun from the room. "Be still as mice!" she told the kids.

"I had a hard time warming them up," she said to Calhoun.

"Will they always be this loud?"

Isabel's throat was dry. "Sometimes. Is that a problem?" She looked over her shoulder at the children, no longer still as mice. "I'd better go," she said, not waiting for an answer.

Back in the room, she split the children into two teams. Sky against the Sea. Half the children held hands, swarming and curling as if they were the tide. The sky children waved banners of blue crêpe high above their heads.

"Are you in trouble?" asked a little boy.

"No. I am not." She spread her arms out and let the fringe of her colorful poncho hang in the air. "Now listen or you will be in trouble. I am a bird," Isabel cawed. She flapped her arms and the poncho flew into the air. "And the Sea team is water and the Sky team, you are the big blue sky!" She flew above the children who were rolling on the floor, back and forth, here and there, rumbling loud as surf. She maneuvered her wings about the banners of noisy tissue paper. And after awhile she sighed, "I'm so tired. I need a place to rest." She scanned the children still rolling about like waves in the sea and, seeing no land, she said, "Where shall I rest?"

"You have to find an island!" a little girl yelled.

"Land in a tree!"

"Land on a rock!"

But there were only two teams—Sky and Sea—and there were no islands, no trees, no rocks. The Sea children wrapped their fingers about Isabel's ankles. Then the Sky children tugged at the fringe on Isabel's poncho. Somebody tickled a flag under her nose. The bird feigned a sneeze.

"Let go!" she yelled. "Let me rest!" But they continued to hold her captive and, finally, the bird began to cry.

And then she had an idea. The bird whispered to the sea of children, "The sky no longer loves you." She sang to the flags of blue crêpe paper, "Ocean called you ugly." Outraged, the sea unraveled its fingers from her ankles and she was free to run. The sky raised its banners in fury and conjured up storms and hurricanes and black thunderclouds. The children swung their arms in wide circles and spun like tornados, raining lightning from their angry sky fists. "That's it!" Isabel called out. "Toss thunderbolts into the Sea!"

"You have to toss them really fast!" yelled a boy hurling lightning at the sea. "Cuz they're hot and they burn!"

The team of Sea children cowered as they imagined bolts of light being flung into their faces. "Oh yeah?" called a Sea child. "Take this!" Isabel rose to her knees and waved her arms at the boy with the blue banner. And then the other Sea children waved their arms too. The sea

7

rose high and higher, crawling onto its knees and finally standing on its feet, spewing water up into the sky's scowling, bitter face. The waves ripped the tissues of blue sky into tiny pieces. And then the sky threw paper rocks and cardboard boulders onto the floor. This surprised everyone, especially the sea, which calmed under the weight of the rocks. So the thrashing of water died, leaving the sky to herself. The rocks rooted themselves to the earth, settled their bodies among the seas and formed seven thousand islands. And the bird rested her wings among the rocks, settled on a hill and found herself a home at last.

That night, the Tidewater community threw a Back to School party at the Philippine Cultural Center. Isabel was the guest of honor.

A montage of hands flew at her like a dream, one after the other. She felt like a politician, nodding, smiling, uttering yes, yes, yes. "Thank you," she said, and "I wasn't aware of that." Faces faded one into the other. "Finally you are here," someone told her. "You will be the role model for the children." Some pulled her aside and whispered, "You are the answer. Now you will fix it."

Fix what, she wondered. She was a drama teacher.

Everyone looked so familiar, like relatives in old photos. Every young man looked like her brother Frankie, every old lady like a version of her Lola Dee, her mother's mother. And the way they talked to her, shooting words and hardly waiting for answers, reminded her of family gatherings.

"How old are you, hija?" asked an old man.

"Thirty-two, po," she answered. He was an old-timer, a very little man with skin as dark as coffee, and thick white hair.

"And already a teacher! Naku! Your parents must be proud."

"Ay, honey," said a woman with a face painted in powder and heavy red blush. She kissed Isabel's cheek and asked, "Wala pang asawa?"

Isabel fiddled with the zoom on her camera, twisting its lens in and out. She was dying to shoot some photos, place the lens between her and these crazy conversations.

"Leave her alone, Wilma," said Tito Romy. "She's gotta work for us and help da kids. How she gonna do that if she's married?"

"Welcome, welcome," said Mayor Wexford. He patted her on the back and leaned into her. "We're hoping to see great things from you."

Isabel grabbed a paper plate, escaped the barrage of voices by standing in line for food. Platters of noodles decorated an entire table. She smiled when she saw Arturo Sanchez serving pansit. He was a boy lean with muscle, and his hair had been shaved to reveal a perfectly round head. Arturo had rolled up the sleeves of his oversized T-shirt. On his left arm, the light caught a thick black-ink tattoo. She recognized the letter from the Filipino alphabet. On skin the color of earth, the tattoo marked the boy like royalty. His mother stood next to him, pointing. "Make sure you get all the noodles. Mix from the bottom, anak," she told him. "Naku, not like that." She took the large metal spoon from him, pushed him aside, throwing her whole body into the work. "So the top doesn't get dry, hijo." She handed the spoon back, and with her hand on his shoulder watched him try. "Yan, that's it. Like that."

"Hello, Arturo," said Isabel. "Did you cook?" She held her plate out as he dished her a large helping of noodles.

"Eat pansit so you live long and healthy among us," said the woman.

Arturo pointed to his mother. "Mommy has a restaurant at the beach."

Mrs. Sanchez winked. "You met already?"

"I haven't met with Arturo's class yet," Isabel said, shaking the woman's hand. "But Arturo and some of the boys helped me unload my truck last week."

"Oo nga," said the mother, "Arturo said he met your parents. Did they go back, na?"

"Yes, Mrs. Sanchez. They flew back last Sunday."

"Anak, call me Tita Chic Chic." She leaned over the table and sniffed Isabel's cheeks. "In this place, we are family."

"Ms. Manalo's mommy makes a dope tinola," Arturo said. He waved to another boy and his tattoo looped and swirled like a black hurricane on legs. She made a note to research Tagalog script. "Right, Miguelito?" he said. "That was some dope chicken soup!"

"Yeah, it was," Miguel called back. "Wassup, Ms. Manalo?" The boy leaned over and kissed her cheek. "Take our picture!" He ran to the other side of the table and stood between Arturo and Tita Chic Chic, wrapping them both in his long arms.

Isabel held the camera up and looked through the lens, at the landscape of their bodies close and fitted like a range of love. Miguel made his eyes big like he was surprised and he smiled. Shifting the focus, she waited for the crosshairs to mark them and then she shot. Flash! "Thank you!" they chimed together.

In Evanston, where she grew up, people were formal. There was no kissing-kissing everyone on the cheek. And adults were doctor this or missus that. A tita didn't have to be your aunt by blood, but she was a close family friend. So this was new to Isabel, and she found it comforting in a way she had not expected.

"You're such a pig," said Elliot North. He gestured with a plastic fork at the glazed lechon sprawled on all fours, stretching its roasted head to the room's fluorescent lights. Elliot shook the hair out of his eyes. He was lean and tanned from the beach. His hair was bleached and messy. He reminded her of a blond Elvis. Looking around at the people next to him, Elliot elbowed an elder of the community, "Get it, he's a pig?" The old man looked at him, confused and somewhat irritated. "That's lechon," the old man said. "Pig."

"Give it up, Mr. North," said Arturo, laughing. "When you gonna realize you neva funny?"

"Tough crowd," Elliot answered, brushing hair out of his eyes. He stood next to her with his feet thrown apart, his left hip out of line with the rest of his body.

"Kid's right," she said. She smiled at him. "What do you teach again?"

"Earth Science." He popped an egg roll in his mouth. "I love this stuff. You teaching too?"

"Yup."

"That's cool," Elliot said. "And you're from Chicago?" He grabbed a piece of toasted pig skin from the table, held it up to the light and examined it before he popped that in his mouth too.

"Evanston. Just north of Chicago. So is this weird for you?" she asked him.

"What?"

"This Filipino culture stuff?" She gestured at the crowd and at the stage, where a Pinoy band dressed in black tuxedos and golden cummerbunds played everything from Filipino love songs to Captain and Tennille.

"You kidding me? I've been living and teaching in this community for almost ten years. These are my peeps!"

Up front, children were dancing with lights and bamboo sticks, coconut shells and brightly colored fans. Elliot glanced over his shoulder and said, "Excuse me, these are my kids. I'm gonna check them out."

At the edge of one table simmered a pot kids called chocolate meat—dinuguan, blood stew. She smelled the vinegar, the chili pepper. Stirring the pot, she watched the small pieces of meat swimming in thick gravy. The fragrance of ginger and garlic made her picture her mother cooking at home.

A small-boned woman with a wide painted smile kissed her on each cheek like they had known each other forever. "Sweetheart, you're so beautiful," she said. "I can't believe you're not married yet." She waved her hand in the air, and called to her child, "Anak, come here." She leaned over and whispered, "I'm Anita Starr, Tita Nita. I want you to meet my daughter. She's gonna love you." She ran her hands through Isabel's hair. "Look at you!" she said. "What do they call you?"

"Isabel." She took a step away. Tita Nita smelled of heavy perfume and nicotine. Isabel pulled her camera strap over her shoulder.

"That's so long. What's your nickname? Isa?"

She hated that nickname. "Bel," she answered.

"That's too American," Tita Nita said. "I'm gonna call you Isa." Then, waving her arms, she screamed, "Anak, where are you? I said I'm calling you!"

"Mrs. Starr—"

"Anak, call me Tita Nita!"

"Okay. Tita, what kind of trouble are they talking about?" Tita Nita smiled as if she hadn't heard her. "With the kids, I mean."

"What kids? Not ours. Our kids are good. They just need a role model like you to show them the way." She smiled again at Isabel and then called out for her daughter.

That's so weird, Isabel thought. She gulped her water down and looked through the crowd. Bodies swam left and right, and then a small pathway opened up and she saw one of the girls sauntering toward her. It was the girl with eyes blue as stained glass. She wore hip-huggers that widened into big bells of black Spandex. Five-inch heels lifted the girl's small body up off the ground so that she appeared to be floating right at Isabel. Her belly ring slipped in and out from underneath a cropped T-shirt. When she reached Isabel, Tita Nita put both arms around the girl and squeezed her tight. "This is my daughter," she said. "Lourdes Starr. She's gonna be a senior this year and her daddy is an American. Louie Starr." She pointed across the room, to a guy sitting at a table by himself. He looked like an unkempt version of Dean Martin. Tita Nita reminded Isabel of her own Auntie Baby, a well-meaning misguided tita. "My Lourdes is gonna learn a lot from you."

Isabel smiled at Lourdes. "We've met. Hi, Lourdes."

Lourdes mumbled a greeting, her eyes shifting back and forth. When Isabel's cat was held against his will, his ears winged backed and his haunches rose up like furry shoulders. That's what Lourdes looked like, she thought, only not as sweet. The daughter crawled out of her mother's embrace. She smiled in a way that Isabel could not read. Flipping her hair back, Lourdes turned and strutted back to her homegirls.

Lourdes hated her. Isabel was sure of it. Then again, when she thought of the week she had moved to town, she remembered that Lourdes hated everybody.

*

Isabel's parents had just pulled into Virginia. They were climbing out of the truck when they saw a group of teenagers walking toward them. The kids wore denim and corduroy pants three sizes too big. Their bums rode right out of the seat, and their legs were drowning in curtains of fabric. Their bodies were lost in T-shirts and flannel—pieces of clothing they must have acquired from their fathers' closets. Every now and then, a gesture of bone, or shoulder blade, or slope of spine peeked out from somewhere inside their shirts. They crowned themselves in backward baseball caps. Some of them wore the brim to the side of their heads. One boy had a bandana tied around his shaved skull. The girls, on the other hand, wrapped their bodies in clothing tight as skin. They approached the Manalos on platform shoes, walking awkwardly as cats on ice. One of the girls tripped, but recovered quickly.

Isabel held her breath. Oh, she thought, they're scary. These are the kids you wanna be when you're in high school, the kind of kids you'd never be, she told herself.

The teenagers stopped just ahead of them. A girl draped herself around a boy. Two other boys play-punched each other in slow-motion. They etched the empty space between them precisely as Tai Chi masters. A second girl stood next to the group, arms crossed, head thrown back. A cascade of hair wild as seaweed ran down her skinny back. This girl, half Pinay, half Caucasian, was the color of pine nuts glazed in honey, and her eyes were a shiny blue—real blue, Virgin Mary blue. She stepped away. She was too cool. Indifferent. The rest laughed and talked at their friend:

"Sup wit choo?" said one boy.

"Girl—come on now. Don't act like that."

Like a dancer in a music video, she spun her body away from them. Strutted.

"Lourdes, why you wiggin' out like dat?"

"Mercedes been waitin' at the beach," she said. "I gotta page her."

They called after the girl in a cool and lazy language. One boy threw his hands up and said, "Whatever." Then, simultaneously, the group turned and sauntered away, letting Lourdes wander off to wherever she pleased.

*

Isabel held her camera to her eye. It's all an act, she thought. A way to keep the world out of your face. A way to keep moving when everyone else lets you down. Now she was thinking about her own life, about Mark and how they would have been married by now. She scanned the room, looking for a shot. The world was small and dark in her lens.

From a corner of the hall, a beautiful ivory Madonna watched.

Next to Her, Lourdes's homegirls leaned against the walls like ladies in waiting. Their faces were painted. Black eyeliner, red lipstick, hair teased into perfect cones. As Lourdes reached them, they whistled and whooped. They howled. Isabel spun the lens, made the images crisp, grabbed them.

The lens wandered into forbidden spaces. Sometimes the zoom distorted the faces before her. She rotated the lens, watched the bodies go soft, melting together like confusion. She liked marking her target and capturing it in a flash. Flash! And the little bulb illuminated the world. Flash! And she had stolen the moment. Flash! Frame. Flash! Isabel shot and the world was hers.

In the darkroom she'd conjure up this community, find the shapes of Lourdes and Tita Chic Chic and the old-timers bleeding from sheets of glossy paper.

*

She had wanted to shoot them on the first day they met because they were the image of cool. The girls had come over with the guys when they unloaded her truck. Mercedes, Lourdes and Marilena hung out of the mouth of the truck's rear, their feet dangling in the air, the heels of their platforms clicking together in sync. They muttered things to the boys as they climbed in and out of the back. "Sup, mahal?" cooed Mercedes. "Why don't cha take a break?"

"Oo nga," Marilena agreed. "Di ka pagod, pare?"

During the pandemonium, the boys laughed and yelled to each other in a language Isabel could not understand. Finally, she asked the girls, "Is that some kind of Filipino dialect?" They looked at her, unmoved.

"Yeah," Lourdes said, swinging her legs off the back of the truck. She reached down and picked at the polish on her toes. "It's called Pinglish—Pinoy English."

The girls burst into a song of giggling. "Oh yeah?" Isabel said. "Pinglish?"

When Camila called everyone to sit among the boxes with Styrofoam bowls of steaming chicken soup, the boys claimed a corner of the tiny beach bungalow. They settled down as comfortable as house cats.

"Kain na," Camila called the girls, climbing down the steps of the porch. "Hoy—mga dalagas—halika na. Kain na tayo."

"Ay, salamat Auntie. Pero hindi ako pwede. Inaantay ako ng nanay ko."

"Ako din, po," said Lourdes. She smiled at Camila, her eyes sparkling like the deep blue sea.

Their conversation was fast and complete. Isabel strained to keep up, but the words tumbled quickly out of their mouths. She looked over her shoulder at the sea, listened to the rhythm of the waves, counted to ten. Breathed. "It's getting late," she mumbled.

"Okay," Camila said. "Maybe next time. Okay?"

Isabel draped her arm around her mother and the two of them watched the girls strut to their car, their platforms clicking against cement driveway like bamboo clapping in a round of tinikling.

"You never taught us Tagalog," Isabel said.

"In those days we thought it would confuse you," her mother said.

When she was little, the adults stayed up late talking Tagalog. Their conversations rolled around the room like tidewater and lulled her to sleep. But that day, among the teens, she'd hear them talking with her parents and every time they broke into it, she felt odd. Like she knew this was her house and these were her parents—but somehow she was the intruder and the teens were the ones who belonged. It was as if they were part of some secret sorority, complete with handshakes and passwords. Pinglish my ass, she thought.

*

On the other side of the hall, directly facing the statue of Mama Mary, was a rattan throne with a back that bloomed up and out like beautiful palm leaf. And placed in the center of the throne was a girl in a silver beaded crown, her hair stacked in curls and her face painted like a porcelain doll. Her dress was a traditional Maria Clara spun of white lace and piña fibers. When Isabel first saw the girl, she thought she was a statue, sitting alone in a corner of the hall, mirroring the stillness of

Mama Mary. She raised her camera to shoot the statue, a wax figure in a hall of colorful beings, and as she zoomed in the statue sneezed. "Who is that?" she asked Elliot.

"That's the royalty," he said smiling. "Miss Virginia Beach-Philippines 1995. She's reigning. Do you want to meet her?"

"Maybe later," Isabel whispered back. The queen teen haunted her, painted up like one of those tragic clowns. She wondered why Miss Virginia Beach-Philippines was sitting all alone. She panned the camera to the other side of the room and framed a shot through the crowd. There she found an image of the Blessed Virgin with all the rest of the girl teens grooming themselves like a litter of kittens, seemingly unaware of their adoring public. A larger girl caught her looking and pointed her out. In a chorus, they looked at Isabel and then they turned their backs to her. She shot the picture anyway. Elliot's right, she thought, it's a very tough crowd. She zoomed in and caught them looking over their shoulders, tossing dirty looks, posturing like they didn't care. She braced herself. Held her breath. So what, she thought. Who cares?

The lead singer in the band shouted, "It's Electric!" and uncles, aunties and children, school board members and teachers alike leapt to the floor. They lined up, row after row and together they moved. Line-dancing. Filipino style. She thought it was funny how everyone jumped in, even the tough girls. Their hips hesitated and then swung as they pumped their shoulders to the beat. Their attitude was cold—tight lips, bored faces, hair sleek and bobbed at the chin.

Out on the dance floor, an older man directed the crowd. He was John Travolta in *Saturday Night Fever,* but old and Pinoy. Isabel ran to the front of the room and framed him in her lens. The room glowed red and he filled her frame, dressed in black satin from head to toe. Even his hair had been dyed and greased off his face to give him that smooth satiny look. Dangling from his open shirt, a thick gold chain shifted like a pendulum on an old grandfather clock. He was the master. The electric of electric slide. "With glamour!" he told them proudly, waving his arms out to them. Isabel captured the frame. "Do it with glamour!" he sang out.

She stood on stage and shot a series of wide shots, caught the community slipping back and forth like the current at high tide. Then, scooting her body from the platform, she marked the steps in place, shifting right, then left, dipping her hips when she bent her knees.

Every family gathering she had ever been to had a moment like this—a giant timeout when whatever fight you were having with whatever family member stopped, when the horns blared out against electric drums and the disco ball shined bright like a Las Vegas moon. The only difference was that in her world she was related to all the dancers.

A man, squat and sturdy as a pit bull, approached her. When she looked up he was smiling at her, one gold tooth shimmering against the disco ball. He held up a finger and whispered, "You don't know how hard we worked to get you here. There's so much to be done." He placed his hand on her shoulder.

Isabel pulled away from him. "Don't tell me," she said. "Ferdi Mamaril?" They had warned her about him. He was a community activist, a fanatic.

The man nodded. "We are all related, you know. We all are blood. Pinoy forever!" he yelled, throwing his fist up into the air. "What d'you teach today?" he asked her.

"The creation myth."

"The one about the bird?" He swung his hips to the music. She danced away from him, hoping he wouldn't be offended. "Or the one about Malakas and Maganda?" She laughed nervously. Was he for real? "You know the Pinoy version of Adam and Eve?"

"I know," she said. "We did the one with the bird."

"I'm into educating the kids too—but none of that island mentality shit cuz we Americans now and the youths gotta know we Pinoy have contributed to America's history."

She nodded at him and pointed the camera at the band. She focused on the middle-aged men with pomade-greased hair, at the way they cradled their electric guitars, all shiny gold glitter. She waited a long time before she shot the picture, hoping Ferdi would walk away. "Why you always taking pictures?" he asked her.

"I don't know," she answered him. "It's my hobby. So you're a teacher too?" she asked.

"Naw," he said, shaking his shoulders to the beat. "I'm a nurse. I just educate the youths for a hobby." He stepped away from her, a bad disco dancer, stuck in the groove of a severely scratched record. "Pinoy forever, sista!" he called again.

"Right," she answered as she walked away. "Pinoy forever." She slipped back to the tables of food. Stuffing another fried lumpia into her mouth, she heard another voice. A guy her age stood before her, his own plate filled with lumpia and pansit. Unlike the others, who were bathed in cologne, and shaven, this one was unkempt, his hair dancing in and out of his eyes. He had a beaded choker around his neck and was burnt from the sun. He wore a T-shirt. Not very tall, but he was lean and Isabel couldn't help but smile. "Pinoy's another word for Filipino," he said, raising his fist to the air and clenching his jaw.

"I know," Isabel answered him. "Are you mocking that guy?"

"Maybe."

She turned away and leaned her body up against a wall, two feet away from Mother Mary's shrine. Pretending he wasn't there, she spun noodles on her plate. She could feel him standing there, watching. She could hear him breathing. They exchanged glances.

"Something the matter?" Isabel asked. "Food on my face?"

"Naw," he answered. "When d'you arrive?"

"Recently."

"Adjusting?"

She felt flushed. She put her foot up against the wall, made a feeble attempt to look cool.

"It's different here, huh?" he said, moving closer to her.

"Different?"

"Than where you come from." His name was JoJo and he said his niece was in her class. "She talks about you. Sez you're all about teaching 'em how to be Pinoy."

"No," Isabel said. "Not how to be Pinoy—more like lessons on Filipino history and myth." She held her camera out to him and asked, "Mind if I shoot you?"

He shrugged, muttered, "Whatever." He was the one the boys told her about. The one who was supposed to be so cool. Kuya JoJo Reyes. Isabel held the lens up and even though they were only three feet apart, she stepped closer and zoomed into the pores of skin; he was brown, burnt like toast. She let the camera roam the landscape of his face, explore a tiny line of scars along his chin. He had dimples on either side of his closed-mouth smile. She snapped the lens out so she could see the way his hair shattered around his face and shoulders. His eyes darted back and forth between the strands of hair; they were the shape of almonds but large. He slipped a lit cigarette into his mouth and took a long slow drag. Then he pulled the cigarette out and, not looking away, blew smoke out the side of his mouth. He was daring her.

"Cuz you know, you can't teach that stuff. You just are." He took another drag from his smoke. "Or you're not."

Isabel raised an eyebrow at him.

"Filipino," he said. "You gonna take the picture or what?" He danced his body close, right there at the egg roll table, right next to Mother Mary. "I changed my mind," he said, pulling the camera away from her and staring her down. "Don't shoot."

She reached for her water, took a step away. What an ass, she thought. JoJo tugged her arm, whispered, "You know what they call our teens? At risk. You know what that's about?"

She was about to answer him, feeling a little weak, a little irritated, when the speakers spat loud and abrasive into the air.

Uncle Romy stood up at the microphone, blowing into it, tapping it and saying, "This on? Hello, this on?" Tito Romy welcomed everybody to the new school year. He thanked the school officials for coming, he honored some young Republican guy for "supporting our Filipino-American youth" and then he introduced Isabel to the community. He went on to tell them how lucky the children were to have a mentor like Isabel—a "beautiful, elegant, and smart Filipina American." The room echoed with his voice as he shouted into the microphone. The speakers squeaked with feedback, electricity gone bad. "The problem with kids today," he yelled, "is that they don't listen anymore to their parents, don't behave. You think you know better, when what you kids don't realize is that we love you, and we say what we say so you will live better lives. So I want you to listen to Ms. Manalo. Pay attention, take advantage of her wisdom. Don't give her trouble. Because soon we will be too old, too tired to watch over you and you will be adults, the citizens of this community. You will be the leaders and you must be prepared."

She was horrified. When she looked around the room, she saw adults nodding and clapping as Tito Romy took a breath. The teens weren't looking at him but at each other. Or they stared at the floor and crossed their arms. She was sure they were not listening. Then he asked her to say a few words. Her tongue felt fat and thick. She was parched. Nodding, she drank a big glass of water and chewed on an ice cube before she made her way to the stage.

"Welcome to Virginia Beach!" JoJo yelled above the clapping.

Isabel climbed the stage, where Miss Virginia Beach-Philippines greeted her with a bouquet of roses and a kiss on each cheek. She felt like she had landed on another planet where everyone around her looked familiar but was definitely alien. She looked into the teen queen's face and thanked her, felt her own stomach sinking when she realized how tired and haggard the beauty queen appeared up close. A thousand clapping hands brought her back to the crowd. She smiled at the audience, took note of the teens in the back of the room, how they leaned on each other, and looked at her askance. The aunties and uncles wore painted smiles, looked hopeful. She realized this was only the beginning.

She tried to explain that, growing up in Evanston, she and her brother and sister were islands floating among classmates who were mostly White Anglo-Saxon or Jewish. She never knew what it was to walk among Pinoy—to utter Tagalog slang in school. "You don't know how lucky you are," she said. She envied that they had friends who shared so much with them. In Virginia children weren't islands. They were the oceans, bodies of water so large and so full, so tumultuous, that no one, not even the administration, could ignore them. "You are so lucky to have each other. And I feel lucky to be here." As she spoke, she felt the movement in the back of the room. She heard the pounding of clogs and platform shoes collide with her words. Ten girls exited the room. She worked hard to ignore their departure, tried not to focus on the echo rising from their shoes. She took a long drink of water. A little stream fell from the cup and ran down her chin. Breathe, she told herself. She shifted her weight and thanked the principal, the school board, and her colleagues for making her move so easy. "I just got here and I've already got two communities—the Filipino-American community and the Virginia Beach Public School System."

Afterwards, she sat away from all the commotion and shot photos of the crowd swarming the dance floor. Samba filled the room, shined from the band's tin speakers. Bodies swirled fast with color—gold scarves and chiffon skirts sailed, brown hands flew up and flared like Spanish fans. Painted lips, wild and red, blurred to the beat. The singer belted out his version of "Torro, torro." Along the walls, members of the school board sat in folding chairs, their stillness framing the wildness of the dancers. Elliot tapped his toes on the upbeat.

Tito Romy held his wife, Wilma, and waltzed her around the ballroom. Isabel followed them along the edge of the dance floor, the lens close to her eye, waiting for a moment that she recognized. They were an elegant couple, and Wilma's chiffon skirt shifted across the parquet like a rush of water. At one point he spun her in circles and Isabel could see the silver slippers on Wilma's little feet. She racked the lens and sharpened the image, holding her finger over the trigger. He whispered something into the curve of her neck and they both collapsed into one another, laughing. Though they were in their sixties, the couple reminded Isabel of teenagers at prom. Click, rewind, click, Isabel stole the moment. Her heart ached for her own parents.

Nearby, JoJo watched her. "Overwhelmed?" he asked.

"No."

"Got your work cut out for you, ha?" He tipped his head back and blew cigarette smoke into the air. When she dismissed him, he nodded at her and left.

What the hell, she thought, watching his reflection in the mirror. He strutted away, his hips rocking back and forth, his feet shuffling to the beat of bongo drums. She hated that he was so smug. More than that, she hated that she felt anything at all.

She was a tourist in a foreign land, a camera around her neck, a Tagalog-English dictionary open in front of her. For awhile, she closed her eyes and listened. Heard the tongues around her whisper like the soft rattle of maracas shaking fast and syncopated on the downbeat. She was thinking of places like Chicago, like Kansas, like Milwaukee, Wisconsin. She was picturing her family at a community event. That asshole's right, she thought: she's never been to anything like this before.

Elliot North crossed the dance floor, bobbing his head and waving his hands completely out of sync with the music. "You okay?" he called. His mouth hung open like a giant cake donut. She laughed.

"There's a name for people like you," she said.

"Yeah," he said, grabbing her hand, "the word is cool." He pulled her up off the folding chair. "Do you know this one?" They whirled their way into the crowd. The bass drum beat loud, so loud she thought it came from inside her, and before she knew it she was swinging her hips, spinning in circles, making cha-cha on a dance floor of Pinoys. She shut her eyes and imagined she was dancing underneath a full moon, a tent of silvers stars winking at her, not here on the floor of this gymnasium.

TWO

Between the tunnels that connected the land and the peninsula, girls attached their bodies to the underpass like spiders crawling up a wall. The rumble of trucks, the whir of tires spinning fast on asphalt, and the wind floated down and drowned beneath the underpass, bled into the bay. Fireworks popped like shooting guns. In the girls' hands, spray cans emitted a fierce red, a cold blue, yellow and a white, light as the first layer of snow. Each girl worked on a section—scales of the fishtail, slope of the hips, brown breasts and nipples dark as chocolate, hair that swam long and black as floating seaweed. Together they tagged the underpass in Alibata, in English, in unison—Las Dalagas. Pinay forever. Forever Pinay.

When the ringing woke Isabel at two in the morning, she knew it was bad. She could tell from the tightness in her belly. She leapt from sleep, her long arm reaching for the phone.

"Hello?"

She didn't recognize the voice, though she could tell by the tone that something was really wrong. "Who died?" she wanted to know.

"A child," said the voice. "He was pretty young."

"Who?" She was afraid the night and this new environment were playing tricks on her.

"One of the boys."

"What," she said, "one of the boys?"

"Afraid so."

Her body shivered and she pulled the cotton sheets around herself.

Outside, the crash of water hitting sand confused her.

"It's me, Andrea Calhoun," said the voice. "From school. Are you awake, Isabel? Are you all right?"

In less than a minute, Isabel was grieving. Tears flowed so fast, she began to hiccup. The hiccups interrupted the beating of her heart. Now she skipped a breath. Now she sighed long and low. She felt grief come over her like waves washing her out to sea—lost and wet and completely overwhelmed.

*

Two years ago Isabel misplaced her baby. Miscarried it so that it skipped certain critical stages of development. The fetus had grown a tiny sleeping face. Its mouth had been set into a grin—as if it were enjoying a dream. And crying, "Uppy, Mama, uppy,"he or she came to grow two long and slender arms flung out in opposite directions. What the baby didn't grow were legs. The child had a trunk that loomed out into his or her ten digits—toes woven together by a membrane thin as spider webs. He or she, her baby, had grown into a semi-human/semi-tadpole. Its fin-like leg kicked inside her, begged for two legs, two feet, ten perfect toes. There was nothing she could do. She tried herbs and special teas. She sought out wise women—a healer and a high priestess. She implored the Mother Mary to intercede. But nothing. And one night she woke because the kicking stopped. The baby gave up and floated out of Isabel's body.

She still dreamed of the unborn baby. Her water baby swam in a maze of large and small intestines. Negotiated its way about the blood vessels, the blue veins, the forest of muscles and tissue woven together like a pretty braid. She saw hands tiny as specks of dust groping for her uterus. But the baby only found its way to a kidney, a bladder, a chamber of the heart—no place to grow a baby. No place to be certain. So the baby had to choose. And what were the options? You can have a set of hands, two beautiful arms complete with biceps, deltoids, and triceps, a chest and a big fat belly—not to mention a trunk, a leg, a tail and webbed feet. And you can be born to this world a special child, anomaly child, a child of challenge. Or you can try again, come back later with legs and arms, a torso, head, shoulders, a perfect set of vertebrae, deep-set almond

24

eyes, hair like silk—the works. You could slip into the world like the rest—healthy and unremarkable. What'll it be? Womb or land, spirit child or baby thing, heaven or earth? What kind of choice is that?

*

The rest of the night was lost. She could not find her way to sleep. When she closed her eyes she saw the ghost of a boy who died in a trance of happiness—among his friends, among the boom-boom-pop of his homies' bass, of rapture, of ecstasy and of escape. When she opened her eyes to lose the image of the boy, she heard the child's mother, wailing, dying, shrieking at God and all the angels. So she got up and walked through the house, closing windows, and shutting doors that had slipped wide open. That's when she felt her baby's spirit floating next to her, swimming alongside of her in the unforgiving blackness of night. That's when she realized this could never end.

La Familia threw a house party, Dr. Calhoun told her, down on 56th and the beach. Music blared and everyone closed their eyes, dancing, rapping, hanging with their homeboys. Then kids from Norfolk—maybe one of the rival gangs—suspected their girls were at that party so they cruised their slick cars down Beach Boulevard, circled the house and shot shot shot. The bullet found its way to a window framed in white ruffles, crashed through glass so clean, so clear, so invisible a bird might've flown right through the pane. The bullet darted into a red-lit dance floor, careened into music so loud so—UH an UH an UH UH UH—that the sound of this shooting gun and the grunt of that falling boy were barely heard over the slow beat of the bass. Shot in the stomach and bleeding, the boy called out and no one heard over the cries of this MC—fly artist of the angry word, repetitive word, the beating word. The boy went down. Died. This was not the first incident.

"Who is it?" Isabel wanted to know. She ran through the faces of the boys she had met. In her half-awake state, they were all a part of her dreams. "Who got hit?"

Dr. Calhoun couldn't tell her. "His father's at sea. We have to contact him before we release his name."

More than worrying for the boy who died, she worried for his parents, for the sleepless nights and haunting spirit of the child. His mother's hands had run the course of him, would have memorized the texture of his skin—all that was perfect and all the flaws too. Isabel could only speculate what her unborn child might have been. And Mark never understood that the thing that died was a child, was something between them. She knew her child was only a dream baby, but this family would have memories.

Usually memories held it together for Isabel. When she lost the baby and Mark, she counted on memories to ground her, remind her of who she was. As bleak as the situation appeared, she would make it through. Her memories would see to that. But how could memories of this boy's life help his family? They would only miss him and their hearts would ache anew every time they thought of him.

She crawled under her bed and pulled out three shoeboxes of photographs. She rummaged through them, looking for an answer, flipping through stacks of black and white, color, and sepia-toned photographs. Friends, family, students, and ex-boyfriends. Little moments of insanity. Her life. She shuffled them like a gypsy reading tarot cards.

In one photo, she had just come in from an afternoon of sunning. Her skin was not its normal hue, but burnt the color of coconut husk. This way, she looked like her dad. Isabel's father had rough and weathered skin, like rich volcano ash. Her mother, light as mother of pearl, was her father's extreme. Those unfamiliar with the Philippines and its mosaic people—the Spanish, the Igorot, the Chinese, the Malay, the Japanese, and the Dutch, the Ilocano, the Visayan, the Pampango and others—would think they were each of a different race, a different nationality. But they were born on the same island archipelago, and their American-born Pinoy children, cast in shades of ginger, bamboo and sugar cane, reflected the faded colors of indigenous tribes marked by foreign blood. In this picture, Isabel looked like an authentic island girl.

"Oh my God," she said, weeping over the box of photos, "that poor family." She kept thinking about what that mom was going through.

After the miscarriage, she dressed herself in jeans and T-shirts. She bathed a little less often. Three times a week instead of every day. Every day seemed like so much work. She stopped curling her hair under with an iron, and then the blow-drying stopped, then the haircuts altogether. Then she stopped with the make-up. Blue went to black, and during the black period her shoulders began to droop. Her nails had dirt under their little moon beds. She looked awful. She stopped going home to see her family, and when she did she hardly said a word. When she stopped playing with her nephews and nieces, they knew something was really wrong.

"What is it?" her mother would ask.

"What happened?" her nephew Max wanted to know.

"What's the matter?" asked her sister.

"Stop that!" her father yelled.

But she said nothing. Mark had stopped coming around with her. So maybe her heart was broken. "She'll come out of it," she heard her mother telling the others, "you'll see."

She was so blue, they didn't know what to say to her. And then she was so black that every time they said anything at all, she seemed to slip a little farther away.

Then one day she came home and her hair was pulled back. And her nails were painted a sheer pink. Instead of being cloaked in black, she had on a pair of khaki pants and a black sweater. She saw her mother and sunk into her arms. Everyone was so happy, they didn't ask anymore. They let her be.

She laid the pictures out before her, scattered them all over the bedroom floor and examined them, listened to them and let their images calm her down.

Frank's Despidida Party. Angeles, Philippines. July 1958.
Photo by Lorenzo Manalo

The whole town fills the gymnasium, wearing their best suits and dresses. The lights in the gymnasium swoon for a second and then rise again. Lorenzo Manalo sets up the camera on the far end of the basketball court as they line up in rows, gathering around Francisco in his wide-lapel jacket, his tie—fat as a pig's tongue—his fancy two-toned shoes. His older brother and sister stand on either side of him like guardian angels. The younger siblings hang onto his sleeves, his pant legs, his belt. Lorenzo's sweetheart wife weeps openly, has not stopped with the crying for two weeks now. "Try to smile for one moment," he calls to her, pretending to wipe her eyes with his hanky. Francisco is the first doctor in the barrio, and so the whole town celebrates. The girls have curled their hair and piled thick waves of black silk upon their heads.

The boys have slicked their messy locks in pomade and sweet-smelling cologne. They have shaved their skin smooth—some for the very first time. The manongs and manangs have held his son's face and kissed him like a newborn. The priest has blessed the food, the journey, and the doctor. They have played records on the phonograph so everyone can dance. From this far away the faces are dots—many blurry dots—except for his son, who is etched into the lens of this camera, never to be forgotten. Lorenzo waves his hand at the mass of people, ready to click the button. Like this, they are the color of tobacco and forever young and beautiful. His heart grows weak with loss, fat with pride. His fingers shake, tremble at the thought of Francisco, his third child, his second boy. The only town doctor.

Her father had warned her this move would not be easy, that separating from family never was. She ran her fingers along the bottom of the photo, where the lab had scrawled "Frank's Despidida Party. Angeles, Philippines. July 1958" in an irregular hand. She squinted at the tiny faces, trying to imagine what her grandmother must have been feeling that night, knowing her son was going to be this far away. She searched the photo—the angle at which it was taken and the very center of it. She knew her lolo had taken the photo; it was his eye, his heart that captured them this way. It's almost like losing a son, she thought. Having him this far away from you. It's like not having him at all.

She spent the rest of the night searching the faces of her photos, feeling the spirit of the boy and her baby hovering over her. Somehow she knew they would all be all right. Somehow the faces were winking back at her; two ghosts patting her on the shoulder, begging her to rest.

Isabel had no idea what to expect as she entered the hallway and traveled around the maze of students and faculty. She walked amid the banging of metallic lockers, and echoes of caterwauling teens.

At the edge of the corridors, a mural illustrated the lives of the youth. Spiked hair was in—the boys on the wall displayed it—white boys, brown boys, black boys. Some of the portraits had round heads, smooth like the surface of a basketball. The girls had curvy bodies—long lashes, bright lips. Fishtails caught her eye, the long strands of mermaid hair sailing across the wall, and arms that moved like ribbons wrapped their way around the boys. The letters LD were tattooed on mermaid fins. Maybe, she thought, they were the high school mascots. Mermaids and sirens. Why not, she reasoned—the Atlantic was just down the street.

Students buzzed at one another, leaning on lockers and pulling at each other as if this day were no different than yesterday. Isabel searched her past, mentally paging through her high school yearbook. One boy died in a car crash. He'd been drinking. Another girl had died of a heart attack. Another one in a ski accident. Not a single one had been shot. Just the thought of someone dead had silenced her school, had fallen like a giant shadow onto their halls. It was different than this, she thought.

She walked into the gym. Took a long drink of water. Breathe, she told herself, breathe. She exhaled slowly and examined a dozen teenagers on metal folding chairs, their arms crossed and their voices hissing into the air like steam. Derek, Lourdes, Marilena, Mercedes, and Miguel sat among the students in the gym. Isabel smiled at Derek, mouthed hello, but he looked past her, his face set, locked in a heroic pose. She felt pain rifling through her bones. Miguel sat forward on his folding stool, nodding his head to some internal rhythm. He locked his thick lips tight as airmail. She wanted to leave the room, never return. Instead she called, "Miguel?"

Miguel raised his eyebrows, nodded. "Sup, Ms. Manalo."

"What'd we do now?" crooned a girl, heavy-set and sad.

"Dis gonna take all hour?"

Lourdes and Mercedes bowed their heads, whispered hot S's into the gym's atmosphere. A few of the boys had shaved their heads, wore dark shades to cover their faces, faces hard and scored like marble gods. The girls slumped down in their seats, tough as their brown brothers, with the exception of lips lined in brown pencil, stained boysenberry, sienna, and chocolate. Some of the girls had dyed their hair blonde, red, and cherry.

"How are you?" she asked, putting her books and tapes on a table. She ran her hands through her hair, made sure it was fluffy, not stuck to her scalp.

Silence. Old heaters spat. Long tubes of fluorescent lights hummed. Outside a cop siren howled like a cat being torn in two. They stared at one another. Oh shit, she thought.

"So why we here?" said Lourdes. She stretched her thin legs out in front of her. Her arm reached up high and exposed a silver belly ring. She shifted her shoulders, cracked a bubble with her chewing gum.

"You not going to try talkin' to us bout Arturo," said a boy in wire-rim glasses. "Cuz ain't nothing you can tell us we don't already know."

Arturo, she thought. Not Arturo. She could feel her insides collapsing. Not Arturo, please.

"Yeah," said Lourdes, picking at peeling nail polish. "An nothing we can tell you either. We don't know what happened, who did it, why it happened. We don't feel nothing."

"What do you mean you don't feel anything?" Isabel asked. She remembered—how he mixed pansit at the table, how he joked as he carried her TV into the house. She could see the curve of the black letter etched into his auburn skin. Alibata for Pinoy. Black ink on brown skin. She had asked him to explain it. How could that be?

They stared at her like she wasn't there. She saw a force field—an invisible dome—hanging over them, keeping them from her. "You don't have to talk about it," she told them. She held her breath, fighting the swell of tears rising inside. She pictured Tita Chic Chic yanking that metal spoon from her son, teaching him how to cook. She heard Tita Chic Chic whisper, "In this place, we are family." She wanted to leave.

"Thas right," Derek answered, "we don't."

Their arms rested against their chests like armor. Their eyes were open, but nothing registered—no light from the window, no book slamming to the ground, no hand to a face. Unflinching. Isabel felt hot, felt her clothing sticking to her skin. Her heart beat wild—pintig, pintig, pintig. It's all she heard. What did they mean they felt nothing? They had to feel something.

"That's the difference between us," said a girl named Maya Antaran. Her face was red, swollen.

"You can't tell us what we feel!" Miguel shouted. He stood up from his chair and, pointing, said, "Who you to tell us what we feel?"

"That's not what I'm doing," Isabel said. "I'm not—"

And then it seemed they were all standing, circling her like a swarm of bees, irritated and ready to sting. She swung her arms at their words, swatting them out of her way, but they persisted. She tried to speak to them, to tell them that she was there for them, but they were shooting: Who are you anyway, they wanted to know, and why should we listen to you? You don't know us and you want us to tell you how we feel? Sup wit dat shit? She felt claustrophobic, their brown arms swirling fast like electric fans, like blades slicing through air, through her. They wouldn't let her near them. She turned away and looked up at the window, breathing deeply. She fought a tumult of tears. Reaching for her bottled water, she talked to herself. Don't you dare, she said. Her mother warned her about teenagers—they were mean, especially when they came in bunches. They were always mean. You too, her mother told her, you were a nasty, cruel teenager. Me too, she had said, leaning over and kissing her.

When she turned to face the class she realized that they had been sitting silently all this time. Silent. Silent. Nothing. Still as a portrait, they leaned on one another, their faces vacant as Barbie dolls. They sat like that for the rest of the hour. No one spoke. No one moved. Just Isabel facing the youth. Like that. For an hour.

Chiu Family Portrait. Manila, Philippines. 1940.
Photo by Tony Estrella Jr., Estrella Studios

The father, a Chinese businessman, came to Manila many years ago. Sugarcane, thinks Estrella the photographer. Very typical. Very wealthy. Chiu's flesh shines, looms fat underneath a white linen suit. Western collar. Tie made of silk. The photographer powders the patriarch's balding head. He smells of expensive perfume. Estrella places Chiu next to his Filipina wife, a woman fifteen years his junior. He has chosen a love seat woven of rattan. Sheer fabrics drape the wife, decorate her tiny body in fine embroidery and pearls. Around her shoulders, a Maria Clara shawl covers her milky skin. Probably, *may Castilla sa dugo.* Her eyes are too round to be pure Filipino, her skin too light. Her black hair has been pulled back into a bun and fastened by a comb made of pearls and silver. Her thick lashes rim a set of eyes dark as the mahogany room divider Estrella has set up as a backdrop. Next to the family he props an old Spanish table, a delicate vase of china and sprigs of white sampaguita blossoms. He places the children around the parents like a constellation of planets orbiting the sun and moon. Three daughters wear traditional dresses. Butterfly sleeves rise from their shoulders and each dress bears a train that flows past their feet like clouds. The older sisters flutter fans carved of sandalwood and cloaked in lace. The youngest daughter hides behind a book—*Summa Theologica.* "Camila," hisses one of the older sisters, "put that down." Camila ignores her ate's command and the photographer must pry the book from her fingers before he takes the photo. Even so, she grabs it back from him. The pages flutter under the studio lights and she folds the binding under her arm, carries it the way the others hold their fans. The father nods at Estrella. "It's okay, na," he says. The flash goes off and illuminates Camila's beautiful face, her skin which is light as the moon, and her eyes which are dark like her mother's, but sad, very sad.

At lunch, Isabel saw them in the cafeteria, huddled together, leaning toward the center of the table. JoJo sat above them, his feet resting on a bench. He wore a ratty T-shirt and combat pants. He looks like one of them, she thought. Though he whispered, she could hear his words. He gestured to the white fluorescent light. What's he doing here, she wondered. She stopped in her tracks. The kids listened to him. They tilted their heads toward him and nodded. Why does he make me so pissed off, she wondered. He pointed at the door, then the teens. And just as he was about to hiss another word, he caught her eavesdropping from across the room. He stopped. His face was void of any emotion. The teens turned their heads, checked her out and, without acknowledging her, turned away.

Isabel entered the principal's lounge and picked her way through the crowd of students sitting on chairs and on the carpet around a coffee table. She smiled at three girls—Lourdes, Marilena, and Maya.

"Hi, girls," she said.

"You can go right in, Ms. Manalo," said the secretary. "Dr. Calhoun is waiting for you."

A door opened and a girl named Angel stepped out, her face red and her eyes swollen. Isabel reached for her. "Are you okay?" she asked.

"What do you think?" Angel said as she walked away.

Inside Dr. Calhoun's office two officers waited for her. Dr. Calhoun propped her arms on her desk, smiled as Isabel found her way onto an early American loveseat. "We're just waiting for Mr. Reyes," she said.

"I thought I saw him here," Isabel said. "At lunchtime."

"He had to step out." The officer speaking had hair so blond and shaved so close to his head, he looked bald.

Dr. Calhoun rose from her seat and gestured toward Officer Macmillan, then Officer Smith.

"You're new in town?"

Isabel nodded. "This is awful," she said.

"Yes, ma'am," said the other one, Officer Smith. He was shorter than his partner, but just as stocky. She looked him in the eyes. They were blue, cool and shiny. He had a kind face. "It's a bad habit your kids are getting into."

"This has happened before?" she said, turning to Dr. Calhoun.

Dr. Calhoun nodded, rubbing her hands as she spoke, kneading each bony finger. "Too often."

"It's always gangs," Macmillan said. "Filomafia, La Familia—those are the boys—then there's the girl gangs, right?" He turned to Smith, who nodded and named other gangs—Triple P and Las Dalagas.

Dalagas, she thought as she pictured the fins of the mermaid, the letters LD scrawled dark as a blood tattoo.

"The girl gangs are actually more dangerous," said Smith.

"What's the P stand for?" Isabel asked.

The three looked at one another and shrugged. "Beats me," said Smith. "Doesn't really matter. Call it trouble."

"Pinay?" she asked. "They fight for territory?"

"Something like that," Macmillan said. "Power, boys, girls, anything. We're thinking the boys from Virginia Beach were mixing it up with the girls of Norfolk."

"And the Norfolk boys got territorial, if you catch my drift," said Smith.

Isabel shook her head. How can I help, she thought. This is so out of my experience.

She heard a tapping at the door. JoJo stepped in and filled the room with his presence. He looked for a place to sit, and settled himself next to Isabel.

"Sorry about that," he said. "Arturo's dad is out to sea and they needed help at the restaurant. Auntie Chic Chic is in a bad way—you know."

"This is serious," Dr. Calhoun began. "Arturo's death is the fourth in three years."

"I agree," said JoJo. "This is senseless, but I don't think that siccing your Beach police onto the kids is the answer."

"We're trying to help, JoJo," said Macmillan. He scratched at his fuzzy head, his hand big and square, stretched like a giant paw.

"You're making them feel like criminals."

"We're trying to solve this," said Smith.

"You're scaring them."

Isabel watched them banter like this for awhile. The rhythm

of their speech was so regular, so easy, as if they had had this conversation often.

"They won't answer the questions," said Macmillan.

She pictured the kids sitting on folding chairs, holding their breath, staring past her at the gym wall, waiting for the hour to end. She thought about the echoes in the room, how she could hear the pipes banging, the whistles blowing outside for a soccer game in need of calming.

"They just lost a brother, cut 'em some slack," JoJo said, his voice getting louder. He spread his legs apart as he leaned onto his knees. He gestured at them. Isabel moved to the edge of the loveseat, giving him space. She glanced down at the carpet, and noticed grains of sand had pooled around his feet.

"Okay, okay," Dr. Calhoun said, waving her hands, calming the men. "We're here working on the same side."

"I'm not so sure about that, Doc," said JoJo.

"What's that mean?" said Smith. "You know we'd get farther with these kids if you'd cooperate, JoJo. You're as bad as they are."

Loud voices called out from the front office. Calhoun's door trembled a little before it flew open. Ferdi Mamaril pushed the secretary away with one hand as he fumbled at the doorknob with the other. "I have a right to be here!" he yelled. "One of the brothers has gone down, and I have a right."

The secretary smiled weakly at Dr. Calhoun.

"It's okay, Lee," Calhoun said. "Leave it to me."

"I wanna know what you're doing about this. I wanna know why you excluded me from this meeting," Ferdi demanded. "I pay taxes, I'm a citizen and I have a right to be here."

Dr. Calhoun rose from her seat and took Ferdi by the arm. "Of course you do, Mr. Mamaril. But this isn't an open meeting."

"This is another example of how brown leaders in this community are being discriminated against. There's a problem when something this big happens and only your elite meet. Why didn't you call me?" He struggled to get out of Calhoun's hold.

"Take it easy," Macmillan called out.

"Man," JoJo said, "you're makin' it worse. Stop it." Ferdi looked over at JoJo. "Can't you let it alone for now, pare? I'll fill you in later."

Ferdi's nostrils puffed in and out. Beads of sweat formed just above his right temple. He dragged a hand over his face and snorted. "Nothing's going on," JoJo told him. "We're just talking." JoJo nodded at Ferdi. "Getting acquainted wit Ms. Manalo."

"Man," Ferdi said. He bobbed his head up and down, like he was finally getting it. Pulling at his jacket, he zipped it up and told JoJo, "I'll wait for you outside. I'll be hanging with the crew."

"Kay, man," JoJo said. "Thanks."

Just like that, Ferdi walked out the door, closing it quietly behind him. The cops threw each other a look and Smith whistled.

It seemed as though everyone paused and then JoJo smiled at them for the first time since he'd come in.

Isabel let out a long breath and sighed. She wasn't sure she could take all this drama. She looked to the window. The bell rang and everyone spilled onto the parking lot and into their cars. So this is my life, Isabel thought. A shooting, a crazy man, and now the cops and my boss. What the hell am I doing here? She watched the kids outside. A group of Pinoy paraded past the principal's window. They leered through the glass and waved at JoJo. Isabel saw the beauty of Lourdes, strutting across the grounds. She saw Maya's fat smile. She saw Miguel's dark curls and the glint of his sunglasses. She saw a boy in a sleeveless shirt, a black tattoo shining, screaming in Alibata, "Pinoy!" She shook her head. That can't be. Or maybe another boy had the same tattoo. She thought of the conversation she had with Arturo. She saw his arm dark from the sun, brown from his mother and father, saw the image of black ink etched onto his skin. She was sure that he was among the kids just now. He has not left them, she thought, he's somewhere in between.

"What do you need from me?" she asked. "What can I do?"

"We hired someone to work with the kids," Dr. Calhoun said, "JoJo works with them out of school, but we need someone here too. We thought maybe if they were given attention, taught something about their culture and history, that this would be helpful—show them we care."

Outside, Ferdi's squat frame chased after the kids like one of those yippy dogs. He waved his arms up and down, jumping at them. The kids ignored him. Some of them were laughing. Maya leaned over and embraced him to calm him down. Isabel wondered what he was screaming at them. She could see his neck straining, the fat veins pulsing, the face red.

"I really doubt you can do anything," said Macmillan, "but if you hear or see something that can help us—"

"That's messed up," JoJo said.

"What he means is," Dr. Calhoun said, waving her pen in giant circles, "maybe they'll open up to you and that would be helpful to the investigation."

"I understand them now," JoJo said.

"I don't know," Isabel said. She looked at the police, who were leaning toward her, waiting. "I mean JoJo's right . . ."

"Doesn't matter what kind of supertoken you bring in," JoJo said. He took a moment to stare into Isabel's face, his black eyes drilling holes into her. She felt herself flush with anger. Fuck you, she thought, fuck you. Without looking away from her, he continued, "Slong as you guys bully them, nothin's gonna change."

Macmillan nodded to the mass of kids swarming the field. "We need to reign them in. Get 'em to behave before Will Peterson puts the pressure on us and makes life hell for everyone."

Calhoun explained that Peterson was the young Republican at the community party. "A nice young man," she said, "who's concerned."

They talk about the kids like they're animals, Isabel thought.

"We need to get to the bottom of this shooting," said Smith. "Can't you get them to talk, JoJo? Maybe you can do it, ma'am."

"If they don't feel like talking," JoJo said, "don't force them. If you want to help, get off their backs." He stood up and threw Isabel a cold look then stepped to the window and rapped on it. "Just back off, okay?" he said as he walked out the door, leaving them silent and staring at one another.

ISABEL? YOU THERE? FERDI MAMARIL. I WAS JUST THINKING ABOUT YOU. YOU OKAY? ARTURO'S DEATH WAS A BLOW. THEM COPS ARE A BLOW. DID YOU KNOW WE WERE HERE BEFORE THE WHITE MAN? TRUE, TRUE. MORO BAY, CALIFORNIA, 1587. OUR PEOPLE WERE ON SLAVE SHIPS UNDER THE COMMAND OF A CAPTAIN UNAMUNO—I'LL SAY IT SLOW,

UNA-MUN-O—PROBABLY PART OF THE MANILA-ACAPULCO SILK-FOR-SILVER TRADE MOVEMENT. 1587 AND OUR PEOPLE WERE JUMPING SPANISH GALLEONS AND SETTLING IN NEW ORLEANS. AMERICA WASN'T EVEN AMERICA YET. AND HERE WE WERE, ROASTING LECHON ON A SPIT. WE PROBABLY TAUGHT THEM VOODOO DOCTORS A SPELL OR TWO—KNOW WHAT I'M SAYIN'? WHEN WHITIES TELL ME THEY WERE HERE FIRST, I SAY, HELL NO YOU WEREN'T. INDIAN TRIBES WEAVE FABRIC LIKE THE IFUGAO—DID YOU KNOW THAT? FILIPINOS WERE IN THE AMERICAS HOOKIN' UP WITH THE NATIVE BROTHERS LONG BEFORE THE WHITIES. SINCERELY. YOU ARE LIKE ONE OF THE FIRST FILIPINOS WHO SETTLED THERE IN NEW ORLEANS WITH CHEF PAUL PRUDHOMME. UNTIL YOU, OUR CULTURE HAS BEEN HIDDEN, OUR YOUTHS IN THE DARK—BUT YOU CAN TEACH THEM WHO THEY ARE NOW. YOU HAVE THE OPPORTUNITY TO INSTILL A PRIDE IN THEIR HISTORY AND HERITAGE. AND I KNOW, IT'S NOT EASY BEING A FIRST, BUT YOU CAN DO IT. DO IT FOR THE MOVEMENT, FOR THE YOUTHS. DON'T LET ANYONE TELL YOU YOU DON'T BELONG HERE—WE CAME ON THE GALLEONS, WE WERE MAKING LUMPIA BEFORE POCAHONTAS AND JOHN SMITH EVER MET. IF ANYONE BELONGS IT'S YOU AND ME. IS THAT THE SHIT OR WHAT?

Isabel baked a rice cake smothered in sweet coconut. She got into her car and maneuvered her way about the beach in search of Tita Chic Chic's little restaurant, TAPISLOG-N-RICE. Entering, she passed a shrine of Mama Mary dripping in gold, a little votive candle at Her feet and a five-by-seven photograph of Arturo and his family next to Her. The restaurant was packed with members of the community, people quietly sitting at kitchen tables, spooning rice and eggs, rice and longanisa, rice and chicken. She didn't see Tita Chic Chic at the register, or walking among the customers. Sunshine blasted in through walls of glass and blurred the faces of the diners.

She carried the rice cake with two hands. The tin foil she had placed on top of the pan rustled like old leaves. She was getting ready to ask a little girl behind the counter where her mother was when a loud moaning issued from the corner table. She saw a woman's arms, fisted and angry, flying up into the air; several women at the table threw themselves on her as if she were on fire.

"This is for your mom," Isabel said to the girl. Her voice cracked and her vision blurred with tears.

"Bring it to her," said the girl. "She's over there." She pointed to the corner, her small arm thin and brown as a tree branch.

Isabel tiptoed to the other side of the diner, her arms stretched out, heavy with the rice cake. "Tita Chic Chic?" she called out. "Tita Chic Chic?" She heard the movement of chrome squeaking on linoleum, the women moving out of her way. She wondered why she'd come, what possessed her to walk into this diner. She placed the pan down in front of Tita Chic Chic, who was so small today, shriveled up from all that crying, her face sinking into pockets of sadness. "I'm sorry," Isabel mumbled.

Tita Chic Chic pulled back the tin foil and stared at the pockmarked surface of the cake, where some of the coconut milk's sugar had burned deep holes or puffed up into air bubbles. And when her gaze fell upon Isabel, she leaned up and pulled her to her, sobbing into Isabel's nest of black hair. "Naku, hija," she whispered, "see how good you are."

Isabel was crying too. "Oh, but I'm not. I'm really not."

They held each other for awhile. They whispered things to one another and Isabel could not believe how close she felt to this woman. "I can't imagine the pain," she told her. "I can't imagine your broken heart."

But she knew she could. She just didn't know how else to say it.

"Can you imagine," said Tita Chic Chic, "if you would have been here sooner? Maybe Arturo would not be dead."

"Tita, don't say that." Her chest was aching.

"But it's true, hija. That's why they brought you here." Tita Chic Chic leaned away from Isabel and looked into her eyes. She pushed the strands of wet hair off Isabel's face. She smiled at her and Isabel felt as if she were losing her baby again. "Why did you move to Virginia, hija? Why did you come?"

And here Isabel did weep. She wanted to tell Tita Chic Chic the very truth: that it was her shame that made her leave home, it was the guilt of what she did. I embarrassed my family, she wanted to say. But she couldn't say it. She only leaned over and kissed Tita on the cheek, and said, "Let me know if there's anything I can do."

She left the diner and raced home. On the steps of her porch, she watched water and sky. She synchronized her breathing to the tide. Felt the breeze.

She thought about the sound water made when she plunged her body deep into its infinite blue. How it roared and swallowed her up. Underwater, the beating of the heart began at the core of her chest and rippled out into the sea. Pintig, it sounded; pintig, it beat. Pintig, pintig, pintig. Immersing oneself in the sea must be like reentering the womb, she thought, must be what her baby's world was like.

Until now, she'd hardly had a chance to think. All she knew was she needed to get out. To pack her things and give up right now. Her insides rattled like the skin of a tom-tom. She hadn't eaten for days. Hadn't felt like it. She hungered for nothing, but was thirsty for everything. Her stomach growled.

She saw Arturo everywhere. His face was a round moon with two dimples creased into his caramel skin. His teeth were big white tiles hiding behind a sly smile. She saw him in the hallways at school, or the aisles at the grocery store. She saw him when the other boys looked past her as if she were the ghost. Sometimes, pausing at a stoplight, the radio in the car next to her blared hip-hop, and she actually imagined Arturo at this party, dancing with one of his homegirls. Slow and easy, his body hinted at the rhythm. She saw his hands come up in front of him, teasing the girl. Two fists sparred at the air, and his muscles flexed to the beat of the music. She imagined his tattoo pulsing like a heart. Once, she caught the kids in the car next to her watching. "Hell you lookin' at?" their faces said. The light changed and they left her idling there.

Sometimes she'd forget the details of his face and wondered if she had made it up. She reached into her pocket and pulled out a fistful of photographs. Some of them were from the other night at the Cultural Center. The picture she had taken of Tita Chic Chic, Arturo, and Miguel had turned out fuzzy. Their faces were blurred and their bodies looked as if they had melted together into one. She was trying to remember what he looked like today. Today he appeared to her like this photograph—something of a ghost, a faceless spirit, a light. He was so kind, she thought. Too bad she never really got to know him.

What was she doing here anyway? JoJo's right, she thought. Mostly she wanted to go back home.

The last photo was a picture she had taken a long time ago when she was a girl. She had only recently found it and was carrying it with her wherever she went. It was a picture of her little sister Millie.

Millie—4 years old. Chicago, IL. May 1976.
Photo by Isabel

Millie gazes at the "Life Before Birth" exhibit—a wall of forty specimens embalmed and jarred and donated to the halls of science and industry.

Busloads of children sprint past the almost-babies, not seeing them. But Millie lingers at each station, searching for signs of life.

"Turn and look at me," Isabel tells her, winding her Instamatic.

A few days old, and the embryo, tiny as a flea on the back of Millie's cat, floats in a crystal monolith—so small it looks like dust. She presses her face up to the window, spreads her own small hands out against the pane and smears the glass with prints.

Isabel gives up. "Okay," she says, "an action shot." Millie studies the heads and the bellies and the tail, which seems to recede with each passing week. At week eight the embryo becomes a fetus, the legs and arms begin to grow, fighting to catch up to its oversized head.

The almost-babies draw Isabel into their world too. The alien bodies develop eyes, and eyelids, fingers and toes, begin to look like babies. The plaques read "Male Fetus at Nine Weeks" or "Female Fetus at Seventeen Weeks." A translucent yellow fin, lit against the black velvet window, flaps lightly in its jar. Isabel points to the sacs of skin, wrinkled and twisted along the thighs. One station displays a set of identical female twins, still coddled in their respective amino sacs, fairies wrapped in magic spider webs. Sleeping beauties. Sisters. The never-to-be-children have flat noses, squinty eyes, little slits tilted up to the temples. "Are these babies Chinese?" Millie wants to know.

Isabel frames her sister leaning into the shelf of babies, her profile looming large against the fairy sisters. She clicks the photo and, grabbing her sister's hand, says, "Let's go. Everyone's been looking for you."

When Isabel looked at that photo, she understood what happened to her baby. She knew what he or she might have been going through, how he or she was just becoming. Sometimes it hurt to look at the picture. She shoved the photos back into her pocket and took a deep breath. She could smell the salt coming from the sea.

Every day there was something different. Since the shooting, she saw gang tagging everywhere, scratched into the wood of school desks, inked onto homework, chalked on playgrounds next to four-square games and tetherball lines. She saw letters swimming big as trout, and images of mermaids at battle. She had entered a world as foreign to her as Africa, or Germany, or the Philippines. Every day she struggled, feeling out of her skin, reading signs she could not comprehend.

Yesterday Ferdi Mamaril showed up at school and handed out flyers to the kids and teachers. He screamed into his bullhorn: "Stop this injustice! The persecution of Pinoy youth! Look what you're doing, America!" When he saw her standing there, he rushed at her and said, "Hey Sista Isabel, you joining the struggle? Whatcha gonna do about the death of our boy, Arturo?"

On the six and ten news, Will Peterson flashed a toothy smile. "We have to fight this," he said to the lens. "Make the laws work for us. Punish the wrongdoers and deter this behavior." He wanted to wipe the streets clean. He wanted a better America. "We've got to send a message to these gangs: you're not wild and free; you're part of this country and you will be held responsible." She knew he swayed voters with that smile, could have been Donny Osmond, a smile that wide, that bright.

When she called her parents to tell them about Arturo, her mother whispered, "Shot him dead?" She didn't believe Isabel.

"You be careful," her father warned her.

"Did they arrest the killer?" her mother continued.

"Don't get involved," her dad said.

"How can she not get involved?" her mother said. "You do what's right, hija."

"How did I get here?" Isabel asked them. "How?"

In the water she saw bodies toss about—small as children, brown as dirt—fluid like they were born in that sea. She saw them chase one another fast as fish. Their voices rose like steam off the hiss of waves. She wondered if they were the girls. She had seen them walking the beaches late at night. She wished she could play in the water like that, had the upper-body strength to swim against the tide, could hold her breath and dance in water to music only they could hear.

Fuck JoJo, she thought, I'll show him. She stood on her porch and breathed. "What the hell," she said and, running to the shore, leapt into a rush of water and swam. In the distance, she heard the voices of the fish girls giggling like dolphins in an episode of *Flipper*. She ignored them. The water filled her up and left her wanting. Hungry.

THREE

Moving to Boone, North Carolina. April 1966.
Photo by Francisco Manalo

Frank and his wife, their three-year-old and their infant son drive across confederate lines, full of hope and happy for their future. He pulls into a gas station somewhere just south of the Virginia state line. It's hot, too hot for April—ninety-one degrees. The sun blasts the metal on the chrome pump, bounces off the tin roof and scatters in sheets of shiny white light across the car. Getting out, he grabs the camera. "Sweetheart," he says, framing the car before pumps and the white storefront window, "put your head out and look at me."

Camila waves him away, frowning. Her face shines with heat. Her belly rises up before her like a beautiful balloon. "Not now," she says.

Their three-year-old waves at him, climbs out of the back seat and into the front next to Camila. "Take my picture, Daddy," she says. She pokes her little head out the window and makes a face.

In the background, he can see a young man walking toward the lens. He is tall. Dressed in baggy pants and a greasy service shirt. Over his heart is embroidered a dull red "Roy." This man is the color of coconut. His hair, crunched up like tiny balls of cotton, is cropped close to his skull. From the back of his pants hangs an oily hanky. He pulls it out and dabs his forehead.

"Fillerup, sir?" he asks.

"Sure," Frank says, clicking the camera. He begins walking toward the men's room.

"Not that one, sir," the attendant calls out. The gravel beneath Frank's feet rolls to silence. The steam from the pavement rises up and covers the boy's skin with sheen. "That door's for whites only."

Frank waits, contemplating the man's words. He holds his breath. His family watches him, looking out the windows of their red beetle, waiting. And then Frank turns around, shifting direction, whistling "Yankee Doodle." He saunters around the corner of the gas station, goes into the bathroom marked "Colored."

Frank Manalo woke up itching all over. He reached around his sleeping wife, squinting at the big red numbers of their digital clock. 2:30 A.M. He ran both hands through his thinning hair and scratched his scalp. Isabel wants to know how she got there, he thought. How does she think she got there? He brought her. He was responsible. He said, "Stop moping around! Get a job! Live!" And then he helped her pack her things—well, he watched her pack her things—and they drove the child east. Oh my God, he thought, what have I done?

And what about that boy, Arturo? He kept seeing that kid lifting Isabel's TV up over his head like he was King Kong climbing up the Empire State Building, and the boy, losing his balance, fell off that tower over and over again. Magkaguluhan sila, Frank thought, as he pictured the boys lifting boxes, their girlfriends hanging all over the mouth of the truck like silver bangles on a gypsy.

*

"Bend those knees when you lift, boys." He dashed down the stairs and scrambled onto the back of the truck saying, "That is breakable." The boys nodded.

"Don't worry, po," said the tall boy, Miguel. His hair, a mop of wild curls, spilled from his scalp like a fountain of water. "I ate my Wheaties."

"Me, I'm Navy. I'm Popeye," said Arturo. "I eat spinach."

"Please, boys. No joking. Dahan, dahan, okay?"

"Oo, po. We're being very careful."

The ocean roared behind them so loud that they had to shout to be heard. So full was the wind that whistled above them, it carried their words away as soon as they breathed them into the air.

"Use your whole body, boys. All of it," Frank warned them.

Tchaikovsky's "1812 Overture" shot across the yard—loud, thunderous, heavy. Frank's music competed with the hip-hop "toom-toom-pow" popping from the speakers of the truck's cab.

Inside, Camila had found the box of spices and the pots and pans. She took her rice cooker out of her assortment of travel things. "I packed it separate," she said to Frank, "in case we couldn't find hers right away. You know how you are about rice." The house smelled of Camila's cooking. Steam floated from the rice cooker and the aroma of jasmine

44

warmed the kitchen. She boiled the chicken in a broth of onions, garlic and ginger, cooked the meat right off the bones so everything was tender.

"Damn, I'm hungry," said Miguel to Derek. Derek swatted him with a cap. His eyes opened up—big, angry, warning. Miguel punched him back with a free hand. "What I mean is your cooking smells like home, Auntie."

"I want some tinola too," said Arturo. "Smells better than home to me."

*

He was just a boy, Frank thought as he tried to reach an itch at the center of his back. What kind of world was this? What is this shooting? And now Isabel was gonna get tangled up in their gulu. Naku!

He hoped she'd use her head, that she would remember the sacrifices he and his wife had made for her. The struggles so they could have this life. Sometimes he wondered what he must have done wrong. He had to fight his own dad to come to America and make this life. True, he thought, she was not yet born, but hadn't he been thinking of his future? Of his family's future?—and that would have to include the children that he would have some day.

*

In 1955, Frank's last year in medical school, the U.S. government sent a letter around, looking for medical residents. When he got the letter, he ran to his father's store, a small shack with dirt floors, hemp-covered walls and a thatched roof. He found his father stooped over a counter, balancing books, counting sacks of rice, bundles of fish and stalks of sugar cane. Frank read the announcement in one breath and told his father what he wanted to do—to go to America. "And think," he said, "I could go there and have a job waiting for me."

His father continued counting pesos, marking the books with his crooked finger. Outside, the wind whistled through the palm trees, cautioned them. Frank tapped him on the shoulder. "Did you hear me, Tatay?" His father looked up slowly and skeptically from his handful of pesos, shook his head. He took the letter from him and read it.

"What do you think, they want you to come to them? What they gonna give you?"

"A job," Frank said. "This is opportunity."

Frank's tatay held the piece of paper up to him and shook it. "Read the letter again, son. They don't want to give you a job. They want you to study. When you finish, you come back here."

It was true, the letter wasn't offering Frank a job, actually. It was an exchange program for foreign medical graduates. They would go to America, the letter said, finish a two-year program and, in the end, be able to return to their motherland to practice the latest in medical technology.

"I know, Tatay," Frank told him. "That's a formality. I'll get a job there when I'm done with my studies. I'll have the training and the education—I'll already be there. No problem."

"So your mother and I educate you so you can gallivant the world? That's how you thank us? How you show respect?" His father ran his hands over his face, rubbed his eyes. Frank knew better than to push, than to raise his voice to his father. He'd get nowhere that way.

"Can't you see, Tatay? It's the greatest honor to work this hard and see your children succeed. I'll send you money—maybe even send for you and Nanay—you won't have to work."

"They want you to work for them for what? Not money."

"In exchange for my education."

"Free labor for them and then you have no guarantee—nothing that says they will get you a job." He leaned over and put his hand on Frank's shoulder. His voice was stubborn and loud, ready for a fight, but rings of skin draped his eyes, folded years of hardship up into his temples like pockets of wisdom. "The barrio could use a doctor. Your family needs you. Out there—who knows how Americans will take advantage of you? Who can you trust so far away from us?"

*

Frank scratched at his head again. Scratched a little faster and let his fingers run down the front of his face. He was sleeping less and less, worrying every night about those kids. That Isabel. Naku! he thought, how did they get here is right. He turned to Camila and watched her sleeping. The stress of the day had receded from her face and left her pale and smooth as mother of pearl. He knew that sometimes she put a little dye in her hair to keep it black. He ran his fingers through strands of it. "You do a nice job, sweetheart," he said. He leaned into her face and stared, hoping she would wake up. He kissed her hand. He jiggled the mattress. "Why can't I be more like you?" He pulled at the sheets, which made her roll a little, nestle deeper into slumber.

Water dripped from a faucet, grew irritating like the itching. Frank got up and checked the master bathroom. Nothing. He walked down the hall to the children's bathroom. Dry. He wandered down the stairs to the kitchen, then the laundry room then, finally, he limped his way down the basement stairs and heard the drip drip drip coming from a pipe. Perfect, he thought, reaching for his tool kit. He took a wrench from the kit and climbed up a stepladder to reach the pipe. He examined its cool metal, rusted and wet. He was thinking about the day they moved Isabel to Virginia.

*

His voice filled the cab of the truck, surged loud above the rhythm of public radio samba. His words were clipped, short and fast, roared louder than the truck's heavy engine. Isabel held a picture of herself up to the truck window, where the cows, red barns and silos blurred like memory.

"None of this dwelling in your misery," he said to her. "A waste of time."

Isabel nodded. She flipped through a stack of photos.

"This is about opportunity," he said, shifting gears to accommodate a hill.

"She knows that, Dad," his wife said. "Why else will she go?" Camila sat on the other side of Isabel, peeling hard-boiled eggs, feeding her family coffee, oranges and cheese. "Why else would you, Isa?"

Isabel kissed her mother on the cheek. "Smile a little, Ma. It's not so bad."

"This place is so far away and I don't see why you think you have to be so far away to have an opportunity."

"This way I start over, Ma. No strings. No past. No nothing from before."

Camila made a face. "There was nothing wrong with your life."

"Take the opportunity," Frank said. The spin of the wheels on tar droned just underneath the radio's crackle, just underneath the heaviness in the cab. "But if I find out you are just feeling sorry for yourself again, we'll be out there to bring you back. No sense wasting time in Virginia when you can do it at home."

Isabel drank water out of large blue bottles the color of stained glass. She doled out photos like a game of solitaire.

"You should put them in an album," Camila said.

"I know."

"Then you won't lose them."

"Yes."

"Don't tell me you're that thirsty," Frank said. "Before you know it, we'll have to stop again."

Isabel drank some more, said, "Want some?"

*

The problem with that girl, he thought as he climbed down the ladder, is that she never listens. He had been watching her for months. Of course they were disappointed when they found out about the boy and that pregnancy. Frank was heartbroken. She was his oldest daughter, still a girl. She should have waited. But what could he do? At least that Mark guy had a good job. His daughter was his daughter. Nothing would change that. And when she lost the baby, Frank had cried.

Last Thanksgiving, when all the grandchildren were at the house, Frank looked through the lens and found his apo looking fat as turkeys. They were variations of a theme with their big heads, chunky legs, skin the color of toast. The older boys crowded the baby, squeezed their faces together close to the lens. In the background a shadow crossed the frame. The shape was willowy and silent, almost nothing. Isabel. "Get in the picture, Sweetheart!" he called to her. But she shook her head and the long strands of black hair sprayed out from her head like the string at the end of a mop. A light from the other side of the room shined on a face distorted and gaunt like the reflection in a carnival mirror. "Can't be," he muttered to himself.

"Come on, Tita Bel," the children called. "Be in our picture."

She waved their invitation away with an arm thin and angular as a chicken wing. "I'm getting a drink," she told the kids, holding up her empty water bottle.

"Aw, forget her," he told them. He tried not to lose his temper, but it was getting harder and harder with her.

Then a few months later, this old friend of his called him up on the phone. "We heard your girl's a schoolteacher," Uncle Romy Alvarez said.

"Something like that," Frank said.

"We have a position here in Virginia Beach and they're looking for a teacher. I bet they'd love to hire Isabel, Pare."

That was all Frank needed to know.

"You could have benefits," he told her. "Steady work."

She picked up the newspaper and rifled through it.

"This is a good opportunity, hija. Put the past behind you."

"But I don't want to move away." Bel shook the paper out. "Where are the comics?" He handed her the papers and threw her a look. "I want to be close to the family—unless you're ashamed of me."

"Why should I be ashamed of you? You're the one who is ashamed of yourself—always hiding from the world like a fish out of water. Naku! Come on, hija. Make a new start."

She tossed the paper down and picked up the TV guide. "Have you seen the remote?" she said.

*

Upstairs, a loose shutter was banging to the breath of the wind. "All right," he said out loud. "I'll fix you too." He grabbed his tool kit and climbed up to the attic. If I had given up, he thought, all those years ago. If I had let those people push me around. Where would we be tonight? He pocketed a screwdriver, hammer and a couple of nails in his bathrobe. Then he pushed open the door to the attic and pulled his old body into a crawlspace where they kept boxes of Christmas lights and decorations. The shutter slammed against the house like a ghost looking for attention. As he opened the window a gust of autumn air swirled into the crawlspace and blew the dust about. He sneezed.

*

On the night of their six-month anniversary living in Boone, North Carolina, Frank walked into the kitchen with a dozen balloons and a handful of red roses. "What smells so good?" he called.

Isabel ran into the room, squealing. "We cooked all day, Daddy. Better be hungry." She pulled on his pant leg as he squatted down to meet her.

"Balloons for you and red roses for Mommy." He reached over to kiss Camila and handed her the flowers. "Happy six months living in Boone, mahal. Boondocks U.S.A., we've done it!"

She wrapped her arms around him and squeezed tight. "Happy anniversary, Daddy."

Classical music exploded from the speakers in the room. Cellos and tympanis, tubas and oboes collided, a rush of white rapids, crashing at the water's end. Isabel ran circles around Frank, dragging the balloons behind her while he held baby Frankie up in the air, flying him like a super-jet. Just as they were sitting down to dinner, the phone rang. Camila snuck around them to answer it. "A moment," she told the caller. "Frank, it's the hospital." Walking past her, he rubbed her belly.

"Yes, Dr. Moorland. Good evening, sir." He waved at her to turn the music down. "Well, sir. I told the patient she—I know, sir—I understand. No—no what I said was—I told her that. But, sir—" His supervisor shot words at him, giving no space for answers, no moment for breath. And suddenly Frank stopped talking altogether. His jaw clenched shut. His eyes were wide. "Now wait a minute. No, now, wait. You can't talk like that to me. No. I know, but you can't—" He put the phone back into its cradle. He felt the heat from the candles and the gas oven fill the room up, scorch the walls red.

"What's the matter?" Camila asked.

"Some old woman said I refused to help her. Said that I was rude and that I couldn't speak any English."

"What?"

"She wanted a refill on her painkillers—but she already had them refilled two days ago, so I told her to see her regular doctor." He sat in his chair and leaned his elbows on his knees. Camila put her hands on his forehead and leaned over to kiss him.

"Well," Camila told him. "Dr. Moorland must've understood once you explained."

"He told me he expected there would be this kind of trouble." She pushed the hair from his forehead. He felt beads of perspiration dotting his temples.

"What kind of trouble?"

"That bastard said, 'You foreigners ought to go back to where you came from!' Can you believe that, Mommy? Demonyo!"

Frank began by pacing the floor. He didn't deserve this kind of treatment, he told her. He worked hard for Moorland—worked late shifts and double shifts and even Sundays, which were his only days off. He worked meticulously, and in between the patients he could always be found sitting with a medical book—a map of the heart set before him—when others were snacking on oranges and chips or gossiping about the hospital's latest love affairs. He circled the room, his voice growing louder with each lap. His arms, long thin arms, stretched high above his body, cast fiendish shadows on the wall. First he knocked over a chair, then he dragged the curtains from the window. The streetlamp filled the room like a giant spotlight, exposing them to the whole world. Frank tore right through the bouquet of brightly colored balloons. The little bulbs of helium broke apart and rose high up to the ceiling like floating mines—each one a tiny bomb waiting to burst. It seemed the house was falling apart.

Frank spied Isabel running from the kitchen table and into the bathroom. He could hear Frankie Junior wailing in the other room. An angry wind spun in the corners of their home, colliding there in the center of the dining room and whistling in their ears and making them ache with its frightful pitch, so that everyone was calling out, crying, screaming.

Camila snatched the toddler from his crib and waited patiently for

Frank to settle down.

The dinner sat cold on the table. When, finally, Frank fell exhausted into his chair, he called out to his little girl. "Come out, hija," he told her. "Let's eat." And Isabel climbed up behind her father's chair and rested her small head on his shoulder while Camila put the food into plastic containers, blew out the candles and turned up the volume on the radio. The three of them listened to the orchestra. The music swelled, grew deep and heavy, like the wind in an angry storm.

*

Frank was hammering the shutters down when he heard Camila calling from below.

"Ano ba yan?" she yelled. "What are you doing up there, mahal?"

"Fixing the shutters!" he answered.

He turned around to see her small head peeking up through the attic door. "It's four in the morning. Can't you sleep?"

"No, this banging banging—who can sleep?" he answered her.

"Exactly, so come to bed," she said, reaching out her hand to him. "There's tomorrow. Fix the world tomorrow."

"After I'm finished," he told her, scratching his head. He was still thinking about the boy—such a dangerous and violent moment. He was thinking about his daughter. "How did you get here?" he said out loud. "I have no idea. But I do know this, you better not get involved. Those people will kill you."

FOUR

Back in Virginia Beach, twenty-five second graders surrounded Isabel on the wood gymnasium floor. "Look," she whispered, scrolling blue paper before them. "Do you know what this is?"

They strained their necks, crawling closer, so close she smelled their breath, sweaty and sweet as milk. She smoothed her hands over the roll of aqua-blue paper and taped the sides down onto the floor. Next to her lay an odd-shaped satchel, bulging with hard edges and incongruent angles.

"Paper," said Tony Muñoz, a boy with a face round as Buddha's.

"No," Isabel told them. "It's the Pacific Ocean!"

"What? That's crazy. Do you have toys in that bag?"

Grabbing the sack, she shook her head. She took out blocks cut into the shapes of major islands—Luzon, Visayas, and Mindanao. She placed the brightly painted wood down on the paper, starting with the northern tip of Luzon and working her way south to Mindanao. She pulled out little plastic trees and vegetables, little animals, fish. She poured a handful of rice over certain islands.

"Before the Spanish came," Isabel told them, "our people were scattered across the islands, separated by rivers and small bodies of water. Our people lived in baranggay—communities of thirty families. Each baranggay spoke a language all its own."

"Barkadas," said Tara Sanchez. Her bangs draped her eyes.

"Gangs," hissed Marlon Asunsiyón.

"Your kuya was shot by gangs," said Pancho Garcia.

"Was not."

"He was! Isn't that true, Ate Isabel?"

Isabel shifted her body and hushed them with her fingers. She felt them stare at her, waiting for her answer. She closed her eyes and took a long breath, grabbing her bottle of water and drinking. What should she tell them? Their legs squirmed beneath them, their bodies wiggled. "Let's talk about that later, okay?"

Tara was Arturo's cousin. She looked to Isabel, her mouth trembling and her hands opening and closing into little fists.

"Are you okay, Tara?"

The girl nodded, combing her fingers through her hair so her bangs would part.

"What happened to Arturo is a sad thing," Isabel told them.

"Are you going to the funeral, Ate Isabel?"

"Sure she is—why wouldn't she? You can go with us," said Tara. "We got a new minivan with lots of extra seats."

"Do you guys call everyone ate?" Isabel asked.

"Only older sisters and cousins and if you're too young to be a tita," Tara said.

"Okay." Isabel pointed to the blocks of wood. "Come on now, you guys. See this? Let's stay focused. A datu was the leader of the baranggay and he decided when to plant, to harvest, to shift the people to better land."

"Like a gang leader?"

"Yeah," she said. Looking at their faces Isabel saw her nephews and nieces—full-faced and dark-eyed and earnest. What would they do if I were shot? Oh God. Please God, she thought, let's move on.

She divided the children into groups, little baranggays speaking in new and made-up languages. Each baranggay named itself, and the people pantomimed a life apart from all the others.

The room was noisy with their voices, with the running together of vowels and consonants, all jumbled and mixed up. She almost didn't hear the commotion. But she felt the energy. It came in a shove, and then a scuttle.

"Shut up," said Tara. She pushed Pancho across the room.

When Isabel looked up, the kids were gesturing with their arms, kicking back on their heels, posturing like gangbangers. "Ate Isabel said we'd talk about that later!" Tara shoved Pancho again.

"Hey! What are you doing?" Isabel asked. She rushed into their circle and pulled them apart.

"We actin' like gangs. Isn't that what you told us to do?"

"Not just any gang," she told them. "Baranggay. There were many baranggay," Isabel told them, "living independent from one another—quiet and respectful of the other. There was no fighting. No landowners. No nation. No need to claim one."

"You mean no Philippines? I never heard of that."

"That's so crazy."

The children passed islands to one another, fingering them, and feeling the weight of them in their hand.

"What island is this?" Pancho wanted to know.

"Luzon," Isabel said. She pointed to a spot on the block. "Manila is right there. Is that where your parents are from?"

"No, they're Visayan," he said.

"That's this one," Tara said, handing him a tiny red block.

"Isn't this also the Visayas?" Marlon asked. "Which one do you come from?"

They pictured their lolas and lolos on these blocks, grandparents they had only spoken to in dreams and in sepia-toned photos. They found their hometowns and provinces in the grains of wood, imagined living on islands floating in the Pacific Ocean.

She let them move the blocks about, floated finger baskets in buckets of tap water and called them monsoon-swollen rice paddies. They hunted milkfish. They salted duck eggs. They built forts made of nipa leaves. They played this way for hours, until the sun paled and moved from one corner of the room to a spot on a wall high above them. In the end, they swept their arms across the floor, gathering the islands, the brown-skinned people, the animals and plants, and packed them back into Isabel's satchel, a magic bag where she kept the oceans, skies and numerous clouds and fishes.

On the morning of Arturo's funeral, the wind howled and whistled above the pitching of the sea. In the distance, a seagull fluttered its wings against the breeze. It hovered above the water like a spirit.

Elliot agreed to pick her up, so that she wouldn't have to walk in alone. His SUV pulled into the gravel lot, dodging members of the community. He hunched over the steering wheel, his shoulders rising up like two little mountains of stress. The fog was thick and seemed to rise from the earth and fill up the whole world. It was difficult to make out the shapes.

Inside, the Ilocano choir stood on risers, moaning love songs in minor keys. Some of them masked their sadness behind sunglasses.

Elliot guided Isabel into the parlor, and the bodies cloaked in black milled around like a carnival of noise, women speaking loudly and rapidly and men humming low. Children ran laps around the grown-ups. Their laughter rose above the other sounds, distracted Isabel from mourning. One or two of the little ones recognized her from school. "Hi, Ate Isabel!" called a little girl in an off-white dress. "Hello!" called the child who was chasing her.

Isabel spied Ferdi pushing an old lola in a wheelchair. "Yo!" he yelled to her. "Isabel!" She waved back at him, and looked away, but he kept pushing the old woman in her direction. "I want you to meet Lola Espie," he said rolling the chair to a halt. "She's an old-timer here, and you—you are a new-timer."

Lola Espie was a woman with skin as delicate as lace, an intricate weave of fine lines around beautiful gray eyes. She held her hand out to Isabel and Isabel brought the old woman's fingers to her forehead.

"Anak," said the old lola, her mouth quivering. "Any friend of Ferdi's is family."

"Are you Ferdi's lola?" Isabel asked. She couldn't see any family resemblance.

"I wish," said Lola Espie. "He's my yaya—always feeding me, dressing me, giving me pills as if I am a baby." She put her bony arms out and Isabel watched them tremble. "Let this old lola kiss you." And taking Isabel's face with her two hands, she sniffed at her cheeks. Isabel felt herself melting inside. She smelled lilacs on the old woman's kiss. She pulled herself away and wiped her eyes, smiled at the two of them, then hurried away.

Metal folding chairs were lined up before the coffin. She searched for Tita Chic Chic. Rows and rows of chairs filled the room, but no one sat in them. The people were standing in corners, or pausing in the aisles, blocking traffic. There was nowhere to go. In the back of the room, a circle of women gathered, and every now and then Isabel saw a hanky waving. Moaning haunted the room like the song of sirens on a moor, howling like a bitter wind. She must be here, Isabel thought.

The powder room was furnished with posh chairs and little day beds. Golden wallpaper warmed the room and tropical fronds peeked from corners. A stream of mourners slipped in and out of stalls. Aunties and lolas gabbed loudly, tsismis ran rampant. Isabel nodded at a few old ladies, mumbling, "Kamusta po kayo?" None of the ladies paid much attention to the teenagers lined up along the powder room mirror like chorus girls. Isabel leaned on the back wall, waiting for a stall. Angel rolled on another coat of lipstick. Her lips were so dark and rich they looked black. Lourdes pulled at her eyebrows and penciled them in. She took a tissue from a box in front of her and dabbed at her eye.

"This sucks," she said.

Stumbling out of the bathroom, Maya smoothed her dress, running her hands over her body. White bulbs soft as eggshells glowed along the edges of the long mirror. Maya glanced down the row of girls to her right and left, then bowed her head onto the counter and began sobbing.

"Your eyeliner's gonna bleed," Mercedes told her. She nudged Maya. "Stop that. You'll get it all over."

"Fuck you," Maya said. She held her head up to the mirror and black streaks dripped from her eyes.

"I think she looks good like that," Marilena said. She took a comb and teased her hair then shaped it carefully into a brown halo.

Lourdes grabbed another tissue and handed it to Maya. "Shut the fuck up," she told them. "Bad enough Arturo's gone." She glanced in the mirror and, seeing Isabel, she snapped, "What?"

"Are you girls okay?"

"Our friend is dead," Lourdes said.

Isabel took a deep breath. "I'm sorry for your loss."

"What do you know? You hardly knew him," said Mercedes.

"I have nightmares," Marilena said. "Ever hear guns go off in your sleep?" They looked at Isabel, waiting.

"Didn't think so," Lourdes said.

Isabel sat next to Maya. She pulled out her compact mirror and checked her face. "The point is I wanna be here for you."

"Yeah," Lourdes asked. "Why?"

"Maybe someday when this is all over," Isabel said, "maybe you can tell me about him."

"What for?" Lourdes said. "So's you can psychoanalyze us or something?" She turned away. The blue silk of her Manchurian dress shimmered like the sky. Though her arms were thin, the muscles were long, lean, well defined.

"Leave her alone, Desa," Maya said suddenly. "She's tryin' to be nice."

"Whatever," Lourdes said. She turned once more in front of the mirror. Her platform shoes made her three inches taller than she actually was. She wobbled. "I'm outta here. Who's coming?"

Several of the girls followed Lourdes, walking past Isabel as if she wasn't there. Maya stayed, a river of mascara and liner staining her beautiful face. "Sometimes she's a bitch," she told Isabel. They looked at one another in the mirror. "Even if she wants to back down cuz she know she's wrong, she won't."

"It's okay," Isabel said. She powdered her face, dabbing at it without really watching. She felt her lip trembling. "I lost a baby," she said. "A miscarriage. And nobody knew. Not my friends. Not my family." She placed the sponge on her cheek, and held herself steady. "So nobody knew to say goodbye."

Maya fumbled with her purse, nodding. "For real? Wow." She pulled out a crumpled-up handkerchief embroidered with pink and yellow flowers. She smoothed it out on the counter, the white linen rising up like old wrinkles. Isabel said it was lovely. "It was my lola's. Sometimes I dip it in her perfume." She handed the kerchief to Bel, who held it to the eggshell light and saw the irregularity of stitches there, beautiful and rough and fragrant as a garden of roses.

In the parlor, she saw JoJo kneeling at Arturo's coffin. The top half of the casket was propped open, and JoJo had one hand on the banister and the other plunged into the casket. The only funeral she had ever been to was a neighbor's who had died of old age. That casket had been shut tight.

JoJo wore black jeans and a black silk shirt which hung over his belt. She imagined this was the same thing he wore when he went clubbing. The boys stood next to him; some of them knelt around him. Miguel rested his head on Derek's shoulder. She envied the way they loved JoJo, stood by him like guardian angels. She closed her eyes a moment, and the heavy scent of flowers wafted around her like a drug, making her feel a little dizzy. The hem and haw of the electric piano faded, and when she opened her eyes the boys were standing in front of everyone.

"He was our brother," said Miguel. One black curl hung in the center of Miguel's forehead, dangled like a satin ribbon. "We love him, and we'll never forget him. This is for you, Auntie Chic Chic."

Their song blew quietly like wind. The voices of people and children spoke over their song, and as their melody took shape, conversations dissipated, kids sat down at the feet of the boys. They began as one voice, eyes closed like angels descending from some otherly place. Then Miguel snapped his fingers in a syncopated rhythm and Derek spun a bass-line, his lips pouting, "Boom, doom, boom-boom. Boom, doom boom-boom." All four boys swayed to Derek's beat. Miguel and Elvie, humming now, provided the background for Edison, whose falsetto voice soared across the room.

Elliot nudged Isabel, nodded to her an "Are they good or what" nod. And she smiled weakly back at him. She knew this song, though she couldn't place it. Their harmony made her want to disappear in its familiarity. Miguel stepped forward, still snapping his fingers and sang, "Dahil sa iyo—sa buhay ko'y labis . . ." When she closed her eyes, she heard her own mother humming to her, rocking her to sleep.

"What's it mean?" Elliot whispered.

"I'm not sure," she answered, but she knew it was a love song.

She looked around the room, at the heads nodding, the bodies gently moving to the music, JoJo crumpled up in his chair, his shoulder falling and rising. Stooped over like that, he didn't look so mean and intimidating; in fact he looked small. She was glad he had a circle of boy angels around him.

Tita Chic Chic Sanchez sat on a long couch in the very front and smiled at the boys as they sang. Drawn to her, Isabel moved through the crowd, weaving between children and old ladies. She made her way to the front, sat next to Tita Chic Chic and took her hand.

"I'm so sorry," Isabel whispered. She felt her heart swelling up.

"It's okay," Tita Chic Chic said. Her hands felt tough and wiry. "He's with God now."

"It doesn't matter what they say," Isabel told her. "You should be proud of Arturo—he was such a kind boy." She could only imagine the tsismis and hiya that must be running through the community.

"Alam ko yan, hija," Tita Chic Chic said. "There is nothing to be ashamed of. He was a very good boy and now he is with God."

Mother's Day Brunch. The Marriott Inn. May 1994.
Photo by Isabel Manalo

The ladies gather around her mother and everyone is chirping like birds. They wear matching corsages on their breasts, and they all have hair that's cut and curled and teased into puffballs. Bel backs up to get them into the shot. But everything seems crowded with their colors, their profusion of flowers; even their laughter seems to clutter the frame. Tagalog surrounds her, and more irritating than the women who seem to shout their conversations at each other is the whispering behind her. Bel feels sick to her stomach; if this were not Mother's Day, she wouldn't have come. But who could say no to her mother?

It's just as well she doesn't understand them. The whispering feels like hot breath on her neck—sticky and irritating. Shut up, you old gossips, she thinks. What do they know about it? They were born in another country, in another time. Things are different now. At least her problems were born of love.

Angel Torres has found her way into the photo and she is tossing Isabel nasty looks. She's not a mom, how'd she get into the frame? For one second, Bel pictures herself sitting next to Angel, community spinster, but with a little baby in her arms. A little toddler who'd squirm and slobber kisses, who'd be sweet and sweaty from naps, soggy Cheerios, and diaper wipes. The ladies would call her baby Siopao like she was nothing but a big old white bun full of sweet adobo meat.

The whispering feels like little stickpins jabbing at Bel's sides, her legs, her armpits. She cannot fit the table of mothers into the frame. She backs so far away from them she ends up on the other side of the room. Why do Filipinos care so much about other people's business? Nothing but tsismis and hiya. Bel waves a hand at the ladies, who keep turning their heads and looking at one another. "Smile!" she yells above the din of motherhood. "Picture!" And they all turn their heads and grin at her like they love her best. "Beautiful!" Bel says and they disperse.

When Isabel's secret was told, the community in Evanston talked and talked about her and that baby. She remembered how women would approach her mom and give their condolences like she herself had died. They had whispered so long and so loudly, Isabel heard those old women even when they had stopped talking. What did they know about love, she thought. What did they know about losing your own baby? Isabel shifted in her seat. She held up Tita Chic Chic's hand and kissed it.

Isabel let the music bring her to another place. The scent of flowers grew even stronger. It was the kind of perfume that soaked into one's skin, so pungent it startled her awake. Candles flickered wildly, as if the flames shot up a little higher, spun out a little farther. Except there was no breeze, only the boys and their song. Arturo's here, she thought, he's here.

When the boys slid into a single voice, their song fading into nothing, there was a cloud of laughter, of thunder clapping. Ferdi threw his fist into the air and hollered, "All Right Now!"

Arturo's mother took each boy's face into her small hands. She kissed each one, stroked their cheeks. She took a moment to examine them the way she would her son. When she got to Edison, who was a big bald boy, she took her kerchief and pretended to shine his head. Everyone giggled at this.

Then Oscar Sanchez arrived. His presence was announced by a flutter of voices. "Nanay," he said, calling out to his wife. It was almost a whisper, but she turned to him right away. When she saw him standing in his Navy attire, the formality of blue and white, she held out her arms. The couple collapsed together, as if all this time Tita Chic Chic had been waiting, so she might fall apart, at last.

"Have you seen him?"

Isabel looked up to see JoJo sitting next to her.

"No," she answered.

"Why not?" He looked at her and all she saw was the red in his eyes. "He'd probably want that."

"You're kidding, right?" she answered him. "I'm the supertoken." She stared at him, ready to fight. When he didn't say anything she said, "I feel him."

"What?"

"He's here. I feel him."

JoJo started to leave. Then he hesitated, leaning his hand on the chair in front of him, tapping at it. He nodded at her and, turning, he walked away. She listened to his footsteps as they grew faint, to his voice whispering under his breath, slipping into prayer.

Outside the rain fell hard on the roof of Elliot's truck. She watched the way the windshield wipers zipped back and forth across the glass, listened for the thud-thud as they brushed all this rain out of their way. The world was so noisy to her right now. Elliot said, "That wasn't as bad as you expected, now was it?"

She thought of the church full of people, his body lying in state before the altar. The Mass was long and full of weeping, loud and uncontainable. She sat with her colleagues, which only made her feel more out of place since she was the only one among them who knew when to sit, to kneel, to beat the heart with a clenched fist. "I am not worthy," she had prayed. "I am not worthy to be with you." It didn't really matter that the rest of the church was in sync with her litany—she was sitting in a pew of visitors. When it came time for communion, she watched the families parading past. She put the children together with the mom and dad, found the resemblance in the mouth, the eyes, the shape of a body. She wondered what went on in their homes. Passing her pew, each child, each teen, looked at her, big-eyed and wondering. They distracted her from prayer.

She made her way past Calhoun, Wedgwood, the officers and Elliot, joining the families in the aisle. She walked among them, a procession of mourners, of lolas and lolos, of anxious parents, of broken-hearted brothers and sisters, holding out for the body of Christ. Waiting her turn, she wondered if it helped to share this pain. If having all these people together weeping like rain somehow made it easier to say goodbye.

She had stood at Arturo's casket and examined his sleeping face, at the way the color had drained, was tinted green, at the shape of the head still round as the moon, at the eyelashes that brushed his cheeks. She tried to reach into the casket to hold his hand, but she couldn't move past the wood. The sweetness of the flowers wafted her way, comforted her. Inside she felt a flutter, like goldfish swimming laps around her uterus, and she thought for a moment, for a very brief moment, that her baby had come back.

Rock 'n' roll shouted from the speakers of Elliot's SUV, bled a guitar riff painful and off-key. The leather in his SUV smelled like him, like eucalyptus and clove and something sweet. "I think the whole thing was kind of nice," Elliot said. "Don't you?" When she didn't answer, he hummed softly to himself as if to say, it's okay, you don't have to answer.

"Can you see where you're going?" she asked him. Before her, the world was washed in gray, and steam rose from hot pavement.

"Sure," he said, pulling into the gravel driveway of her beach house. The windows of the truck were all fogged-up. Everything here is so dense, she thought.

"Okay, Elliot," she said, wanting to get out. "Thanks." She grabbed the handle of the door, and yanked at it.

"Hey," Elliot said. She stopped and looked at him. "Are you okay?"

"Sure I am," she answered. Her voice felt small, like it was about to shatter. She blinked. "I just want to go inside now. Thanks." She was weeping, tears chasing down her face. She looked up at the windshield, at the torrents of rain spilling onto the glass. She felt so stupid, crying like this. Elliot moved closer to her. "I only met him once, you know—no, twice." She wiped her face with the back of her hand. "God, it was just weird. Wasn't today weird?" she asked.

She looked at him for the first time, at his eyes, which were so round and sad. "Yes it was," Elliot said. "Of course it was."

"Not just that," she stuttered. "It isn't just—it's . . . well." She pounded on the seat, her fists bouncing up off the cushions. "Aw, Elliot," she cried, "I just want to go home."

He leaned over to embrace her. "I know," he said. "We're here now. You're home." Most of his cologne had worn off, but she could still smell a hint of clove in his shirt collar.

"No, I want to go home," she said, her fists still pounding, this time on Elliot's back. He held her tight, told her things would be okay. No it won't, she thought.

"It's all wrong," she told him.

"What?" he asked.

"Everything, every goddamn thing."

He tried to quiet her. "Comere," he said softly. "Just comere." And then he kissed her, just like that—he kissed her as if he always had. And when she pulled away from him, she found herself a little weak, a little embarrassed, a little dizzy from his cologne, which was sweet and fragrant like cedar burning up north.

FIVE

An alcove of rocks tucked behind the ocean bore the many colors of the crew. A fat white candle burned, emitting white plumes of smoke, cluttering the air like ghosts traveling the night. The girls posed like fallen stars. They locked arms and rested weary heads on one another. There was moaning. A song. The boys scattered—Derek silent, Elvie shouting, Edison weeping in the distance. Miguel climbed the wall of rocks, his face shining from the surf, his eyes wide, angry, wet. We gonna let them get away with this, he wanted to know. We gonna let this slide? When no one answered him, he pulled a wrinkled piece of paper from his pocket. Sniveling, he wiped his nose and he told them, "Me and Arturo made this rhyme." He balanced his feet on the rocks and, holding the note to the sky, he began to rap.

> *Pintig is da beat of the Filipino heart.*
> *Pintig. Pintig. Pintig.*
> *Pintig is da beat of the Filipino heart.*
> *It's the primal bang of bamboo rappin'*
> *to the off-tune strings of my daddy's mandolin.*
> *It's da clap-clap-clappin' of da lolas*
> *when we dance.*
> *It's da bee-bop-boppin'*
> *of homies when we rap—*
> *It's da pukpukin kita*
> *of Nanay's slipper when we bad!*
> *It's da magbabarílan poppin'*
> *when the crew has all gone mad.*

Pintig. Pintig. Pintig.
Can you hear my heart?
Filipino heart. Pinoy on da beach heart.
Homeless unanswered heart.

Weeping answered him, soared from some place deep within the circle of girls. The wind blew and took with it the light from the burning candle.

Elliot brought her to a place on the oceanfront, where they took their shoes off and stumbled across the sand, climbing warped sets of stairs, to a bar where you could see the tide rolling underneath the floorboards. A local band played, twanging songs in memory of Hank Williams and country-fried rock. He held her hand and dragged her through a crowd of people in stonewashed jeans and cotton shirts. The sea air, salty and pungent, fought the stench of beer and heavy perfume.

He told her to wait while he got them drinks. "Is this fun or what?" he said, pushing his way past shoulders and the poofs of big-haired women.

He came back with two bottles of beer and five single men. "These are the guys, Isabel," he said proudly. "Guys—Isabel. She teaches with me."

They were a motley crew—skinny and fat and short and towering. They nodded to her, shook her hand, held up their bottles of Miller and Heineken.

"It's loud in here," she said.

They listened to rockabilly and she danced with Elliot like she was from the mountains—barefoot and hot from too much liquor. Once she glanced out the window, looking for the moon. And there they were: Lourdes, Maya, Mercedes and Marilena. Bright as the Big Dipper. Some pack of she-devils, giving her the evil eye. Like she had stepped into their world with the sole purpose of making their lives unbearable—even when she was minding her own life. Who asked you on this date, she thought. These girls were everywhere and nowhere, and this was her everywhere. Get out, she thought, closing her eyes and turning away from the window.

She tugged on Elliot's sleeve. "I'm sort of tired," she said.

"What?" His arms and legs were tumbling out of whack, a puppet without strings.

"It's getting late," she tried again. She looked over her shoulder at the window, which was vacant as night.

He nodded, and waving goodnight to the guys they began their climb down the stairs. He leaned against her, the weight of him pulling her down each step. When they neared the bottom, they fell forward, laughing at one another, giggling.

He whispered to her, said he hoped his friends didn't bore her, said she smelled of pretty seashells. She squeezed his hand, told him no, what a good time she'd had, what a crazy man he was.

Strolling down the beach on the way to the car, they saw a bonfire's orange flames dancing against the night. Guitar music wafted their way, the voices singing something of a lullaby. As they neared the light, she saw JoJo and the kids gathered about the fire.

"Hey, you guys," Elliot called out.

"Don't," she said, covering up his mouth.

"What?" he whispered. "Gotta say hi."

She saw their faces lit by the fire, the warm tones making them flushed. Lourdes and Edison cuddled up under a blanket, falling into a dream, while Mercedes, Marilena and Maya sat just outside the circle, whispering to one another. Closest to the fire, JoJo squatted, his knees popping up like a grasshopper's legs. He stoked the fire with a piece of driftwood. Miguel and Derek winked at each other as they approached.

"You guys jamming?" Elliot asked.

They turned to look at Isabel and Elliot, expressionless. She felt the heat from the fire, and the flush of the beer made her uncomfortable. Casually, she slipped Elliot's arm off her shoulder.

"Something like that," answered Miguel. "How you doing?"

The tide banged up against the shore, beat white under the full moon. "Hurricane season's here," JoJo said. "They say that one is on his way."

She could smell the ocean swelling full and pregnant with South American winds. "What's his name?" Isabel asked. "This new one they're tracking, what's his name?"

"Daniel," Miguel called out.

Elliot began to talk about the hurricanes. His words streamed loud and rapid against the water's cry. This year the hurricanes would be boys. All boys. Every few weeks since she arrived, the weather reports predicted the arrival of one of the boys. Alvin, Bertrand, Chester, and now Daniel. Soon as the weather people named him, the Tidewater community rushed out to stores and bought up all the water, fresh fruits and vegetables. Stocked up on canned goods, candles and flashlight batteries. Hurricanes always threatened Tidewater—always pumped the ocean, full of wild energy, diving pelicans, leaping fish, always drove the dolphins a little closer to shore. And though the community looked for him, he never arrived. Never got there.

"Sort of anticlimactic," Elliot said.

The ocean pulled Isabel away from the kids, distracted her, made her want to float out to meet the dolphins. Made her wish she were completely alone.

Finally, she looked up and caught JoJo's eye. He was staring. "Have the police found anything out?" she asked. Derek stopped strumming the guitar. Beyond them, waves were crashing. They all looked at her and waited. "I mean about Arturo's shooting. Have they found anything at all?"

JoJo looked at the sea. He spat tobacco onto the sand. "Don't know," he answered.

"That was awful," Elliot said. "Tragic."

"Well," she said. "We shouldn't intrude. Elliot, we ought to go." She pulled him away from them, wanting to escape.

Later they sat on her back porch and tracked clouds shifting across the night sky. Elliot asked, "What made you say that? They were perfectly cordial."

Isabel nodded. He was right. They were cordial, polite and distant. Exactly. She gazed at Elliot and the freckles on his fair skin. He was kind, she thought. Nothing like Mark—that showy, macho, run-from-the-truth ex-boyfriend of hers. She kissed Elliot on the cheek.

"What's that for?" he asked.

"Nothing," she said. "For making me feel home when I'm not, I guess."

Sunday Mass for Foreign Graduate Students. Chicago, IL. 1959.
Photo by Camila Chiu

Two hours before, Camila sat behind the sisters in Mass, whispering Hail Marys and Our Fathers, dreaming of home. She focused on the altar and the candles' yellow flicker. Standing with his back to the congregation, Father Andrew lifted the chalice. He sang the Latin Mass, called out to God, and just as he was about to reach for that high note, the one he could never seem to get, he gasped and fell to the floor. His body fell with a thud that echoed throughout the church. The sisters screamed, a flock of geese in white habits with wooden black beads hanging from their skirts. By the time Camila got up to see what was wrong, a slender Filipino was stooped over Father Andrew. A stethoscope plugged to his ears connected him to the priest's massive chest. The sisters surrounded the site, getting down on their hands and knees. Their hands flew across their chests as they uttered the sign of the cross and waited for the ambulance. Afterwards, the sisters guided the young Filipino to the church basement to eat a pancake breakfast.

Now the nuns stand about him, stroking his arms, blessing his forehead. Sister Mary Margaret hands Camila a camera. "Look through the lens, dear, and take our picture," she instructs. "Dr. Manalo is a hero." The doctor is a dark-skinned man with almond eyes and a wide smile. His arms stretch out to hold onto the sisters. He grins into the lens and with a thick Kapampangan accent says, "Taga saan ka?" Where is she from? And for the first time since Camila has arrived in America, she feels at home.

For the repose of the soul of Arturo Sanchez, Isabel joined the families, kneeling before Mother Mary, rattling a series of Hail Marys and Our Fathers. The novenas took place for nine days. Mourners gathered at the house of the dead, in his living room, near the spot where every year his father placed a lighted evergreen tree, where they sat to open gifts or snap a family portrait. The Sanchez home filled up with members of the community. Some nights there was hardly any room at all, and the heat of the bodies made it difficult to breathe, to focus on Mother Mary and the large portrait of Arturo, which sat above the Lady, guarding her. Candles added to the heat, flickering from tables, lining the shrine of photos. Arturo had become a saint.

She had to call her mother, to ask about procedures. "I know the Our Father, the Hail Mary, the Glory Be," she said, "but what's all this other stuff they rattle off—another prayer, something they have memorized?"

The first night she attended, she acted as if she had been to novenas all her life. She knew how to recite the rosary. She had one in second grade. She even knew the different mysteries. What she wasn't used to was the way everyone would touch her, kiss her, make her eat as if the gathering were a party, and then came the time to kneel on the hard floor and everyone would do it, and the light in the house would go from celebratory to solemn. They chanted prayers and then the leader would ask a question, and the room of mourners would answer. She was lost; she felt like a complete fake.

Sometimes the teens showed up, sometimes not. They never prayed, though—they only sat in the back of the room, a figure of faces, sometimes with heads bowed, or hands masking their grief. Leaning on one another, they'd drift into sleep, always silent.

The room buzzed, chanted, "Holy Mary, Mother of God, pray for us, sinners now and at the hour of our death." Our death, she thought, our death. The chanting numbed her. She felt herself going light, and just as she was about to float right out of her body, a hot wind blew, like someone blowing in her ear. Someone had grabbed her hand and held on, squeezing it as if to comfort her. She pictured Arturo dancing around the pansit table, teasing his mother and kissing her on the top of her head. "Holy Mary, Mother of God," she whispered, "pray for us." The person squeezed her hand even tighter, and she opened her eyes to see who it was. There was no one. But the feeling was still there, like a giant hand wrapped around her palm. Oh shit, she thought. What is that? she thought.

JoJo stepped through the screen door, banging it behind him. Perfect, she whispered, rising up off her knees. She met him halfway into the room and whispered, "I need to talk to you." He nodded and followed her into the kitchen. The voices floated underneath the tension between them. She looked up into his eyes, at his face serious as always. She felt anxious. "Have you heard?" she asked him.

"What?" he said in his regular voice. She pointed to the other room, held her finger to her mouth. He stepped a little closer. His breath fell on her.

"They're dropping the investigation," she said. "Can you believe it?" She smelled the saltwater in his hair.

"Bout time," he whispered.

"What's that mean?"

"Ain't nothing gonna bring him back."

"Calhoun says the family's dropping it too."

"Right, I knew that. Of course. What's the point?"

She moved even closer to him now, whispering in his ear. "The point is whoever shot Arturo is getting away with it, and could maybe do it again."

"You're talkin' like a white girl. Ain't no such thing as justice for all."

The voices outside were deep and powerful, pushing them close together, so close they became a whisper. "Our Father," the others chanted, "who art in heaven . . ."

"I am not," she hissed. "Do you want this to happen again?"

"You don't get it, do you?" JoJo said, smiling now. "You totally buy into that shit Calhoun feeds you. Next you're going to tell me you want a rap session with the crew."

The chorus of mourners begged forgiveness. Promised to forgive. Like a deal they were cutting with God. She waved the prayers away. The look in JoJo's eye made her so mad.

"Stop making fun of me," she said, slapping his arm. "We can't just let it die."

"Why not?" he said. He put his hand on her shoulder and told her he understood she meant well, but, "Leave these people alone, please? Their son is gone and any more talk only hurts 'em. Just leave it alone." He patted her on the head, smiling. "Besides, I hear you got your hands full with that new boyfriend of yours."

"He's not my boyfriend," she said.

"Right," he said, leaving her as the voices filled her up with language loud and foreign.

She decided to leave; she was so mad. But just as she walked away, Tita Nita Starr cornered her with a plate of egg rolls.

"Why aren't you married, anak?" she wanted to know.

Isabel shrugged. Why do they always think you should be married, she wondered. What if you don't want to be married? Maybe you'd rather shack up or sleep around. She smiled politely at Tita Nita. "I guess I haven't found the right guy," she said.

"What about that handsome Elliot North? I think he's kind of sweet on you, no?"

"Tita, he's my colleague."

Anita Starr ran her hands along Isabel's arms. "Anyway, you come with me." She dragged Isabel into the living room. The prayers were breaking up for the night, and people were snacking. Tita clapped her hands loudly and asked everyone to listen.

Bel grabbed a plate and filled it up with pansit, egg rolls, pan de sal. She heard Tita Nita's voice above the others, calling them to order. In the corner of the room, Lourdes, Mercedes, and Marilena sat with their backs to the wall. The three sat exactly alike—slumped in their folding chairs, eyes half closed, arms crossed against their chests. She wondered if they were breathing.

Tita Nita gathered the group, ushered them onto folding chairs, quieted them down. Isabel remained standing, picking at her pansit, dipping lumpia in sweet and sour sauce.

"So anyway," Tita Nita said, "we are so lucky to have Isa Manalo, who is a trained actress, and beautiful like a model." Here she waved to Isabel to come up to the front of the room. "Parang artista, di ba?" she asked the group. A wave of whispers floated like butterflies. "We would like to know if you will honor us and help produce our Miss Philippines-Virginia Beach 1996 beauty pageant." She indicated the teens sitting in the back. "The girls are very excited to work with you, to learn about glamour." Isabel smiled and looked to Lourdes, Mercedes and Marilena, who collectively rolled their eyes at her. "Stand up, Lourdes," Tita Nita said. "Stand up, anak." Lourdes rose from the folding chair, kept her arms crossed against her chest. A strand of hair fell into her eyes. She kept her focus on the ground, studied her shoelaces. "You can teach her how to act beautiful."

Millie as Miss Teenage Sampaguita. Chicago, IL. April 1981.
Photo by Isabel Manalo

This is the craziest thing she's ever seen her sister do, but there she is, Miss Teenage Sampaguita. A white gown cascades down her body and billows at her feet. She has curled her black hair into tiny ringlets and gathered them up and stuffed them like posies on top of her ridiculous head. Bel squints into the lens. She focuses on her sister's sash, a garish white satin banner with harlot-red lettering. Their parents stand on either side of Millie. Mom has to step out of the way so that the rose's thorns will not jab her. Dad has his arm around Millie, but Millie gives Dad a look and says,

"Queens don't let anyone touch them for pictures, Dad. It crumples the dress." And just as she says that, Frankie Boy emerges from behind, his fingers held out like bunny ears over the reigning Miss Teenage Sampaguita's big fat head. It is at this very moment that Isabel snaps the photo.

Isabel took a deep breath. She tried to explain—diplomatically, of course—that her training wasn't really in performance. Besides, she thought, teaching Lourdes beauty and glamour scared her. What a nightmare. "It's called creative dramatics. The idea is to use improvisation to learn about history and literature. I've never done this kind of work—beauty pageants, modeling. I wouldn't know where to begin." She looked out into the faces of the group, at the smiles frozen on their faces. She glanced over at Tita Nita, who nodded her head. She wondered why she was doing this, asking in the middle of a novena.

"But you can try," Tita Nita said. Isabel shook her head. "You've been in pageants, di ba? It's part of growing up Filipino." Isabel drew her lips into a line, shrugged an apologetic no. She felt them looking at her, all of them, checking her out. She felt so red, white and blue, though she knew for a fact she did grow up Filipino.

*

Millie was always the good child. She studied harder than Isabel or Frankie Boy ever did, she took up folk dancing when her parents suggested it, she took science when her siblings were taking music and painting. And Millie never stayed out past her curfew.

When Frank suggested Isabel enter the beauty contest during her senior year, she laughed and said, "No way, Dad. I've got things to do!" Millie watched the way her sister's answer planted a seed in him, angry, disappointed, hurt.

"That girl is too good to listen," he ranted. "Too smart."

So years later, when he asked Millie to sign up, she told him, "Already have, Dad. Wanna see my talent?"

Every Friday night for two months in the fall, she joined twelve other girls from the area—promenading up and down the lunchroom runway in platform shoes; waving and flexing and fanning her wrist; smearing lip balm across her teeth. They'd rehearse for three hours at a time.

Tita Elena, a sultry auntie and ex-Mrs. Philippines U.S.A., danced her body across the stage and directed them. "Like stars, girls, like stars!" Sometimes, in a fit of impatience, she'd stomp her high heels one after the other, and slam her papers to her sides. "No Millie, darling, not like that! Not like you're dying. Graceful—like a butterfly, darling!" During the talent section Millie marched up to the microphone and sang a shaky, shrill version of "Wind Beneath My Wings," popping p's and k's into the microphone, straining to hit the long high notes. The other girls were older than her, and in between the numbers she tried to squeeze her body into their circle of laughter. She could not compete—these girls lined their lips before they painted them, these girls knew how to backcomb their hair to pile it high, high, high. Isabel said they ratted their hair.

"Don't be catty, hija," Camila warned.

"It's true, Mom," Isabel said. "Your baby's running with the big girls—the BIG HAIR girls, that is."

"You think you're so witty," Millie snapped. "You're jealous—and, Ate, it isn't pretty."

But the truth was the girls had big hair, painted toenails, padded bras, and boyfriends. Millie started bringing her books to rehearsals, alternating between her paperback novels and chemistry text. No one noticed her, no one paid attention and she was bored. She sold the most raffle tickets, and got the biggest crowd at the pageant. She won.

Isabel thinks of the night her sister walked down the runway, her rhinestone tiara slipping off the side of her head, and the Vaseline dripping from her teeth. She saw Millie squinting at the blinding lights, her scrawny shoulders hunched-up and awkward. The past Miss Teenage Sampaguita's voice rang from house speakers. Applause rippled from the audience, and the girls on the stage kissed Millie generously, whispering under their breath, "Unbelievable—What a rip—Who knew?"

Years later, Isabel asked her why she did it and Millie told her it was something she was told to do. It made her parents happy. She figured it was the least she could do. They were her parents.

*

Tita Nita begged Isabel to think about it, to be a team player and do it for the girls. And Isabel, not knowing what to think, looked around the room, searching for an answer. A sound from the back—chairs rattling forward—startled her. She looked up just in time to see Lourdes, Mercedes, and Marilena dragging their bodies up and out of the room.

Isabel wondered if Millie would have walked out with them. She doubted it. The night of Millie's crowning, Bel watched her little sister standing with a crooked crown on her head, a glow-in-the-dark sash and a chrome scepter with cubic zirconium bobbles glued at its crown. I should have been there for her, Isabel thought, never should have let her do that to herself. Let her be Miss Teenage Sampaguita, a queen without subjects.

The following day, she fed Elliot sandwiches and chips. They were sitting on her back porch, reading the morning paper. The tide was high and rushed in giant white waves toward them, its fingers of soapy bubbles retreating gently to the sea. She handed him a turkey sandwich on a paper plate, chips falling like leaves on the table. "It just pisses me off," she said.

"I know," Elliot said, turning a page.

"He thinks he's so smart, like he's in it for the kids," she said, sitting down, facing Elliot. She put her palm to her face, and leaned toward him. "But he's willing to act like nothing happened. Like everything is fine. Fucking denial."

Elliot looked up from his paper, reaching for her hand. "Calm down," he said. "I know he makes you crazy, but it's not worth it."

"What do you mean? This boy dies and everybody knows another boy shot him, and that's it?" She sighed, looking out to sea, to the pelicans flying high overhead.

"And then that crazy Tita Nita Starr—a name straight out of the strip at the beach, I might add—asks me to run a beauty pageant—in front of everyone." She waited for him to look up from the paper. "I mean everyone. Right after they said 'Amen.' Then she was at it."

He told her to calm down. He told her she would have to pick her battles, or go insane, but she didn't want to hear it.

"And you know the thing that makes me really ticked?" she said, squeezing his hand and waving it up and down. "He says I talk like a white girl."

Elliot studied her face, looked at her with those eyes. "Honey," he said, "so what?"

Ferdi left twenty-minute messages on her machine every week. Just dialed her number and started lecturing. At first his messages irritated her, but then her days were always full of tension and worry. The messages grew interesting, like books on tape. She had been through the Spanish galleons, the canaries in Alaska, the ships' kitchens of World War II and the destruction of the International Hotel in San Francisco, an old structure that used to house Chinese and Filipino immigrant railroad workers. Ferdi barked from the speaker of her machine, winding in and out of tangents, misspeaking verbs and nouns like crazy. She began looking forward to his lessons. She let the machine run as she took off her shoes, and changed into sweats and her Chicago Bulls T-shirt. She cooked rice, measuring grains with a plastic cup, rinsing white pebbles of rice. She never called him back, but he continued to leave her messages.

HEY, ISABEL. JUST CALLING MY LOLO ON THE WEST COAST TO WISH HIM A HAPPY BIRTHDAY—HE IS NINETY YEARS OLD NOW. ANYWAY, I CALLED TO SEND HIM SOME LOVE AND I THOUGHT OF YOU. ARE YOU FIRST- OR SECOND-GENERATION FILIPINO AMERICAN? I AM THIRD. DID YOU KNOW MY LOLO WAS AMONG THE SECOND WAVE OF U.S. NATIONALS TO COME TO AMERICA FROM THE PHILIPPINES? HE ARRIVED IN 1922. HE WAS AMONG 45,000 FILIPINOS SEEKING THE GREAT AMERICAN (QUOTE) OPPORTUNITY—BETWEEN THE YEARS OF 1920-1930. NOW THEY ARE SO OLD WE CALL THEM THE MANONGS, BUT BACK THEN, THEY WERE DAPPER YOUNG MEN COME TO MAKE THEIR FORTUNE. KNOW WHAT THEY FOUND? THEY COULDN'T MARRY WHITE GIRLS. (HAD TO GO TO MEXICO FOR A BRIDE. WHICH IS WHY WE'RE SO TIGHT WITH OUR LATINO HERMANOS.) THEY COULDN'T BUY LAND. THEY WERE U.S. NATIONALS, BUT THEY WERE DENIED

CITIZENSHIP. AMERICANS CALLED THEM MONKEYS WITHOUT TAILS. SAID, "MONKEY GO HOME!" WHENEVER THEY WALKED INTO PUBLIC VENUES. PROFESSIONALS—TEACHERS, DENTISTS, DOCTORS, LAWYERS—WERE NOT ALLOWED TO PRACTICE THEIR TRADE AND WERE REDUCED TO MENIAL LABOR. THEY PICKED GRAPES, CANNED SALMON, BUILT THE RAILROADS WITH THE CHINESE. THIS SO-CALLED "LAND OF OPPORTUNITY" BECAME A NIGHTMARE FOR OUR FOREFATHERS.

BUT HEY, THAT'S JUST MY FAMILY HISTORY. WHAT ABOUT YOURS? DO YOU KNOW WHERE YOU CAME FROM?

She knew he meant well, but Isabel couldn't help feeling offended by the question: DO YOU KNOW WHERE YOU CAME FROM? Of course she did. Her father was always reciting their passage to America. How he came from the provinces and Mom came from the city. How they would never have met had they not traveled to the States. How many times had her father gone over his struggles, landing work as a surgeon only to be treated like an orderly?

She remembered a night long ago where her parents were shadows stretched over the curtains and walls of their little apartment in North Carolina, arguing about what they should do next. The boss had told him to go back to where he came from, was having him throw needles away and replace surgical supplies when he should have been assisting in surgery, if not performing it himself. This was her legacy. She didn't need Ferdi Mamaril barking at her, shouting his histories into her phone as if she didn't have any of her own.

"Where is everybody?"

They stared at Bel. Shrugged. Angel, light as Chinese tea, pulled a baseball cap over her eyes, slid her body down into the metal folding chair. Her legs stretched out in front of her, crossed and weary. Her shirt rose up and revealed the olive hue of her skin. Next to her, Miguel, hiding behind a dark pair of shades, rocked back and forth on the heels of his seat, a headset attached to his ears, bass guitar bleeding from him in hisses and beats.

"Flip time," Maya said plainly.

"Right," Isabel said. She let her eyes roam the empty gym, followed the streams of light from windows that kissed the floors. The clock hung above the basketball hoop, big as a full moon. "Well," Isabel said. "I suppose it's just the four of us then."

Maya dropped a notebook. Initials were scratched onto the page. LD written in script, or printed big and bloated on the cover. Little fish girls swam in between the letters. Fishtails covered the page, seemed to snap at Isabel. Maya caught Isabel's eye, turned the notebook over and picked up a magazine. She began leafing through its glossy pages. Isabel saw black rappers in ski caps, silver chains draped along their torsos, sterling crosses sharp as swords dangling from their thick necks. Hip-hop gangs held arms up high over their heads, like the end of the alphabet, a giant Y or V or something that made the body look big and strong. There were fans in colorful garb standing at the foot of the stage, hanging, cool as winter.

From underneath the baseball cap, Angel's voice floated up. "So you kick it with Mr. North?"

Silence filled the room and echoed like electric feedback, muffling sound. Isabel waited. Was she talking to her?

Angel sat up, lifting the cap from her face. "Di ba?" she asked again. Her eyes were tiny almonds, half closed, half-moons of light. "Last weekend, you and Mr. North, right?"

"We're friends."

"Looked to me like you were together," Angel said, smiling.

"Yeah," Maya said nodding, "Thas a trip, man." Now she was grinning. She sat up and leaned her body forward. She was a big girl—thick-boned and steady. Her broad face shined, dark and fertile as earth, half-cocked, full of mischief. "That for true?" she asked. "What you see in him?"

Angel nodded her head up and down. "He ain't all bad, not for a whitie."

"That's just it. He's a whitie," Maya said. "Don't that bug you?"

"Should it?" Isabel asked.

"Guess not," Maya said.

"He's really very nice," Isabel said. They stared at her, faces blank as paper.

"He's different," Maya said. "You deserve a hottee like Kuya JoJo."

"A hottee?"

"You know," Angel said. "Somebody who is da bomb?"

Isabel looked over to Miguel, who appeared to be napping under his shades. His body pulsed to the beat of the radio, lulled him onto some other plane. Then she asked, "You think JoJo's a hottee?"

"Phat," Maya cooed.

Miguel sat up and yanked the plugs out of his ears. "Did you know," he said, squinting at her as if the sun were blinding him, "that Elvis is a fake? He appropriated black culture. Those moves? Black. His hair? Dyed. His music—black. Gospel. Blue suede shoes? Not his." He shook his head, sat back in his chair and crossed his arms.

She smiled, surprised at this and said, "Appropriated? Says who?"

"Says Kuya JoJo an all them books on Elvis."

"You study Elvis with Kuya JoJo?" she asked.

"We study all kinds of things," Miguel said. "Part of his gig with us, ya know? Magkasama. He likes to kick it with us, and show us stuff 'bout history an shit." He said this with such authority, like Elvis was part of history the way the Boston Tea Party and Betsy Ross, and Martin Luther King, Jr. were part of history.

The others trailed in like beads of rain. They slipped into the gym one at a time. Mona, Derek, Ria, and Mercedes. Like spirits, like shadows. Vince, Elvie, and Edison. Each silent, as if mute by nature. Marilena, Nando, Lourdes, and Irma. Each with his or her hands flung into pockets, tucked under arms. Heads bowed and faces hidden behind masks and attitude. Every now and then, Isabel glanced over her shoulder to see them enter the room. They talked about music. They talked about first kisses. They talked about dating. They talked about how their parents believed they were incapable of dating. They talked about sex. The pros and cons of celibacy. The impossibility of maintaining their virginity. Isabel ignored the tardy as they entered. She let them find a place on a folding chair, against a wall, or on the edge of the stage. They slid onto the floor, their backs flat against the wood grain, their faces lifted up to the skylights and the web of metal grids and girders. They listened to Maya, Miguel and Angel, and slowly they began to respond. Some nodded and whispered, "Talaga?" like Maya, wanting to know, "For real?" Others rocked their bodies, rolled onto their sides, and teased each other—"Elvie still dreamin' of that first kiss," somebody laughed. "Talk to Ria—she's nothing but a sista waiting for trouble."

Lourdes and Mercedes sat in a corner of the room, whispering to one another, checking Isabel out with a tilt of the head, the arch of a brow. Now and then they emitted a small chatter of giggles. Isabel let them play the role tough girls play, knew that despite their whispers, their secrets, their nonchalant glances across the room, they were listening. Good enough, she thought, good enough.

She thought about asking them what they thought about Arturo and the investigation that would never be. Did it make them mad? Did they want revenge? But she knew it was a dangerous topic. She was lucky because today was the first conversation they had ever had. She decided not to push it. So she and the teens began like rain—first a drizzle, then a shower. Who knew, maybe someday they would sweep the gymnasium, a hurricane running, a monsoon devouring palm trees and ferns—entire jungles. Someday they would upset the clouds above, thunder clapping loud and angry, threatening to break the skies open once and for all.

SIX

Isabel walked into her third grade classroom, tossing scraps of rugs from her arms. "Imagine," she said to everyone, "that these patches of carpet are the archipelago of the Philippines." There were gold shag carpets, and rags tied and braided together. There were thick beige rugs and patches of astro turf. There were bathroom towels and welcome mats of hemp. There were seven thousand pieces. "Who can arrange these," she said, "into las islas archipelago?" The children scrambled to the task, spreading the pieces of turf across the entire gym floor into a distorted range of islands like a cobra stretching long and lean.

"Now," she told them. "Look at me. Pretend I'm no longer your teacher; I'm a Spanish conquistador!" She stepped onto the rugs with two hands on her hips. She walked with a swagger. "You guys be islanders, okay?"

They giggled at her and nodded their heads and watched her stepping on and off the multicolored rugs. "Has anybody ever been to the Philippines?" Some of their hands went up. Some of them jumped. "Did anyone have to get shots?"

"I hated that part!" said Noah Montenegro.

"Me too," said Marilu Gimenez, rubbing her arm. "But I like when they give you the suckers afterwards."

"Why did you have to get shots?" Isabel asked.

They told her so they wouldn't get sick. They told her so that mosquitoes with strange germs could bite them and they wouldn't catch fever.

"Aha!" she said. "But back then, there weren't shots. And back then, the ones with the germs were the visitors, and the islanders did not have the medicine to fight the germs. So, say I am coming to your island and I am bringing all kinds of things from Spain, even germs," she told them. "And you can't get shots!"

She touched a boy named Pepito and called out in a thick Spanish accent, "Cooties!" Pepito looked at her and rubbed his hands. He scratched the top of his head. "You're it, Pepito," she said. "You're one of the villagers and I just infected you—you're it. What you gonna do?" Pepito ran around the room yelling, "Cooties! I don't want cooties!" He tagged his cousin Nina.

Nina ran off and tagged another villager, spun in circles, grabbed onto another child, a make-believe husband, warrior, datu. He became infected too. Several villagers fell onto the hard-lit floor, feigned death by disease, and the surviving members of the tribe broke into tears, smashed their fists to the floor, raised their faces to the skylights, wondered why.

"Stupid natives!" yelled Isabel, "Don't you know how to handle Cooties?" She raced around the makeshift village, dodging tables and chairs that came to her knees. Waving a giant matchstick made of poster board, she tagged the artwork they had made that afternoon. "Fire burns germs!" she said. "This'll stop the germs from spreading."

"But wait," the children yelled. "Our stuff!" The children ran to get documents they had carved on tree bark, on bamboo and on banana leaves. But it was no use—she had tagged their things with the match and the whole civilization burned.

She put her hands on her hips and surveyed the room. Children were scattered on the floor, lying still as corpses. Other children ran to the bodies and covered the faces of the dead. They leaned over them and pretended to cry into their hands.

Soon the spirits of the dead villagers floated up off the floor, arms wafting and heads rolling back and forth. "What happened?" droned the dead spirits. "Where are we? Why are we here? Why are we not here?" They wandered about the room, bumping into desks and chairs, tripping over the pieces of carpet. Dead family members, forced to join the land of wandering anitos, were lost and could not find their way. Who would guide them?

"We can show them where to go," Isabel said. "We can let them

82

know it's okay to leave us." She brought out dog bones she had picked up at the pet store, and the children washed the bones.

"Are you still a Conquistador?" Pepito asked.

"No," she told him. "Now I'm one of you." She pulled out plastic buckets. "We can put their bones in burial jars and send them off with special things that will make them feel like they're going home," she said.

"Like what kinds of things?" Marilou wanted to know.

"Things that make the journey from this life to the next life easier," Isabel answered. "What kinds of things do you need when you go on a trip?"

"Toothbrush."

"Money."

"Something to eat."

"Maybe some music?"

"Exactly," she said.

Isabel and the children painted bones the color of fire and moss, the color of wild birds, tropical flowers and mango. "Usually when people die, we just put them in a casket," said Pepito, "and then God takes them home."

She imagined Arturo sitting with them, gluing beads onto the bones, etching Alibata letters that spelled kapatid, pamilya, sa atin, words connected to home. Was he finding his way to the other side?

That day, the children took their burial jars to the river and gave them to the sea. The bottles wobbled and turned, threatened to sink. "Send them off," she said, thinking of the boy who died. The children whispered goodbye and in this way they sent the painted bones, the coins and the little shells floating out to sea.

JoJo maneuvered his pickup through the broad avenues of Virginia Beach. The streets stretched three lanes wide, and strip malls lined the boulevard. On corners there were gas stations with huge yellow shells and oceans of pumps the colors of stars and stripes forever. The colors of Virginia Beach popped out of long and skinny storefront windows, loomed large from used-car parking lots. He sped the truck in open lanes, swerving in between traffic.

"Not so fast, hijo," his mother nagged.

"What do you mean? We're barely moving."

He hit the gas and the truck surged. Gracie Reyes' small body lurched at the dashboard. Flew back into her seat.

"You see that?" she said, pinching him. "You're gonna kill your own mother."

They charged past a billboard where a half-dressed girlie straddled a missile. Her comic-book wink addressed the drivers, said, "Hey, baby. Buy me a drink?"

"I hate this town," he said. He pushed the car lighter into its socket. "Look at that shit."

"That's no way to talk, anak."

"What?" he said, glancing at her. "It's true." He pulled out a cigarette from his shirt pocket and lit it.

"Anak," Gracie said, pulling the cigarette out of his mouth. "What are you trying to do, kill me?" She slipped it between her fingers and took a drag.

"Very funny, Ma. Give it back."

JoJo slid the truck under an overpass. On tunnel walls, graffiti blossomed like ivy clinging to damp concrete. Faces sprawled before them—slits for eyes, dots for noses, giant squiggles for wide smiles. These words marked the passage: Pinay, Dalagas, Filomafia, Pamilya.

"You see that?" he said, yelling and pointing. "You see that? That's what I mean. That's why I came back—to stop that shit. Look where it's got us."

She told him to slow down and to stop being so hard on the world. "You gotta be patient," she said. "Things don't change one night. You should know that by now. And anyway, why you gotta rush everything? Where we're going, doesn't matter if we're late. They're waiting for us. But they're not going anywhere. So slow down already."

For two years, JoJo drove his mother to the cemetery. Sometimes they went in the morning, sometimes after supper. Sometimes he took her there in the middle of the day so she could see what it looked like in the light. On occasion he would visit on his own, sitting cross-legged at the foot of his father's grave or at the headstone of his brother's, snatching at patches of grass, thinking. Since Arturo had died, he went twice a day.

This morning, they brought cleaning supplies with them. JoJo hauled a bucket full of cleansers and rags, a little tool kit in case something needed to be screwed on or pried off. You never knew what to expect. His mother carried an armload of flowers —so big they seemed to overtake her.

They dumped their goods at the side of the graves. Kneeling together, they made the sign of the cross and rattled off the Our Father, a Hail Mary and a Glory Be.

"Have you seen Arturo?" Gracie asked Jay. "Has he been to see you? He left us last week, you know."

"Stop that, Mom," JoJo told her. "That's disrespectful. Walang galang yan."

"Bakit? Di ba dead siya? Di ba patay rin ang kapatid mo? Maybe they can help each other on the other side. Did you ever think of that?"

He reached into the bucket and pulled out a tube of polish. Squeezing it onto a clean diaper, JoJo felt it oozing through the tube. He gently soaped Jay's headstone and thought about how ill-tempered he had been lately.

"Son, you cannot blame yourself for what happened."

"Who says I'm blaming myself?"

She cut the grass between the graves with a set of hedge clippers, squatting like an old rice farmer. "Eh, kasi you act like you're mad at all the kids—your brothers and sisters—you act like you're mad at everyone—even me. Naku—and you ignore people when they are talking—you are brooding over this Arturo thing. Even being mean to that nice new girl—ano ang pangalan niya ulit—Isabel?"

"Isabel Manalo?" He scrubbed the marble, leaning his whole body over the grave. "She probably deserved it," he muttered, circling the rag over the headstone, carving out the letters of Jay's name with his fingertips. JASON ARNOLD REYES. March 27, 1977 – July 10, 1993. He pushed the polish onto the marble, scrubbed harder. He could feel his face getting red. He could feel the anger burning him up.

"His death is no more your fault than Jay's death."

He applied more polish on the stone and shot his breath at the smooth surface, rubbing with new vigor.

"Anak, are you hearing me?"

"Ma, you're so callous," JoJo said. "Like you don't know what

Tita Chic Chic is going through."

"Ano? You want to talk about walang galang? Ikaw! Wala kang galang! Where's the respect for your old widow mother? Ha? You don't know how this week is my nightmare happening all over again. How I go to that funeral house and I don't see Chic Chic, I don't see Arturo. I see myself, I see Jay. I see all of you kids broken and confused. Naku! If you only knew my heart." Now she was weeping too, her old jaws clenched, her hands fisted and striking at the air. "How dare you think I cannot feel this." She pounded her fist at her chest. "Don't you know that if I show it—even a little bit—baka wala na rin ako. I'm lost for good, son."

He reached over to her, but she pushed him away. "Finish what you are doing," she said.

When JoJo left his law practice, he did it for Jay. He'd been with a big entertainment law firm in Manhattan, catered to the stars—rock, pop, funk, actors. He sat in with the partners when they were making deals with record producers, movie houses and presses. Man, he thought, that life was killer. Now he knows he should have been in Va Beach. He should have been watching over Jay, Julia, Jenny, Justin, Joy and Jing— not gallivanting with actors and models and other fancy whities. But in New York, he could afford to send money for the kids. He sent money for lola and lolo. And for Papa's treatments. Too much going on. Too many kids. Papa died. Jay got lost. Jay was only ten when JoJo went to law school. He was twelve when he joined his crew. He was sixteen when the bullet knocked him down and tossed him from the top of the car where he was rapping to his boys.

On the night Jay was shot, the family called JoJo's little studio in the Village, and couldn't get a hold of him. They paged him, but he was too high to get the page. They called his number every ten minutes but he was clubbing that night, doing the nasty with some singer he had met at a session. He couldn't even remember her name. But when he got home that next afternoon, there were twenty-two messages on his answering machine.

After the funeral JoJo disappeared. Packing one of those giant knapsacks full of jeans and T-shirts, he climbed aboard a 747 and headed for Europe and Asia.

86

All my life, he thought, I did everything this family asked. What good was that?

He didn't tell anyone. He paid his ticket and left, sent postcards from Paris and chocolate from Germany. He found himself surfing the waters near Manila Bay. He was drawn to the mountains and he hiked along the hills of Mindanao and found himself.

Two years later, JoJo came back, a little browner, a little less polished and a little more charged. He was a revolutionary, a nationalist. His ideas, his language, his very eyes were rooted in the history of his people.

Pulling out another clean diaper, he squeezed the tube of polish all over the rag and began washing the stone again. "Brother," he whispered to Jay, "our people have been fucked over."

His manner confirmed his family's suspicions—he had gone mad. Even still, they welcomed him home, their prodigal son. They gave him back his bedroom and he began his new life, hoping to practice immigration law.

Day late, dollar short, like they say, but here he was. Every day. And every night he dreamed of that moment, the way his brother's scrawny figure must have looked perched on the hood of that car, that beat-up blue Civic, Jay's arms stretched out, embracing the whole world. His voice must have reverberated and echoed against the underpass. How his song was the song of a rebel angel. And then JoJo dreamed the squealing tires of an angry car as it peeled around the corner, the gunfire popping like fireworks on a night named after freedom. Each night Jay fell from the hood of that car: heavy thud, heavy thud, heavy thud. And then silence.

"Ma, you remember what Magkasama means?" he asked her.

"Of course. How am I going to forget that? It's Tagalog. My first tongue. Bakit?"

"Bakit? Because Ma, isn't that the group we put together in Jay's name—a group for teenagers to help them make it. I left my practice in New York so no more kids—especially my brothers and sisters—would die like this. And what happened?"

"You are not God, hijo. That's nice that you came back here for the kids and for me. Your dad would have been so proud. But you are not God and you do not get to say who lives and who dies." She put her hand on his back and she rubbed. "You are my sweet boy," she said. "I thank God you came home, but anak, stop brooding already."

JoJo rubbed at the marble, wiping tears away with the back of his hand. How was he going to make the kids understand? He ran a sleeve across his runny nose. He thought hanging with them was enough, being an example. And then he tried reading history books and magazines to set them up with their own Pinoy pride. The deaths were so senseless. The dreaming was endless.

"Ready, anak?" his mother asked him. JoJo nodded. He folded the rags up into neat little squares. He pulled out two glasses filled with white wax and lit each candle then laid it at each of the headstones.

"Maybe," Gracie told her husband's grave, "your son has met a girl. She's a Filipina from Chicago—petite and pretty— very American."

"Stop it, Ma," he said to her. "I'm sure Papa would rather hear about the kids. Besides, that girl is not my type."

"Oh really? What's the matter with her?"

"Too skinny," he said, kissing his mother on the cheek. Then, taking her hand, he bowed his head, and because it was Monday, they meditated on the Joyful mysteries, Gracie's holy rosary clicking like bamboo chimes.

SEVEN

The View Outside Camila's Window. Oak Park, IL. 1959.
Photo by Camila Chiu

By the end of February, when the afternoons grow dark and bitter, winter loses his charm. Camila searches through the lens of her camera out the window of her dorm. In the lower left-hand corner of the frame, edges of books written by Kierkegaard, Camus, and St. Tomas Aquinas peek at her. Snow frosts the windowpane. Outside the landscape offers nothing but white hills and, occasionally, the twisted branches of naked trees. In the morning she often hears the ugly caw of black birds diving in and out of skeletal trees. Since arriving, the sisters have treated her well, but still, Camila dreams about the rainy season. How the water beats down on the roof in a rush, like the beating of her mother's heart. She dreams of banana trees waving their leaves like giant fans cooling the earth. She conjures up her parents' house, the way their kitchen smells of freshly steamed rice, pan de sal, cassava and rice cakes. In her sleep, white sampaguita flowers blossom and overwhelm her father's garden. They climb fences, the bark of palm trees and the Santa Maria's small grotto so everything is white and fragrant. Camila used to complain that the clamor of their Sunday afternoon fiestas made it difficult to study her philosophy, but these days she wakes and the silence in the dorm makes her ache for all that noise. Camila spins the lens, blurring the white outside the windowpane. She searches the skies for a single snowflake. Impatient and bored, she takes a picture of nothing but the empty sky.

Isabel blew up a picture of the Midwestern skies and plastered it on her bedroom wall. It was an old black-and-white that her mother had taken when she first got to America in the late 1950s. There was nothing brilliant about it—just a sky with a gesture of clouds, maybe the hint of snow. It was more like a gray-and-gray than a black-and-white. She liked it because it calmed her, made her a little less homesick. Virginia Beach was only twenty-some hours away from home, and yet everything felt foreign to her. She spent most of her days answering to her boss, Dr. Calhoun, or taking calls from the community. Never mind that she still had to plan her lessons and teach to motley tribes of six- to seventeen-year-olds. Her teaching seemed secondary to her role as community liaison. Tita Nita was a never-ending loop of chitchat. She was starting to hear them in her sleep. Once she dreamed Ferdi's big face was floating right at her, his brown finger wagging at her. "And how about it, Isabel, are you Pinay or what?"

Isabel returned calls in the middle of the day when she knew Tita Nita was at work. "Come on," Tita Nita said on her machine, "don't tell me you're so Amerikanized already."

Pulling the blankets up to her chin, she kissed Flounder's pink nose. She snuggled closer to the cat and stared at the picture on the wall. Beauty pageants a part of growing up Filipino? Whoever heard of such a thing?

On Monday morning, Dr. Calhoun summoned Isabel to her office. "Of course this isn't exactly the Bible Belt," Dr. Calhoun warned her, "but still we need to be careful." She was worried parents might worry.

"I thought the idea was to teach the Filipino-American kids something about their heritage."

"Yes, but this lesson on making care packages for the dead is very pagan. And isn't the Filipino community largely Catholic?"

"They aren't care packages—they're burial jars. That's what some of the indigenous tribes—who weren't Catholic—did: they filled clay jars with gifts for their loved ones." She asked if someone had complained.

Dr. Calhoun shook her head and smiled a very fake smile. Parents have not complained, she assured her. In fact, many had called to commend them for hiring Isabel. One woman, an Anita Starr, raved about her, said she was looking forward to her help with their upcoming pageant. "I'm glad to hear you're making friends in the community," Dr. Calhoun said. She hoped this talk would encourage Isabel's work.

Isabel felt the little veins in her body pumping hot and furious; her heart was beating, beating, angry, beating. "Well," she said, "Mrs. Starr must have misunderstood. I'm not working on the pageant."

Dr. Calhoun pulled her glasses from her face. Her blonde hair had grown coarse with age and years of setting and teasing. Her eyes were large and vacant as the blue sky. "Perhaps you can see what you can do for Mrs. Starr, anyway. She believes you are the perfect mentor."

Isabel looked away for a moment, feeling tired. "What's going on with Arturo's case?" she asked. "I haven't heard a thing about it."

"Nothing's going on. I told you. It's been dropped."

"Dropped, not solved?" Isabel asked.

"Time to move on, Isabel," said Dr. Calhoun. She shuffled a few manila folders on her desk. Isabel couldn't understand why so many people related fixing a problem with dwelling on the past. "We are appointing you to be the administrative delegate to the Parent Teacher Association. Since you float from school to school within the district, you are the perfect candidate for this assignment." She handed Isabel a two-page list of dinner engagements, board meetings, and fund-raising activities.

"What am I supposed to do?" Isabel wanted to know.

"Nothing," Calhoun told her. "Just be your charming self, try not to be political—rather be diplomatic. Be a team player."

"But I am a team player," she answered. "Isn't that the point?"

Calhoun looked down at her paperwork, dismissing her. "Then maybe you need to figure out the game plan," she said.

Fine, Isabel thought. She would play the game, mentor the students. They would be chieftains, datus and warriors bearing spices and sugar cane. They would be rice farmers, peasant women, migrant workers following the seasons. And yes, they would be resistant and independent thinkers when she was through with them.

The lights at the County Board Meeting blared fluorescent bright. The people rose from their seats to yank a static-ridden microphone to their mouths. Most of the people spit their p's and t's out so that the speakers popped with their saliva.

Tita Nita had the floor. She was suggesting that the community and the school board join efforts to produce this year's beauty pageant. She waved her hands and swayed as she talked like the beauty queen that she was. "It is perfect. The pageant provides an educational perspective for non-Filipinos. You can learn about our young people, their talents and their energy. The Filipino community can in turn, through advertising in our program and supporting our efforts, make their businesses known to the Tidewater community. We can give to each other."

The school board treasurer, an old southern gentleman, nodded. His long fingers reached for his mic. The thing crackled as he brought it to his mouth. "With all due respect, Mrs. Starr, I fail to see the educational value of tiaras and gowns."

Isabel was dying. She shrunk low in her wooden chair. She closed her eyes, hoping no one associated her with Tita Nita's suggestion. She made herself think of home, how it was autumn in Evanston now and pumpkins would be in full bloom—orange globes of light glowing along the driveways and entrances of people's homes. She imagined the barren trees, the skies. She thought of her mother's photograph of the sky and wished she could crawl into it.

"Recognition of beauty and the attributes of womanhood are part of our culture, Mr. Brojan. As Ms. Manalo will attest, this is a way to transmit the dances, the stories, and the influence of our heritage to our young."

"Ms. Manalo," Mr. Brojan said.

"Well," Isabel said, spinning her mic close to her. "Pageants are a part of the culture—" She surveyed the board members, mostly older people, mostly southerners. In the chambers, the seats were split between members of the white community and members of the Filipino community. She felt all of them looking at her, waiting for a diplomatic answer. "—to be sure. And if the board and the community are hoping to raise revenue through this event, I'm sure this is possible. But actually," she said, pausing and glancing over at Tita Nita, "I was hoping we could sponsor a play. Say at the Independence Day picnic in July. It could be historical and cultural, and it could illustrate the relationship between the U.S. and the Philippines. I understand that's a big event in the area—the Independence Day picnic."

Applause filled the room, and she breathed a sigh of relief. She'd managed to put off the pageant one more time. The board members nodded in support. Brojan doffed his imaginary hat to her.

"If I may," Will Peterson said, approaching the podium, "incorporating the boys as well as the girls in such an activity will keep those gangs off the streets. I think it's a great idea."

"You mean the children?" Tita Nita said.

"No, ma'am," Will Peterson said, "I mean the gangs. The teen gangs."

Isabel held her breath, waiting to hear how Tita Nita would deny the existence of trouble, of gangs and crews. Tita Nita continued to smile, never breaking character, forever the reigning beauty queen.

Then she said, "Well, the Independence Day picnic is such a long way off. I still think there's the opportunity to do both the pageant in April or May and then the play on the fourth of July." Applause again. Isabel sighed, long and heavy. The battle she fought wasn't against the white administration, but her own people, if she dared to claim them at all.

Looking for Housing. North Carolina. April 1966.
Photo by Isabel Manalo

Isabel looks at Mommy in the front seat. Camila closes her eyes and rubs her hands in circles around her tummy. "Is the baby moving?" Isa asks her.

Isa leans over so she can feel her mother's skin, soft and powdery. Mommy removes Isa's hand and says, "Sit down, anak. The car is moving." She takes a tissue from her pocket book and wipes the perspiration from her forehead. The air is sticky and hot and smells of egg sandwiches.

"Try not to drive over bumps, Daddy. I'm getting dizzy reading this thing."

Isa focuses the camera on Frankie's leg, on his fat skin, the color of sand. Zooming in, she takes a picture of the tiny holes and fine lines.

The car jiggles up and down. Camila looks out the window at the houses— yellow brick and orange stone, aqua siding, blue linoleum.

"We're nearby, aren't we? Why don't we just stop and ask?"

"Mahal, just look for 13th Street. Just look at the map."

Isa can see the baby inside her mommy rolling, making her kind of sick. She thinks the baby's doing somersaults. Her mother rolls her head from side to side, drops the map on the car floor and then she bursts. Just like that. "I don't know where we are!" Mommy cries. "I don't know what we're doing."

Frankie Boy joins Mommy. Wailing, they sing out. Rebel. And then she doesn't know why, but Isa too. They all cry, loud and angry, and all their faces are wet with tears. Feels kind of good, she thinks. They cry until Daddy pulls the car over to the side of the road and holds all of them in his arms, and sings them a song from home.

When she got home from the meeting, she slipped into the shower and let hot water run down her back. The water was hard and pounded at her neck like a thousand miniature fists. She cried. The whole day flowed out of her at that moment, made her think of those days back in North Carolina, where her family spent a week looking for housing. Every time they followed a lead, they'd get there and the house was just rented or the owners had changed their mind, or nobody answered the door. "You see," she told herself as she climbed out of the shower. "These things just happen. But you gotta just keep on going, you gotta just go."

She threw open her closet doors, fingering shirts and skirts. Her day was not over. She was heading back out to chaperone the Tidewater Youth Dance.

She felt so Midwestern, so Mary Tyler Moore. At dusk, she stepped her way around the bodies of souped-up cars. The parking lot reeked of whiskey. Cigarettes hanging from their mouths, the youths grunted at Isabel as she walked by. They nodded hello.

Inside, the music beat against the walls and floated up into the rafters, banged against the panes of skylights, fighting to get out. Boom, ba boom boom—bang, bang—ba boom boom. The rhythm of bass called forth the various tribes. Several hundred teenagers bumped and shifted to the beat. Everybody danced. Everybody moved. Every beat made itself known. Underneath baggy jeans and skintight Lycra, hips popped like metronomes. The music made everyone want to explode. Led them into new levels of consciousness. The DJ, the bartender (who delivered cokes and lemonade), the parents who chaperoned the dark corners and cubbyholes of the room, the little baby sister someone had brought—all moved. It was as if everyone could understand at least this much: rhythm.

She stepped up to several college boys, who cased the room, stood at doors, legs thrown apart, arms crossed—warriors guarding the young. She shot extreme close-ups of their faces, their eyes, their broad nostrils. They nodded to the steady boom ba boom boom—bang, bang—ba boom boom. Their jaws were set, ready for a fight. They were all business. They were the kuyas looking out for their younger siblings, their little cousins.

A red light floated in a shaft across the crowded dance floor— searched out trouble, caught the spinning disco ball on occasion and glittered brightly.

Outside two police cars patrolled the parking lot, waiting for the inevitable—or so they thought. Last time, two rival gangs rumbled with switchblades and surgical knives they'd taken from their fathers' offices. Someone sliced an ear, scarred the apple of someone's cheek, almost killed a brother. Time before that, the sisters from one of the tribes jumped a girl for talking trash, beat her till her eyes went from brown to black and blue. And nobody had forgotten the year before, when several brothers from Pamilya circled the Cultural Center, shooting bullets into the windows and doors of the dance hall. No one died. Several fainted. Mostly aunties.

Bel felt Arturo's presence filling the room. She wondered if the others saw him shifting among them, bumping hips with the pretty girls, swirling fast with the other breakdancers. To utter his name would validate the circle of cop cars; to mention his death, a threat to everyone there. So no one named him, but Isabel knew he was there. He was a guardian angel now, he was a spirit, forever caught in the mix.

Isabel wanted to enjoy the music, but the tension was too distracting. The song floating from the speakers haunted them. No telling what would happen next. She wandered the dance floor with a camera in her hand, shooting images of teens dancing to escape.

On stage, two boys in black ski caps and basketball jerseys rapped into the microphone. The rhymes were sloppy, and sometimes they had to rush the words to make them fit the line. One boy was big, bear-like. The other was small and skinny. The small one had a loud and angry voice. The larger one was as mellow as an old-time jazz singer. They swung one arm low, leaning their bodies down to the crowd as they spat words out. They hid behind dark glasses, but every now and then one of them peeked over the top of his shades, winked out into the crowd.

Isabel climbed onto stage and crouched below the boys. She got red lights shooting out from behind them, and the rappers loomed large and loud from the low angle of her lens. The dancers cheered the rappers on, even though many of the words were lost to the deafening beat of the music. The energy of the room filled Isabel up, her chest expanded with every beat from the bass. Her fingers moved fast like the music—zoom, rewind, focus, click. Zoom, rewind, focus, click.

DJ Boy spun records, scratched vinyl against the rap. Every now and then Isabel picked up a line: "Lookin' at me you think I'm a Chino, but I am (beat beat) FIL-A-PEE-NO." Back-up rappers chanted, "Brown is the power, now is the hour" in between the bleeding of bass and the thick strokes of a steady electric beat. In the center of the gym, breakdancers tumbled like a set of children's jacks, whirling in different directions, twisting limbs, knotting bodies.

She shot photos of JoJo perusing the crowd. He stopped at the doors and checked in with the college boys. She saw how they deferred to him. He placed a hand on one of the boys' shoulders. Patted each of them on the shoulder or arm, moved on. Every now and then he nodded at her. His face remained expressionless. He walked laps around the youth and she shot pictures of him moving constantly, waving at kids— hello, watch out, stop that. At one point she asked him how he was doing. Too worried, he said, too anxious. He wanted to know where Elliot was.

"Why?" she asked.

"Just wondering," he said. He was rocking on the heels of his running shoes, looking over his shoulder, his hands still waving at kids around him. "Is he picking you up or do you want a ride?"

"I have a car," she said.

"Great," he said, his face breaking into a smile. "Then, can you give me a lift or what?"

She told him, "Okay, find me later," and then she wandered around the dance floor, counting the youth. Must be two-hundred, maybe more.

Fifteen years ago, Isabel and her friends worried about stupid things—dance routines, crêpe paper for the gym, in-depth articles on submarine races, cartoon strips that would catch the essence of their class. They had hall passes, yellow slips of paper that granted them permission to go to the bathroom or the library or nurse. They'd steal a pack of passes and get Jody Anderson to place counterfeit signatures there, on the bottom-right corner. They dealt with teachers—not security guards.

Her students at Westover had to walk through metal detectors every morning, just to get to class. She'd been there at lunch when security guards announced random searches, frisking freshmen for scissors and blades, for guns. They lined the students up along a wall, spread their legs and arms wide like they were sure the kids had something on them. They checked everything, even the insides of their socks and shoes, the linings of their jeans, the spaces along their inner thighs. All this, just to have lunch.

There was never that kind of trouble when Isabel was in high school. Out in the east parking lot, they got high on pot, or made out between periods. They divided themselves not by the color of skin, since that would have meant Isabel against all of them, but into categories—jocks, freaks, actors, and video nerds. Isabel floated in and out of the categories, defying labels, depending on the season. During her last year they drank or cut classes, because they were seniors. The behavior was traditional, expected.

At the dances she attended, the boys stood against the walls, too cool to participate, while the girls were the ones scattered in the middle of the floor, moving without pattern—in many cases without rhythm—to the likes of "American Pie," "Brown-Eyed Girl," and any song by the Eagles. What a change, she thought.

She heard voices coming from the stairwell, so she stole up the stairs in her soft-soled shoes. Two female voices hissed to each other in a mix of Taglish and street talk. She had a hard time understanding and so she hurried to see what was happening.

"You keep homegirl away from my boy."

"No, you tell him to keep to hisself."

On the third landing she found two girl crews. Lourdes, Maya, Mercedes, Angel, and Marilena stood with other girls from Westover. Tough girls, they clenched their fists, their jaws. They stood with their feet spread apart, claiming territory. The other girls, from Norfolk, faced them with equally strong stances, equally beautiful faces filled with hate. They didn't notice Isabel right away, didn't see her spying on them. She caught a word or two. Someone trash-talked someone. Someone's getting jumped for something—a boy, a comment, most likely an attitude.

They faced off, but only Lourdes and another girl were speaking. They glared at one another, growled like two cats threatening to fight. For the first time since she'd moved to Virginia, Isabel realized that her girls were part of something larger.

"Sup?" Isabel said.

The tension fell away as the girls leaned back against banisters and bricks. Some of them smiled at her. Some walked past her, down the stairs.

"Nothing," Angel said. "Girl talk is all."

"Yeah," Maya said. "You know—boys an shit."

The stairwell was dark and only a light from the floors above illuminated their shadows, threw expressions on their faces. Isabel had a hard time recognizing her girls. She felt their attitude more than anything, knew something bad was going down. Lourdes and the girl from Norfolk smiled. They flung an arm over each other and passed Bel silently. Slowly the girls descended the stairs, one and two at a time. They whispered to one another. Chit-chatted as if they were all sisters. They left her standing there alone.

Isabel was not sure what she had witnessed. She could feel something was up and it made her nauseous. She uncapped a bottle of water and drank long and slow. Why didn't she realize her girls were Las Dalagas? She stood for a minute and listened to the fading sounds of their shoes as they flip, flip, flipped their way down the stairs. A small army of girl soldiers mad at something. Someone. She hated feeling like Mary Tyler Moore. She hated knowing she had more in common with the career girl from Minnesota than her own Pinay sisters, who were younger than her but just as brown.

They stopped at a burger joint on the way to JoJo's house. It was a trailer, long and skinny. Everything was soaked in grease—the leather stools at the counter, the black-and-white tiles on the floor, the plastic-covered menus.

"I love this place," JoJo said.

"You do?" Isabel said, dragging a napkin across the counter before her. "Why's that?"

"Unbelievable," he said.

"What?"

"This place not good enough for you? Clean enough?"

"I never said that. I asked you why this is your favorite place," she told him. "Besides, I have a hangout in Chicago. Leo's Lunchroom. It's dirtier than this."

"Yeah, whatever. You said you were hungry. You gonna order or what?" He looked over his shoulder, at the voices outside of the trailer.

At first it was difficult to make out the bodies. They were connected and hooked one into the other, and in the dark they appeared to be one giant monster.

"Shit," he said, putting down his cola. He ran out the door.

"We think she sprained her ankle," Derek was saying. He and Angel held Maya between them. Behind the three, Marilena floated quiet as an angel, a trail of scarves and jackets dragging at her feet. Maya's body was limp and shifting in all directions. Hair covered her face so it was hard to tell who she was, except for her large bones and the wide heart shape of her face. She appeared unconscious or drunk or maybe high.

Isabel unlocked the back of her station wagon. "What happened?" she asked, pulling at Derek's sleeve.

They stretched Maya from one end of the back seat to the next. JoJo shot to the opposite end of the car. He flung the door open and slowly examined Maya's ankles.

"Her right ankle's swollen," he said.

"What happened?" Isabel asked again.

Words spilled out of Derek, fast and incomprehensible. He ran his sentences together—one breath, one word—and Angel swatted him. "Stop it," she said. "Let me tell it." She looked to JoJo and Isabel, threw Derek a dirty look. She said they were walking down at the beach by the strip of hotels and restaurants. "We were chasing each other and we got to the concrete part of the boardwalk. Maya fell down the stairs."

"No wonder," Isabel said. "Check those heels out. No one ought to be in these at all—much less running."

Bel's throat felt dry. She needed water. Her heart pounded so loud it competed with Angel's voice. She ran her hands over Maya's body, calming her down. Tears scattered everywhere. Maya's blouse fell open and Isabel recognized the fishtail tattooed on Maya's chest. Oh shit, she thought, oh shit. She pulled the strands away gently to get to Maya's skin. Maya's lips were still stained berry from several applications of lipstick, a habit Isabel noted she had whenever she was anxious. Isabel found blood streaking down Maya's cheek. The blood mixed with the tears, made the hair even stickier.

"What's this?" she asked. "JoJo, look."

"She scraped her face on the pavement," Marilena said.

"It's burning," Maya cried. "Make it stop!"

"These are fingernail scratches," Isabel said. "She didn't hit any concrete."

"Stay cool," JoJo said.

Isabel flung the glove compartment open and rummaged through the mess of maps and receipts, looking for her first aid kit. The tin box was no larger than a carton of eggs. Inside, everything sat in perfect miniature. She pulled out a little spray bottle and a couple of tiny Band-Aids. Taking a small swab of cotton, she dabbed at the wounds, a row of scratches trekking red down Maya's face.

Isabel's stomach turned. "She didn't fall down," she said. "Did someone beat you up?" She looked to JoJo for the answer. "Right? She was in a fight."

"Could be."

"This is nuts," she said. She pulled at Marilena's sleeve. "Who did this? Those girls from Norfolk?" Marilena looked away from her, but Bel followed her, stooped low to catch her eye. Nothing.

JoJo rolled up Maya's wide pant leg. A bruise, long and wicked and the color of eggplant and red wine, spread the length of her shin. Maya's cries were small now, quiet and to herself.

"Let's take her to the hospital," Isabel said. "We should bring her in." She looked up at JoJo, then at the others. "Have you called her parents?"

"I'll take her home," JoJo said. "I'll talk to her parents." He leaned down to look into Maya's face. Isabel saw how his gaze comforted the girl. "It's okay," he whispered.

"You should take her to the hospital," Isabel said. "You should get her to tell you what really happened. Somebody scratched her face."

JoJo spun around. His eyes were dark and full of anger. "She'll be okay."

"Thanks, Kuya," Maya said, reaching her arms around JoJo. He held her tightly and she let out a heavy sigh.

Morning After Frankie's Prom. Evanston, IL. May 1982.
Photo by Isabel Manalo

She wants to get even. She hears him sneaking into the house. Spies his ruffled shirttail hanging over polyester dress pants. He smells of stale alcohol. He smells gamy. Perfect. She sneaks down the stairs, a camera in her hand. It's six A.M. and the sun is still lost to them. Looking through the frame, she sees the width of his broad back, the hair frayed and standing on end. Behind him stand their parents—staggered, wearing pajamas and robes. She cannot see her mother's face, but she hears her voice trembling. The moon shoots through a window and casts a streak of light on their father's jaw, reveals it clenched in anger. He waves his arms like one of those air traffic controllers at O'Hare.

"You ruined your future!" her father yells.

"It's my life!" Frankie Boy answers. He waves his arms back at his dad. Just like Dad, she thinks.

"This is how you repay me?"

"My life!"

"Walang hiya!" their father yells.

Their mother reaches for Dad's arms, like it would somehow quiet him. But it's useless. "Walang hiya! Demonyo!" their father screams and the house howls. The voices make Bel jump. She hits the button and emits a flash as electrical as lightning. The figures streak across the frame. The room's frenetic energy dazzles the lens like white noise.

Elliot was already in her bed, sleeping and happy in the warmth of the comforters. She rolled him over and cried to him like a teenager coming home from a bad night of drinking.

"And then I said, no, let's take her to the hospital, and JoJo insisted we take her home. And then he wouldn't even let me out of the car, said he'd take care of it. I have no idea what he told her parents."

"It's your car," Elliot said, washing his hands across his face. Sleep was a mask hiding him from her. "You could have taken her to the hospital."

"That's not the point," she said, slamming her fist into a pillow.

Elliot didn't want to talk about it, not right then. "Calm down," he told her. "Get some sleep."

That was his answer every time she was upset. Calm down, get some sleep. Calm down.

In her room, there were wardrobes built into the walls—so big and wide everything she owned fit into those walls. Her bed floated in the middle of the room, tilted at an angle, irregular as the beating of her heart. With a life of its own, the bed rolled its way right then left, ebbing gently as if there were wind.

Isabel was convinced Arturo was seeking her out. His soul roamed the tiny bungalow, sleepless and hot with fever, looking for water or something cool to drape across his brow. She could hear him rummaging in her kitchen, or knocking about in the bathroom. He too was tired, desired sleep, and finding none he fumbled about the house. Isabel tossed and turned so much she must have kept him up. And then she thought— so what? Like I haven't lived with ghosts before.

Perhaps Arturo was asking her not to give up, to keep on trying. "You'll get it straight," he hummed from the walls of her room. "You'll work it out." The screen door bump-bump-bumped around two in the morning, the hour when teenagers were best known to sneak into houses.

But it was Maya's image, and the sound of her moaning, that kept Isabel up tonight. She felt so naïve when it came to the girls. How stupid was she not to see it? They were water spirits. Mermaids. Fish out of water. How could she not know? Maya Antaran was a girl drowning. Bel pictured the dalaga's hair dark as seaweed. She was expanding. Her arms floated weightless as the plants rooted at the bottom of the sea. Her breasts were cupped in glitter the color of gold. And then the hips. The bellbottom slacks tapered in and out like a shimmering fin.

When Bel lost the baby and nobody knew, she cried every night for months. Keeping the secret was like holding her breath. But if she told her family, they would be disappointed, they would be ashamed. The family would be disgraced. Walang hiya. So she kept it a secret. So she knew this much: the girls had secrets and the secrets were wrecking everything.

Isabel leaned over and kissed Elliot. He slept like he never worried over anything. He rolled over and rested on her shoulder. She felt the burn of his stubble against her skin, and the flight of something unnamed and frightening rushed through her.

"Get up," she told him, shaking his arm. "Get up, Elliot."

She made his long body crawl out from under the covers. He moved like a giant cricket unfolding its legs to the wood floor. Stumbling to the bathroom, he tripped over Flounder, who chased him, thinking he wanted to play.

Bel slammed the bed against the wall. Her cousin Pearla told her that beds placed in the middle of the room left their owners up in the air, destined to travel away from sleep.

"Bel," Elliot said, yawning. "What are you doing?"

"Just come to bed," she said. "I'm trying to sleep."

She wondered if it would help. If the bed up against the wall would keep her where she wanted to be—safe and rested and home.

EIGHT

Hip-hop hit rolled-up windows. Wu-Tang rapped. Inside the hatchback, five dalagas—Lourdes, Mercedes, Marilena, Angel and Ria—flipped open compacts with secret lighted mirrors. They painted lips the color of blood, etched their brows high and thin. They traced each eye with liquid the color of charcoal, and pressed their lashes into curls. All the while, they rocked to the rap, nodded to the beat, pulsed and teased their perfectly coiffed bobs into brown halos. Five girls crammed into four bucket seats, adjusted pants made of black Lycra, smoothed scoop-neck T-shirts, hoisted up five sets of miracle bras. Ten legs kicked around a five-speed joystick. Strapped in clunky platforms, fifty toes painted dark cherry wriggled to the beat, to the beat, to the beat beat beat. Someone's beeper stuttered electronic bells and everybody reached for a hip, a purse, a pocket, pulling out five neon pagers. Lourdes fingered the tiny screen, read upside-down numbers like words. She raised an eye to Marilena and nodded. The girls slipped on shades cool as the deep blue sea. Ready to attack.

The following morning, Isabel wrapped herself in blankets and slept on the shore. The sea howled. Inside, Elliot was making her brunch. "You had a tough night," he whispered. "Go lie on the beach." She opened her body to the sun, bright and blinding despite the November chill. She breathed in and out, slowly and methodically. Tried not to think of the evening before, of the dark colors and the heavy beat of electric drums, of the girls confronting one another, of Maya. But the images flashed like a montage of the photos she'd shot, the figures zooming in and out of focus, the contrasts hard-edged and grainy.

She concentrated on the Kulintang, the gongs from the islands, the bells and chimes of indigenous tribes and how they must have accompanied the ocean's chanting. For years she had read books and listened to tapes of the Muslims and the mountain tribes. She studied pictures of Igorots and Ifugao. She wondered what it would have been like to have lived on the islands before the time of King Philip. To be part of a community where everyone was in support of everyone. This was how she imagined the tribes, the baranggay. A people without conflict.

Last night, on the way to the burger joint, she shared this idea with JoJo and he called her a petit bourgeois brat. Said she was dreaming if she believed there was ever a tribe that didn't fight.

Growing up upper middle class, a brown seed in a white landscape, Bel never belonged. People were nice, she thought. But she never felt like she was one of them. Senior year, the class voted her homecoming queen, but no one dared to ask her out. She was queen without a date. Even in her own family, she was a loner. She never had any reason to complain, but she didn't know what it was like to be among her people. Come to think of it, until this year she wasn't even sure she knew who her people were. This community was the first opportunity Isabel had to be part of something, and it was nothing like her dreams.

Enough, she thought. She was getting a headache. She concentrated on the sound of the water rushing in and out. She let her mind float up and out to the sky, where the wind gently guided clouds. But even then, she saw ghosts in the sky—her baby swimming in the clouds, two arms stroking at air, his feet tied together and going nowhere, and Arturo rapping with his hands up, raising the roofless sky. Why couldn't she rest? She hid under a sweatshirt hood, wore glasses with thick dark lenses. At least she had the ocean, she thought; at least there was the sea.

In class the girls posed their bodies like beautiful statues in an art museum. They knew how to sit so the boys would notice. Their perfume infiltrated the air, seduced everybody. They were like blossoms, smelling all pretty and perfect. Isabel would look them in the eye, lower herself to catch their gaze and what did she see? Eyes made of glass looking right through her. They were there but not there. They were everywhere but nowhere. She could see them, she could touch them, she could speak to them, but their souls were gone. They practiced reading each other's minds with their hands, and with the way they leaned on a shoulder or stooped over a desk. They did it in the way they shifted their eyes and they made it pretty clear Bel was nothing but a waste of time.

Last night, when she took JoJo home from the dance, they got into it. He stared out at the roads, one hand hanging out the window, threatening the night. He was deep in thought, as he seemed to be all evening long.

"Did you have a good time?" she wanted to know.

"Okay," he answered. "But that's not really the point."

Dances like this made him realize how much work there was to be done. Made him anxious, thinking of how insurmountable the work was. "You're doing a good job," she had said to him. But he ignored her, seemed impatient with her. And when she asked about the girls, and told him about the incident on the stairs, he shook his head. "Why didn't you tell me the girls are Las Dalagas?" she asked.

"I didn't know you didn't know," he answered.

"How would I know?"

"How could you not?" Las Dalagas was a name she must have seen written on walls, scratched onto desks and cement sidewalks. Teenagers who had been jumped would jump to be one of the sistas.

"Jumped?" she wanted to know.

"Beat up." His face was cold, stern.

"Why are you so rude?" she wanted to know.

He didn't answer.

So Maya had been jumped. She was torn apart like a paper doll.

Isabel took a deep breath. Try not to think, she told herself. The beach was one place she came to where trouble would float away. She imagined carrying a basket of trouble to the edge of the beach and pitching it far away.

"Ay, anak, there you are," called out a shrill voice. Isabel heard sand swishing. "Look at you, how you dress. You look like one of the kids. People are gonna start talking about you like you are one of those boys in the gangs."

Now who would do that, Isabel thought. And why would they bother? She rolled her eyes and braced herself.

Tita Nita and two other women were making their way over sand dunes and driftwood. She was carrying a plate of something in one hand, her shoes in another. A bright green chiffon scarf sailed in and out of her painted face.

"I brought you some cassava cake," she said. She indicated the two aunties. "I don't know if you remember meeting Tita Mercy and Auntie Wilma."

Isabel greeted them. Blankets fell from her body and tangled at her feet. She nearly tripped as she leaned over to hug each of them. "Of course I know Auntie Wilma," she said as she gave them kisses. "I'm staying in her beach house. How's Uncle Romy?" she asked.

"He's fine," Auntie Wilma answered. She had a big smile and chubby cheeks. She held Isabel's face in her hands and studied her. "Why are you freezing yourself out here, hija? It's so cold."

"She probably finds it refreshing," Tita Mercy said as she reached over and pinched Isabel's cheek. "You're so healthy."

Isabel guided them back over the sand, holding their hands as she walked. The blankets hung over her shoulders. The beach chair sat abandoned and lonely on the shoreline. She gathered the aunts into her house and sat them around her kitchen table, where they ate up all the cassava cake and drank glasses of cola and cups of Chinese tea.

Elliot shuffled into the kitchen, his hands shoved into his back pockets. An apron dangled around his neck. He was shirtless. "Ladies," he said, bowing. "How are you today?"

The women giggled. "Mr. North," Auntie Wilma said, "I didn't expect to see you here."

Isabel felt hot. She went to the fridge and poured herself a giant glass of ice water.

"Sure I'm here. I'm Isabel's chef. I'm happy to serve you."

Tita Nita winked at Isabel and whispered loud enough for everyone to hear. "He's such a nice guy. And good with the kids."

Sitting at the table, the aunties doted on her. Called her beautiful. They caressed her hands, patted her head. They treated her as if she were one of their kids. And soon the matter was brought to the table.

"Isabel," Tita Nita said. "You know how much we admire you, and how grateful we are that you are here." Isabel nodded. "Anyways, we really think you are the most qualified individual. We have elected you to be the Miss Philippines-Virginia Beach 1996 pageant assistant director."

"You're perfect," Auntie Wilma said.

"The girls will listen to you," Tita Mercy added.

"No problem," Tita Nita said. "Kind of exciting. You know?"

"I'm flattered," she told them. "That you would entrust the pageant to an outsider like me."

"You are not an outsider, hija," Tita Nita said.

"You're one of us," Auntie Wilma told her. "Your father and my husband were residents in Boone, you know. You're really one of us, anak."

"Sure she is," Elliot said, offering them a plate of scrambled eggs. "That sounds like it would be fun, doesn't it, Bel?"

"Ay, your nick name is Bel? In the Philippines we'd call you Isa," Auntie Wilma shouted. "EEEE-SA. Like the number one. Isa. Isa-Bel."

"I told her that before," Tita Nita yelled. "Ako, I like to call her Isa."

Isabel tossed Elliot a look and said, "I'm sure there's nothing Elliot would enjoy more than to work with bathing beauties. But aunties, I'm no good at beauty pageants. I've only seen one, and I didn't even stay for the whole thing."

"Didn't your community have pageants in Illinois?" Auntie Wilma asked. "Wasn't your sister Miss Teenage Sampaguita?"

"Right," Isabel nodded. "Right, that was my sister. Not me."

She looked into the circle of faces seated at her table, and her heart grew weak. They wanted the kids to glamour up. To learn about the traditions from home. A pageant was what they wanted.

"Kasi," said Auntie Nita, "the kids become so American and they forget who they are, why we do things the way we do."

"They get into trouble," Tita Wilma told her. "Not just little things either—sometimes they get in fights, or they get chased by police. Minsan, may baril. You know, guns." She clicked her tongue three times. "Nakakahiya naman."

"Some of the girls don't have any idea of our Filipino morals—you know they get influenced by this MTV," Tita Mercy said. Tita Mercy sneezed—"Chewchewchew!"

"Oo nga," said Auntie Wilma, "that's how some of these girls get pregnant."

"From MTV?" Isabel asked.

"It's those rap songs," Tita Nita said. "And then they get confused—are they black or are they Mexican or what."

"You mean like Arturo?" Isabel asked.

"No, that shooting was not about a baby," Auntie Wilma said.

"No, mare," said Auntie Mercy, "I think it was. Di ba, they said that girl in Norfolk was pregnant and then the brother warned Arturo to stay away?"

"Iba yan," cooed Tita Nita. "You're getting the kids mixed up, mare. I heard that was one of the Norfolk boys stalking one of our dalagas. Si Maya, di ba?"

Maya? What did they know about Maya? Isabel straightened up. Her heart hit the sides of her chest, blocked her hearing and made her ears pop. She felt like she was watching a telenovela report. Her heart ticked loudly—pintig, pintig, pintig. They sounded like the old aunts from Evanston. The way they took a seed of truth and sprung all kinds of fiction around it – not only fiction but judgment too. She had been on the receiving end of this and she knew what it felt like to walk into a room and for the conversations to hush. Sometimes at a party or community function, standing at the food table or sitting with the other doctors' daughters, she felt the women staring from the other side of the room, whispering. She hated the whispering. She didn't trust the painted smiles.

Flounder leapt onto the table and sniffed at the bits and pieces of cassava cake, of coconut milk, of sweet cream that garnered the plates. His sudden appearance scared Tita Mercy, who screamed, "Ay!" Isabel picked the kitty up, and held him close to her chest. Then Tita Mercy sneezed and the cat jumped out of Bel's arms and onto Tita Mercy, who screamed a second time, and then the phone rang.

Isabel was surprised to hear JoJo's voice. Are you calling about Maya, she wanted to know. Are you calling with a plan? He advised her to forget what she saw. But the commotion behind her and her sleepless night, and this loss of control made her frantic, and all she could say was, "We need to talk." Flounder was running amuck, and the women were squealing like he was a mouse. Elliot waved his hairy arms like a conductor, trying to calm the women down. "If you don't fill me in," Isabel said, "I'll ask the aunties about it. You hear them don't you? I'll go to Macmillan. What are you doing anyway?"

"Heading out to kick it with the kids at the Cultural Center."

"Can you pick me up?"

"What for?"

"Come as soon as you can." Not waiting for an answer, she hung up the phone. She turned around, picked Flounder up like a child and shooed him out the door.

These aunties were still in tsismis mode, despite the Flounder disturbance. Isabel watched their round little faces light up like they had drunk from the fountain of youth, how the words spinning from their mouths like beautiful incantations smoothed the wrinkles away. They put up a good fight, but she held her ground. No, she couldn't work on the pageant. She had limited time, she told them, limited experience. "But you know," she told them, "I think we should try and find out what happened to Arturo, not just gossip about it, but make sure it doesn't happen again."

"Ay, but why?" Tita Nita said. She gasped and held her breast. "Don't you know that would only make things worse for Chic Chic?"

"Oo nga," said Auntie Wilma. "Parang si Gracie Reyes when her boy Jay was shot. They tried to bring that to trial and it was in the papers and on the news and the whole family was on TV and she was so disgraced. Di ba?"

"Gracie Reyes?" Isabel asked. "Is she related to JoJo?"

"The mother. Jay was the brother."

"That's why JoJo is so angry all the time, di ba?"

What did any of this have to do with her teaching position or her need to serve the community? She bowed out gracefully, but felt they were not convinced. She suspected they would try again.

She washed the dessert tray they'd brought, scrubbed it sparkling clean to demonstrate her good Filipina upbringing. Then she sent them off without a pageant assistant director. Dutifully, she kissed each of them at the door and they left the beach house a little less talkative, a little less friendly.

Isabel's Going Away Party. Evanston, IL. August 1995.
Photo by Mark Olsen

You try fitting fifty Filipinos into a thirty-five-millimeter camera. They cram onto a love seat and one long leather couch that bends like a comma at the end. Their bodies press against one another, pile up fat like pillows. Arms and legs hook and overlap. Toddlers rise up into the air. The old ones—gray-haired and fine-boned—sit on a row of metal folding chairs before the sofas. They wait like passengers on a train, accepting the babies that land in their laps.

It's hard to focus. Everyone talks, gives loud directions. I understand some of it, but mostly it's just noise. Even the English.

I push my back against the wall and squint into the lens, but I still can't get them all into the shot.

There are ladies directing the teenagers: "Dat's it. Moob closer togeder. Dat's it." I think about how much space there'd be if they would just shut up. "You have to hold still," I say. No one hears me.

"Look at Mark, look at Mark!" Isabel yells.

"Sino si Mark? Boyprend ni Isabel?"

"Yoon, the boy with the camera. Si Mark yan!" shouts Dr. Manalo.

I hold my breath. "Okay," I say, more to myself than anyone else. I glance at the mound of cameras next to me. I'm trying to figure out how many times I'm going to have to take this picture. "Say cheese," I say.

"Say money!" calls out one of the uncles. Isabel rolls her eyes at me and I wave at her. When a baby cries like she's been stepped on, I snap the picture—blur the faces with a single click, smudge the brown and yellow and coffee-colored copper-shiny faces. The shutter stutters and flashes, and for a moment the world freezes. All that noise streaks across the photo, culminates in a chorus of old and young. "TENK YOU!" they sing as I pick up the next camera.

"Why do you always do that?" Isabel said, tossing plates into the sink.

Elliot looked up from the stove, bewildered. "Do what?" A shaft of light fell across his shoulders, softened the lines around his eyes. Like this, he was beach-movie Elvis in cutoffs and a surfer T-shirt. At least Mark worked with her. He didn't always understand the ways of Filipinos, but he never betrayed her. He always followed her lead.

"Make me look bad." She grabbed mugs from the table and flipped the water on. A gush of hot water rushed forth as she dumped cold coffee. "I don't want to do that beauty pageant."

"Why not?" He broke a piece of toast in his hands, munched

on it. "Could be fun."

"Why not? Where do I start?"

He wrapped his arms around her. "You make too much out of every little thing," he said.

"Oh," she sighed, peeling herself away from him, "stop it." She walked away, leaving him with the rest of the dishes.

Out in the yard, she found JoJo leaning on the hood of his blue pickup. The wind wrapped his hair up around his face, and his shirt rippled like he was going to fly off. He sort of looked like a Filipino version of David Cassidy when he was on *The Partridge Family.* She always had a crush on that guy.

"What's got you so riled up?" JoJo asked.

"Nothing. Can I come with you?"

"Why you want to do that?"

She wanted to escape, she wanted out, so she told him, "Take me for a ride." They flew down the highway in his beat-up convertible and the wind washed everything away. The world was a blur. Finally.

"Did you leave your boyfriend for good?" JoJo yelled.

"None of your business."

"I thought you wanted to talk."

He drove her to the Cultural Center, a neighborhood with white pillars and red brick buildings, a little colony away from the beach. This was where many manongs and manangs retired on Sunday afternoons. The Center had a porch that wrapped around the building so old lolas and lolos could play mahjong and poker, rounds of dominos, so they could flirt with one another under a hot southern sun or watch people on the street.

"What are we doing here?" she asked.

They walked around the deck, greeting elders. They found a wicker loveseat and sat across from an old woman. "Kumusta ka na, Lola Evelyn," JoJo said, making mano. He took her hand and brought it to his forehead. "Naku!" she whispered. "Halika," she said. She put her skinny arms around his neck and kissed him. "Ang sarap ng buhay ko."

"Ito, si Isabel Manalo, lola," he said. He pulled Isabel close to her and the lola took her hand. She was small—not much taller than four feet and very thin. Her salt and pepper hair was pulled into a bun. She wore silver earrings and a wedding ring. "Anak ko?" she asked, looking at JoJo.

Their voices slid up and down like waves, calm and melodic. Isabel opened her eyes a little wider, studied Lola Evelyn's face, her little body draped in a floral jersey, her perfectly combed hair. Isabel was hoping that if she could see the old woman exactly as she was, she would also understand her words. No luck. The language was still familiar noise, but noise without meaning.

"Hindi, po," said JoJo. "Nasa New York pa yung daughter mo."

"Wala siya dito?" said Lola Evelyn. "Kamukya niya ang anak," she said, leaning over and sniffing Isabel's cheek.

"She says you look like her girl," JoJo said.

Isabel smiled at the old woman, who reminded her of her father's photos of the relatives back home. She had never met her own lola. They were too far away from the Philippines, and it was too expensive to fly the family back and forth, so her grandparents grew old without her. She smiled and said, "How are you, Lola?"

Ferdi wheeled an old man onto the porch. The manong was in his nineties, frail as rice paper. He was talking in Tagalog, maybe telling a story. Actually, it sounded like he was yelling at Ferdi.

Ferdi waved at them. "Sup Sista Isabel? Be with you guys in a second."

The last person she wanted to deal with right now was Ferdi. He rolled the manong to the edge of the porch so the light bathed him. He combed the old man's hair and straightened his shirt. Crouching at his feet, he rearranged the manong's legs so he could stretch them.

"Ferdi!" JoJo called to him. "Psst!"

The manong waved his hands as he yelled at Ferdi and Ferdi laughed at him. He answered the old man and the lolo swatted his arm.

"What's with you?" JoJo asked her.

Ferdi leaned over and kissed the old man's forehead and the manong swatted him again.

"What?" she answered, but she knew he was referring to the big fat tears rolling down her face. "Does he work here?" she asked.

"Volunteers. He's a visiting nurse, hangs with the old ones at their houses, but he likes to come here on Senior Sundays. You know."

They waited for Ferdi on the porch, and talked with some of the elders. Every time JoJo introduced her to an old lola or lolo, they wanted to touch her, to embrace her, they wanted to sniff her cheeks with a kiss.

"Where did all these lolos come from?" she asked.

Most of them were Navy cooks, JoJo told her. Some of them were veterans from WWII.

"So they speak English?" she said.

"Sure, if they wanted to."

"Why don't they?"

"I'm going to guess they don't want to," JoJo answered. "What do you think?" He stared at her for a moment and then he told her, "Sometimes, I bring the kids from Magkasama down here and we hang with the lolas and lolos. We play poker and dominoes and we bet. You wouldn't believe how many of them cheat."

"What's Magkasama?" She remembered the kids had mentioned this before.

He told her it was a nonprofit organization for youth. "Like an after school-club, or a—"

"Program for at-risk youth," she finished. "Was your brother Jay a member?"

JoJo turned away from her and chewed the ice from the bottom of his Styrofoam cup. "None of your business."

"Sorry." She grabbed his cup from him and refilled it with soda. "Have you talked to Maya?" She looked him in the eye, offering the cup like an apology.

"What if I have?"

"So what's going on?" she wanted to know. He was looking less and less the tough guy, she thought. She examined his blank face. She thought she saw dark patches of stress floating beneath his eyes.

"Nothing," JoJo said.

"She's fine," Ferdi answered, joining them. "Her ankle was twisted. No broken bones. She just needs time to chill out."

"You didn't take her to the hospital?" she asked.

"Oh yeah," Ferdi answered. "He brought her in and I took care of her."

She couldn't understand why they didn't report the incident to the police. "Those girls shouldn't be doing that to each other," she said.

"How come you never answer my phone calls?" Ferdi asked.

"If we got the kids to talk about what's really bothering them, maybe they wouldn't need to act out like this," Isabel said. She looked at Ferdi and said, "Phone calls? That's you?"

JoJo told her to stay out of it. None of your business, he told her. "If you want to be helpful, why don't you join Ferdi on Sundays, visit the lolas?"

She rained questions on them—why do they do this, why don't you stop them, what can we do to get to the bottom? But they were indifferent. You wouldn't understand, they told her. You grew up different, you live like a white girl, they said.

"What the hell does that mean?" she asked.

They smiled at her. "You know," they said.

But she went on—can't you see you aren't helping, don't you worry for their health, don't you wonder why they do it?

She could tell from the way they talked that this was how they treated all these incidents—like secrets, like something to be proud of.

Maya stopped coming to school, and nobody spoke about that night. They went about the class, acting out parts, calling on elders from the Ifugao tribe, playing out the roles of conquistadors like Magellan and resisters like Bonifacio and Aguinaldo.

Isabel stood before her high school kids, their faces blank, their bodies slumped over, leaning lazily one against the other. They were broken toys, pretty but nonfunctioning. They stared at her. Row after row of hostility. Like she had done something to them. Okay, she thought, I am not going to let them get away with this.

Maya had not been to class for a week. Her absence weighed Isabel down like a bad bellyache, and made for distance between her and Elliot. Isabel asked and they said she was visiting her lola on the West Coast. What for, she wanted to know and they shook their heads, shrugged "Don't know."

The night before, she'd seen Lourdes walking down Beach Boulevard, holding hands with Edison. "It was like a scene out of a music video or something," she told the class. The kids whistled and whooped.

The guys leaned over and patted Edison on the back.

"Thas my man," Derek told him.

"I can't believe your mother lets you out of the house like that," Isabel said. Lourdes rolled her eyes. "She had on this half shirt thing, and pants that were hanging off her butt."

Lourdes muttered, "Whatever," and shifted her body away.

Isabel took a breath and continued. "Mine would never have let me out. 'Get bock in da house. What are people going to say, huh?'" She saw a smirk curl onto the lips of two or three kids.

"Yeah," said Mercedes, "Why they always like that—'What are people going to say?' Who cares what other people say?"

Miguel leaned forward, smiling. "What are people going to tink?" he mocked.

"Don't embarrass your pamily . . ."

"Stop galibanting around." A couple of them sat up, nodded their heads. Derek punched Edison in the shoulder and laughed, "I'm telling your padder."

Isabel stood up then and paced before them. "It's called tsismis, right? Gossip."

"Walang hiya," said Derek. No shame.

"Yes," Isabel told them. "It's about gossip and shame. Tsismis and hiya govern our people."

"Yeah," chimed Marilena. She leaned on her boyfriend's shoulder. She was the quiet one. "Like no matter what else you do, you gotta make sure you look good."

"Better to look good than be good!"

"Do you think it matters," Isabel asked, "if you're good or not?"

"Hell no," answered Derek. He sat like a monk in his vestments, a sweatshirt hood pulled up over his bald head, sunglasses over his eyes. "Just don't get caught so people won't talk."

"Ferdinand and Imelda Marcos," Isabel asked, "walang hiya?"

"Oh yeah," said Mercedes. "My mom and aunties always talking 'bout those two."

"Tsismis," Isabel said. Marcos and his wife looked real good—prayer and council and treasures in their palace, and in reality there was bargaining and stealing, lying and cheating.

"You oughta know," Lourdes mumbled.

"And those shoes!" said Elvie from beneath his hooded sweatshirt. "Sup with that?"

This was how martial law survived, Isabel told them—on tsismis and hiya. First the Catholic church and conquistadors planted it in the palaces and in the giant cathedrals next to statues of Mary and Joseph and little baby Jesus, then gossip and shame trickled like wet paint down the socioeconomic ladder, so that everyone alike—the peasant, the farmer, the ya-ya, the tailor and the fisherman—lived under the rule of tsismis and hiya.

Tsismis, Isabel told them, a dangerous monsoon rain, traveled fast as a hurricane wind, drenching everything in sight, ruining all that it saw, regardless of truth or fiction. Pinoy gossip inflicted its pain. While hiya, a hot flower in bloom, kept them from speaking up. Flower of shame helped each of them die a slow and painful death. "Too timid to stand up against the monsoon, too insecure to leave without their compares and comares, tsismis and hiya keep us in our places."

"No," called out Edison. "Keep our parents trapped, not us. We don't care."

Isabel nodded at him. "Do you talk to your parents about this?"

"What do you think?" Lourdes said. "Gimme a break." She shook her head and stared out the window.

"Why you ask Desa?" Derek said. "She only half gets it cuz she only half."

"Shut your mouth," Lourdes snapped.

"Cuz she's half an half. Little bit white, little bit right," Derek teased. He leaned over to mess her hair, but she shoved him away.

Lourdes folded her arms and looked at the ground. Then, smiling, she tilted her head, her hair falling over one shoulder. "All those titas were at my house and you know the tsismis? They say Mr. North is all naked and running around your house like he lives there. 'Baka lovers sila!' They all singing that tune."

"Who lovers?" Edison wanted to know.

"The teachers!" she answered, and the girls broke into giggles.

Some shook their heads, some laughed, some stared past Bel. A long silence ensued. They waited to see what Isabel would do. She paced the room, zigzagging her way between their metal folding chairs. She was looking at the tops of their heads—how shiny the bald heads were, how artificial the girls' hair color. She imagined them with halos of white laid like crowns. Duck, duck, goose, she thought. Duck, duck, goose. When she got to a corner of the room, she found herself walking through a pocket of warm air. A white image chased across the room. Like a bird, Isabel thought, or a spirit. She took a deep breath. No, she thought, like Arturo. She summoned her strength.

"Do you think that's appropriate, Lourdes?" she asked. She took a long swig of water from her blue jar.

"You talkin' bout tsismis and hiya?" Lourdes asked. "Ain't you got no hiya? Don't you know if you gonna ask us, we gonna ask you?"

"Fair enough."

"So you want us to trust you? You start," Lourdes challenged her. "You come clean and tell us: did you and Mr. North hook up or what?"

"Yes."

A chorus of ooos and ahhhs rose from the metal chairs.

"Okay? You happy? Yes. I went out with him. But more importantly, don't you think that what happened to Maya and to Arturo might not have happened if we all weren't so afraid of tsismis and hiya? If maybe instead of mistrusting one another, we opened up? No secrets? Not even from your parents?" She stared at them. "Do you talk to your parents when you have problems?" The gym floor shined yellow under the fluorescent lights, and gray sky peeked into the windows. The faces of the teenagers hid in the afternoon shadows. Silence.

Isabel took a deep breath, let it out slowly. She imagined they didn't talk to their mommies and daddies. Their expressions told her they were older than anyone suspected. They kept secrets, banding together, fighting this war on their own.

"We ain't talkin' about our brotha and sista like dat," said Derek. "Ain't gonna tsismis on them."

Then Miguel said, "Anyhow, what are the choices? None. Can't talk cuz when you talk at all it's talking back, and you know we can't do that. Talking back—talking—thas disrespect."

Miguel was right, and this is why she let it slide forever before she told her family about the miscarriage. Whatever she said, she knew it was going to hurt them, disappoint them, be a sign of disrespect. She walked around the room, searching for that white light, for that pocket of hot air. What do you think, Arturo, she wondered.

When the bell rang, they wandered out of their seats, a little slower than before. They said goodbye to her. Some even thanked her. She felt like she had crossed a major line. Inside, the energy buzzed and she was happy.

Lourdes was the last to leave, lingering by the doorway. "Ms. Manalo?" she said. "Whatever. Just cuz you read lots of books about the Philippines doesn't make you Filipino."

Isabel's heart ached. "I know, Lourdes."

"Good, cuz I didn't want you to think that cuz you knew something about our history that it meant you was one of us."

"That's great, Lourdes. Thanks for cutting me some slack."

Lourdes shifted her weight, threw her hip out to punctuate her point. She smiled at Isabel and then she strutted out the door, like she owned the whole world.

SOMEONE TOLD ME YOU ARE TRUE MIDWEST. YOU KNOW WHAT IS A MIDWEST PINAY? I SUPPOSE THAT BECAUSE YOU ARE PRIVILEGED—COME FROM UPPER MIDDLE CLASS "ASIA AMERICA"—YOU'VE BEEN TO FANCY HOTELS AND RESTAURANTS. WHEN WAS THE LAST TIME YOU LOOKED AT YOUR BUSBOY? WAS HE AN OLD-TIMER, A FILIPINO COME TO AMERICA TO FIND HIS SILVER LINING, ONLY TO FIND HE IS WASHING YOUR SILVERWARE? WHEN WAS THE LAST TIME YOU LOOKED AT THE DOORMAN—DID HE RESEMBLE YOUR GRANDFATHER, YOUR FATHER'S UNCLE, YOUR ANCESTOR? AND BY THE WAY, YOU KNOW IT'S WRONG TO BUY INTO THAT ASIA AMERICA BULLSHIT, RIGHT? ONLY MAKES YOUR PINAYNESS LESS VISIBLE, LESS VIABLE. WE ARE NOT "ORIENTAL." WE ARE NOT LIKE THEM—JAPANESE, CHINESE, KOREAN. WE ARE OF MALAYSIAN DESCENT. A BROWN PEOPLE WITH LATINO BLOOD. WE WERE U.S. NATIONALS. WE DESERVE TO BE CALLED WHAT WE ARE: FILIPINO AMERICANS. MIDWEST MANONGS DID NOT SUFFER ANY LESS THAN WEST

COAST MANONGS—BUT THEY CAME TO AMERICA AND
WORKED JOBS I KNOW YOU WOULD NEVER DREAM OF
TAKING. ELEVATOR MAN. TAXICAB DRIVER. HOUSEBOY. HOW
MUCH OF OUR PAST COLORS YOUR PRESENT? DON'T SHOO
ME AWAY. I CAN HELP YOU. I CAN EDUCATE YOU AND DIRECT
YOUR WORK IF YOU LET ME. DON'T YOU KNOW THAT UNTIL
THIS GENERATION, EVERY FILIPINO WHO WAS A ROLE MODEL
WAS RELEGATED TO THE BACK OF THE BUS, THE SINK AT THE
KITCHEN? HE WAS A BARTENDER, A COOK, A BELLHOP. NOT A
DOCTOR, NOT A LAWYER, NOT A TEACHER. OUR LIVES WERE
BUILT ON THE BACKS OF THE MANONGS. MIDWEST. EAST
COAST. WEST COAST. WE ARE NOT—AS THE SONG
CORRECTLY STATES—AN ISLAND. WE ARE A COMMUNITY.

In the grocery store the dalagas ran in packs of six. Lourdes and her
other mersisters stood around the aisles, browsing at yogurt and cheese.
Meanwhile, the unsuspecting Bel charged her cart around a corner and,
suddenly, a showdown.

Marilena held a carton of yogurt in her slender hands. The others
were huddled around her, reading the flavors. Strawberry. Banana
Cherry. Kiwi. Vanilla Nut Bean.

"Check it," Angel said. "They gots coconut and mango too."

"Hi girls," Bel said, rolling the cart to their feet.

They looked up at her like gapers cruising past an accident. A
wreck. She pushed the cart left and right. She was hinting. But they were
rooted to the aisle.

"Yum," she said. "Yogurt." Lourdes gazed her beautiful blue-eyed
gaze. "Could you let me through?" she finally asked. "I'd love to chat,
but I'm in a hurry."

They shifted their legs and expanded their stance. There was a
breeze from a shaft above and their windbreakers sailed like butterfly
wings. Bel couldn't make it around them. They tossed her the look. The
one that says, You better off dead. So don't even.

A young mother with a cartful of children slid down the aisle. She
yelled at her kids. The children stretched their arms out and grabbed at
the shelves, pulling at cereal boxes and packages of Oreo Cookies. The

woman squeezed through a narrow pathway between Lourdes, Mercedes and Angel, who were posed like dancers at the end of an MTV video. Bel was amazed that the woman had passed through undaunted. She took the moment and ran with it, rammed the cart close to the mother's heels.

Everywhere and nowhere, Isabel thought. The image of the girls burned like an eclipse of the sun. What's up with that, she wondered as she tossed goods onto a black conveyor belt. She imagined fishtails flapping in the breeze like flags on the fourth of July.

NINE

Tidewater fourth graders hung old linen on broomsticks glued to carton boxes, called them Chinese ships. They packed their makeshift boats with plastic teacups, old green bottles, thrown-away tennis trophies and brightly colored plastic beads. "We better pack chopsticks," said Alex Martinez. "In case we get hungry. Chinamen eat with chopsticks."

"What are we going to do with all this stuff?" Benny Ramos asked. "Sailors don't use teacups or flower vases. Sailors don't wear jewelry."

"You'll see," Isabel told him. "You can trade your stuff for other stuff."

"Whose gonna wanna trade with Chinese sailors?" asked Coco Cabungcal.

"You are," Isabel told her.

"But we don't even speak the same language," Coco reasoned. She pointed to the boats. "They speak Chinese, you know."

"So figure something out," Bel said. "How might you communicate with someone who speaks another language?"

"Let's get going," Alex said. He climbed his slight body into the cardboard box. "Row, oarsmen, row!" Two boys shoved the box and Alex across the floors in Room 204, sailing smoothly from the South China Sea to the northern tip of the archipelago. When they reached the other side of the room, they pulled their treasures out of the boxes and left them on the floor like offerings to gods they had never met.

"Should we wait?" Benny asked. "Where are they?"

"No," Alex said. "What if they are scared of us? Let's hide."

Isabel stood at the light switch as they slipped behind their desks and hid behind the room dividers, while another set of fourth graders crept out from behind the map of the world. She dimmed the lights, brought night upon their story as they pointed to a moon made of white tissue paper, strung like a kite just above fluorescent lights. Coco led the mountain people out from their hiding places and packed the vases, the beautiful glass beads, the statues of iron and gold into hemp baskets and sacks.

"Look at all this stuff," whispered Clara Estrada. "Who left all these things here?"

"The yellow gods," Coco said. "Shhhh." In exchange for the Chinese treasures, Coco and her crew drew cotton swabs, golf balls, tortoiseshell combs and betel nut from their satchels and left them on the shoreline.

"Okay," hissed Clara, tiptoeing back under the map. "Let's go."

Bel opened the curtains of the room, shifted the blinds to let the sun stream in. The Chinese traders returned, put the goods into their brown canoes with paper-bag bark—and headed back to China.

"I love that," Coco said.

"What?" Isabel asked.

"How we talked without words."

Isabel pulled into the driveway of her beach house, sat in the car and breathed. She waited, listening to the wind howling. She could see the sand flying through the air, little particles of twigs and maybe even stones. Even from inside the car, she could feel the bitter wind; she closed her eyes and listened to it moan. Okay, she thought, I'll run in, brew a pot of tea and rest.

Inside the house, everything was gray and dull. Flounder lounged on the kitchen table, his face buried in his paws. When he saw her, he raised an eyebrow and sighed. "Like you have anything to complain about," she said, patting his head. "Get off the table!"

The kettle was not on the burner. She ran her hands under the cupboard where she kept her French press, her espresso maker, and her traveling coffee pot. "Where are you?" she hissed. All she wanted was a cup of tea. The house shook as if the heavens were breathing down on

124

her roof, rattling everything inside. She must have searched twenty minutes, her blood pressure rising higher and higher. She found the kettle hanging from a hook above the island in the kitchen. Who had put this there—Elliot?

The blue flames licked at the kettle's chrome. The pot rocked and threatened to explode into outer space. She reached for her favorite mug, the one Max, her five-year-old nephew, had made her.

She loved that mug because he had painted it himself. It was the color of the sky, all patchy and irregular blue, with a very misshapen smiley-face sun. Max had painted two squinty eyes and a long crooked smile. "There's no nose," he had explained, because it was a Filipino face. "So, no nose." The mug was not in the dishwasher. She checked all the countertops—the bedroom dresser, the bathroom vanity. She panicked a little because she was certain she had poured her morning coffee out that morning, rinsed the mug and placed it on the top rack.

Auntie Baby once told her that sometimes the dead liked to visit the living.

"Why?" Isabel wanted to know.

"No reason," her tita said. "Just to play hide and seek or something like that."

She called Elliot. "Hey," she asked him. "Did you come by the house earlier?"

"Nope."

"Are you sure you didn't come by the house earlier and make yourself some coffee or tea or something—maybe used my smiley-face mug?"

"Me touch the beloved smiley-face mug? And risk my life?"

"Forget it," she said.

The kettle howled and steam spewed from its spout, filling up the tiny kitchen, fogging the windows. She ransacked the cupboards, leaving doors wide open, letting plastic containers and little cups litter the floor. Was she going crazy? She placed her hand on the island counter and raised herself slowly, glancing down at the ground, at the wastebasket by the corner. Her eye caught a shiny blue something. She felt a twinge in her gut. A kick. The baby that was. And there she found the mug all shattered in pieces. Here was her beautiful blue sky and the mangled face of a smiley-face Pinoy. Who the hell did this, she thought.

After searching her place, she found her television remote was not where she left it. Her wireless phone was in the bathroom, but the last time she had used it was in the bedroom.

Later that night, Elliot rolled his eyes. "Relax," he said. "You're overreacting."

"Did you move my coffee cup?" she asked him. "Did you lose the remote?"

He shook his head. "You know you've got so much going on these days, you probably don't even know what you're doing anymore."

She handed him a compact and a lipstick. "Is this yours or have you been bringing girls over when I'm not home?"

"You know technically this isn't your house—Romy and Wilma and their kids have lived here forever. Maybe its Jenny's—you know their daughter?"

"Elliot, stop messing around. Who else could have broken my mug?"

"Sure, blame it on me. Look, is anything else missing? Anything of value? Why don't you check with Romy and Wilma? Check with their kids."

He said she was paranoid, but when she went into her darkroom, her pictures were thrown all over the counter—some had fallen into baths of chemicals. They were ruined. Flounder's paw prints were all over the countertops, the floor. He had chewed several contact sheets. She held up a photo and looked through the holes he had made in the corner of the sheet. It took her an hour to clean up the mess, and when she finally developed the last roll of film she found a series of blurred images of the ocean.

She tossed the photos onto his lap.

"Think Arturo did this?" he said.

"No, I don't," she said, tired of his sarcasm.

"Clearly, you left the darkroom door open and Flounder —whose prints are everywhere, I might note—went nuts. It's exactly the thing a cat would do."

"Okay, say Flounder got in and trashed the prints—who shot these? They are totally out of focus. I did not shoot these."

"You've never misplaced a roll? Shot a bad one? Shot one and forgotten about it? Your memory's that good?" He whistled at her. "How'd you get to be so perfect?"

"Why don't you ever believe me?" she wanted to know. "Why do you always fight me?"

She went to the kitchen and played with the door. A rush of wind from the sea blew the curtains up like parachutes. The newspaper on the table fluttered. "Have you been leaving this open?" she asked, pushing the lock down. It popped up in her fingers and the brass knob swirled around like a skirt two sizes too big. "It's broken," she said. "Could you fix this, E, or should I call a repair guy?" She waited for an answer. And then, "Do you think we should call the police?"

Someone had been in the house, or Elliot was messing with her, or maybe Auntie Baby was right: Arturo and her baby spirit were haunting her house. She believed it was Elliot. When she called Tita Wilma, she laughed and cooed into the phone, "Da kids? No, they wouldn't go there. They know you are living there now." The rush of the white water beat the sand and she felt small and unheard. She stepped onto the wet sand and watched her toes disappear under the weight of mud. She knew it was dumb, but she really loved that mug. Why would Elliot do that? Didn't he get anything?

Above her, pelicans soared like jets. She spent the rest of the morning watching them scouring the waters. On occasion, a bird would spot his prey and fly in the opposite direction, only to turn sharply in the wind and divebomb the fish. She nodded, understanding that to catch fish you had to snatch them unawares, make them think you didn't see them and then slaughter them with a sneak attack from the sky.

*

It rained for a week after she miscarried her baby. The sky was able to do what she and Mark could not do. They didn't know how to share this grief. They did not know how to cry. At least together. After awhile, they couldn't even sleep together. One time, she remembered waking to the rain running down her windowpane, to her voice pushing at the glass, trying to break free. She was so frustrated, trying to get Mark to understand.

That morning, she sat at the kitchen table, stirring her teacup over and over, weeping. The kettle was howling again, but she left it alone. She let it rock on the burner, knowing Mark would silence it in a moment. The rain seeped into the house through a crack in the window and ran sideways along the kitchen floor. She heard Mark shuffling across the wooden floors, moaning. He came into the kitchen and took the kettle off the burner.

"Did you sleep?" he wanted to know.

She traced her fingers along the edge of the crooked smiley face, ran her hands along the blue cup. "Are you going to have coffee or tea?"

"All that rain," he said, "who could sleep?"

"Yeah," she said, holding out her mug to him. "Who could sleep?"

The rain leaked into her dreams, drizzled a pool of water into her sleeping uterus. She saw a tiny baby swimming in the cavern of her body, trying very hard to surface, to lift its head, to breathe. Who could sleep?

He slipped his arms about her waist, pulled tight the ties around her robe. He stole a glance at her, but she wouldn't look at him. He buried his face there in the nest of her hair. "Do you wanna talk to someone? If not me, maybe Frankie?"

She shook her head. She didn't think she could tell anyone.

She remembered standing there with Mark, staring out the window at the water falling. The rain blurred everything, made her feel like she was drowning, that they were swimming toward each other, but the storm made it impossible. She stood there. Didn't answer him. Lost him in the rain.

Two years later as she lay on the sands of the Atlantic Sea, staring at the shifting clouds, she recognized this feeling, this distance between her and Elliot. She knew it was happening again. That talking and not-talking-at-all thing couples go through. She was mad at him for not trying harder. For always being funny with his smartass comments. She was mad at him for trying at all.

*

Isabel felt like one of the tribe exchanging treasures with Chinese traders.

The visitor had been leaving her items—a mirror, some lipstick, glitter gel pens on tables and countertops. Sometimes she'd find things tucked away in the cushions of her couch. The intruder would leave her things and take food from her cabinets. Elliot insisted she had taken her drama classes too seriously, but the food on her shelves seemed to disappear quicker than usual—milk that lasted a week was gone in five days, two-dozen cookies on a cookie sheet felt more like a half-dozen.

She should have been scared. She should have been edgy. "If it's what you think it is," Elliot told her, "call the police."

But she liked having guests. She knew it didn't make any sense, but she had a feeling and she welcomed it. Part of her imagined that it was those spirits coming to haunt her, keep her company. She imagined Arturo hung out in the middle of the day, dozing on a little MTV and munching on chocolate chip cookies. She considered her baby spirit was guzzling milk out of the refrigerator. Why not, she thought. Who said it couldn't be?

Two weeks before Thanksgiving break, she came home and found the television screaming rap from its blue window. She came into the house, calling Elliot's name. Sunshine glared into the tiny beach house and she could hear the wind whipping against the glass. There was a body on the couch. Flounder was curled up, napping on the body. When she got close enough, she peered over the side of the sofa and saw a mass of black hair splayed across the cushions. Flounder purred like they did this every day.

And then Isabel saw her, eyes closed, face soft and rested like a brown cherub. Maya Antaran was crashed in front of her TV.

Maya was surrounded by bowls of chips and salsa, magazines. Acetone-soaked cotton balls, emery boards, and glitter-blue nail polish lay scattered on the coffee table. Bel's thirty-five-millimeter camera rested in the girl's lap. The wounds on her face, four little roadways, had risen into bumpy scabs running north and south, the length of her face. She stretched across the couch like a princess waiting for her ladies. On television, a rapper in a giant Afro cruised the city streets with nothing but a pair of long shorts, gold chains and a convertible. Oh my God, thought Isabel. What the hell.

She leaned down to get a better look. What was Maya doing here?

She shook her arm, and the girl's shirt revealed a small patch of bruises around the navel. What had happened? The child slept. Isabel shook her harder. "Maya," she said, "wake up." She took the camera out of her hands and placed it on the coffee table. "Maya," she said again, "what are you doing here?"

When Maya opened her eyes and saw Isabel leaning over her, she jumped like she was being attacked. "What are you doing here?" she hissed.

"This is my house," Bel answered. "What are you doing here?"

Maya refused to talk. She curled up in a ball and lay her head back down. Bel kneeled down on the floor next to Maya and waited. She felt her heart pounding, filling up the room. Pintig, it shouted, pintig. Pintig. Pintig. Maya was swollen and blue, a cat lost in the wild. Bel reached her arm out to the girl, but Maya reared back, ready to swat her. "Come on now," she whispered. "This is my house, I have a right to ask you, don't you think?" Pintig, pintig, pintig.

"You ate all my chips," Bel said. "And here I was blaming Elliot." Maya turned her head so she wouldn't have to see Bel. She drew her legs up underneath her. Tried to make herself very very small. "Do you want something to drink?" Maya picked up the remote and turned the volume on the television up high. "Hey listen, Miss Thing. This is breaking and entering. The least you could do is tell me what you're doing." She had fixed the lock. How had Maya gotten in?

"I'm sorry," Maya whispered.

"What?" Bel said. "I'm sorry, I didn't hear."

"I thought you'd be in school. I thought you wouldn't care."

Actually, Bel was relieved. Even if Maya wouldn't talk to her, the child came to her. That was something, wasn't it? "How did you get in?"

"Jenny gave me her key."

Isabel thought of all the other possibilities—the burglar theory, the haunted house phenomenon, Elliot messing around with other girls in her house. This was a possibility Isabel had not considered. All this time she was looking for Maya on the beach and in the hallways at school, worrying about her, and the girl was sneaking into her house, napping. She hoped that maybe this meant Maya was going to let her in. Talk to me, she thought. Tell me what is going on with you.

Isabel's Senior Year. Evanston, IL. Fall 1980.
Photo by Frankie Boy (the Obnoxious Brother)

Ate Isa has draped dirty clothes on every chair, bedpost, and doorframe. Whatever. Psychedelic peace signs spin and swing yin yang over her mattress like giant butterflies. She lies face down in the bed, her butt wide as the whole earth. Her jeans fray at her feet. She spreads her body into a giant X. Her hair has not been washed today. Black sheets of her hair fan out in all directions.

"Ate Isa, I'm going to shoot."

"I told you not to call me that."

"Sorry! I mean BEL!"

"Go away."

A needle scratches at her vinyl album. John, Paul, Ringo and George—her gospel singers—play out their sad songs. Rocky Raccoon, Sexy Sadie, Julia, Prudence, Martha and her favorite of all, that damn Blackbird. He's pretty sure she thinks they really are singing about her. The record is skipping where the birds are flocking, chirping like they got the hiccups.

"Come on, Ate, turn that shit off!"

He focuses on her figure, a lean corpse, lying in the bed. Light from the window casts everything blue. "Get out!" she calls, not even lifting her head. He snaps the picture and she throws a pillow at the door. He shakes his head. "Don't worry, ugly duck. Someday you'll grow wings," he tells her. He spins away, his arms stretched out, singing deliberately loud and off-key, "Blackbird, fly—into the night of the big black sky!"

He can hear her yelling from across the hallway. Like he cares if the words are right. Like she would know.

Isabel decided not to push Maya. Instead she said, "Look, I don't know what's going on with you, or why you thought you could sneak around here like I didn't live here—but at least you're safe."

Maya got up to leave, mumbling an apology, a please-don't-tell-my-family prayer. "Hey," Isabel said, "You don't have to go."

"I don't?" Maya had been trying to intimidate Isabel, acting tough and angry, but Isabel could see she wasn't scary, she was scared.

"No," Bel said. "Sit, sit." She tried to make the girl comfortable, brought her a huge pillow from the bedroom and a lightweight comforter made of down. Secretly, Bel felt like a ten-year-old having a sleepover. She felt like she had finally made a friend.

Maya sank into the couch, drinking soda and munching chips. "You're outta salsa too," she told Bel.

"I'll say this, you've got some nerve. Do your parents think you're in school?"

"Nope. They think I'm at home, recuperating. They're like all embarrassed their girl's all beat up an shit."

Isabel watched her for a long moment, at the way Maya took over the whole couch, at the marks on her arms and forehead, the bruises and the scars on the girl's face. "Naw," she said, "I'm sure they just want you to get your strength back. Tell them I said it was okay for you to come here, all right? I mean if you want."

Maya nodded to Isabel, rocked her body slow to the beat of the bass on the color TV. "Cool," she said, crossing one leg over the other, leaning back like fish girl on the rocks, sunning.

Maya started to come over every day. She sat on Bel's couch like a cat who didn't want to be bothered but didn't want to be left alone either. She followed Bel around the house—shadowed her in the kitchen, slept on the couch when she vacuumed, hung on the porch when she pulled at the weeds. One Sunday, Isabel sat on the floor, folding white undergarments and T-shirts. Maya lounged upside-down on a couch, her hair falling to the ground, her cheeks floating like two balloons.

"Teach me some of that slang," Isabel told her. She sorted the clothing into little piles.

"Like what?"

"Sup wit dat?"

"Oh," Maya said, nodding her head. She raised her finger to her mouth. "Watch," she said. "WHAT IS UP WITH THAT?"

Isabel laughed. Maya's face was round and full of light— a plump moon teasing her with words. The bruises on her belly and arms were turning blue to yellow now. "I don't see where you get sup from what."

"Say it like one word: supwidat?"

"Supwidat?" Maya nodded so she asked her, "How about talaga?"

Maya sat up and crossed her legs under her. "Thas Tagalog. You oughta know dat. Means really." She tilted her head back and smiled. "Say it when you can't believe it—like this." She opened her eyes wide like she was surprised and clicked her tongue. "Talaga?" She smoothed her hair back, the scars rising up her cheeks. "Or if you're real cool you say it like you don't give a shit." She squinted at Bel and frowned. "Talaga."

Isabel told Maya about the time when she was little and living in

North Carolina and they had walked into a dry-cleaning store.

"How old were you?"

"Maybe three or four," Isabel said.

"And you remember it?"

"Kind of hard to forget," Bel told her.

She had walked into the dry cleaner with her mother, little brother and sister. An older woman stood behind the counter.

"Was she white?" Maya asked.

Isabel nodded. "Does that matter?"

"Just wondering."

*

The old woman's hair was set in loopy curls and teased into a giant nest balanced on her head like a golden tiara. Next to the woman, a younger man in thick glasses counted money, recording the figures in a notebook beside the cash register. When Bel's mom, Camila, walked into the shop, arms full of laundry stuffed in pillowcases and children at her side, the woman threw the young man a glance, rolled her eyes.

The man stopped what he was doing and opened his mouth. "Ah—M—sooree, ma'm."

Camila dumped the mound of white linen onto the counter.

"WOO—EE," he slurred, pointing to the air, the woman and the counter. "AH KAH—LOSED." He clapped his hands together in one gigantic slap. "FAH DEE DAY." Frankie was singing, "Old McDonald Had a Farm" at the top of his lungs, dragging Millie, who was just beginning to walk about on her own, around the tiny shop. Bel stared at the man, at the way his mouth moved in slow motion. She listened to his voice moaning each vowel, long and whiny. She felt like running around the counter and slapping him on the back as if hitting him would jar something inside him and make him move at normal speed. She watched her mother turn and look out the window, at the noonday sun pouring in through the glass and onto the black and white linoleum floors. Camila took a deep breath and sighed. Bel copied her mother, letting the air run out of her belly. She wanted the moment to be over, to tell her mother not to look so sad.

"I don't think she understood, Willie," the woman said. "Maybe you should just take the shirts."

He drummed the pencil onto his notebook. "LAY—DEE," he continued, tapping her on the shoulder. He was yelling. "WOO—EE NAUGHT," he shook his head and waved his hands in the air, "NOAH OPEN."

"Fine then," Camila said, making sure to articulate her vowels and consonants. "We'll just go back to Spic and Span, where they have regular business hours." She stuffed the shirts back into the pillowcases she had carried them in. "Come on, kids," she said, gathering them up like a handful of wild flowers. "This establishment isn't open."

Her mother pulled them out into the sun and Bel remembered the heat singed their skin, made them ache inside and her mother weep all that day until her father came home from the hospital.

*

"Ah, man," Maya said, "thas so intense. That really happen?'

"Talaga."

Isabel stacked the white shirts up into a pile, then the underwear and bras, and finally the socks, which she rolled into tiny balls. "What do you think?" she asked, winking.

"Aw," said Maya, "thas too intense." She picked up Bel's camera and fingered the buttons and switches. "This really work?" she asked.

"Sure it does," Bel said. "I can teach you how to use it. If you like."

Maya pulled a lever on the camera, held the viewfinder to her eye, said, "Okay." She fiddled with the zoom. "The darkroom too?"

There was a week before Thanksgiving break. Maya had not come back to school, and Bel was hoping something would happen. She hoped Maya would spill, would be so overwhelmed with her generosity, that somewhere between apertures, shadows and light, she'd feel like bonding, like talking, like filling her in. She'd give Maya the things she needed most in the middle of her crisis—time, space and someone to talk to.

For dinner, Bel had made chicken adobo and rice. The house still smelled of garlic, vinegar and soy sauce. Adobo was a comfort food her mother always made when they were kids. Inside, Maya was clearing the table while she and Elliot sat on the porch and watched the moon. She could hear the water running in the kitchen sink, and the pots banging against one another. It felt good. Normal. Like how a house should sound.

The sky above them was plastered with little stars that blinked white as Christmas lights. The moon was slinking out from a covering of clouds—quarter moon, sexy moon, moon as jagged as an icicle.

"How long you gonna let her stay?" Elliot wanted to know.

"It's not like she's living here. She goes home at night."

"Yeah," he said, "but how long you gonna let her do that?"

She turned to watch Maya through the window. Maya's face scrunched up like a rag as she scrubbed at the rice cooker. Her berry-painted lips were set in a scowl, and her scars marked her cheek like war paint. "She needs time," Bel said.

"Time for what? Has she told you?"

She slapped his shoulder. "Obviously, you've never been a teenage girl." She kissed him. "Time to figure stuff out. Just time."

"How do you know she's not taking you for a ride?" he whispered, pulling her close. She put her arm around his waist; she could feel his love handles growing. She thought he'd be happy that the burglar wasn't a burglar. But he was more skeptical than ever.

She pointed at the house, and told him to listen to that. He tilted his head, closed his eyes and what came from the house was the cling and clang of pots, the tinkling of silverware being rinsed and dropped into a dishwasher. "That, my love," she whispered in his ear, "is the sound of a teen cleaning up. What child would take you for a ride and then do your dishes?"

"Look at her," he said, turning Bel to face the window. "Do you see the scars on the girl's face? Can you see the bruises running down her arms? That, my sweet, is a vision of trouble waiting for something." He warned her. He cautioned her. He kissed her several times and then he asked, "You playing house, Ms. Manalo?"

She gazed at him, at the lines around his eyes and the stubble on his beautiful face. He had never known it this way. "Growing up," she said to him, "did you ever have a curfew?"

"Nope."

"Did your parents know your every move?"

"Nope."

"Did you feel comfortable telling them your secrets?"

"That's what therapists are for, my sweet."

He didn't know what it was like to have so many secrets, and feelings growing inside with nowhere to go. He didn't know what it was like to have parents worried about your every move for fear of ruining your own future or, worse yet, your reputation. "Do you know what it's like to be told every single day of your life not to forget where you come from and then you fuck up and you can't tell them because somehow that will show that, once again, your disrespectful behavior has revealed that you have indeed forgotten who you are and where you come from?"

"Whoa," Elliot said. "Why so hostile? Don't take it so hard."

"Yeah, right," she said. Then she slugged him really good and left him on the porch alone to chase the half-naked moon, a teasing moon, a moon drifting far from reach.

Isabel bought Maya a cheap used camera. "You're really good at this." Maya weighed the camera in her hand, peeked through the viewfinder, pulled all the silver toggles. "Talaga?" she asked. She was so excited she nearly dropped the thing.

"Yes," Bel said, "for real." She told Maya to go capture the world. "Show it to me," she told her. Isabel wanted to see everything. She wanted to know all of it. If Maya couldn't speak it, maybe she would capture it.

Maya shot pictures of starfish, of children running on the beach. She shot beautiful portraits of Flounder. The first few rolls were either over or underexposed. Everything was always in focus, but the lighting was off.

In the darkroom, Bel showed Maya how to bathe the images. They soaked the paper and watched as a smudge emerged, a shape defined itself, and finally there it was, a photo of a life.

"Timing is everything," Bel told her. "You have to make sure you let the chemicals take." She told her that when she was shooting the pictures she needed to pay more attention to the light. "Don't just shoot—figure out where the light is coming from, right?" Maya nodded. She poked at the photo paper in the tray with a plastic tong. "So exposure is important and getting the aperture right—all that."

"How long have you been doing this?" Maya asked.

"Since high school," Isabel told her. "I shot pictures for the yearbook."

The timer ticked away the seconds and the room reeked of sour vapors, pungent and deadly. "It's like magic," Maya told her. "Like what you really have is nothing—just a white sheet of nothing—and then you count to ten and there it is."

Isabel watched Maya's plump hands float the paper in the tray, and as she talked the shadows on the page floated to the top, moved around, finding areas of gray and white and in-between black and white. Maya's eyes got big, glossy. The sun began rising from the page, and streaks of white clouds ran like words across the morning sky. Below the sky, white surf splashed at the horizon.

"Do you ever think of Arturo?" Bel asked.

"Why? He's dead—what's to think about?"

"Were you there that night?"

"What if I was?" Maya wanted to know. She picked the photo up with the tongs and hung it on the line. She took another sheet from a bath of water and placed it in the chemicals. "I don't know what thas got to do wit anything."

"Well," Isabel said. "I thought maybe you'd seen him."

"What? I told you he's dead." She hovered over the tray, started humming to herself.

"But sometimes," Isabel said. She hesitated. "Sometimes I think he's here, visiting."

"Nah-ah," Maya said, laughing. "That's whacked. He's dead."

Isabel couldn't believe Maya'd never heard him rapping in the walls of her little beach house. Sometimes when Maya followed her from the kitchen to the living room and out the porch, Bel could sense that it wasn't just Maya and Flounder trailing behind her. There was another. Maybe two. "You don't sometimes walk through this old house and walk right through a pocket of hot air?"

Maya shook her head. "Unless you trying to scare me from ever coming back here, you better stop right now, Ate Isa. Focus on the pictures, ya know what I'm sayin'?" Another shape began to emerge. This one filled the glossy white page.

Isabel stopped. She didn't want to make a big deal out of it, but inside she was spinning in circles. Yes, she thought to herself, yes.

Maya held the finished photo before Isabel like a trophy. Chemicals still rained from its edges. "You'll want to rinse that in water," Isabel told her, "before chemicals splatter on your clothes."

"Do you see what it is?" Maya asked.

Two bodies—one male, one female—filled the frame, locked in an embrace, twisting together like two long pieces of red licorice. "Oh my God," Isa whispered.

"Does he sleep over every night?"

"That's sort of personal, don't you think?" Isabel asked. "When did you shoot this?"

"You ask personal questions all the time."

"This is different." Isabel grabbed the photo and tossed it into the water tray. "Don't do that again," she said. She watched the image floating, coupling before her, shimmering under red lights. She and Elliot locked in a smooch.

TEN

One-hundred teenagers swarmed the beach. The moon lit everything—
sea, sky, sand. Everything glowed. A long arm balanced a camcorder
above the crowd, panning across bodies of boys and girls pushing up
against one another. The lens zoomed into a cluster of finely dressed girls,
fragrant as Sampaguita blossoms. A clenched hand rose. Then a flurry of
arms flew up and down upon the girl who was planted at the center of
the circle. The crowd whooped and oo-ed and ah-ed as if they were at an
Olympic event. Someone kicked and the rest followed. The camera went
blurry, and only the dull thud of heels kicking against a body could be
heard. The girl muffled her cries, held her breath. She winced as a hand
clawed at her face. This the camera did not see, but the way the crowd
cringed suggested something. The girl held up two arms and curled her
legs into her belly. Her hair, wild and tangled, disguised her identity,
though everyone knew who she was. The camera panned into a sky the
color of Virgin Mary blue. Slowly, the crowd dispersed and she lay still
as a bird who had broken a wing. The voices melted into the rush of
water beating hard against the rocks. Her voice, shrill as the high-pitched
seagulls floating above her, wondered why she ever agreed to this.

*

Maya kept everything inside. Shut everything down. Kept them out. She
could sit at her mother and father's kitchen table, the whole family
pummeling insults and orders at her, and she would stare at a spot on a
wall just under the clock and feel nothing. Maya bore this like the rest of

the abuse. She was numb. She was fat. She let them ruin her beautiful face. How could she do that? She threw away the family honor. She was kinahihiyan and a Demonyo. What kind of example is this for the little ones? She moved too slowly. She slept too much. She overcooked the rice. She burnt the leche flan. She didn't know how to listen. How will they show their faces? She looked straight ahead. Her arms rested on the table, the spoon and fork in her hand, shoveling rice into her mouth. She drank her water. She watched that spot on the wall grow. Sometimes she thought she saw a face there—like a man-on-the-moon kind of face, like a lady-in-the-wallpaper face. That was how to make it through the day.

Tonight, the family surrounded her and talked at once. Her father Gregorio handed her an empty plate. "Why do you put so little on there? Put it all on the plate. Don't wait to be asked." She served her kuyas, her father, her mother and younger sisters, scooping the white grains from the cooker, peeling the sticky goo from the white plastic spoon.

"As soon as those bruises go away, you have to go back to school," her dad was saying. "They're gonna think something bad has happened to you."

"Naku naman, I don't care what she looks like," said her mother. "I want her to feel strong before she goes back. Who cares what she looks like?"

"I do. She walks out of this house, she represents us—you, me, the family, everything my papa ever worked for. That face is my mother's face. She even has Mommy's body too—taba, so fat."

"She's got Lola's pwet too," laughed her Kuya Dave, pointing to her ass.

"So when that girl walks out of here like that—and that body black and blue—how ugly you make your lola appear."

"Daddy, naman!" her mother yelled. "You over-exaggerate." She leaned over and waited for Maya to hand her the plate of rice. "Why would they hurt my baby like this? Who did this?"

Walking back to the table, Maya handed the rice to one of her brothers. He gave her back the ulam.

"We need more adobo, Maya."

Maya replenished all the plates—the chicken, the beef, the rice. Finally she sat down, and before her father had a chance to notice, she got back up, worked her way back around the table, got him his beer. "Ay salamat, hija," her father said, taking the cold glass.

After dinner, after she had cleaned her mother's kitchen and bathed her little sisters, Maya locked her bedroom door and cranked the music. At the end of the day, she was a diva draped in a silver mini-tank dress, complete with shiny breasts, hips and a full bottom. She imagined a crew of homeboys chasing after her. She didn't give them the time of day, though she sang and danced and shooed them away. "Neva gonna get it, neva get it." When the pounding on the door began, she pretended not to hear it. Leaning into her boom box, she turned up the volume, belted out even louder: "No, ya neva gonna get it . . . no, ya neva gonna get it . . . ah ah ah."

She slipped away someplace deep into that song, and the words vibrated in her skin, turned her body in zigzags and swirls, made the pain rise from the darkest part of her and flow out first in the lyrics of the song, and then in the movement of her body. All the while, there was the pounding at the door. But Maya was too far away by now, trying so hard to forget what happened that she didn't hear the rattling at the door, the banging growing louder, her father bursting in, angry and loud. Maya didn't see him see her standing in the middle of the room, tears dripping from her face, from her hands, didn't feel the wounds on her face ripped open and bleeding.

*

The night of the Tidewater Youth Dance, Maya's crew gathered round her and protected her from the Triple P. Pure Pinay Power my ass, she thought. Motherfuckers. Las Dalagas faced off with the girl gang from Norfolk, posturing on the gym balcony. Their arms and legs moved slowly, deliberately. Elbows jutted out from hips thrown to the side. Heads, cocked to the left and right, threatened to spit out nasty words, killer words. They strutted around each other like beautiful peacocks, their chests and asses puffed up and out, their feathers spread wide.

"You keep your girl away from Kenny," spat Inday Romero. Long strands of cherry bangs were draped over her eyes, criss-crossed with heavy black lashes curled and pasted on her thin eyelids.

"What makes you so sure," Lourdes said, leaning her face right into Inday's, "she's lookin' fah him? If you all that, you tell yo' boy ta stay away from Maya." Marilena, Mercedes and Angel leaned their bodies on Maya, took one breath and sneered. "If he can help it, that is."

"Whatever. That cow?" Inday's girls chirped, slapped Inday on the back.

"Tell it," cooed the one with twenty pigtails sprouting from her tiny head, "like you see it." She said it slow like she was slicing into chocolate cake.

Downstairs the bass from the DJ spun in fast circles, made heat rise, muffled everything but the drum. It was beating loud and strong. Like a heart on the warpath.

Maya could not remember what she felt, she was so busy looking tough, wearing her anger like a crown. I can take you, she thought, but really she was scared shitless.

"You know In-DIE, you the one that's gotta watch it. You the one that got our boy shot in the first place—playin' him against Kenny. Why should Kenny want you anyhow?"

"Cuz I ain't no cow." She turned and smiled at Maya, slowly like that look alone would kill her. "You keep your fuckin' mermaid tail away from Kenny or we jump you. Easy as that. You heard it here. You know it. And nothing anyone can do."

"If you'd a kept yo bitch hands to yo'self," Lourdes said, "Arturo be downstairs rapping right now—so don't you even go there."

"Shut the fuck up."

"No, for real. You the reason that boy died. And you not worth it. Now you comin' round here trash-talkin' our girl? How come you so cold?"

If Ate Isa had not snuck up the stairs at that moment, maybe they would have gone down right there. If Kenny had kept to himself, she'd be whole right now. But he was fine. He was older and drove his own car, liked to take her spinning on the beach. To places her body never been to. That was it, she knew she'd die for him and she nearly did.

The first week after the jump, her parents nursed her in her room, didn't let anyone come in. She'd lay in bed, all that blood coming out of her in drips and drools. Her head felt like it was stuffed, and she could barely breathe. She felt her mother's hand, soft and worn, rubbing her skin, taking a cool washcloth to her body.

Mommy hummed a lullaby in her Tagalog tongue. "Who did this to you, hija? You know the police said if you tell us we can put them away."

Maya rolled her body away, and the aching of the bruises traveled inside her skin. She thought she saw the colors moving like liquid along her arms, filling up her fingers and the palm of her hand all royal purple and midnight blue. She closed her eyes and started dreaming. She saw figures dancing at the house party. She saw fire shooting through the curtains and at the air, bursting into little flames. She was dancing with Arturo, all fly and phat with the beat. He was spinning around, joking her, and then he was falling to the floor. She thought he was still joking her. She thought he was making fun of the beat—sounded like guns going off, boom, boom, boom. Sounded like some homes scratching the beat on vinyl. But it was a real gun and he was not joking on her. She saw the heat rising from him, smelled that boy's spirit lifting right out of him and floating above her, sending her light.

"Maybe you're afraid you're in trouble. No hija, pero, I tell you, sometimes I think it's better to let things pass like they never happened. So I don't blame you." Her mother brushed her hair for a long time, and she was too weak to tell her to stop, too weak to tell her that same light she had seen on the night of Arturo's shooting was there, hovering over her bed like an invitation to follow.

Her older brothers Kuya Alan and Kuya Alex popped in the door, and when they began making cracks, Mommy shooed them away. Called them makulit. "You just sleep, hija. So you can heal and be strong and beautiful again."

Maya didn't have to do chores, she didn't have to watch the babies. She didn't have to come to dinner. She didn't have to explain a thing. For once in her life, they left her alone and she wondered if maybe this wasn't such a bad thing after all.

After a week, she could sit up and move around, but her body bore the scars of the beating. She was a figure of navy blue, of eggplant, of mahogany. She had scratches all along her arms and her breasts and four thin tracks of burgundy scabs marking her like a warrior woman. They wouldn't let her go to school. Her family couldn't bear to look at her; how could they send her out like that? They ordered her around like she was better, but they wouldn't let her out of the house. She didn't give a fuck what she looked like. She didn't want to be home anymore, but her parents were embarrassed and they kept her locked up in the house.

That's when she started sneaking off. She'd wait for her mother to leave for work, for her brothers to get out of the house, and then she'd hop a bus and go to the mall. Who bothers girls at the mall? But she had a black eye and people kept staring at her. So she ran off to the beach and found her way onto Ate Isabel's back porch. Jenny once told her that their family kept an extra key underneath a plant in the back. And she started hanging with Ate Isa's gray kitty.

That baby was sweet, all fur and kisses. That baby would plant himself right on top of her fat lap and nestle in all day long. She called the kitty Homes, as in I am coming homes.

Kenny paged her, but she wouldn't call him. Sometimes he paged her every ten minutes. After awhile it was every two minutes. How she gonna forget him that way?

He smelled sweet. Like Boss aftershave. Like heat. He talked to her and called her Love and shit. Never mentioned her weight. Never put her down. Called her scars beauty marks.

"You the one that got me like this," she said to him one day. She was calling him from Isabel's house. "You the one that all this trouble is about. Why you wanna cheat on Inday anyway? Ain't she yo girl?"

"Naw," he said, "not since she cheated wit Arturo. And not since you, baby."

How she gonna stay away from a boy like that?

She held out, though, because at night, when all her wounds came back to her fresh and bleeding and full of pain, she'd see Arturo dancing on the walls of her bedroom, she'd hear him singing, "Neva gonna get it," and she knew his spirit was telling her to hold out. Girl, she thought to herself, what is the matter with you? Ain't you got it yet? She knew he was coming over from the other side like a guardian angel watching her, whispering the future to her.

But no spirit dream was as real as Kenny's pulling at her hair, making her squirm under the pressure of his body all hard and warm like that.

144

"Okay," Maya told him. "You can meet me here—ain't nobody here in the day. But you watch yo back cuz I don't wanna hurt like this again."

He knew how to coo in her ear and make everything melt away. He knew how to make her feel like taking her clothes off in the light. She liked the way his hands would massage her and he would sing to her all Backstreet Boys, soft like love, all whispering and she would let him do anything. Go anywhere. Yes, she thought, months after she'd been jumped. I'd die for him all over again.

ELEVEN

Isabel drowned. She opened her mouth and swallowed the Atlantic sea. She gasped for air and inhaled silvery fish, stingray and the finest grains of east coast sand. The ocean bloated her body and traveled to all her extremities. She felt herself sinking. She was at once underwater and water. She hiccupped and drank the Indian Ocean, the South China Sea, the Black and the Red Seas. She was working her way to the Pacific.

The linen of her king-sized bed wound around her legs, torso and arms and tangled her up. She punched at Elliot, a great whale of dead weight, woke to find herself rolling back and forth against him. But he remained asleep, didn't even know she had swallowed five of the seven seas. He was oblivious.

"ELLIOT!" she screamed. "Wake up! I want to quit."

"What do you mean you want to quit?"

"You heard me," she said, still kicking and swimming her way to the surface. "I'm going home." She was tired of all that drowning, of the way the salt from the sea stung, made her raw and numb. She wasn't cut out for this after all. "Not all of us are mermaids," she told Elliot.

That Wednesday, she made Elliot bring her to the airport. She didn't even wait for the engine of his SUV to stop. She leapt out of the front seat, threw an overnight bag around her torso and blew him a kiss. "Hey!" she could hear him calling, "that's it? Happy Thanksgiving to you too, sweetheart!"

Two and a half hours later, Isabel climbed aboard the elevated train in Chicago, lugging her bag like a sack of dirty laundry. She collapsed in a seat and closed her eyes. The stench of grease and of people who hadn't bathed surrounded her. She smelled urine. Another train ran tandem with hers, glided past like a slender piece of film. Between the sprockets, she saw passengers. Some were reading papers. Others slept standing, holding onto rails, slumped into their chests. Always, they appeared to be almost falling. The colors of bright scarves, hats and mittens popped against the passengers' drab winter coats. The train picked up speed, began rolling downhill, coasting farther underground. Riders passed like streaks of light as their trains crossed.

The rocking soothed her and she found herself drifting in and out of sleep. She welcomed the gray Midwestern sky, congested with clouds. In Virginia every day was a sunny day—there was no respite from the heat, there was no depth, no shadow. The bright sun flattened everything. Isabel was going home, she could feel it. An autumn chill and the rush of city dwellers bumping gently into her comforted her.

Maybe she should come home for good, she thought. Maybe she had been out east long enough. There was something so familiar and comforting about the ride, about the colors of winter travelers popping against the dreary Chicago sky. But even at rest, she saw her teenage students between the cars—wild, colorful, loud Miguel, Mercedes, Angel and Elvie—passing on the Dan Ryan. Arturo's face was etched into a windowpane. She found herself looking for Maya—her wide smile, her fat berry lips all painted and shiny, a trail of purple scabs tracking her face.

She made up her mind to dream about her family, to consider them waiting at the front window as the el train prattled down the tracks. But every time she shut her eyes she saw Arturo's casket or Tita Nita's painted face. Drifting off, she dreamed the children were floating burial jars in baths of blue Kool-Aid. She felt her ghost child drowning in the fourth chamber of her heart. She heard the skin tearing from Maya's face. In the distance, boom boxes blasted in the subways.

The Manalos filled the house like warm rain spilling into steel pails. They dropped in, one at a time, gathering first in syllables and sighs. They arrived in a pattering of kisses and grew heavy and loud like the beginnings of a storm.

They took almost an hour to settle down, to fill their glasses full of fizz, to heat a kettle of water, to frost the mugs. "You want beer, sweetheart?" her daddy offered. "You want beer?" It took nearly an hour for everyone to find a place to sit, to pull out napkins and baskets of chips, and pretzels and freshly fried lumpia. An hour to look into each face, to see the changes, and exclaim, "Ay!" and "No!" and "Naku, naman!"

"OH!" Auntie Baby screamed. "Get the Minus One tape, Daddy." She stood before them, her lips resting on the microphone, her long fingers caressing the cord. "Hurry, Daddy, they're waiting," she whispered into the mic. Her voice wafted out to them amid electric feedback. What a trip, Isabel thought. Uncle Leonard pushed the play button and a couple of trumpets rang, a sexy samba boom-chick-a-boomed from the speakers and Aunti Baby bowed her head, waiting. Slowly, she lifted her eyes to the ceiling. "What do you get when you kiss a boy . . ." Oh no, Isabel thought, looking over at Millie—can it be? "You get enough germs to catch pneumonia." Auntie Baby swung her hips in time to the samba, rocked her heels, lifted her long skirt to reveal a pair of ankle-length animal skin boots. "After you do, he'll never phone ya!" the audience sang.

"Why is our family so weird?" Frankie Boy whispered into Isabel's ear.

"This is not weird," she told him.

"Oh-oh, I'll never fall in love again!"

"This," she said pointing at their family, "is normal. Trust me."

Calamity, confusion, chaos. Magkaguluhan. What Isabel missed most about living alone.

Rachel and Frankie Boy's Wedding. Chicago, IL. May 1991.
Photo by Millie Manalo

Rachel's sitting on the steps of Lulu's Hawaiian Luau with her arms wrapped around the trunk of a coconut tree. Her white gown spreads like bed linen down the steps. Her red hair falls in ringlets around her full face. The beaded veil has been pulled away so she looks like an angel in an old-fashioned Bible painting. Fake palm tree leaves dip into the frame, surround her and Kuya Frankie Boy. He is sitting on the step below her, rubbing her belly like she's a Buddha and he's wishing for luck. Underneath the gown, a small world is rising, filling out like a promise, like a sunrise, like the beginning that has already begun.

"This has been a good year," her father announced.

He was carving the turkey with a large silver knife, piling white meat on beds of jasmine rice. "Millie has begun her residency program, Frankie Boy's auto repair is thriving." He paused, looked over at his son, who was fussing over Lucy, his three-year-old. "Right, son?" he asked.

"Yeah, Dad," said Frankie Boy, stooping to pick up Lucy's fallen silverware.

"And Isabel's home, safe and sound from Virginia." Her father stretched his arm like Ed McMahon introducing Johnny Carson on late-night television. He made the sign of the cross. "Thanks be to God!"

"Frankie's having a great year." Rachel said. She ran her hands through her husband's thick head of hair. "Come winter, everyone needs a tune-up, a new heater," she said, "something."

"So, Cousin," Pearla said, turning to Isabel. "What kind of drama do your students perform?"

Isabel described the history lessons and creation myths and the beauty pageants.

"Don't you think what you're actually doing is self-exoticizing our culture?" Pearla said in a dry tone. A strand from her messy ponytail slipped and swung into her face like a pendulum. Last Thanksgiving, Pearla had announced she was an activist. She questioned everything.

"Is that really a word, Pearla?" Uncle Leonard asked. "Self—what is self-exoticizing—is that like self-eroticizing?"

There was an awkward silence. A breath. Isabel smiled, swallowed a mouthful. "I see you're growing your bangs out," she said.

"It's too bad you're no longer acting," Auntie Baby said. "Because you're a good actress, and so beautiful."

"Well, I don't really teach acting, Auntie. I teach the students stories and history and I use acting to do it."

"Can there be any money in that?" Leonard asked. "You'd be better off getting married."

"In theory, what she's doing is a good thing," Frank said.

"What do you mean in theory?" Isabel asked.

"Eat," Camila called out. "Your food's getting cold."

Isabel felt her chest tightening, her stomach filling up hot and full of bile, ready to explode. "Anybody thirsty?" she asked. She got up and filled a pitcher with ice water.

"Did anyone find the chicken heart yet?" Max asked. "Did you put the heart in the misua soup, Lola?"

"You know," her father said, waving the serving fork about him like a magic wand, "all I hear about Tidewater is bad things."

"Of course I did," Mom said. "Let's see who'll find the heart."

"What place?" Uncle Leonard asked.

"Yoon, sa Virginia," Frank answered. He pointed east with his lips. "Laging may trouble—there was that shooting." He turned to Camila and clucked his tongue. "Sayang. Such a nice boy."

"They dropped the investigation," Isabel said, pouring water in her father's glass. She felt everyone looking at her.

"Somebody shoot somebody?" Uncle asked.

"Some homie," Frankie Boy said. He winked at Uncle.

Looking over her shoulder, she threw her brother a look. Ice from the pitcher tumbled out of the glass and splattered everywhere.

"Careful, anak," her mother warned.

"Was it a driving by?" Auntie Baby asked. "Susmariosep! Ang dangerous naman."

"It's not like that," Isabel said, swallowing quickly.

"Can you imagine the poor parents?" Auntie Baby asked. "What people must be saying."

"I never pay attention to what others say. I never have," Camila said. "Life is too short already."

"You know, Isabel," her father said, "this isn't worth it. I think you should come home."

"I'm not in danger, Dad," Isabel said. A grain of rice flew from her mouth.

"No kidding," her dad said. "First this boy gets shot, and then that girl—the one who is taba—gets beaten up and she breaks into Isa's house."

"She didn't break in—"

"Daddy," Camila warned.

"Yeah," Frankie Boy added, "and to top it all off her kids keep telling her she's a white girl."

"A white girl?" Uncle Leonard asked. "Ikaw, Isa? What's a white girl?"

"Daddy," Pearla interjected, "she wants to be called Bel."

The children waved their hands in the air. A fork dropped. Auntie Baby sighed like she might swoon.

"Forget it, Pearla," Isabel said. "Whatever."

"They're probably referring to your petit bourgeois attitude," Pearla said.

"Bet you're an expert on that, Pearla," answered Frankie Boy.

Millie looked like she wanted to beat someone up. "Why would anyone call you white?"

"It's not worth it. Those kids are trouble and looks like you get no support from your supervisor—ano ang pangalan niya—si Calhoun?"

"The trouble with Isa is that she's always pleasing everyone around her," her mother said.

"You mean Bel."

"Which is generous, but not so practical, hija."

"You don't understand," Isabel answered. She raised her arms, creating space for her words, but her father cut her off. Her brother jumped on her breath. Pearla and Auntie Baby interrupted her, loud and out of tune.

"Get yourself mixed up in their gulo and next time a gun goes off—Ha! Ikaw na. Maybe you're next."

Their words flooded the air. Isabel wanted to plunge into the sea, to swim away from all of them. The kids were not bad kids. She tried to explain, "Nobody listens to them."

"What do you mean?" said Auntie Baby. "Who doesn't listen to their kids? How can you not listen to your kids?"

"Maybe because—"

"Oh come on!" Frank said. "Are you crazy? You mean to say if I'm busy earning a living and you ask me a question and I don't answer you right away because I'm preoccupied with work, that gives you reason to shoot your classmate? Ano ba yan? You call that reasoning?"

She held up her arms to shield herself, but that was useless. "No! It's more complicated than that. If you could see them—"

"You need to look out for your safety and your reputation, anak."

Isabel looked at the people around the table. She wondered how she could look so much like them, share blood with them and still feel

152

completely alone. How was that? Frank always needled Isabel, began small and unintentional, and when she resisted, he pushed harder. She felt herself going numb. She closed her eyes, held her breath and the words all blurred together. What was the point of trying? They were never going to get it.

"Can't you see? I think I can help."

"Help with what, hija?" her mother asked. "You said yourself you wanted to quit."

She heard the bang of rap music and bamboo splitting into thin strands of fiber. She felt her tummy swelling. She felt the baby she should have had tugging at her insides, trapped by shame and fear. Above the table, she felt a heat, a white light she had come to think of as Arturo's guiding presence.

She straightened up. "I don't know, Mommy. I just know I can't quit right now." She guzzled her water and made up her mind not to listen anymore. Her father's voice faded, garbled. She didn't hear when he called her stubborn. Didn't hear him call her hardheaded. Didn't hear that she was destined to ruin everything. Her eyes wandered the table. Her mother began to weep. The bones of the turkey—yellow and nasty—stuck up and out of plates and platters.

"Isa can always go back to acting," Auntie Baby sang above the noise. "She has star potential, you know. She reminds me of my younger self."

"Bel, Ma, not Isa."

"Let it go, Pearl," Isa snapped.

She got up from the table, taking her half-empty plate with her. She dumped her dish in the sink and picked up the phone to check her house for messages. She heard her father in the dining room, charging words at her as if she were still sitting among them.

"You kids have no respect," Frank said. He slammed his fist on the table, and plates rattled against the clatter of silverware. "You make me feel old," he said, and, dragging his chair out from under him, he left the room.

IN WORLD WAR SECOND THERE WERE TWO INFANTRIES OF FILIPINOS FIGHTING FOR THE AMERICANS. THAT'S RIGHT:

153

TWO INFANTRIES. ONE CAME FROM CALIFORNIA—U.S. NATIONAL FILIPINOS WHO VOLUNTEERED AFTER GENERAL MACARTHUR PROMISED TO—AND I QUOTE—RETURN. AND THE HAWAIIAN BOYS—STATESIDE PINOYS CALLED THEM THE WILD BUNCH CUZ THEY WERE SO MUCH YOUNGER AND BETTER LOOKIN', SINGIN' HULA SONGS AND PLAYIN' AROUND AND SHIT. ANYWAY, WHAT I'M SAYIN' IS BEFORE AMERICA EVER GRANTED THESE BOYS THEIR RIGHTFUL CITIZENSHIP THEY WERE FIGHTING FOR AMERICA AND FOR FREEDOM. THEY WERE GOING ON MISSIONS AS SPIES AND SPECIAL UNITS CUZ THEY WERE SKILLED, LOYAL AND CUZ THEY HAD ASSETS THE WHITE SOLDIERS LACKED—IF YOU CATCH MY DRIFT—WHICH ALLOWED THEM TO INFILTRATE AND DO THE JOB UNNOTICED. OUR FOREFATHERS WENT TO WAR FOR A COUNTRY NOT EVEN WILLING TO CALL THESE BOYS THEIR OWN. HOW MESSED UP IS THAT? DO YOU KNOW THAT AMERICA NEVER WELCOMED HOME OUR FIGHTING FILIPINOS IN THE TRADITION OF TRUE MILITARY HEROES? IT IS ON THEIR BACKS, ISABEL, THAT WE CLIMB TO GET OUR SO-CALLED EDUCATION, OUR JOB OPPORTUNITIES, OUR UPPER MIDDLE CLASS STATUS—AND WHAT HAVE YOU DONE TO BETTER OUR PEOPLE'S LOT? HOW HAVE YOU CONTRIBUTED TO THE MOVEMENT SO FAR? YOU IGNORE ME, THAT'S WHAT YOU DO. YOU KISS THE WHITIES' BUTTS, THAT'S WHAT YOU DO. DON'T YOU FEEL RESPONSIBLE?

Isabel slammed the phone down and marched through the house, leaving the voices spinning behind her. She paced around the yard, kicking at leaves that had fallen ruby and orange and pumpkin from their hundred-year-old trees. She liked the rustling sound moving under her feet, how she could easily clear the path by swinging her legs. She watched her breath, pale and smoky, rising from her lips.

"Stressed?"

She turned to see Mark standing on the sidewalk. He buried his hands deep in his pockets, hunched his shoulders up in a giant question mark. She didn't answer him.

"Did you have a fight with your dad again?"

"Not much changes," she said, smiling.

He made his way into the middle of her yard and kicked a pile of leaves. "Not hardly enough," he said. He leaned over and kissed her on the cheek. "When did you get back?"

"Yesterday," she said, but felt like she had not arrived at all, that somehow she was still back in Virginia and this whole night was a bad dream. "What are you doing here?" she asked him.

He was thinking about the past, he said, how the last memory he had of her was the silence between them, and he didn't want that to be the last of it.

"But it is," she told him. "We're moving on, remember? You told me to get over it. The baby was never a baby. He was—oh, what was that again?—a mistake." She leaned over and hugged him. She closed her eyes and tried to remember her life with him. She knew he was once the one she loved the best. "Remember," she asked him, "how I wanted to make another baby?"

A month after the miscarriage, when she was seeing babies everywhere and longing for them, she seduced Mark every chance she got. Once he came home and she was lounging in a tub of rosewater, drinking fumé blanc. He shed his clothes on the floor and slipped his lean body around hers.

"It's a stupid idea," he told her, not understanding that she didn't want any baby—she wanted to bring back the other one, the miscarried child.

It was never the same after that.

"Okay," he answered her now.

"Okay what?" she asked him.

"Let's make another baby."

She pulled away from him then and shook her head. She studied his face and she realized that she no longer knew the eyes, the shape of the face, she no longer remembered his cologne. She found herself looking for Elliot.

"I'm a fighting Filipina now, you know. I don't have time to make babies."

"You crack me up," he said, brushing the hair out of her eyes.

"I missed you."

"No, I'm not kidding. I'm over it, Mark. My job's not easy, but I gotta do it."

"Why?" he said, holding her tightly.

"I have people depending on me." She felt something heavy inside her spinning slowly to a stop.

His face went dark. "What do you mean?"

"People," she said. "At my job, in my life." She smiled at him. She could tell he no longer recognized her either. "I have two things to tell you," she said, leaning up to whisper in his ear. "No, make it three. I won't forget you; I am too a fighting Filipina; and last but not least, that baby that was ours, he's still with me . . . like an angel."

She waited for him to discount the three things of her heart, but he was silent. Around them the starlight filtered the sky and it was as if the shifting clouds had come from the mouth of the moon, floating like breath, chilled by autumn and the night.

The rest of the night the dishes rattled and the silverware fell one upon another like stars crashing from the sky. Isabel could not believe she'd told her parents she didn't want to quit. She was dying to quit. But they had made her so mad, how they ran words at her, pummeling her, not listening to her. In that moment she saw the rage of Tidewater teens. She also heard their families—all of them sailing accusations and twisted renditions of things they had meant to say. Shutting down was easier. And Ferdi was right too. Fighting Filipinos had come too far to die in the field like this. Lost. Misunderstood. Accused without trial.

Water spewed out of her mother's faucet. Traffic moved easily between the dining room and kitchen, and all the little children found reasons to chase one another from room to room. In the family room, the men gathered on leather sofas in search of football scores and other sports-related items.

Isa was in charge of wiping all the counters and tabletops. She worked silently, listening to the women chat as they swept the floors and filled the dishwasher full of china. Their voices buzzed softly like hornets hovering.

"Is everything okay?" Millie whispered as she dragged a broom across the floor. Isa looked at her and shrugged. "At home. Is everything okay?"

"You mean in Virginia? Never mind."

"Why do you say that?" her mother asked. "You know we only mean well. Why do you shut us out?"

Isabel grabbed a big metal pot and ran a towel over its surface, wiping away all the little drops of water. She could see her face in the chrome, the way her cheeks puffed out and her eyes spread in two distorted directions. That's how she felt. Luminous and stretched in two directions. "What's the point of talking, Mom? You already have your minds made up."

"Look," her mother said. She scoured the kitchen countertops with a wet rag, her little body stretching into corners, her hands moving fast like moth wings. "You're just like your dad. You think because we don't understand right away, you are wasting your time." She pushed hair off her forehead with her forearm, the water from the rag dripping into the sink. "But if the people you love don't understand you, you should make it a point to explain."

Auntie Baby sat at the kitchen table, cracking peanut shells with her teeth, reminiscing about the past.

"Your dad stood up to that Dr. Moorland," she said, popping a peanut into her mouth. "Remember that, Ate Camila?"

"Yoon!" Camila said. "That is a perfect example of how Frank and Isabel are alike. He was going through all this trouble with Moorland, his boss. And do you know that man kept it to himself? I was so mad at him."

*

In North Carolina, Frank worked all the hours given to him, studying between his shifts, night into dawn. Sometimes, he'd come home after sixteen hours, kiss the sleeping children, whisper stories to them in their slumber, and then, with hardly a break, he'd read the latest journals on heart implants, cardiac arrests, and new theories on dieting and medication.

All the while, Camila watched him, the way his small body seemed

157

to lighten with each passing month, the way lines carved themselves around his eyes and in the corners of his mouth.

One night, Camila tiptoed behind Frank and, wrapping her arms about his waist, whispered, "What is happening to you?" He moved out of her embrace, left the tiny living room and headed for the kitchen.

He stuck his head in the refrigerator. "Where's the beer?" he asked her. His voice, muffled and full of agitation, floated out to her from the second shelf of the fridge. "All day long I'm under pressure. Why can't I come home and find cold beer?"

"It's there," she told him. "Look harder. Look in back of the milk." She sat down at the kitchen table and watched him move a few bottles aside, slam the door shut and walk across the room.

Sometimes she'd wake in the middle of the night and gaze at him. She'd press her body against his, let her breath rise and fall with him. Under a crescent moon, his face relaxed. The slope of his cheek was a beautiful golden apple. The eyes, big eyes, slept under heavy lids with long sweeping lashes. Like this, he was himself, the man she loved. Like this, she would hold him, feel the weight of him against her. She'd kiss his arms, his chest, the back of his ear and wish him back. Like this, she'd cry for hours, not knowing what to do.

"Francisco," she said, "I thought operating would make you happy."

"I'm happy," he told her. "I'm just tired."

"You aren't happy."

"I said I'm happy." He stomped his foot, to emphasize his point, threw an insincere smile, mocked her concern. He stared at her, hand on his lower back, the other toting his beer, as if to challenge her, as if to say, "Tell me again I'm not happy, you'll be sorry."

Then, unexpectedly, it was she who let out the howl, who burst the tension, the whispers, the unspoken changes in their lives. "This is not how I want to live," she told him.

Frank stood in the middle of the room, the beer bottle dangling from his fingers like a man hanging from a tree. Meanwhile, Camila drew a circle around him as she paced, shaking her hands at the air. "Demonio," she hissed. Everything spilled out of her then. "None of this was my idea," she told him. She listed the sacrifices. All the opportunities she had given up for them. For Isabel, Millie, and Frankie. For him. For his ridiculous dream. And for what, she wanted to know. And what about her? What about her studies and her ambitions? What about the life that was waiting for them back in the Philippines? Whatever became of that? She spun around him, spewed her anger out at him, like a priest spraying holy water from his scepter on Good Friday. She cried till she felt her face heavy with tears. "What's happening to you?" she asked again. She felt hot, and the room grew big and Frank looked small, small, small.

"This is not how I want us to live our lives, Frank."

His face froze for a moment, red and confused. He reached out to touch her and she walked away. For weeks after, he followed her around the house, planting small notes of affection in the pockets of her aprons and slacks. She continued to play with the children, continued to sing them songs and flatter them with stroller walks to the park. And when he entered the house, she encouraged them to greet him, to kiss him, to love him with all their might. But for a time, she refused to speak to him. His shadow would fall upon her, or the smell of his cologne would sneak past her, and she acted as if there was no one there.

Then one night, he slipped into bed next to her, running his hands along the length of her body, and she heard him crying, could almost taste the salt from his wet face. "I'm sorry, mahal," he whispered. He never expected his days would be so difficult, he wasn't even sure if they were as bad as he thought, so he kept to himself.

"You mean you were too ashamed," she said to him.

"No," he insisted, "it isn't about shame. I just didn't know how to explain it."

He told her he was afraid of what she would think. That he might appear weak and a coward—not a man or the head of the family, but a fool. She kept her back to him, crying with him as he spoke to her. His voice was uncertain, cracking now and then, faltering. He spoke in Tagalog and then in English and then the languages fell together and mixed—one word spilling out after the next. She realized he had been living in those white hospital walls all by himself, confused and broken. She turned to him, finally, wrapping her arms about him. Forgiveness.

*

Isabel sat still. She felt her mother's hands and, somehow, she drifted back into her girlhood. She tried to stop the trembling in her bones, to shake the vision of her young parents fighting. She remembered them back then, the days when there was no conversation, no making kwento, only silence. It always scared her, it scared her now, but sometimes she couldn't help it.

"You ever hear of the Fighting Filipinos?" Isabel asked.

"Anak," Auntie Baby said, "we are all Fighting Filipinos."

"That's not what I mean."

"So why don't you tell us?" Camila said, rubbing her back. "Make kwento, anak."

Isabel held out one of her black and white photos. She laid it on the table and she began to speak.

Arturo and the Boyz. Virginia Beach, VA. September 10, 1995.
Photo by Isabel Manalo

Three homies line up on either side of him, wearing dark suits and white gloves that pop like flashbulbs. Each boy hides behind a pair of shades. The mouths tremble as they pass. They rest a hand on six brass handles, roll the cart down the long aisle. The wailing ebbs as they pass, as they carry their boy home.

TWELVE

Isabel flew back to Virginia determined to set a fire under her students and groom them into fighting Filipinos who would one day rise up and stretch their limbs to the sky.

One sunny afternoon, she bundled up the kids in their scarves and thick sweaters and led them to the playground.

Mikey Viernes, the smaller twin, buttoned a white shirt all the way to the collar. Squinting into the sun, he measured the distance from the ground to the top of the jungle gym. Maybe fifteen feet high. The structure would be his jail. It was the color of copper, shiny and fitted together like a maze of house pipes. He pulled his vest to his waist and ran his hands through his hair so it would lay flat on his head. He climbed. When he reached the top of the gym, he heard Mia Hidalgo and Ligaya Tan wailing and pounding on their chests. The girls sat at the edge of the sandbox, cloaked in veils, masking their fake tears with white hankies. Every now and then, Ligaya peeked out from under her hanky to see what everyone was doing.

"Stay in character, Ligaya!" Isabel yelled from a park bench.

Mikey pulled out a marker and a little notebook and wrote a letter to his people. *Put down your weapons,* he wrote; *think about our people. No matter what happens, don't forget I love you.* He prepared himself. For today he was not Mikey Viernes from Virginia Beach, Virginia, but Dr. José Rizal, national hero of the Philippines, leader of the Propaganda Movement.

"Way to be in character!" Isabel yelled. "You look just like the picture, Mikey!" Seeing him on the top rung of the copper bars, writing into his pad, made Isabel's chest expand with hope. "You're my hero!" she cried.

Meanwhile, beyond the jungle gym, kids jumped up and down, screaming and chanting as they rode high on seesaws and teeter-totters. Andres Bonifacio, played by Manny Viernes (the bigger twin), stopped raking gravel on the playground and yelled, "Who wants to beat Spain? Who wants freedom? Calling the oppressed. Come by me!" Ten children came running, and as they drew near him, Manny demanded a formal separation between the islands and Spain. "You are not the boss of me! Free our children from pain! Free our children from Spain!" He lifted a fist to the sky. The children ran to the swings and, climbing onto the seats, they began to pump, kicking their legs higher and higher to the sky. No, Isabel thought, no matter what the grown-ups think, you are the Fighting Filipinos. We are.

The revolution grew; the children came in masses.

"Go get 'em!" yelled Isabel. "Show 'em what you got!" She felt the energy rising within her, she felt the kids were making her stronger. The louder the kids yelled, the stronger she felt.

Meanwhile, the Spanish soldiers climbed the rungs of the monkey bars and pulled Dr. Rizal down. They made him walk a plank, shoot down a ladder, fall to his demise. And still the people rose—Kataastaasan Kagalang-galang na Katipunan mga anak ng bayan—Freedom to the people or die!

The hall echoed with the clash of pins knocking against one another. Bowling balls roared like doom down gutters and freshly waxed planks of wood.

She watched Elliot caress a fat blue ball. Kicking his elbow back, he walked his way to the line, released. His fingers hung long like Michelangelo's hand of God. The ball spun.

CRASH!

Ten pins tumbled down. Elliot danced, punching at the air, hissing, "Yes!"

His friends—the same motley crew from the bar—howled at the whirling disco ball. Midnight bowling: what could be better than this, she thought, rolling her eyes.

"Come on, honey," Elliot said. "Your turn."

"I don't think so."

"Let's go, Isabel," the tall and skinny one said. "Can't let your man show you up now, can you?"

She had cramps, and would rather be soaking in a hot tub of bubbles, but Elliot had begged her to join them. "The guys really like you," he told her. "They want to see us again. You can meet their wives."

"Can't I just watch?" she said. "Cheer my guy on?"

Karla, one of the wives, handed her a ten-pound ball. "Humor them," she said. "It'll go quicker if you do." She winked at Isabel.

Sighing, Isabel got up and said, "Okay, I warned you."

The walls of the Bowl-a-Rama Bingo House vibrated, taking them back twenty years. The speakers spat out a flash-flash-beep-beep rhythm. She focused on the pins, their fat bellies and little red bows. The black light strobe made them nuclear and slightly animated. Her backhand twisted and the ball shot out crooked onto the alley, teetering on the edge of the gutter, almost dying. Then, suddenly, it spun to the center lane and shot the pins dead. All ten of them.

Elliot's friends chanted, "Hoo! Hoo! Hoo! Hoo! Hoo!" like a tribe of owls. She laughed at them and, dusting off her hands, she said, "Told you."

At the bar, she ordered a pitcher of beer and grabbed a basket of stale popcorn.

"Who knew you could bowl?"

Oh no, she thought. But, turning, she smiled at JoJo, asked him if he wanted a beer. His teeth glowed in the dark. His face was a black mask. He was like that disappearing cat from Wonderland.

"Naw," he said. "I've had enough."

She craned to see how the bartender was doing, like she was supervising or something. "Okay," she said, not looking at JoJo. "Don't say I never asked."

"You having fun?"

She nodded, digging into her pocket for cash. The lights in the room twirled, flashed red and blue. She nodded to the music.

"Don't think I've ever seen you this relaxed," he said.

"Why wouldn't I be?"

"Those your friends?" he asked, nodding toward the alley.

"Yeah." And then she looked him in the eye and off she went. She didn't know what he was getting at, but did he always have to be on her back? So she was out with her boyfriend, and she was out with his friends, and they were loud and drunk, but they were nice to her and they didn't give her shit the way he did, the way Ferdi did, the way the kids always gave her shit, so get off her back, she told him. "Just get off my back."

"What makes you think I care?"

"What makes you think I don't?" she said. JoJo's smile grew and he leaned toward her. She said, "You're not the only one who's lost someone, you know."

"You hardly knew him."

"I'm not talking about Arturo."

He stared at her, as if wanting her to go on, as if daring her to explain herself.

"And if you gave me a chance," Isa said, "I could help you and the kids—but how am I supposed to do that if they see you mocking me?"

"I don't mock you."

"Hell you don't. Then why haven't you asked me to one of your club meetings?"

"Magkasama? You interested? It's wide-open, homegirl. Why don't you come?"

"Maybe I will." She wanted to help, but something about him made her so mad. She had imagined this conversation differently.

She tossed a twenty-dollar bill on the bar, grabbed the pitcher in one hand and the popcorn in the other. She turned away and took off before he could say a single word. The bartender called out to her, "Thanks, lady." The music pounded who-who, beep-beep.

Isa walked up the stairs and heard the teens giggling. They were scrambling together, piled like throw pillows on the stage, and they were yelling, "Picture! Picture!" She hesitated before entering, holding back long enough for Maya to focus her lens and shoot. When they saw Isa, they tumbled off the stage and onto their folding chairs and left Maya standing alone in the front of the class.

"Welcome back," she called out as Maya took her seat in the back row. "You know," she said to the group, "the children are doing some incredible dramas. If this were a stone statue contest, you'd win, but it isn't, and you are very far behind." She crossed her arms and mirrored their expressions. She set her mouth into a straight line, and focused on the window behind them. Clenching her jaw, she tensed all her muscles. She mimicked them for almost two minutes and let the silence smolder like a volcano ready to explode. Then she shrugged at them and said, "No wonder the cops are always picking you up. Who could trust a face like yours?" She walked over to Derek and grabbed his chin. "This is a mean face." He cracked a smile then, revealed a row of teeth, large as tiles of Chiclets gum. "Do you think people make assumptions about you?"

"If me and my brothers are walkin' Military Circle, buyin' shoes or sumthin'—" Edison said, "you better believe the salesmans or whatever wants us out of their store 'fore they even know what we want."

"Right, right, right," Angel said. "Or if we're waitin' at Pizza Hut and they're like—sorry but we're all full right now. We can't seat you. Sup wit that? Like no one's ever going to finish up an leave?"

"Why do you think they do that?" Isa asked. "Send you off before they even know your business?"

"Ts race."

"They think we're gangbanging."

"Are you?"

"If we're walkin' around with our friends," Miguel said, "and we're all Pinoy, white cops stop us and they think for sure we've got guns or drugs on us."

"We ain't that stupid."

"Ts ignorance."

She felt their comments coming like a battery of punches because she couldn't draw from her own life. She couldn't say, "That was me! I know what you mean." The more they shared, the more she realized how different her world was. When she was the only brown girl in a group of white girls and all those white girls thought she was white, she took it for granted. She thought she was one of them. Not white, but one of them.

Isabel encouraged the kids to talk by nodding and muttering, "Yeah?" and "Right." She told them about the time she was in Rome and someone mistook her for a maid.

"A maid?" asked Maya. She was sitting in the back row. The scabs were gone and in their place were four thin scars.

"You know like one of those Filipina maids who've gone abroad?" Isa said. She was pleased to see Maya there, participating.

"Thas messed up, Ate," Maya said, and Lourdes, Marilena and Mercedes leaned forward like a company of dolls and leered at her. Ate?

"Sup wit dat?" Mercedes whispered.

"Maya, dat you?" Lourdes said, poking her ribs.

Maya pushed the hand away, muttered, "Fuck off."

Meanwhile, the others sketched at the air, made illusive pictures of frustration, of common experience. The kids seemed to relax, except for Lourdes, Marilena and Mercedes, who sat in the back, whispering. Their heads were bent toward one another. Mercedes had pulled out her nail polish and was touching up Marilena's fingernails. Isa could hear a file zipping back and forth as Lourdes sanded her nails down with a silver emery board.

"You know," Isabel said, raising her voice, "you three need to stop that. Come up closer and put that stuff away."

The girls continued to whisper, to file their nails and beautify. Their voices rose and echoed like prayers.

"I'm serious," Isa said. "This is my classroom, and if you girls are here, you've got to participate."

Nothing. She took a stack of cards out of her bag and handed them to the kids, asking them to write down a moment when someone made an assumption about them. "We're going to roleplay," she told them. "Do you know what that is, to roleplay?"

"Act it out?" Maya asked.

"Like if Miguel and me were doing a card, maybe he can be the gangbanger and I can be the cop?" Derek asked. Isabel nodded. "Coo-cool."

When she got to the makeshift house of beauty, she took a deep breath and then she went for it. She reiterated her rules. "Either join us— or leave." She gazed at them, at their beautiful faces. "I mean it," she said. "Or better yet, just go before I call security."

There was no announcement, no moment of public humiliation—she sent them away quietly. She gave them the option to stay so the others would never have to know. The girls laughed nervously as they threw their things together and grabbed their purses. They snorted as they flung their bags over their shoulder and tossed their hair into their eyes. They acted like they didn't care, like band groupies caught in a dressing room. "Whatever," Lourdes whispered. She looked at her classmates and, nodding to Angel, Maya and Ria, she asked them, "You coming?"

"Where you going?"

"Just outta here."

The girls shook their heads. Then Mercedes, hesitating a moment, took a breath and brought her things to the front of the class. "Cedes," Lourdes said, "we outta here." But Mercedes held out her hand and waited for Isa to give her a card, then, sitting down with the others, she began to write. Lourdes and Marilena stormed out the door, their shoes clicking against the floor, steady as a tribal drum.

HELLO? THIS MESSAGE IS FOR FERDINAND MAMARIL. IT'S ISABEL MANALO AND I'M CALLING TO ASK YOU TO STOP IT. STOP CALLING ME, PLEASE. JUST TO WARN YOU—IF YOU DON'T STOP, I'M GOING TO HAVE TO NOTIFY THE POLICE. THANKS.

She stood under the hot flush of water, trying to calm her body. Adrenaline still surged through her veins, and she was shaking from the day. Until today, she had let these people disrespect her —ignoring her when she spoke, calling her at all hours of the night, staring her down like she owed them something. But today was different. Today she kicked the troublemakers out of her class. Today she answered Ferdi's phone call with a warning. She might even call Tita Nita and tell her to back off. The water beat little rhythms on the nape of her neck, settled warm on her back, and calmed her down. Out of her window she could hear the ocean roaring. She surrounded herself in water, in the sound of water, in the image of mahogany boats floating out to sea. Like a jellyfish, she thought. Dead man's float. Relax. She was nervous. JoJo would be there in an hour.

Out of the shower, she stepped through the fog. She made her way to the mirror and stared. She hadn't looked in a long time, hardly recognized that girl that began to emerge from under the steam. Long hair, wet and black, slicked back so that the face filled the mirror's frame; so that first thing she saw were her eyes. They were round, not almond. They were brown and sad and empty. She had her father's high cheekbones, her mother's full lips. She had the dark skin of an indigenous woman, browner now, morena. Her long thin neck curved like a reed of brown sugarcane. Two diamond studs glistened at the very tips of her ears. Stars.

She thought of Lourdes, Mercedes, Angel and the other girls. They could be her sisters, her nieces. Their beautiful faces hid under cover girl paint and attitude. Never into make-up, Isabel used the stuff to blot out pimples, black circles, and sleepless nights, but that was it. She put her hands up to her face, held her hair up and away. I'm so uncool, she thought. Her face had lost the fat of youth. Theirs were ripe, waiting for something big to happen. She turned her head again, looked at herself out of the corner of her eye. Not that bad, she thought.

Saturday Night. Evanston, IL. February 1980.
Photo by Millie Manalo

Millie spies on Ate Isa through the lens of Dad's Polaroid camera. Ate slumped over a leather recliner—her limbs flopping over the armrests. Her zits look bright red through the lens of this camera.

"Put that away. Now."

"Dad's gonna kill you," Kuya Frankie says. He's watching TV upside-down, popping Cracker Jacks.

"How come you don't have dates tonight?" Millie says, framing them both in the shot. "How come you're both home babysitting me?"

They shoot her a look like they're going to kill her, but she knows better than that. Millie has the power and it goes like this. Zzzzzip! And zing! Her kuya and ate fly up off their seats and grab for the camera. Zing! Zip, zing! She takes another shot and they chase her round the house as she waves the pictures in the air and cries, "Touch me and I'll send these to the *Evanston High Gazette!*"

When the photo develops, two faces loom into the frame, nostrils big and cavernous. Zits the size of craters. Ate's shiny braces burn her mouth white. Kuya's hair is so curly he looks like a giant Brillo pad. Their arms reach out like walking dead. The flash makes their faces glow—all head and nostrils and arms and legs. No body.

JoJo and Isabel walked the teens to the beach. Trailing after them, Mercedes and Lourdes carried buckets of chicken and a pot of rice. Edison and Miguel dragged a cooler of sodas. The others shuffled their feet in the sand, laughing as loud as the sea. The night was warm and a hot breeze blew through their hair, through their lightweight jackets and sweaters.

Isabel figured that if she concentrated on the sound of the waves, on the black motion of the water rushing to shore, her anxiety would float away. So distracted was she that the heel of her sandal caught on a rock. Slipping, she stumbled forward and JoJo steadied her before she hit the sand.

Edison's guitar was strapped to his back and it shined like the moon surrounded by a company of jingling stars. JoJo had on hiking boots, a worn pair of jeans, a sweatshirt.

Every week, after school, JoJo met with the youth, planning Magkasama. JoJo told her they were working together, identifying problems, educating themselves on class and race struggles, looking for solutions. "Each member is integral," he said. "Each one is vital."

She watched them set up camp, moving silently and diligently. Angel spread large blankets on the sand, and lighted clay pots of citronella candles. Her lithe body moved quickly. Candlelight flickered in her eyes. She was a water sprite come to shore. The boys settled the cooler into the sand and Edison sat down, pulled the guitar from off his back and began to pick at the strings. He played bits and pieces of songs, but nothing completely. Although the melodies were small, they pierced the tumble of waves, found a way to rise above the wind. Meanwhile, Mercedes and Lourdes knelt toward one another, spooning rice from the rice cooker, pulling chicken wings, breasts and legs from the bucket, pouring cups of cola into Styrofoam cups. The light escaped the girls, and what Isabel saw was a silhouette of two peasant women working rice fields, putting out meals for farmer husbands, barefoot children, lolas and lolos. In the dark, the ancestors came to them.

"Where's Marilena?" Isabel asked.

Angel fussed over her blankets and called out, "Babysitting. With Maya."

Isabel was amazed at how quickly they worked, how little they spoke or played with one another. Their somber mood reflected another side of the teenagers, a side she had not witnessed until now. Her Lycra pants were wet from the sand, stuck to her legs and her bottom, felt tight against her waist. She felt a little lost. She moved toward Lourdes and Mercedes, gestured with her hand, but Lourdes only raised a brow at her, warned her to sit back.

"It's okay," Mercedes told her. "We've got it."

"Yeah," Lourdes added. "You don't have to worry—if you don't help, we won't kick you out."

"Fine," Isa answered. "Fair enough." She uncapped a bottle of water and took a swig.

They sat in a circle, nibbling at their plates of chicken and rice, sipping on ice cubes and cola. She watched the way the girls gazed at JoJo, as if in a trance. The boys furrowed their brows and listened intently. JoJo asked them how their research was coming along. Were they talking to young brothers and sisters, were they reading any good articles, were they making phone calls?

"What are you doing exactly?" Isabel asked. She held a small shell in her hand; its iridescent blue-green colors seeped through the oyster white of its shell.

"Two things," JoJo said. "Who wants to tell her?"

"First we're educating ourselves," Miguel said. "We spend part of the time studying the struggles of other races."

"We started with the Black movement," Derek told her, "and now we're checking out our Chicano brothas and sistas."

"We're looking to the brothers and sistas living at the res," Miguel said.

She looked at JoJo, who told her, "Indian reservation." She nodded as if to say, Oh yeah, the res.

"And then we're trying to identify our own problems—youth and community. We know we have them, and Kuya JoJo said until we can identify them, we won't be able to fix them."

Each student was in charge of one discussion group: Miguel hung with the middle school gangs; Angel was the link between the adult community and the youth; Lourdes and Marilena led discussions with the girls on sex and pregnancy; Edison looked at class issues and conflicts between the community's doctors and the military; Derek researched the political and historical struggles of other people of color. "Then twice a month, the leaders meet with the rest of their peers and we conversate."

"We don't actually do all that, Kuya," Angel said. "We ask questions and then we bring the questions back into discussion groups."

Isabel looked over at Mercedes, who sat silently, nodding. "What are you in charge of?" Isabel asked.

"Food," Mercedes laughed. "I get the food together and I make all the phone calls to the members."

They called themselves Pinoy, but Isabel had cousins from the islands—and they were real Filipino. Those cousins would not fit in with these kids. These kids—like Isabel, like it or not—were part western; they were hip-hop and MTV, they were street smart and they were not about messing around. And while she knew she was not urban and hip, she knew the kids were more like her than the cousins back home. They are Amerikano, she thought, straight up.

"So I have a question," she said. She looked into the girls' faces, at the way the fire illuminated their cheeks and made their eyes deep-set. "What's so different between the things you are learning from Kuya JoJo and what I teach in the classroom? You're all so into this and so resistant to that."

"Ain't no difference," Miguel answered. "You teach us about Filipino history and this is about Filipino-American history—but no difference really after that."

"What? Thas a major difference, man," Derek said.

"But I can't get you to participate in class."

"Thas cuz it's you," Lourdes said.

Isa and JoJo exchanged a look. "You gotta show your ate some respect," JoJo said. "What'd she ever do to you?"

"Exactly," Desa answered. "My question exactly. What'd she ever do for me?"

The wind blew gently on them, the light from the moon fought its way from the cloudy sky, onto the waters, and reflected on their faces. The boys spoke earnestly, but the girls, while forthcoming, still wore their masks. JoJo cast a spell on them and they did as he asked, but they also kept their secrets. The sea sprayed a cool mist at Isabel's back, made her feel damp, chilly. Lourdes bowed her head and her hair fell like a waterfall over her face. She rocked back and forth in her seat.

"Uncle Romy's giving me shit," Derek said. "He sees me at the library carrying all these books, man, and he sez—What are you doing, Derek, you and your Kuya JoJo and those kids wasting all this time on Black history? We are not Black. So I tell him, this ain't Black history, we're moving into Chicano history. La Raza, Tito, and I hold a book and say—it's cool and he sez—Boy, we are not Mexican either. I wish you would concentrate more on your math and science."

"Same ole colonial mentality," Miguel said. He shook his head and sighed. The night had grown so cold, Isabel swore she saw a trail of smoke rising. A small prayer of frustration floated up to God, begged for patience.

Lourdes raised her hand, and strands of hair fell across her face. "What's she doing here?"

JoJo nodded his head. "You mean your Ate Isabel?"

"She ain't our ate," Lourdes answered. "She's one of them."

"No she's not," Miguel snapped. "Why you always makin' trouble?" He threw a towel at her and it blanketed her face. "Like the other day—you homegirls makin' trouble when all she tryin' to do is teach us sumthin'."

"You're such a kiss-ass, Migs," Lourdes shouted back. "She kickin' us out of class and you call that teaching sumthin'?"

"Yeah, she teachin' you who's boss," Edison said, laughing.

"You kicked them out?" JoJo asked. He smiled at her. "You did that?"

"I gave them a choice," Isa answered. "Lourdes and Marilena chose to leave."

"Still want to know what she's doing here," Lourdes said.

"I want to help."

"Help what?"

"Magkasama."

"All right then, crown the next Miss Virginia Beach-Philippines," JoJo said, laughing.

"What?"

"I'm serious. Help Tita Nita, man. Start acting like one of us. These pageants identify our people, good or bad. It's one way we come together. If they want you to do it, do it. Don't be all high and mighty an shit."

She surveyed their faces, tried to read the light behind their eyes. What could it hurt, she thought. But how could it help? She'd think about it, she said. And they all sighed—yes, and all right.

Then JoJo pulled her away from the fire and walked her up and down the beach until the sky grew light and the kids had burrowed their way into sleeping bags.

"I want to help," she told him.

"All right then," he said, holding onto her hand.

Isabel felt full, as if she'd been eating all night long. "I might not know exactly why you are so committed," she said, "but I have a feeling I know."

"You do?"

"Yeah. I told you, you aren't the only one who's lost someone."

"I hear that," JoJo answered.

Under a newborn sky, the sea calmed down, lulled the birds to silence, and they sat on her steps, looking at one another, and when the sun came up he leaned over and kissed her on the cheek, goodbye.

Crout Creek Park, North Carolina. October 1967.
Photo by Camila Manalo

Isa and Frankie Boy play in the sandbox. Next to them, Millie's stroller is parked so she can watch. Camila holds the camera up and spies on them from faraway.

Behind the sandbox is a bench of women. One lady, draped in a pink woolen coat and polka-dot scarf, hides behind cat-eye sunglasses. Down from her sits an older woman. She's pale, yellow and slight. Blue glasses perch at the tip of her long nose and a red wig covers her head like a veil during Sunday Mass. Every now and then, she holds a cigarette to her painted lips and takes a heavy drag.

Two boys—one Isa's age, the other a little bigger—roll tractors through the sand. One of the boys runs a truck right up to Isa, who squeals and says, "Can I try?"

"You live in my same building, don't you?" shouts the old woman.

Camila thinks she's talking to someone else.

"Okay, but you have to do it like this," the boy says, instructing Isabel.

Looking into the frame, Camila calls to the kids. "Smile!" she says. They all show their teeth—even the little boys who are not hers. The children shut their eyes tight like they're all waiting for kisses.

Then the lady points to Camila and, still shouting, says, "What's the matter? Don't speak English?"

After Isa agreed to help with the pageant, she started having nightmares. Ill-formed mermaids swam against the tide, palms spread wide and stiff as starfish. Their fanned-out tails whirled like giant propellers spinning out of control. Isabel floated on a giant wooden barge, dipped her butterfly net into seawater. She was catching wild girl fish. She dragged them out of the water. Fighting with all her strength, she hauled them across cool sands. Sometimes she had to maneuver around blobs of stinging jellyfish. Slowly the mermaids died. Between the curses from their foul mouths and the gasping for air, their blue skin turned brown, their eyes dilated. Their gills, fine etchings slashed at the fleshy curve of their hips, flipped and flopped, resisted. Metallic scales flashed in the sunlight, and the girl fish howled sharp siren pitches, sent urgent signals.

Afterwards, she stood high on a ladder, balancing on an ailing pier somewhere on Virginia Beach. With two hands, she held one of the beautiful mermaids upside down. She got the girl by the tail. A crowd gathered around her, applauding her catch, taking flashbulb pictures and cooing, "That's a big one, all right." Everyone was happy. Dr. Romy, Tita Nita Starr, Edna Gebhart and Ferdi. Isabel woke from her nightmares, trembling.

Next morning, she rushed down to the Cultural Center, her foot pressing the gas pedal, thinking of how to back out. She could be weak, tell them her life was too busy, too crazy to add something new—or she could tell them the truth. That their kids needed something else—not a pageant so much as a forum, a place where they could go and be understood. She'd suggest a dialog, a community speak with all generations of youth and adults. And maybe, in between the sessions, they'd have a program where any of them could get up, play a song on a guitar, or dance to music, or read a poem. She worked the whole thing out in her head. JoJo would be so proud, she thought. She'd incorporate Magkasama and then everyone would understand.

In the main meeting room, folding chairs were lined up in rows of ten, and twenty deep. The room was half-full of people. Manongs and manangs of the community, gray and small, sat in places of honor all along the sides. Most of them were widows and widowers. Some spoke Taglish, others no English at all, but dialects from Ilocos, Visayas,

Pampanga. They nodded to her as she walked past them. "Morning, po," she called to them. "Kamusta po kayo?" Up front, Tita Nita talked fast and loud as usual. If Isabel could get to her before the meeting started, if she could tell her the plan in private, the whole thing would work out smoothly. She crossed her fingers, leaning over to give Tita Nita a kiss. "Good morning," she said.

"Morning, hija." Tita Nita put her cheek next to Isabel's and sniffed her skin. "We have so much to do, and we have many contestants this year. Come here, let's get going."

"Well, actually," Isabel told her, "I have an idea."

"Good, good, good," said Tita Nita as she flipped through a stack of papers. "That's why we asked you to join us. We need your young blood, hija."

For the next five minutes, Isabel followed Tita Nita around, told her about her idea. "What about a forum?" she suggested. Tita Nita ran back and forth from the aluminum folding chairs, hissing directions at mothers, carefully examining the faces of young girls.

Without looking at Isabel, she patted a teen on the hand, speaking rapidly in Tagalog: "Whatever you say, Isabel. Just make sure it doesn't go too far over half an hour. We can use that time for costume changes. Maybe last year's reigning queen can host the show. What do you think, anak?"

"What costume changes?" Isabel asked. "There'd be no costume changes. I was thinking it could be more down to earth than that. Jeans, or summer skirts or—the boys like to wear athletic warm-ups and baggy pants."

"Boys," Tita Nita said, looking at Isabel for the first time. "Since when are boys running for Miss Virginia Beach-Philippines?"

Tita Nita scurried over to the girls, and, kissing them all, she said to Maya, "Nice to have you back, anak." She ran her hands across Maya's face, pushing the tendrils of hair behind her ears. "How's your lola doing?"

"Fine, po," Maya said, fiddling with her camera.

"Too bad about your face, anak," Tita Nita said, kissing her cheek.

"Tita Nita—" Isabel interjected.

"What?" Tita Nita said. "It's not so bad. Nothing make-up can't hide."

Maya nodded and said, "Yes, Auntie."

Something inside Isabel ached. Tita Nita hadn't heard a word of what she'd said. She glanced over her shoulder and saw Ria, Mercedes, and Marilena sitting on a row of chairs, their hands folded over their laps, their gazes fixed on outer space. She made her way over to them and asked, "Hey girls, whatcha looking at?"

"Lourdes," they told her.

"Lourdes?" Isabel said. "Where's Lourdes?"

Ria puckered up, her mouth became a tiny Mount Pinatubo. She pointed with her lips to the other side of the room, where a young white woman dressed in an ivory suit sat with her back against a hard aluminum chair. Her hair had been set and teased to ride high on her head. From her ears two drops of pearls hung on either side of her. The sunlight hit them just so, made her sparkle. Around her neck a string of pearls wept in droopy loops. She had bright rouge smeared across the apples of her face. Her expression emitted a certain kind of loneliness.

"Who's that?" Isabel asked. "Who is it?"

"Lourdes," Mercedes told her.

"No it's not," Isabel said, laughing. "Where's Lourdes?"

"That's her, Ate Isabel," Ria told her. "Look again. It's her. No shit."

"So far," Angel informed her, "Lourdes has sold the most raffle tickets. She's definitely won Miss Congeniality."

Isabel looked over at Angel.

"Whoever sells the first one-hundred raffle tickets wins Miss Congeniality. It's how they raise money an shit."

She couldn't believe the change. Lourdes had that polyester office-girl-makes-good look. Every little bit of her had been cleaned and polished. Still, she was very beautiful.

When Isabel got up to talk to her, Lourdes turned her head away and acted like she wasn't there.

"That's quite a look," Isabel said.

The girl watched the air in front of her, breathed steady and calm. Alone.

"It's for your mom?" Isabel continued.

176

They gazed at each other for a moment, and Isabel thought Lourdes looked so uncomfortable, constantly pulling at her shirt, or tucking her puffed-up hair behind her ears. The silence between them was fat and weighted like a cake donut. "Well, you look great," Isabel said. "As long as you're doing this for yourself." Lourdes shifted around on her ivory heels, and for a moment she almost lost her balance.

Then Lourdes's mother called her and she stood obediently, crossing the room with her head held high, her shoulders spread like wings. She strutted the floor as if that crown were pinned to the top of her head. She made mano to the elders, and kissed all the aunties. At this moment Isabel knew. There was no turning back, no saying no, no youth forum. And even if Isa walked, the show would still go on.

AH, HULLO? ISABEL. WHY DON'T YOU EVER RETURN MY CALLS? IT'S LIKE YOU'RE NEVER HOME, SO WHERE DO YOU GO? YOU BETTER NOT WORK TOO HARD. WE NEED YOU TO STAY HEALTHY. BUT YOU KNOW ALL ABOUT STAYING HEALTHY—BEING A DOCTOR'S DAUGHTER AND EVERYTHING LIKE THAT. DID YOU KNOW THAT YOUR FATHER AND MOTHER ARE PART OF THE THIRD WAVE OF IMMIGRATION TO THE UNITED STATES? THEY WERE PART OF WHAT WE CALL THE BRAIN DRAIN. AMERICA NEEDED DOCTORS TO GO TO THE GHETTO, TO GO TO RURAL AMERICA—THE BOONDOCKS, AS THEY SAY IN PILIPINO. (DID YOU KNOW THAT THE WORD "BOONDOCKS" HAS ITS ORIGINS IN PILIPINO?) WHITIE DOCTORS WOULD NOT GO INTO AMERICA'S HARLEMS AND CREAM CITIES. AND NOBODY WANTED TO LIVE WITH THE HICKS SO YOU KNOW WHO THEY GOT, DON'T YOU? PEOPLE LIKE YOUR DAD. PEOPLE LIKE MOST OF THE NURSES AND DOCTORS IN AMERICA TODAY. TOOK THE INTELLECTUALS OUT OF THE PHILIPPINES AND BROUGHT THEM ALL HERE AND PLANTED THEM IN RURAL AMERICA, IN GHETTO AMERICA. CUZ THIS IS WHERE THE MONEY IS. THAT'S WHAT THEY TOLD THEM, ANYWAY. THAT'S WHY YOU CAN GO ANYWHERE IN AMERICA AND FIND OUR PEOPLE. MOORHEAD, MINNESOTA; LITTLE ROCK, ARKANSAS;

APPALACHIAN MOUNTAINS; BOISE, IDAHO; MILWAUKEE, WISCONSIN; LONG ISLAND, NEW YORK; JACKSONVILLE, FLORIDA. FILIPINO AMERICANS EVERYWHERE. EVEN IOWA. MAN, THAT'S A BEAUTIFUL THING.

Isabel wondered if all those pockets of Filipino community also took to holding beauty pageants with the same energy the community in Virginia did. In Tidewater, Little Miss Philippines, Miss Teenage Philippines, Miss Philippines, Mrs. Philippines and Lola Philippines of Hampton Roads—they all ran from beach to mall to dining hall in sashes and blinding crowns. They sang, they danced, they cartwheeled through the tunnels that connect Portsmouth, Hampton, Chesapeake and Norfolk. They brought the community together and displayed their wealth in the raffle tickets they sold and the sequins sewn across their breasts.

"Was it like that for you?" Isabel asked Millie on the phone. "Was it awful?"

"It was a pain," she told Isabel. "But it made Dad happy, and it was only a year."

Isabel told her sister about the beauty queens who strutted the streets of Virginia, described their big hair looming large as peacocks' plumes at picnics and dinners and hospital benefits. "Even Little Miss Philippines wears rouge," Isabel confided. "And she's only six years old."

"So what's with those beauty pageants?" Millie wanted to know.

"They do it to raise money. To build buildings and churches and, if they had a chance, I think castles."

"They must have a village by now."

"They have nothing." All the money they raised melted away, slipped into the linings of their fishtail dresses and the hoods of their royal capes. There was never any money.

Once, at a park fiesta, she wandered into a booth of hemp wall hangings, woven planters and coppice place mats. "Are you married?" asked an old lola. The woman had an unmarried son. "You'd make a wonderful Mrs. Philippines. Or if you're single, we can talk about Miss Philippines." She took Isabel's face into her bony hands and sighed, "Talagang maganda ka."

"If you think it's so weird, why are you doing it?" Millie wanted to know.

Her sister sighed, and said, "To win them over. To infiltrate and make it different."

Millie was skeptical, but Isa insisted that it was the only way to make the change. "You know, infiltrate and then—when no one's looking—change things."

"You sure you're not just trying to be a crowd pleaser?" Millie asked.

"That again?" Isa answered. "I told you things are gonna be different. And JoJo says this is the way to get in, to change."

She spent hours convincing herself that this was going to work. She was thinking about Maya and she was dreaming about Arturo.

THIRTEEN

Magic hour. On the west side of Virginia Beach, Lourdes ignored her mother. Back pressed up against a chair, she folded her arms and focused on a dot on the wall, staring until a narrow tunnel appeared before her. The room blurred and she imagined shooting herself through the long tunnel, out into space. She heard the television in the room below, the neighbor's dog barking outside and the beating drums in a garage band down the street. Her mother spun about her, casting a long and disagreeable finger into her face. Anita Starr rained words upon her daughter. "Kakahiya naman!" Here was another lecture on ladylike behavior and respecting her elders, and tonight her mother added a special bonus—her homage to shame and gossip. "Walang hiya!" But the louder Anita's voice got, the farther away Lourdes traveled. Her eyes turned into glass. Her hands numbed like long and slender icicles. She drained all the color from her complexion. Soon, her mother leaned an angry face into hers, but Lourdes saw only the tunnel, a black, skinny hallway shooting off like the viewfinder of a telescope. She hummed to a radio down the street, and soon she sang out loud. "I'll make love to you, like you want me to . . ." When the sting of her mother's hand crossed her face, Lourdes turned away. Did not blink.

Meanwhile, at that same moment, Isabel strolled through the aisles of Albertson's parking lot, a cartful of vegetables and fruits and yogurt before her. She ate less meat when she was away from the family. Sautéed chicken in olive oil. Mashed potatoes. For breakfast, she liked yogurt and bananas—the kind with fruit on the bottom and granola sprinkled on top. She hadn't time to stir-fry leftover rice in garlic, no time to toss an egg sunny side up, to sizzle a little tocino on the side. That stuff was for holy days when she was home and her mother cooked Philippine-style.

Tonight she gazed at the sun as it melted into deep strokes of reds and oranges. Even this ugly parking lot with its faded pavement, its rusted cart corrals and chrome bumpers, was beautiful in the light. The grocery store was lit like a magnificent museum. She breathed the air, fragrant with salt from the ocean just down the block.

At last she had slipped into a rhythm, a life that was becoming comfortable, hers. The girls were slowly opening up, even Lourdes smiled on occasion, looked at her and saw her. It's not much, she thought, but it's a start.

She reached her station wagon, and leaned over to unlock the front door, when the wind blew hard, and pushed her over the hood of the car. Someone grabbed her by the shoulders and spun her around, pushing her back into the metal hood. She struggled, the keys flying out of her hand. Someone held her down. At first she reacted only with her body, pushing and pounding on this weight, on this being. He held her down, muttering words so fast, so tattered, she lost all balance. The bruised sky whirled above her, the clouds spinning in and out of red then yellow and midnight blue. Catching her breath, she took a hard look at her attacker. His face was pushed up close to hers, brown and difficult to name. It was his voice she recognized. She knew this.

"What the hell!" she was screaming. "What the fuck!" His breath was hot. Smelled stale as smoker's breath. "Ferdi, you asshole," she said. "Get off me."

But he was strong and he held Isabel down on the hood of her car, spitting words into her face. She could tell he hadn't bathed in days. His yellow teeth. His red gums. His wide nose. Everything distorted from this vantage point. Rage drowned them, fell upon them like a net, and, captured like this, she only heard fragments. He was calling her a coconut. Now he understood not all Filipinos were Filipinos—some of them were whiter than others. Some of them were white. Thank you, he said, thank you for pointing out to me that brown skin does not mean we are kin. It only means we are better-looking than the whities around us, but that is all. He's mad, oh yeah, he's really mad. What makes you so good you don't see me, sista, I'm standing right there, and you don't see me? Like all whities—you only see what you wanna see—white is light an I'm not white—don't you see me everywhere, lookin' at you, talkin' at you? What's it gonna take? Don't even return my calls, don't answer when I call your name, don't see the little things I leave. Coconut girl, who the hell are you?

She kicked, but he had her legs pinned down and all she felt was the heavy weight of his body, his words. How does it feel, he wanted to know, to look so Pinay then walk and talk just like a Barbie? Can you not hear the cry of the oppressed, the dispossessed, the people who were your blood? Who the fuck are you?

She screamed. Was there no one who could hear this? Was there no one walking by? Was anybody calling the police?

He leaned in so close their eyeballs nearly touched. He whispered and the words fell slick and wet against her skin. What's it like to lie in whitie's bed? Was the linen crisp? Was the pillow fragrant? Ever shiver cuz you too poor to buy one of them duck-feather blankets?

His tirade shook her. Of course, even now, she understood he was crazy, but his words, like the ghost of Arturo, haunted her, made her crazy with rage. He held her down like this until the moon washed the sun out of the sky and magic hour was over.

After he had gone, she slipped into the front seat, the cart of produce knocking gently at her door, the wind tossing the antenna quick like a conductor's baton. Copper lights flooded the blacktop parking lot. She had forgotten the time. From her windshield she stared at the crescent moon, at the stars fighting their way out of cumulus clouds. She could see them up there, straining, tiny flashes of light, like the seed of an idea.

Her body felt bloated. Numb. Soaked in so many tears and all those ugly words. He slithered away, satisfied she had heard him once and for all. He left as suddenly as he appeared. She could not stop the weeping.

She breathed, cupping her face with the palms of her hands. Everything tasted like salt. Like ocean. Everything was sticky and wet. When she opened her eyes, there were faces of concern, fingers tapping at her window. Marilena, Mercedes, Lourdes.

They appeared to be floating just above the glass, three spirits, a halo of copper framing their faces. Their words seeped into the wagon, muffled and alien. Their beautifully painted nails tap tap tapped at the glass.

Isabel wouldn't answer. She was sure they were a dream.

"Sup, Ms. Manalo?" Mercedes said.

"You cryin'?" Marilena wanted to know.

Lourdes peered from behind the other girls like a pale ghost swimming underwater. Her hair floated over the glass and shimmered like it was wet. Her eyes were round, sea-colored, lined with concern.

"Open up," Mercedes said. "You don't look so good."

"I don't feel so good," Isabel told them.

"Open up."

"This your cart?" Marilena asked. "This your food?"

She wanted them to go away. To let her be. She'd get it together sooner or later. She'd load up her groceries.

"That's okay," she yelled through the glass. "I can get it."

"Open up, Ms. Manalo," Mercedes said, then, turning to the other two, she said, "Whas wrong with her?"

Isabel closed her eyes, decided this was not happening, that when she woke she'd find herself at home, in bed with her gray cat nibbling at her elbow.

She opened her eyes. Two faces now hovered over her. She could see smudges where he'd placed his hands flat on the glass, streaks of fingerprints. Knocking startled her. At the passenger's window, Lourdes's face appeared like a portrait in a fine art museum. "Please," she mouthed to Isabel, "open up now."

Bracing herself, Isabel leaned over and grabbed at the handle, and the door swung open. The girls crawled into the station wagon one at a time, stroked her hair, her hands, put their heads on her shoulder. "You okay, Ms. Manalo?" Mercedes asked her. Isabel nodded. "Wanna talk?"

Mercedes turned to Marilena. "Her hands are so cold," she said.

Isabel could hear Lourdes loading the food up into the back, and then the trunk slammed shut. Isabel watched how Lourdes negotiated her skinny body around the parking lot. Her wide-leg denim trailed her as she rolled the cart into one of the corrals. "How 'bout we drive home with you?" Marilena said. "Hang with you awhile?"

"You don't have to do that," Isabel said, gathering her strength. "I'm just having a bad day. That's all."

"What kind of food's this?" Lourdes said, climbing back into the car. "Apples and yogurt an shit. Don't you have anything to munch on?"

She brought the girls back to the house because they said they wanted to go to the beach. "Give us a ride?" Marilena asked, though everyone knew they might just as easily have walked.

They carried her bags into the bungalow and placed broccoli into vegetable bins next to fresh tomatoes, carrots, celery, red peppers and a giant eggplant. "Why you wasting your money buying water?" Mercedes asked. "Faucet gives it for free."

Isabel refused to talk about what had happened. Instead she talked about being seventeen, a girl who hovered around the popular crowd, who did all the right things and wore all the right clothes, but who, in the end, was not the right girl at all. "I was never in," she told them. "I was the only one like me, and that made me almost in—but I wasn't in. You girls are so lucky."

"What you mean, the only one like you?" Mercedes asked.

She tried to explain it this way. At home they took their shoes off at the door, ate rice with all their meals. Her mother chased her brother with a slipper when he was bad, did all the things you'd expect—"But when we walked out the door and into the school, my brother and sister and I, we walked into another kind of existence."

The girls sat at her kitchen counter, staring at her.

"We were the only Filipino family, and when you're the only one— it's like at first the kids looked at you funny but after a couple of years you become like them in a way and they become like you and everyone forgets that you are different. And maybe you aren't so different."

"You mean you were embarrassed," Lourdes said.

"No, I mean it just didn't matter."

"For real?" Marilena asked.

"Sure," Isabel answered. "For real."

How do you explain, she thought, what it's like to be this alone? You gotta find ways to survive. To be like your peers even when your peers were not yours, not really.

"Whatever," Lourdes muttered. "Doesn't matter how many friends you got or how phat you is, cuz if your parents ain't cool, then whateva."

"What?" Isabel asked her.

"Nuthin'," she said. "Just whateva."

Isabel smiled at Lourdes, who had taken Flounder and placed him in the cradle of her arm. She's not so tough, she thought. "What happened to your new look?" Isabel said.

"For the pageant," Lourdes said. "Thas all. It's not my look. It's for my mommy."

The Girls at Grant Park. Chicago, IL. July 1982.
Photo by a passerby

He's passing a gathering of girls clustered in front of the water fountain at Grant Park, their legs all pulled together and their bodies leaning over like the stems of tulips and daffodils. A pretty blonde holds up a camera to shoot the girls' picture. Everyone's giggling, so the passerby says, "Want me to shoot the picture?" The blonde squeaks, "Okay," and hands him the camera. Their faces all shine orange and red from a long day in the sun, blue eyes popping like little stars off the page. One girl at the center of the photo, an Asian girl, sits like the center of a sunflower—brown, round, the color of earth. The passerby smiles and shoots the photo. Hands it back to the teenage girls and says, "Hope it turns out."

"Where's this at?" Mercedes asked.

"That's Bluesfest."

"Whas dat?" Marilena said.

"Damn, look at all that bleach." Lourdes said. She pointed to the girls, at the variations of blonde blossoming against Isa's straight black hair. "You weren't kidding about that. You were the only one."

A rapping on the door startled the girls. Marilena found Maya standing there. Her hair was hung in wet strands across her face. Her breathing filled the room.

"Wassup wit you?" Marilena asked, pulling the girl in. Maya struggled out of the girl's grasp and when she saw Isabel, she broke into tears.

"I'm okay," Isa told her. The other girls called Maya a baby.

"She always iyak iyak at movies and weddings and she always the first to break down when we're in trouble."

"Dalagas don't cry," Lourdes told her.

"Fuck off," Maya hissed at Lourdes. "Who did this, Ate?" she asked, throwing looks at her sisters.

"Don't look at us," Mercedes said. "We found her like that."

Isa held out her arms to Maya and asked her not to cry, asked her if she was hungry. "Want something to eat?"

Maya pulled out of Isa's arms, wiping her face with the sleeves of her jean jacket. "Where's your camera?" Isa asked and the girl shrugged.

"Left it somewhere," she said, and then Isabel knew there was something wrong. Maya always had her camera with her.

"Okay," she said, handing her a tissue. "Let me know if you need anything."

Then she fed them bowls of stirfry vegetables on a bed of yellow couscous, handing them a spoon and fork.

Lourdes spooned food into her mouth, mumbling, "This shit ain't half bad."

"Better with beef," Marilena said, nodding.

"Rice," Mercedes said. "This be good with rice."

Maya picked at her food and offered to clean up the rest. And they comforted Isabel this way, sitting at her kitchen counter, cleaning up their plates, listening to her and hearing her for once.

That night, she could not sleep. Ferdi's pug-nose face, inflated like one of those Macy's Thanksgiving Day floats, charged at her, brown and bulbous, a porous volcano hissing hot air. The nightmare was that he had saved her from the ocean and had begun mouth-to-mouth resuscitation. Elliot spent most of the night holding her, telling it wasn't real, not real. He's not here. Not real. Mostly she heard Ferdi's words distorted like he was spitting into a mic and there was feedback blaring into the tiny bedroom in her bungalow.

"We should call the police," Elliot said.

"What for?" she said.

"We should have him locked up."

"And you think this will help me sleep?" she said, pulling herself away from him. She looked at Elliot, who was pale and slight as the distant quarter moon. She had to get over this, had to tell herself that

Ferdi was nothing more than a crazy man. His words were lies, but she could not stop wondering why he chose to hold her down like that, to shoot them at her like pellets from a bully's BB gun. "I have to do this myself," she told Elliot.

"What?"

"Will you go away?" she asked him. She handed him a pillow and her comforter. "Will you go to the living room?"

He didn't understand, wouldn't leave her, had to touch her, and this only made the nightmares bigger than the screen at a drive-in theater. The tufts of brown hair on his arms irritated her skin. His palms were cold and sticky. "If you turn him in, you'll feel safe. You'll sleep," Elliot said.

But she knew he was wrong. If she turned Ferdi in, she'd never have peace.

All night long, she was running. First the dreams entered through her temples. The sea crashed and swirled, rushed white like anger, charged at her and JoJo where they lay on the oceanfront. JoJo whispered histories into her body, breathing each word, each syllable, slowly into the pores of her skin. They lay at the mouth of the ocean, and tidewater slipped over them. Sand stuck to their spines in strips. They stretched out under the stars and watched the sky, while JoJo spun stories of the Igorot, the Ifugao, the Negrito, their complicated civilizations, a life and a people more advanced than the textbooks have dared suggest. JoJo drew datus—wise chieftains—warriors, and tall mountain royalties who stood at the edge of her days, like spirits—anitos—guarding her, warning her, watching.

In the dream Isabel was falling in love and growing wise. Red, yellow and blue flags rose quick as the sun on their dried bamboo poles, waved valiantly toward heaven. She and JoJo were on a mission. They journeyed to places she had never been. She slipped in and out of his tales: a warrior, a fisherwoman, a migrant worker picking grapes for white America.

Isabel felt her body slipping, sinking deep into a consciousness she could not shake. His body hovered over her, directed her, led her, and she thought she'd lost control. What is this, she thought? And how do I stop? Dreaming ran her ragged so that she woke in the early morning, eyes stinging with tears that traveled just below the surface of her flesh. She was exhausted. Awake, she forgot the dreams. JoJo's voice, his humming, his lessons escaped as the moon floated away. She called for Elliot, who slept on the sofa where she had banished him. Completely confused, she opened her eyes and the dark filled her up like helium in a child's balloon.

When she told her father and mother, her dad begged her to come home. "Quit," he said, "it's not worth it." She calmed him down, assured him she was okay.

"He's crazy. He's harmless."

"Right, he's crazy," her father said.

He only used words. She could see now how frustrated he was, how hurt he had been and so he got carried away. That's all. "He probably didn't even realize what he was doing."

"Hija," her dad said. "That's what worries me."

She knew her father would react this way, she knew he'd want her to come home, and even though there was a part of her that wanted to, she knew she couldn't.

"Did you report him to the police?" Camila asked.

What would the police report say, Isabel wanted to know. He held her down and screamed at her for dating Elliot? She won her mother to her side, knew that it wasn't just about her now—it was about the kids and getting in with them and doing her part.

"Who cares about your part," her father wanted to know, "when you are dead and lying somewhere in the street?"

"Let her work it out, Daddy," Camila said. "She knows what she's doing."

By now, Isabel's heartbeats were louder than her own thoughts, shouted above her speaking voice. Pintig. Pintig. Pintig. And when she hung up the phone, she saw that Elliot had been watching her from the sofa, his eyes fixed upon her, listening.

"I bet you could hear him from there," she said about her dad.

"Why'd you even bother?" Elliot asked. "You're not going to do anything about it, and you only got him worked up."

The television cast blue light across the room. Elliot's skin looked green from here. Canned laughter spilled from the TV.

"You make it difficult, you know," Elliot said. "Should have kept it to yourself."

In her family, there was no keeping it to yourself. There was no minding your own business. "They'd know," she told him. "Even if I said nothing. They'd know."

He shook his head. Disbeliever. Blanket-statement maker. Outsider. She left him sitting there in front of the television, blue-green skin and all. She saw his future, cast in late-night TV light—a beer in his right hand, the remote in his left. She bid him goodnight, said he could stay on the couch if he wanted, but that she wanted to sleep alone.

FOURTEEN

The phone rang. "Where is it?" Isabel said, climbing her way around the cartons. "Who can find it?" Suddenly everyone was up and searching, peeking underneath coffee tables, folding chairs, coat racks. Everyone crawled about the bungalow—her mother, her father, the three boys, even Flounder sniffed about. The phone rang and rang. "Saan ka, telepono?" Miguel cooed, like he was talking to the kitty. "Saan ka?"

When the phone stopped ringing, a machine rattled. Then Uncle Romy's voice came from nowhere. Like God, Isa thought. He told the caller to leave a number. Rewind, click, rewind. She was turning boxes over, pushing them aside. And now the voice began like this:

HELLO? ANYBODY THERE? THIS ON? HI, UNCLE ROMY. THIS MESSAGE IS FOR ISABEL MANALO—FIRST FILIPINA AMERICAN TO TEACH OUR PINOY YOUTHS. WELCOME TO THE MOVEMENT, MY SISTA. LEMME INTRODUCE MYSELF. MY NAME IS FERDI MAMARIL AND I WANT TO WELCOME YOU TO VIRGINIA BEACH. DID YOU KNOW THAT THE TIDEWATER AREA HAS THE HIGHEST CONCENTRATION OF PINOYS ON THE EAST COAST?

Everybody froze, still as children in a game of red light green light. Flounder spun in circles, chasing his tail. Like the voice had made him crazy.

"Aw," said Arturo, "just Kuya Ferdi. Ain't no bother." The boys folded themselves up, sitting down on boxes and in little clearings on the floor.

The voice seemed to be coming out of the corners of the room, as if the answering machine were set to surround sound.

OUR COMMUNITY STRUGGLES WITH THIS GREAT BLESSING—YET OUR YOUTHS ARE STILL SEARCHING FOR THIS THING THEY CALL IDENTITY. DO YOU KNOW YOUR IDENTITY, MS. MANALO? DO YOU KNOW THE SIGNIFICANCE OF YOUR APPOINTMENT IN VIRGINIA BEACH? WHEN THE SUPERINTENDENT HIRED YOU, HE WAS SAYING, "YES, I SEE YOU FILIPINO AMERICANS."

Her mother and father collapsed into each other's arms and snickered. "Oh—you better listen, Isabel," her father said.

She shook her head at him. Smiled.

YOU ARE HERE BECAUSE OUR YOUTHS NEED YOU. WE ARE SEEKING YOU TO HELP OUR YOUTHS FIND THEMSELVES.

Derek reached out his thick arms. "Where am I?" he screamed.

"Over here!" Arturo shouted. "Man, you are over here."

TO BE FILIPINO AMERICAN IS NOT ONLY AN HONOR, IT IS A BURDEN. IT IS NOT ABOUT FOLK DANCING, IT IS NOT ABOUT THE BEAUTY CONTEST, IT IS NOT ABOUT PANSIT AND LUMPIA—IT IS ABOUT A BROWN PEOPLE LIVING IN AMERICA, INVISIBLE TO MOST. YOU ARE HERE TO HELP US CLAIM OUR VOICE, OUR COLOR, OUR PEOPLE. WELCOME TO THE MOVEMENT, SISTA MANALO, MAY GOD BE WITH YOU (AND ME) IN THE STRUGGLE.

The tape machine clicked.

"He's harmless, Ms. Manalo," said Miguel. "He's all about love. Really he is."

"Is he for real?" She said it like she didn't care. Inside, her stomach moved as if she carried the entire Atlantic Ocean. Maybe this was more about risk than opportunity.

They told her stories about Ferdi's antics—how he was always making noise and how nobody ever paid attention.

"He's like a great big fly," said Arturo. "You know, the big green and black and blue shiny fat fly. Huge buzz, no bite."

"Ain't nothing you can't handle," Miguel said.

*

Ferdi had high hopes for Isabel Manalo. On the day she moved to town, he sent her his most special welcome, introduced himself and said she could call any time and he'd be there because that was what it meant to be part of a community. He had been living in Virginia Beach for twenty years and he knew all the history of his people living along the lakes, the tributaries and the shores of Tidewater. Before that, he had been raised on the Pacific West Coast, been indoctrinated into the movement by the son of an old manong living in Seattle. Fernando Mamaril had dedicated his whole life to his people—not those Filipinos on the islands, but to his people here, in America. Filipino Americans. He shook his head, thinking, Man, we are a special tribe. Unnoticed, unloved. We should be indivisible like the pledge, but looks like we invisible. Mang Ciso schooled him on his Filipino-American history and he'd been using the lost pages of American history to nurture the sick and dying elders, the troubled youths, the petit bourgeois Pinoy who were upwardly mobile and shit. Sometimes he teamed up with JoJo Reyes, cuz JoJo knew how to get to the youth with his smooth talk. But it was Ferdi who had the knowledge. And he knew that it was knowledge, not smooth talk or pretty-boy faces that held power. When Isabel got there, he thought the circle was complete— she'd bring the movement that woman's touch and, finally, the whole world would know the truth and the power of his people. Man, he thought, shaking his head, she let him down.

This morning, he began his nursing rounds, same as always. His first call was at Lola Espie's home. He lifted her out of her chair and gently placed her in a tub of warm water. He bathed her and she shared her life with him. This was not the first time this happened. He knew where the stories would end. He soaped her brittle hair and she gave him advice, "You should find a nice girl. What happened to that nice one from before? What was her name?"

"Which one, Lola? You know I've had so many."

"That's my point. You are too choosy. You don't keep them long enough to love them."

"Hey, Lola, they leave me. I guess I'm too radical."

"Then be less radical."

He massaged medicinal oil into her joints, into the parts of her that didn't move so good anymore, and she confessed her greatest heartache. "You are the only one who cares for me. Five children and they are living the high life in L.A., in New York, in Bangkok."

"You helped them be successful, that's why they're there."

"They abandoned me in my old age. Only you come to me, and it's your job."

He shook his head and told her how much he loved her—"Like my own lola," he said—and she wept so passionately, he had to take a wet towel to her face to smooth away the sorrow. Before he left her fresh and sweet-smelling, she sniffed his cheeks many many many times. She told him, "You help me be a little less lonely, hijo. That is a miracle."

He went to the first pay phone off Virginia Beach Boulevard and he called Isabel, just to say hello, check in with her and her machine. He was feeling inspired. Maybe today she would pick up the phone and say, "Thank you, Ferdi. How are you, my brother? What can I do to help the Filipino Americans of Tidewater? Lay it on me!" As usual, she wasn't there and so he left her a message. What would he tell her today? There was so much he wanted to say, so much history in his blood. He decided to tell her about the old-timers who were living in San Francisco's International Hotel. Those manongs were among the first. He wasn't sure if he had told her before, but he thought it wouldn't hurt to tell her again. Seemed like she never heard him anyway.

During the daytime, he pulled bedpans and flushed waste into the sea. He bandaged injuries and doled out pills—counting and recounting. He injected the sugar in and out of their systems, depending on who they were. He cleaned the fluids that ran from their bodies.

His second stop was Lolo Ben. The old man lived in a basement studio. His walls were covered with old newspaper clippings and photos of his youth as a Navy cook in the Second World War. Ferdi rattled through his circles of keys and unlocked the front door. He tiptoed across the basement, to a leather recliner where Lolo Ben was lounging before an afternoon episode of JEOPARDY!. Ferdi heard the clock ticking, the chimes of the quiz show ringing a melody of questions. The game kept Lolo Ben alive, made him recall all the things he had forgotten.

"Hey, Lolo Ben," Ferdi yelled. "What is the American Revolution? What is Hello Dolly? What is an amoeba? What am I still doing here?"

Lolo Ben turned his head and nodded at him. His eyebrows rose up into two humpback kitties.

"What is tribe, Lolo? They ask you that one?" The old man coughed. "What's going on, Lolo?" Ferdi called out. He took the lolo's sleeping hand and raised it up to his brow. "I make mano to you, you gonna wake up and bless me?" He winked at Lolo Ben, who was only now opening his heavy eyelids. "What's your heart got to say to me today?" He wrapped an armband around Lolo Ben's frail arm, put the stethoscope to his ears. He pumped. He listened. The old man sighed. And then Lolo Ben began to speak his heart.

"Naku," he told Ferdi, "Parang I dreamed the morning away." Lolo Ben told him he filled his head with a house back in the Philippines. A big house in the province with open windows and high ceilings and slow rotating fans. He dreamed of the giant fronds outside the bedroom window swaying gently—shoosh, shoosh, shoosh. He smelled salt from the Pacific, which was somehow warmer and sweeter than the cold Atlantic. He dreamed he was twenty-two and that his family surrounded him. He lived with his parents, his four brothers and three sisters, both sets of grandparents and two single aunts. His uncles' families lived in the same compound, and every morning his people would gather for Mass and then a big breakfast. He dreamed he was sitting with his grandmother, reading books. His grandfather sat in a wicker chair, trouser legs hoisted up to his knees. Lolo lectured them about the importance of prayer, the role of the family, the politics of province life. "O'po," he answered out loud. "O'po." He dreamed his lolo's voice and the voice of his mother and the whistle that came from his father and the laughter of all his dead brothers. He dreamed the aunts were singing like angels, but out of tune. He covered his ears. He wrinkled his brow. He dreamed until there was no morning left.

"Whatchoo doing dreaming about the past? This is the future. You are in America. You ain't got time to be sad and lonely. You ain't got business living in your head like that. Don't you know you are a living treasure? A veteran of WWII—a hero?"

"Bakit then, I don't feel like that. I feel like I am a boy again. A child. Baka I'm dying already."

Ferdi watched the old man's eyes, how they teared up and rained on his old face. He felt his heart following the old man back to the islands and to the place where he thought he was so happy. "But you should be happy you are here, Lolo," he said. He stroked the man's arms and patted his knee. "I love you, you know. You risked your life for me—for all of us."

"Ferdi, I was a cook."

"Best cook in the United States Navy, too. Without you, those sailors would have been weak. Don't you know that food feeds the soul, the fighting spirit? Without you, we might have lost the war."

Sometimes when he was out on calls like this and he could see the old were dying, Ferdi also saw the faces of the youth. He could see history repeating itself, and he worried that Filipino Americans would remain forever invisible. Once or twice he came upon an old lolo or lola who had died in the middle of a dream. And that was the easy part. That was the part that didn't bother him. It was when he listened to them tell their stories, and he held their hands and stroked their arms. It was when he embraced their stories. He was always so amazed at their lives.

And then it was the youths—younger versions of the elders, newer models. Not as strong. Not as equipped, somehow. So many of them fell to gunshots and car crashes, some high on drugs and alcohol. Why did they do that? Didn't they know their lives were built on the backs of their lolas and lolos? If he could connect them—the youths, the old ones, the generation between—if he could fuse them with the history of their blood—would that lessen the pain? Would it make getting old easier? Would it make the dying more dignified? Would it keep the youths alive? It made him crazy, what he knew. So when he wasn't visiting his patients, he spent his day making connections, writing letters, filing protests, marching.

He checked his machine every hour. And when he found no messages waiting for him, he'd feel his heart grow a little more anxious. He called Isabel seven times. Where the hell was she? What was she doing for this community anyway?

After his last call, he drove around the beach and visited all her haunts. He wanted to express to her the urgency of their mission. The old ones were really dying and he was afraid they would not get the tribute they deserved. The young ones were tempting death and he was afraid that death would win. They would be a people erased from the history of Americana. He drove past her house. He went by the school. He even drove by JoJo's to see if he had seen her. He went to the YMCA, where she liked to run on a treadmill. A telling activity if ever he saw one. Sometimes when he was waiting for her down on the streets, he'd look up and watch her running and running, always in place. He'd watch the way her hair would slide from its ponytail, the way her face would grow red and moist. Sometimes he thought about giving her a push—j ust a little one—to get her moving beyond that same spot. How she gonna help the youth if she takes up those petit bourgeois sports, he'd say to himself.

He parked his car on Pleasure House Road and he walked the shores of Chick Beach. The water was calm and the waves sounded like whispers. He pulled a black-beaded rosary from his trousers and he recited five decades of Hail Marys and five Our Fathers and he sang five Glory Be's to the wind. He closed his eyes and he let the breeze run through his body, and he saw visions of youths dancing at house parties and on tables and the hoods of trucks. He saw them shouting out, and, in between the dancing bodies, he saw the ghosts of former patients, of youths now dead. The lolas and lolos floated over homies, bent down and kissed foreheads, placing bony hands on them, blessing them. He saw Arturo slipping his thick body into skinny spaces. Arturo chanted with Ferdi. Called out to him. Warned him that if he didn't move, if he didn't reach Isabel soon, the youth would be lost. JoJo would be taken from them like Arturo was, like JoJo's brother was, and the community would slip into the lost pages of history. Nobody ever reads the lost pages of history. When Ferdi opened his eyes, he saw nothing but miles of water slipping back and forth underneath the Chesapeake Bridge. His heart was beating three times its normal rate. He was hot and flushed and filled with the Holy Spirit.

The last spot he went to was Albertson's grocery. He saw her station wagon parked in the third row closest to the south doors. By this time, the sun had spread its light into rainbows across the gray sky. All he wanted to do was talk to her, get her to understand and to agree. How come she never answered him?

She came out of the store still in her workout clothes, sweaty from running in place. Her hair sprouted from a loose ponytail on the top of her head, errant strands drifting into her eyes and down her long neck. She pushed a cartful of bags. He had been waiting so long and he had grown tired and irritable. When he called her name, she walked like she didn't hear. When he reached out to her, she pulled her shoulder away like he was dirt.

Didn't she know what kind of man he was? When the lights on the harbor glimmered like the sleepy eyes of an infant and all anyone could hear was the water washing up on shore, Ferdi got down on his hands and knees. He pulled out his Bible, a present from his old lola on the occasion of his Confirmation. He read passages. He liked the parables. He liked the psalms. He was memorizing all 150 of them so he could recite them when he was stuck in traffic, in between visits to the old ones. The Gospels were his favorite. The brothers had sat themselves down, recorded their own perspective of history—Matthew, Mark, Luke, John. They got the Truth. Ferdi knew too much. He knew it all. Everything he knew kept him up at night. That's the kind of man he was. Didn't she know that?

Once or twice he met a Filipina who seemed interested in his mission. He'd court her. He'd bring her flowers. He'd introduce her to the elders and the youths. But after awhile they always lost interest. Said there was more to a relationship than revolution. He wasn't sure what they meant by that, or why they'd say those things to him. Some left in the middle of the night, like thieves, taking with them his affection.

This time she was not going to get away, not going to turn a deaf ear to him. He placed his hands on her shoulders like an old lover, like a big brother, like one of the lolo ghosts talking to the youths. He talked right into her face and he spoke his words deliberately. "You are too old to be acting like the dalagas, deaf and full of attitude," he said. "You gotta take up your share of the load. What is your responsibility to your people?" He looked into her eyes, at the dark brown pupils, so brown they were black, so black they were the whole sky. He waited for an answer. Kept close to her, while she thought about it. She was silent. "Okay," he told her. "This is really important. Maybe you want to think about it before you answer. Take some time before you commit. That's cool," he said. "You just call me when you know. I'll be waiting for you."

Afterwards, he ran to church, stumbling onto a kneeler before the Mama Mary, and he prayed. He was sorry about the Midwest Pinay. He didn't mean to come on so strong. But she was so deaf. She was so white. How could anyone so moreno be so white? He could hardly believe she was one of them. He sort of lost control. But if she knew what he knew, would she sleep at night? Would she rest? Or would the knowing keep her up? Would prayer be the only thing to ease her mind, to make her see that even at night, through God, he was working for his people twenty-four-seven?

FIFTEEN

For Valentine's Day, Isabel took her sixth graders to the St. Louis World Exposition of 1904. She brought in old photos and paper clippings with advertisements meant to entice Americans to explore the exhibitions. She laid out a poster of a dark-faced man, his hair pulled up to the sky and standing like arrows from his skull. His eyes bulged out from his sockets as if horrified. There were crazy letters and carnival-looking sketches around the man. "Come and see the savages! Real live Tribes of the South Pacific!"

"He's Filipino?" asked one of the girls.

"Why do they call him a savage?"

"What is a savage?"

"What happened?" the kids wanted to know.

"Let's see," she said, and they scoured her artifacts and made the story come true.

The kids took jump ropes and strung them together in a corner of the gym. The tribe members were not allowed to leave the grounds of the St. Louis World's Fair. Elders, chieftains, and children milled about an area no larger than a four-square court. Everything felt crowded. They watched a paper moon circle the sky thirty-six times. The American scouts trailed in and out of their lives, climbing under the jump ropes, crossing the barrier of see-through walls. They took large magnifying glasses and examined the eyes, the teeth, the skin of the island people. They tapped the bottoms of their feet with plastic hammers.

"I know," Julia Mendoza said, petting the top of an islander's head. "This is like a zoo. The Filipinos are animals and we are the zookeepers. Right?"

She caught Isabel off-guard. "And who are you?" Isabel asked.

"The Americans, of course," Julia said. "See—we can go look at them, but they can't come look at us."

The caretakers fed the tribes hard kernels of grain and called it rice. "Over here," Julia told people at the fair, "we have real live tribes. We call them the Igorot, Ifugao, and the Bontoc Tribes."

The Americans said "Oh my!" and "Look at that." Tommy de la Guardia pried open José Reynaldo's mouth. "Looks like he's got just as many teeth as we do!" No one spoke to the villagers directly. No one made friends. Julia reached out to touch a member of the tribe, recoiled at the coarseness of the hair, the black pigment of the skin. "It's like they're people, but it's also like they're animals."

One Bontoc boy, who lived on hope, smiled at strangers when they passed.

Isabel fell under the spell of the actors, at the way they donned the roles of scouts, scientists, and civilized citizens of the world. She watched the children playing tribal members and noticed their bodies begin to fold, their shoulders drooping forward, covering up their hearts. She watched as they went from standing upright to crawling on their knees. Where they had once talked about escape and negotiations with their captors, they now lay down in their imaginary jails, quietly coddling each other like newborn kittens. She knew they were only playing, but still her heart felt heavy and uncomfortable. She realized she had stopped breathing.

"Not too rough," she called out to them. "Remember it's only pretend."

That night, Isabel stood at the foot of the stage, watching the teenagers primp and posture before full-length mirrors. They stretched their skinny arms high above their heads and gazed at their bodies askance, sucking in their bellies or pushing out their breasts. They checked each other out, and Isabel watched their faces contort—some pleased with the images before them, some worried. Tita Nita Starr ran along the edges of the runway calling out commands like a tiger trainer, cracking a long leather whip, moving wildcats through their paces.

Tita Nita waved to her imaginary crowd, her court, her people. "Toss your arms out, like a fisherman's net, and gather the love to your heart," she told the girls.

She lined the girls up along the runway, had them casting nets over and over again, had them gathering love. None of the girls were any good at it. They were awkward, their shoulders rose to their ears, their bums were hiked up like cats on the run. Tita Nita picked on Lourdes quite a bit. "Smile, anak," she told her.

"It's only practice," Lourdes said. "I will when it's the real thing."

"Anak, this is the real thing. You must always smile like a beautiful Spanish jewel." Tita Nita walked over to Lourdes and, with her painted fingers, she pried Lourdes's lips into a smile. "Yan," she cooed, "like that." She tapped her under the chin, made her hold her head high. Using her daughter as an example, she instructed the girls: "Lift your hands high to the sky to show you are indeed a rising star. Stand tall and firm. Don't wobble, don't hesitate. Maya, why are you lying down on the runway? Get up. That's no way for a beauty queen to act. Ka ka hiya naman!"

"Lighten up, Ria," Isabel said. "That smile's plastered on your face. Relax a little, huh?"

Ria nodded at her nervously. "Sorry."

The others tossed Ria dirty looks.

"Maybe she's into it," Angel said. "Maybe she's happy and that's why she's smiling."

"Sup wit that?" Maya said to Ria. "Shoot dang."

During the break, the girls splayed themselves on folding chairs, or they curled up on the runway tarp like tattered alley cats. "Psych up a little," Isabel pleaded with them. "Do it for me?" She was trying to wash the grimace from their painted faces, to quell the curses leaking from behind their Vaseline-greased teeth.

They told Isabel about the reigning Miss Virginia Beach-Philippines 1995. She tried to take her life, she hated practice so much. And when the family found her, they blamed it on the Alvarez boy.

"Alvarez boy?" said Isa. "Is he related to Uncle Romy?"

The girls nodded. "His nephew!" they whispered.

The beauty queen's parents told her to get over the Alvarez boy, to pull herself together, to march right down that pageant aisle. They pushed her to sell over one-thousand raffle tickets. The month before the pageant, she lost so much weight she fainted under the lights of the evening gown competition. She slithered onto the floor, her ball gown crumpling down around her just like the melting witch of Oz. In the end, they crowned her anyway. After all, who else could sell that many tickets?

"Really?" Isabel whispered in disbelief.

"Talaga," they answered her, nodding in sync. "For true, for true."

"Check this," Marilena said, as if that wasn't enough. "Now homegirl's a freshman at the local junior college, four months pregnant."

"What's she ever done to you?" Maya wanted to know. "Why we tsismising like them old titas?"

"No big thing—but come on now—girl's got to show up and crown one of us," Angel said. "How embarrassing. Di ba?"

When Isabel asked the girls if they were doing the pageant because they wanted to, or because they had to, they raised their shoulders and cocked their heads. "Dunno," some of them muttered. "Got to," others whispered.

Tsismis said certain girls binged when they ate. Isabel saw each one yearning to win. It didn't matter if the young sister was doing it to please her parents, or if she was into it. Nobody wanted to lose.

"You kidding?" Lourdes said. "If I don't win, I'm fucked. I mean that."

Isabel didn't know if the tsismis was true. She didn't want to accuse anyone, so she decided to counteract the pageant thinking. "This one's different than all the rest," she told them. "In this year's pageant, everyone's a winner. As long as you have fun."

"You call this fun?" Mercedes said. "My mom is all, 'Watch out, I think you got new pimples again' and 'Don't be in the habit of rolling your eyes—Ay soos! So ugly naman.'"

Marilena laughed. "What about the time my mother said, 'How you gonna hold a crown on that head if you are always looking at the floor?' Man, it's twenty-four-seven."

"Shoot dang, yeah," said Maya. "My daddy thinks I'm getting too taba and he won't let me eat rice."

"NO RICE?" they all said.

Isabel said. "Beauty is on the inside."

The girls shook their heads, said, "No disrespect, but you, brown Ate, with yo' white ideas. Thas messed up."

"Who sees your insides?" Angel wanted to know. "That's gross."

"Nah, man," Mercedes said, "thas private. I don't want everybody lookin' inside me."

One Friday, before rehearsal, Isabel took the girls to Tita Chic Chic's diner and ordered big pans of pansit noodles. The girls sat around two checkered tables, slurping noodles off paper plates.

"That is good," Tita Chic Chic said, bringing over a plate of egg rolls. "I like to see you girls eating for a change."

"Maybe you do," Lourdes said. "But then again you're not my ma either."

Isabel pulled out health magazines of women running or biking, eating at tables with lots of food, and kissing sexy men on glossy pages. "Marilyn Monroe was no Twiggy," she told them.

"Who dat?" they asked her. "Who Twiggy?"

The women in the magazines had full faces, luscious bodies where curves of flesh twisted and turned like a road race in the country. "Personally," Isabel told them, "I'd rather err on the side of plump than bony." She was giving the beauty queen image a makeover.

Isa stood by the door, waiting for Elliot to pick her up. The girls gathered behind her, combing and re-combing their hair. Marilena rested all her weight on one foot so that her hip swerved out to the right. In one hand, she held a compact and in the other she took a bobby pin and separated her lashes. Mercedes gazed into the glass door, checking her shirt, the back of her pants. Ria's song of scales echoed in the halls, her voice haunting and dreamy.

"That's the third time you messed wit that hair, Desa," Angel said. "First it was pigtails, then it was twisted up, then it was all on one side like a hula girl. Face it, who's looking?"

"Someone's always looking," Lourdes said.

Maya groaned. She sat with her back against the wall, her face buried in her hands. "Why does someone always have to be looking?"

Isa watched their reflections in the hall mirror. She smiled and said, "And here I thought we were getting somewhere." She could hear a male voice on the other side of the hallway.

"Sup, Kuya Ferdi," chanted the girls, all at once.

"You girls have a good rehearsal?"

Like bells they rang: "Yeah" and "You know it."

"Your Ate Isa being a good role model, is she?" he asked. He was rocking back and forth as he walked, as though he thought maybe he was a gangbanger himself.

"Ask her yo'self," said Lourdes. "She right there."

He turned toward her and she gazed at his reflection, at his meaty back. He had a cigarette in his hand and the smoke seemed to curl from his fingers. She ignored him.

"Catcha later," he told the girls and, sauntering past her, he said, "You behaving?"

She didn't look at him, but she felt his presence and it crowded the doorway. "That's a hell of a question, coming from you," she said.

"I just want to thank you for all you're doing for our youths. These girls count on you."

She couldn't get over his audacity. How little he suspected that she could file charges, could sic Macmillan and Smith on him so easily. He smelled like garlic and leftover lechon.

Elliot's truck pulled up just then, and she walked away from Ferdi without saying another word. The bass seeped out the cracks of the window, pounded at her head. Elliot was listening to The Who again. When the door opened, a blast of electric guitar and the tenor yell of "Teenage Wasteland" came shooting out. She slammed the door and told him to drive.

"What were you doing talking to that guy?" Elliot asked.

"He was talking to me." She dug in her bag, searching, and when she couldn't find what she was looking for, she reached around her seat, then below her feet. She felt her way along the pockets of the door. Elliot handed her a new bottle of water.

"You crazy?" he asked her. "You should have called the cops a long time ago. You should have turned that mother in."

She peeled the plastic off the cap and turned the volume up even higher and she sang at the top of her lungs. She really didn't care. Elliot shook his head and spun the wheel. Patting him on the knee, she offered him a drink, told him not to worry. But when she wrapped her hand around the blue bottle, her fingers quivered like a child left out in the snow.

One day Isa took out a really old Polaroid camera—the kind that pulled open like an accordion. The kind where you shot a picture then pulled out a strip of paper before the photo itself, then, after it developed in your hand, you peeled a chemical page off the print. She shot a portrait of each of the girls standing against the wall of her beach house. She let them decide what to do with their bodies. Some girls chose to stand with their arms held up like wings, hips cocked to one side. Others chose to sit down, arms folded across their chests, vacant expressions on their faces. Ria stood with her profile to the camera, hands in her pockets and looking over her shoulder to the lens. Isabel gave each photo a minute to develop and then the girls peeled a black sheet off the photo. It was sticky and the girls' images ghosted across the film, revealing mirror images of their arms, their legs, their eyes made up of powder, liner and false lashes.

The girls pasted the Polaroids next to the negatives, and underneath they described how the world saw them—tough or sassy or naughty. Some of them talked about how dumb they were, how ugly they were. They wanted Barbie features—long spindly legs and buxom chests, curly blonde ponytails and dolly-like lashes. Isabel gave them extra pieces of paper and asked them to write themselves on that page. Underneath the negatives they answered the statement, "Who I am For True." Under their spirit photos, the girls scribbled themselves into being.

Maya shot a photo of Isabel strolling around the girls. She pulled the picture apart and handed Isabel a positive and negative image of herself. "Here's the way the world sees you," Maya told her. She pointed to the negative and said, "And here's how you really are. Do you know the difference?"

"Not now," Isabel told her.

"Then when?" Maya wanted to know.

They had been watching Suzie Wong and other notable Asian beauties, picking apart their characters and saying, "No wonder the world looks at us and sees them."

"Shoot, like they're all that?" Angel wanted to know. "I don't think so."

The girls bowed their heads, stretched their bodies long on her floor. She could hear their pencils scratching across the page. Some of them giggled, but some of them went places they had never been before, and Isa could hear those girls sniffling. She fetched boxes of tissue and handed them out. She placed a hand on Mercedes's back, and let her weep all over the wood floor. She pushed the hair out of tear-stained faces and cried along with them. She didn't think they'd react so strongly to the exercise. Maya brought her pictures to Isa and traced her fingers around the words. She wrapped her arms round Isabel and thanked her.

"Do you guys want to share what you did?" she asked them. "Or do you want to keep them to yourselves?"

"Mine looks like shit," Lourdes said, holding hers aloft and ripping it up before anyone could see.

"Your house is like a zine or something," Maya said.

"A magazine?"

"Yeah," Maya said. "Like the kind of place you see on TV—all matching an shit. It's pretty."

Marilena poked around in the fridge, said, "You got so much stuff. All those books about the Pinas."

"Ain't no matter how many books you read," Lourdes said, grabbing a bowl from the cupboard. "Nothing's going teach you how to be Pinay. You either is or you isn't."

Isabel looked at the girls in the kitchen. JoJo once said the same thing to her. That's JoJo talking now, she thought, that's him. They moved comfortably about, knew where everything was kept. Still, she couldn't help feeling their judgment. "Those books don't teach you how to be Filipino," she told them. "They talk about our history, our past."

"They don't help you be Pinay," Lourdes said. "I know that."

"No."

"It's all right," Angel said, swatting Lourdes. "We understand. Just like you tryin' to show us some of dat white life."

"Mr. North?" Marilena said. "Right?"

"I'm talkin' yogurt and carrot sticks," Angel said. "White food."

"Exercise," Maya said. "White."

"Saging?" Isabel said.

"Brown," said Mercedes. "Di ba? Bananas, brown."

"New Age CDs?" Ria said. "White."

"Dieting," Isabel said, laughing, and they all answered, "White."

The girls burst into laughter and the pitch of their screams made her think of dolphins giggling. Marilena slapped her knee, then snorted, sending everyone into a crazy fit, a can't-stop-me-now-no-matter-how-not-funny-this-is fit. Maya sighed and, fanning her face with her hands, said, "Aw man, I don't feel so good," and she ran into the bathroom. The girls continued laughing and Isabel said, "Was it my cooking?"

Isabel slept in her giant bed, floating in the middle of the room, nightmares playing like reruns. She saw Las Dalagas growling, mad dogs warring with the Norfolk girl crews. These dreams ran through a red filter. Blood stained their arms, their hands, their beautiful faces. Sometimes the girls were stuffed into sequin gowns, their bodies powdered with stardust, their faces frozen into perfect smiles. It didn't matter if homegirls were ready to jump another crew, or if they strutted down that catwalk—in each of the dreams, Isabel sat at the edge of the picture, her hands and legs heavy as two-ton weights. She was yelling but her words came out backward, non-words, completely alien. Then Ferdi appeared in a white leisure suit: its polyester fibers shined in the light, the edges were topstitched in gold and his hair was greased back. He followed her and whispered songs to her—slow jazz and rhythm and blues, Barry White love songs—but he was no Barry White. His singing was irritating, like flies buzzing in the dark. When she woke, she and Elliot were struggling and he was saying, "Calm down, baby. Calm down."

"Don't," she told him, pushing him away.

"But you were dreaming."

"Why'd you wake me?" she asked, rubbing her hands across her face, and this was when she noticed the tears, the ache heavy in her chest. "I was trying to work something out."

"You don't have to do this," he told her. "You can quit."

"Why would I do that?" she asked him, rolling her body to the edge of the bed. Why would she stop what she had begun?

I FEEL LIKE TALKING, ISABEL. FEEL LIKE TALKING TO YOU
ABOUT ME. I AM A LITTLE OLDER THAN YOU—BUT HEY,
DON'T WORRY, YOU DON'T HAVE TO CALL ME KUYA. MAYBE
YOU ARE TOO WHITE TO CALL YOUR BROTHERS KUYA, YOUR
SISTERS ATE. TO EACH HIS OWN, I SAY.

WHEN YOU WERE A LITTLE GIRL IN THE SIXTIES AND
SEVENTIES, I WAS FINDING MY IDENTITY ALONG WITH
OTHER PINOYS. WE WANTED TO KNOW—WHO ARE WE,
WHAT DO WE STAND FOR, WHERE ARE WE GOING? IN 1970
THE U.S. CENSUS COUNTED 350,000 FILIPINOS IN THESE
UNITED STATES OF AMERICA. THAT'S A HELLUVA RISE FROM
43,000 BACK IN THE 1930s. LOOKING AT YOU, COMING FROM
MONEY THE WAY YOU DO, YOU'VE PROBABLY NEVER KNOWN
RACIST AMERICA, SEGREGATED AMERICA, GO-BACK-TO-
WHERE-YOU-CAME-FROM AMERICA. IF I CLOSE MY EYES AND
LISTEN TO YOUR OUTGOING MESSAGE, I HEAR A WHITE GIRL
IN BROWN SKIN TALKING. GROWING UP, I DIDN'T HAVE
OPPORTUNITIES THE WAY YOU DID, THE WAY OUR YOUTHS
DO NOW. MAINSTREAM AMERICA'S ROLE MODELS WERE
WHITIES—EXCEPT MAYBE MARTIN LUTHER KING, JR., BUT HE
WAS BLACK, NOT BROWN LIKE YOU AND ME. IN MY YEARS OF
GROWING UP, WE CAME TO REALIZE IT WAS NOT ENOUGH TO
JUST BE CITIZENS, BECAUSE AMERICA STILL SAW US AS
FOREIGNERS. OUR ULTIMATE GOAL WAS TO BE ACCEPTED AS
AMERICANS, BY AMERICANS. AND TO DO THAT, WE KNEW WE
HAD TO BE EDUCATED, BECOME PART OF THE SYSTEM, START
MAKING SOME OF THE DECISIONS. LUCKY FOR ME, THE
BROTHERS AND SISTERS OF THE WAR BRIDE AND BRIDGE
GENERATION GOT AMERICA TO CALL ME A MINORITY. GOT
ME INTO SCHOOLS UNDER THE GUISE OF AFFIRMATIVE
ACTION. PROVIDED ME WITH AN EDUCATION MY FAMILY
COULD NOT AFFORD. NOW LOOK AT ME. LOOK AT YOU.
DIDN'T WE ALL BENEFIT? WHAT IS OUR DUTY TO OUR
FUTURE? TO OUR PAST? TELL ME, ISABEL. WHAT?

His voice looped its way around her head. She leaned over to press the button and erase the message, but even after it was gone, she heard Ferdi spitting out facts, shooting accusations her way. She didn't need him to remind her that she had a duty to the kids.

As Isabel watched the mothers and fathers nag the girls about their skin, their bodies and the image they presented, she found herself eating a little bit less, paying a little more attention to the shape of her brow, the color of her lips. She looked into the mirror and sucked in her gut. She wondered what the girls saw. "Not this, I hope." The more time she spent with the girls, the less she had to say, the more she found herself listening as if she were the student. She felt so naïve. She was the reigning queen of hope, of change, and dare she think it? Inner beauty.

Isa found seven full-length mirrors in junkyards, second-hand stores, and abandoned tenement halls. Some of the mirrors had been shattered and fragmented, distorting images that passed before them, multiplying faces, hands, whatever showed up in their broken way. She dragged a chest of fabrics into the light—red indigo weave, orange tassels, satin corsets, veils trimmed in golden threads and delicate Spanish lace.

She lined the boys up—Derek, Edison, Miguel, and others. She placed three at half-court, and lined up two more rows of boys at angles so they stood in the shape of a triangle. Then she handed each of them a full-length mirror. The reflections of glass bounced across the gymnasium, one into the other, infinitely reflecting light, mirror, glass. She placed Elvie in the center of the house of mirrors and handed him the last looking glass, spinning him around like a revolving door.

Then she brought the girls in. Lourdes, Angel, Mercedes, Maya, Ria, and Marilena stood frozen, awkward and uncomfortable. Their eyes looked beyond, gazing into nothing. They held their breath, remained lifeless for the drama. She deposited each mannequin girl in front of a mirror, stretching the arms into odd shapes, bending the legs into unnatural poses.

"Now," she told them, "when I put you in a pose, don't move."

"Why?" Lourdes wanted to know.

"You'll see."

Isabel draped a simple cloth around Angel, a skirt that hung down straight, a slit for movement. No shoes. She peeled Angel's shirt off and revealed a skin-colored leotard with ink markings like tattoos. Angel was an action figure, sprinting up mountains in search of healing herbs. She was beauty before the Conquistador. She was dark-skinned and bare-chested. She wore wooden trinkets around her neck and wrists. She smoked a pipe.

As Isa turned Angel into a woman of the Ifugao tribe, she described the mannequin's history to the class. She told them about the way the datu of a tribe would relegate work to all members of the baranggay, so each man and woman contributed something of value to the community. The indigenous woman wasn't only beautiful, she also held equal status to the other members of her tribe. "Imagine that," Isabel said.

Finishing her work with Angel, Isa moved on to the next girl. She dressed Mercedes with fabric from the chest, wrapping her body in petticoats and a big puffy skirt. Mercedes became the Doña of the house. This beauty, this mestiza, wore garments that flared out wide, encompassing three times the space of the indigenous beauty. With the Spanish came the weight of clothing and heavy jewels, came tiny tiara combs and rosaries dripping in mother of pearl. Isabel raised an open fan up to Mercedes's chest, sent her eyes looking to the ground. Because the Doña was confined by petticoats, corsets, and yards of fabric, she was not an action figure like the Ifugao woman. To accommodate her new look, the houses grew bigger, hallways fatter, workloads lighter—all to compensate for the beauty's new outfit.

"Can I move?" Angel called out.

"No! Just wait."

Isabel pulled Ria before the mirrors and painted her face with hot red rouge. She streaked blue eye shadow across her lids and dabbed fuchsia lipstick on her mouth. She teased her long hair so that it rose high and wild like the plumes of a peacock. Ria became a girl from Olongapo, a dancer at Clark Air Base. She seduced soldiers, shifting her body under red lights and spinning disco balls, moving to the beat of Donna Summer.

"Shoot dang," Miguel said, "Ria can move!"

"Mirrors don't talk," Isabel warned him.

Isabel dressed Marilena like a nun, washing the blush from her face, dabbing a cotton swab at her eyeliner. She covered Marilena's hair with a lace veil. Folding the girl's hands close to her heart and weaving rosary beads around them, Isabel let the crucifix hang down and dangle close to Marilena's womb. She closed Marilena's eyes and fixed her like a beautiful statue of St. Theresa.

Isabel left Maya exactly as she was. She let the girl's jeans hang low to the ground, propped her up on platform shoes. An oversized windbreaker, wrapped around her waist, accented a torso bursting from a tightly fitted baby-T. She crossed Maya's arms, pulled her fingers and stretched them into some imaginary gang sign. "Gimme some of that attitude," Isa told her.

"What attitude?" Maya asked, rolling her eyes.

Maya filled the mirror with curves and beautiful flesh. Isa asked her to gaze directly into the looking glass—eye to eye, no smile, no hint of that dimple, no emotion. Standing behind, Isabel pulled Maya's hair away from her face and revealed the beauty of a ripened mango. "Look how powerful you are," she said, running her fingers over Maya's fine scars. "Look how beautiful. This becomes a way of documenting your struggles, a beautiful sign of your strength."

"Tell my pops that one," Maya answered her. "He just calls it ugly."

Black liner smudged around her almond eyes made Maya mean-looking, but the eyes were pools of black, brimming with tears.

"You gonna be okay?" Isabel whispered. She looked at their faces, thought of Maya sneaking into her house, remembered Coco Cabungcal's love of talking without words.

"Ain't nothing," Maya whispered back. "Intense is all."

Isabel squeezed the girl's arms. She sensed the boys in the background, shifting the glass. In the cracked reflections of a broken mirror, she thought she saw Arturo smudged and dancing in the shadows.

Finally, she placed Lourdes in front of the last mirror. Lourdes was Filipina Barbie, draped in jewels and silver-sequined evening gown, crowned in cubic zirconium, painted full-lipped and Western as Miss U.S.A..

The girls stood frozen, a foot from their reflections, studying their own eyes, mouth, and waist. Behind them, the human walls revealed the flip side of their bodies—figures wrapped in various cottons, silks and piña cloth. In the looking glass, a girl saw the expanse of her back, the length of her neck, or the shine of blue-black hair. Some of the mirrors, cracked by a bat, or shattered from being dropped, or pierced by a single BB gun, projected several images of the same girl, distorted her face, magnifying a lip, an ear, the contour of a breast. Isa felt something growing inside, like the color of ink as it spilled from a pen onto the floor of someone's purse.

She watched the images floating on the sea of mirrors, and the light moved in such a way that the boys' faces came to her too, one at a time—Elvie, Nando, Miguel, Derek, Edison and, every now and then, a boy who was the image of Arturo.

"Stand perfectly still," Isabel said.

"My foot's asleep," called Angel.

"Shhh," Isabel told her. "Just a little longer."

In that moment, Maya turned away from the mirror. Her platforms punched at the wood floor. She shoved the heavy doors open, muttering, "I gotta pee."

Isa waited a beat then looked around at the girls, who stood so still they trembled.

214

SIXTEEN

A saw buzzed through a two-by-four and set dust and wood chips swirling in the air. For weeks the yard had been noisy with pounding and buzzing, and the voices of Las Dalagas shouting over all of it. They were building a floating fort to hide away from the world. Sometimes they chanted to the rap of hip-hop on Ria's boom box. Holding two pieces of wood together, Marilena and Angel cringed as Ria swung a hammer up and down. "Hold still," she told them. She steadied another nail and pounded inches from their hands.

"Be careful!" Marilena warned her.

"Aray!" cried Angel. Ria stopped pounding, gave a look.

"Whatever," she said, "I didn't even come close."

"Picture!" Maya said. She held a thirty-five-millimeter camera up to her eye, squinted at her sisters. When she looked into the lens she didn't see homegirls, she saw warriors. Ria held the hammer mid-air, glared all mean-like into Maya's lens. Lourdes leaned on a plank, arched her back and stared while Marilena and Angel folded their arms across their chests. The sky above swirled in brilliant reds and oranges, reflected a golden light on all their faces.

"Take it already," Ria said, waving the hammer. Maya pressed gently, the shutter blinked and the girls resumed their work against the setting sun.

On Millie's first night of spring break, Elliot and Isabel treated her to sushi. They took their shoes off and lined them up along a bamboo mat, then snuck their bodies through a door screened in rice paper. Elliot crawled on his knees, his tube socks trailing after him as if they were too big. He squeezed his legs under the table.

"I like this place," he told Millie. "These tables are a total fake." He pointed out the window and said, "From out there it looks like we're sitting on the floor, on top of our knees, Japanese style. But look." He indicated a drop in the floor, a place to dangle his legs. "Makes it easy on the oldsters."

The waitress, dressed in a traditional kimono, handed them a bowl of steaming hand towels wrapped tight like egg rolls.

Isabel grabbed one and handed it to her sister. Then she took her own. They peeled the towels open and the steam rose, a tiny white cloud trailing up in wisps. They wiped their hands clean, discarding the towels in the bowl. Elliot told them again: "I love this place." Unraveling his towel, he draped it flat against his face and rubbed vigorously against the stubble on his cheek.

"You're not supposed to do that," Isabel told him.

"Why not?" he said. "That's why they give it to you." He grabbed a corner and rubbed behind his ears.

"Elliot," she said, pulling the towel from his hands. "That is so disrespectful."

"Oh come on," he said, laughing. He tickled her under her chin. "To the Japanese? You're too much."

"Was your trip okay?" Isa asked Millie.

"We had a two-hour delay—they had to de-ice the plane at O'Hare." Millie groaned. "Then I had to sit between people who talked the whole time. I could barely study."

For Millie, it didn't matter that she was on spring break. She brought her books everywhere. She'd loved medicine all her life, had followed their father's work even as a child.

"You should lighten up," Isabel told her sister. She tugged at her sleeve and kissed her on the cheek again. "You're a total geek. For one week, you're not going to get away with that. You're going to relax."

"Look who's talking," Elliot said, pointing at Isa. "Your sister is a workaholic."

"I am not," Isa said.

"She is too. Intense, always thinking about those kids and reacting

216

to every little thing. You need to let it go, Bel."

"Let what go?" she asked. She was looking at Elliot, giving him the most evil evil eye, sending him telepathic messages.

"I'll lighten up if you get real," Millie said.

"What do you mean by that?"

"You know," Millie told her. "All of a sudden you're Ate Isabel with a capital A, running around like the leader of the pack."

"Exactly," Elliot said. "Was she like that in Chicago?"

"Not at all."

Isabel gazed at her sister, at the way she cracked that crooked smile. "That was over the top," she told her.

"Oh God!" Elliot said, raising his hands up. "Here it comes now!" A white woman in a Japanese kimono placed a bamboo ship before them, its deck covered with rolls of tuna, yellowtail and soft-shell crab. Elliot sang like a vaudevillian, "If you knew sushi like I knew sushi—" and Isa rolled her eyes at him, cuffed him on the ear.

The rest of the night, Elliot continued to make cheesy chopstick jokes. Millie giggled, her feet dangling down into the fake floor's pit, while Isa held her breath. The more they joked around, the more irritated she got, until finally Millie wiped her eyes and said, "Aw Ate Bel, you're the one who needs to lighten up. Come on now, admit it, he's a riot."

On Sunday Elliot dropped Isabel and Millie at St. Anthony's, a sand-brick church tucked behind a strip mall just behind Virginia Beach Boulevard. They walked among a swarm of people, and made their way to the front doors. "He doesn't come to church?" Millie asked.

"Who, Elliot? He's agnostic."

It was a modern church with stained-glass skylights. The altar was made of oak and sat in the middle of one large room. Pews lined with soft red cushions surrounded the altar on all four sides. At the center of the altar, a long brass crucifix hung from the ceiling. Jesus floated there, his half-dressed body bent and bleeding, his wounds open for all the church to see. Standing in the corner of the church, a small brown statue blessed everyone. He was life-like in his stance—black hair, broad brown face, squat body. He wore a Barong Tagalog, a delicately embroidered white shirt, long-sleeved and formal. Months ago, when Isabel first attended St. Anthony's, she thought he was a church volunteer. When he didn't move, not once, she realized he was a statute of San Lorenzo. Millie yanked at Isabel's arm, pointed to the statue, bewildered.

"Why does that surprise you?" Isabel whispered. "Look around you."

When the congregation prayed, their voices blended and spiraled up to the stained-glass ceilings. They united as they rose, and what became clear was a strong Filipino accent. The vowels were short, the consonants crisp, the words rattled forth fast. There were no h's. Millie slowly scanned the room and Isabel nodded at her. "See," she told her. "We're everywhere."

"I feel like we're in a foreign country," Millie said.

Isabel swatted her sister on the leg. "Behave," she said. She glanced around the church and saw JoJo a few rows back, holding his two-year-old cousin in his arms. He winked at Isa, who promptly turned away.

After Mass, many of the aunties in the church swooped down on Isabel and Millie. "Who's dis?" they asked. "Who is your prend, Isabel?"

"My sister, Millie."

"Beautiful too—sopistikated."

"She's a medical resident in Chicago," Isabel told them.

"Is dis da beauty queen?" asked Tita Nita. She reached out to rub Millie's arm, pat her there, examine her. "Of course she is."

"She's so American," said Auntie Wilma.

Millie smiled at the women, but didn't say anything. She tossed looks at Isabel, who only smiled a see-what-I-live-with-every-day-of-my-life smile. Grabbing her sister by the arm, Isabel ushered Millie out of the church, where they found Ferdi staring right at them from across the parking lot.

"Don't look," she told her sister.

"Who the hell is he?" Millie asked. Ferdi sat on the hood of the car, leaned back against the windshield with a baseball cap pulled over his eyes.

"Don't look."

"Is that the guy?"

"Yeah." Isabel tugged Millie's arm and they walked around the cars.

"Creepy," Millie said. "Has he . . ."

"Just leave it."

The aunties in the parking lot chattered like roosters ready for a cockfight. "They're kind of nosy."

"They were right," Isabel said. "You're too American." She thought about the gathering, how crowded and noisy the people were in her church, how they whispered to one another, and sang loudly. She considered the times she had caught a mother crying, or a teenager pulling at her father's sleeve as if she were ten. The church was a living church, she thought, a place where children crawled in and out of pews and scrambled up into the arms of their aunties and uncles, or ates and kuyas.

She studied her sister's profile, and shook her head. "You shouldn't be such a snob, Millie. They mean well."

They waited for Elliot to pull the car up.

"How'd it go?" Elliot asked. "You pray for me?"

"Always," Isa said. "You know you need it." They drove the rest of the way home in silence. Not the kind of silence that's reverent, or the kind that sat between two so comfortable and familiar, but silence meant for strangers, for people without a single thing in common.

The sisters lounged on short beach chairs, their toes exposed to the cold March sand, their faces pointed to the sun. Isabel had covered her body in leggings and a long-sleeved shirt, while Millie, making the most of her long weekend, had stripped down to a swim top and shorts. They sipped glasses of Merlot and nibbled on cheese and crackers, on chips made of sweet potatoes, on carrots and tarot root. Millie sprawled a giant textbook across her lap.

"Give it up, Millie, you're on vacation."

"You understand," Millie answered as she sipped from her plastic cup. "I have to. Otherwise I won't sleep."

The wind moved fast that day, whistling high-pitched. It was warm for early spring. Isabel leaned back and watched white puffs of cloud running across the blue sky. She breathed deeply and thought how nice it was to have Millie there, even if she was completely obsessed with her text.

"What is that you're looking at?" Isabel said, leaning out of her chair. "What's so great about that book?"

She saw the red and blue veins of a heart—an anatomically correct vessel diagrammed in two dimensions and utterly unromantic. "Have you figured out how that thing works?" she asked.

"More or less."

"Like every time a guy breaks my heart or the kids let me down—why do I feel a tightness in my chest?"

"Funny, ha, ha." Millie scribbled into a spiral notebook, her gold pen reflecting sunshine into Isa's eyes.

High tide battled with the wind, and waves crashed like cannons at war, over and over again. The sisters had to shout and use their arms and hands to communicate. They moved like two mimes in the middle of a drama. Isabel was glad to have someone like this to pal around with.

"Dad wants you to come home," Millie said.

Isabel leaned back, sipped her wine said, "What he wants and what has to be are two different things."

"I saw that guy, Ate. He's messed up."

"Ferdi?" She leaned over and traced one of the heart diagrams with her long finger. "Always studying," she said. "Always Daddy's girl."

When Isabel was growing up her dad would say, "You gonna be a doctor," and Isabel would shake her head, whipping her hair back and forth across her face, the ends stinging her cheeks. She'd say: "A dancer!" or "A singer" or "I'd rather be a mommy."

"You got to take care of yourself," her father would lecture. "Depend on nobody but you—especially here in America. It's not like back home where people take care of each other."

But at what cost, Isabel wondered. When she was little he was always at the hospital. She and Frankie Boy would wake up and he would be gone. They'd play all day long, eat their meals and go to bed before he got home. Millie was a baby then, so she never felt his absence the way they did. She didn't know that he wasn't always so strict and mean. Before, he was fun to play with, to tackle, to chase about the house.

In the distance, Isabel saw JoJo and some of the kids making their

way from among the cars. JoJo was with Miguel, Edison, Mercedes and
Lourdes. At the edge of the beach, the girls kicked off their shoes. Edison
ambled his way across the sand behind JoJo and Miguel.

"Sup?" Isabel called out.

"Hey," JoJo said.

"Who's that?" Millie whispered.

"Shh," Isabel said, "Shh. He's no one."

When the crew reached Isabel and Millie, they stood in a circle
around them, hovered over the sisters. Isabel introduced Millie and the
kids mostly grunted at her or nodded. Except for Edison and JoJo, no
one seemed to be smiling.

"You guys look nothin' alike," said Miguel.

"You don't think so?" Mercedes said. "She looks just like
Ate Isabel."

"Yeah, you can tell she's a baby sista."

Isabel stood up and waved her hands in their faces. "Hello there,
we're right here, we can see you. We can hear you."

"I don't see it," Miguel said.

"You don't have to," JoJo told him. "Now sit down and chill out."

Edison plopped himself next to Millie, smiling big and wide. He
picked at the plate of crackers and cheese. "What's this?" he said.
"Cheese and crackers? Wine? How bourgei."

"Bourgei?" said Millie.

"Bourgeois," Isabel told her. "And it's not bourgei. It's good." She
pinched Edison's arm and he feigned an ouch. "This is Edison," she
told Millie.

"Yeah," Edison said, smiling big and toothy. "I was named after
Thomas Edison—in fact, I am Tomás Edison Villanueva."

Millie nodded and smiled politely. "Interesting."

"Very Filipino," Isa said. "His brothers are Dwight Eisenhower
Villanueva and George Washington Villanueva."

"How do you figure that?" Millie said.

"You ain't never heard of how Filipinos always naming their kids
after great American heroes?" Miguel said. "I gots me an Uncle John
Kennedy Garcia."

Isabel watched her sister, made note of how she hardly said a word. The kids were themselves, talking nonsense, making little jokes that Millie didn't seem to get. Lourdes said nothing the whole time. She watched Isabel, then shifted her attention to Millie, as if she were looking for a sign or something, a lesson to be learned. Finally, she said, "So you grew up with Ate Isabel?"

"Sure did," Millie said.

"Was she cool?"

"I'd say bossy most of the time, all right the rest of it."

Isa rose up to get some ice, some coke to heat up steaming buns of siopao filled with chicken and pork adobo.

"Want some help?" JoJo asked.

"Uh," she whispered. Felt her face going hot. "Yeah, sure, why not."

Inside, she kept her distance, brushing her palms against her sweats, stepping around him.

She hadn't really talked to him since she'd had that dream. The dream that visited her now at least a few nights a week. The dream that had kept Elliot on the couch, patiently waiting for her to get over it, whatever it was. She could only look at JoJo when his back was turned, at the way his hair trailed onto his shoulders, loose like a hippie boy's. She sneaked a peek at the curve of his jeans, and instantly an image from the dream—the texture of flesh, of tendons and muscle—came to mind. Shit, she thought as she scooted to the other side of the room. He followed her, said, "What can I do to help?" He was an echo away from her, shadow-boxing in her tiny kitchen. They danced about one another, and for a moment their hips brushed softly. She excused herself. Apologized for the tiny quarters. "Tsall good," he said, smiling. "No worry."

She glanced out the window and saw her sister sitting among the kids. The figures were small against the expanse of the beach, looked tiny under the smoky sky of winter's end. She imagined their faces shining, that they were getting to know her little sister, their bodies leaning into one another.

"You know I've been meaning to talk to you about Ferdi," Isa said. She reached into the pantry to grab some paper plates and, as she did, JoJo nuzzled at the base of her neck, kissed her there. Isabel breathed deep, savored this moment, felt everything was in its place.

"Forget Ferdi," he whispered into her ear.

"Well," she said, breathing deep, "maybe for now. But we have to talk."

Then, gathering plates and napkins in her arms, she said, "We better make sure we have plastic spoons or something."

JoJo pulled her back. She felt uncomfortable, because she liked the weight of his hands pressing her hips, fitted to her bones just so, because she would rather have stayed frozen just like that than join the group again. "They're cool," he told her. "They can eat kamayan style."

"Kamayan?" she asked, as he leaned in to kiss her, biting the bottom of her lip.

"With your hands. Kamayan. Besides, it's siopao. Who uses silverware with siopao? What kind of Pinay are you?"

"Okay, then," she told him, pulling herself away. "You carry the cooler with the food and we won't use spoons and forks." Still clinging to the plates and napkins, she used her free hand to pack the cooler. She wrapped her hands around the hot buns, felt the steam rising from white dough. The fragrance of sweet bread and soy sauce reminded her she was hungry. Her hands moved quickly, before he could kiss her again. The napkins fell like bunches of leaves.

"What's the matter?" he asked her. "Why you scared?"

"I'm not," she told him. "It's just they're out there and we're here and they're waiting for their merienda. Plus," she said, as he kissed her again, "my sister's out there."

He laughed, picking up the cooler, giving in. "Oh yeah," he told her, "no doubt, sister: you're Pinay." With his free arm, he pulled her body next to his, held her for a long long moment. He studied her face, and for the first time she felt calm. And then he whispered not to worry, that this was just the start cuz every Sunday he went to God's house and kneeled down and then he saw her—the shape of her hands pressed together like a beautiful brown tower, the lilt of her mouth as she prayed, and this sight made him talk to God, made him bow his head, made him whisper all his dreams out loud.

Barbecue at Mark and Isabel's Coach House. Chicago, IL. September 1985.
Photo by Millie

Ate Isa and her boyfriend Mark are rolling on the grass in their courtyard. Her brother's three-year-old son, Max, is tumbling out of nowhere, ready to attack. Millie crouches low to the ground. She can smell fresh-cut grass. The sun falls on their shoulders and catches their mouths wide open.

"Look here!" Millie shouts. "You guys are so cute. Max could be your boy!"

Behind them, she can see the legs of the rest of the family—high tops, sandals, golf shoes—kicking up into the air like the fourth of July. The smoke from the grill has seeped into everyone's clothing and they all smell like roasted pig and corn.

Later that night, when the sisters were alone, she confessed that JoJo kissed her.

"God," Millie said. "What did you do?"

"Kissed him back."

"Why?"

The look on Millie's face told her how little she cared for JoJo. "Don't you think he's cute?"

"He's nothing like you," Millie said. "And what about your boyfriend?"

"He's not my boyfriend."

"Elliot's not your boyfriend?" Millie said.

"Not really," Isabel confided. "Not for a long time." And here she stopped because she knew that Elliot was good, was kind. Besides, he looked so much like beach movie Elvis—why wouldn't he be her boyfriend? "Change the subject," she told her sister.

"I saw Mark again. He's still asking about you. Why don't you call him?"

"Change the subject."

"But he was your best one—not as funny as Elliot, and not as skuzzy as JoJo."

Isabel threw her a look, stopped her from going on.

Millie nodded. "Okay," she said, "and what's with your kids?"

Isabel brushed past her, gathering sections of the morning paper, stacking them on countertops and windowsills. "What about them?"

"Why do those kids talk like they're black?" Millie asked.

Isabel picked up an empty glass. "What?" she said.

"Like they're black. Your students talk like homeboys—

Supwitdatshit?" Millie said, mocking them. "It's like if someone didn't tell me they were Filipino, I'd think they were black."

"Change the subject."

"Fine," said Millie. She shut her textbook and smiled. "Come home."

"Yeah, right."

"No, really. Come home. What the hell are you doing anyway?" Millie put the book to one side and told her sister just what she was thinking. "Look at yourself," she said. "Look what you're doing. Kissing scruffy men when you have a perfectly good boyfriend, crowning teen queens, hiding from crazed bullies, talking like a black girl." This was not her sister, this was not her. "What's keeping you here? It isn't your boyfriend. I'm sorry. It isn't Elliot, the guy who's not your boyfriend."

Isabel left the room, pulling dishes into the kitchen sink, running water, boiling green tea in the kettle. But Millie continued like a radio announcer with her very own talk show. "You know," Isa yelled out to her, "this whole time I thought you missed me and wanted to come hang out, but Mom and Dad sent you here, didn't they?" She felt so ganged up on.

"Mom and Dad are worried!" Millie shouted from the next room. "The guy attacked you and you haven't called the police, you haven't said anything to anyone. He's sneaking around town and he knows he's got you."

"He does not have me," Isabel said. She leaned over the countertop, reaching for her boom box. She cranked hip-hop. "He won't do it again."

"How do you know?" Millie said. She leaned into the kitchen. The light hitting her from the living room cast her petite frame against the walls, where she was long and black, a shadow filling up the entire bungalow. When did her sister grow so old?

"I'm your ate," Isabel said, finally pulling rank. "I know. Now leave me the fuck alone." Isabel turned away, and she felt Millie stop. She felt her sister watching, but continued to scrub the dishes, to bathe each glass under hot water. She was thinking of the girls, of Arturo and Maya, of the ones she'd never met, how hard it was to open them up, to get them to see her, to begin. She was thinking of JoJo. She was thinking of that kiss.

"What's it matter?" Millie said. "Let someone else do it."

She was thinking of Ferdi, his hot breath on her, his accusations pricking at her skin like a thousand needles. His actions were out of control, but the words—the words had stayed with her, and some days she questioned her choices, her ways, her very identity on account of those words. Some Filipinos were white.

The house filled with so much noise. The rattle of MC Any Boy crashed one word into the other, struck uneven rhyme. Shriek shriek zippity zip, toom toom now, toom toom now. Noise scratched the air— toom toom now—divided her thoughts—toom toom now—comforted her, made her think of Arturo and that beautiful tattoo dancing on his brown skin. Her dad was right about one thing: you couldn't depend on community to support you the way you could in the Philippines. Well, she thought, maybe we are Americans, but we're Filipino too and I am not going to let you down, Arturo. Promise.

"You think you're so smart!" she yelled to her sister. "You don't remember." She was thinking of the nights in Boone when doctors from so many countries took up the rooms in their house. Late-night meetings and strategy planning, pamphlets and speeches—grown-ups talking loud, and Daddy standing in the middle of the room, his arms waving in the air, pointing at imaginary bad guys. "In America," she could hear him telling everyone, "we have rights. We can speak up and fight. This is what opportunity is about, this is what this country is about." Millie was still sucking formula from a bottle at the time, but Isa dreamed of those nights even now, heard the debating in her sleep. She knew she would never walk away. How could she?

In the other room, Millie slammed drawers, banged books, spun like a small tornado. Isa stood at the door, watching her turn over pillows on the sofa and reach her hand under side tables and bookcases.

"What are you doing?"

"I lost my gold pen." Millie whirled around the room, fingers spread wide open.

"What gold pen?"

"The one I got for graduation—you know, for being valedictorian?

"Do you have to trash the house?"

"Where is it, Ate Isa?"

"Did you look in your book bag?"

Millie stopped turning around and stared at her. "What do you think? The last time I used it I was on the beach, but I thought I put it in here."

Millie dragged her sister out the back door and to the spot where they had been hanging out with the kids. The wind was blowing hard, making their hair fly up. They had to shout at one another. "I already looked here, and nothing." The sun had left them all alone, and the grass and the sand appeared to them in versions of gray.

"I don't know," Isabel said. "Does it really matter? It's just a pen." She knew it mattered a lot. That pen was all about Millie's grades and her grades were all about med school and med school was all about Mom and Dad.

"Why are you such a bitch?"

"It's just a pen."

"I was right here—and then those little gangbangers of yours came over—"

"Watch it."

"Well, they are, and remember they were all this is bourgei this and that is bourgei that and the little one with the shaved head said, 'Check it, she even writes in gold.'" Millie walked in a circle, her head down and her hair whipping across her face. She held the strands down with her hand, bent close to the earth. "I wonder if that hoodlum took it."

"I can't believe you just said that." Isabel pulled Millie by the shoulder.

"What? Like that's not a possibility? They have guns, they break into your house, why wouldn't they lift a gold pen?"

Isabel got so angry she left Millie standing by the seashore, digging in the sand. Sometimes she wondered how she and her sister could have been raised together. Millie was so closed-minded and arrogant. How dare she accuse Edison of such a thing?

Hours later, Isabel sat on the sofa, flipping through channels, the remote in her hand. Millie slid open the patio door and a gust of wind hissed through the living room. Isa dropped the remote into a crack in the cushions. When she pulled it out, the gold pen came with it. "Ah, is this what you're looking for?" She held up a thick ballpoint pen with an ornate cap. The light from the television hit the pen and made the lettering difficult to read: Camila Francisca Manalo, Class of 1988. "Man, how do you write with this? It's like a cigar."

Millie stormed over and yanked the pen from her hand. "Yeah, that's it."

"You don't even know about these kids," Isa said. "You haven't even given them a chance."

"To what?"

Isabel pulled out the notebook that carried the girls' Polaroids—the negatives, too, and the words scribbled on lines of loose-leaf paper. Some of the pages were tear-stained and wrinkled. She wanted Millie to see what she saw, how the girls felt about themselves, small and voiceless, ordered around. The world looked at them, their skinny bodies and their baby faces, and either they saw children or they saw thugs. And in the girls' own mind's eye, the world hated them and so they struck back, strutting around like they owned the world, kicking ass and claiming territory that belonged to no one.

"This girl," Isabel said, pointing to a photo of Ria, "was kicked out of her school in Norfolk because the principal insisted she and her brother were gang members."

Ria had written her entry in tiny letters, perfect figures of art all aligned in one long sentence: "The world is scared a me cuz I am brown and I walk around with an 'attitude.' Hell, what am I suppose to do—cry like a baby—like I already given up without trying—well hells no I am not going down without a fight. Cuz this is my life."

Angel said her parents gave her the name because they expected her to act like one for the rest of her life. No matter how old she was getting, they were still acting like she was too young to understand anything. She wasn't allowed to date, to drive, not even to babysit outside of her own family. "What kind of life is that," she wrote. "I got all these things turning inside me and they want me to pretend I'm still ten years old. How you think that makes me feel?"

What Isabel wanted to do was remind Millie of her own days as a dalaga. "Don't you see?" she whispered. "It's all the same, just a little edgier now." There were always three girls inside of you, she told her sister: there was the girl they thought you were, the girl they wanted you to be, and there was the real you. It seemed to Isabel that everyone had been through it, but just as soon as people made it through that in-between, three-faces-of-Eve stage, people forgot. Even pretended it never happened. But Isa finally understood, because she was still in-between herself. There was the way the community saw her—a role model, a Pinay, a responsible adult. There was the way the kids saw her—a whitie in brown skin. And there was the other Isa, the one she had not yet figured out.

After awhile, Isabel felt her sister's shadow recede into the living room, felt the pages of Millie's textbook fall open to a diagram of a heart—fat, yellow, rubbed in butter and choking.

SEVENTEEN

Isabel sent articles about overseas contract workers home with the teens—clippings on women who had moved from their provinces in Luzon, the Visayas and Mindanao to go abroad to Saudi Arabia, Greece, and Egypt. The women left their families living in houses without electricity, sleeping on dirt floors and eating bowls of rice, fish eggs, and greens harvested from muddy riverbanks. They had dreams of earning enough to feed their babies, to fix their houses and care for their elders.

The women were not much older than the VA Beach teens. Their faces were plain—no lipstick, no eyeliner. No phat haircut. They had long ponytails and slender faces. Full lips. Flat noses. The women looked like any of their relatives from the Pinas.

"What would make a girl leave everything like that?" Isabel asked them. They were sitting on the grass just outside the lunchroom. The Virginia Beach sun was hot but the air that blew their hair about was cold and unfriendly.

"Maybe her life sucks," Lourdes said, pulling a weed from the ground and twisting it.

"Maybe yours," Elvie said, laughing. He high-fived Miguel.

Maya sorted through the articles, holding the newsprint up to the sun. She squinted and said, "Naw, says that they needed the jobs. They needed to get something on the table for their kids."

"Yeah," Miguel said, "they needed that dough."

"But that's so far away," Isabel said. "Why not just go to Manila? Why go to Egypt?" She scanned the circle to see if anyone was listening. A bus crawled past, spewing fumes of oil and dirt.

"Ain't no jobs in Manila either," answered Edison. "Ain't no jobs anywhere."

"Thas why my daddy got on a boat," Derek says. "Thas why we here. To work. My daddy left for ten years, cooking on ships, and then he sent for us."

"But your daddy is no maid," Mercedes said. "In the Pinas, my dad is a doctor, but here he's a nurse."

"Right," Isabel said. "These women are maids and cooks and entertainment girls."

"You mean hookers."

"She mean Japayuki."

"My tita left our barrio outside of Tacloban to be a singer in Japan," Derek said. "Then she sends money to my cousins and her husband. And now they get new threads and go to school and even got a car."

"You sure thas all she doing? Singing?" Lourdes asked. She smiled and then peered at him from underneath curly strands of bleached hair.

He made a fist and punched the air. "You talking about my tita."

"Okay," Isabel said. "Don't listen to her. She must not have had enough to eat today." She turned to Maya and waited. "Maya, what are you thinking?"

"Kuya JoJo says the Greek dictionary says the word Filipina means maid," Miguel said. "That messed up or what?"

Maya held the paper up and watched the sun stream through the newsprint. "Nothing. Just that they say there are thousands of women coming back to the islands every day in pine boxes. Thousands. How they dying like that? Why?"

Isabel didn't answer immediately, but watched the kids—their eyes half-closed and their bodies kicking back on the lawn. They leaned a head on a belly, an arm on a leg, a leg on a leg like they were pillows supporting one another. "Well, the truth is," she said, "many of the women go overseas thinking they are going to be maids or singers or dancers, but well, look at Flor Contemplacion."

"Awe, that sucked," Angel said. "Her boss raping her like that and she just watching out for herself, stabs him and now they hang her like that."

"So they get there, right? And they're ready to work and then they're forced to have sex with their bosses or to service their clients in ways they'd rather not."

"Ain't right." Miguel said. He stretched his body to the ground, crossed his legs, settled his head in the cradle of his arms. He sighed.

"And then because they've given their passports to their bosses, and their bosses hold their money, they can't leave. They can't go home."

"So what happens to them?" Ria asked.

The wind rushed through their circle and Isabel held her hands to her eyes, blocking the dirt that was flying at her. She waited until the air was still and when she looked at the kids again, Maya had laid her head in Angel's lap and was crying. Angel placed her hand on the girl's shoulder, and shook her. "Man, you always iyak-iyak. Get a grip, Maya. It's just a story." The wind blew again and this time it howled.

Isa woke up ready for a fight. Maybe Millie was right. She wasn't doing a good job of handling the situation at all. What kind of feminist is silenced by brute force, by intimidation, by some weird desire to be accepted? What made Ferdi's little club so cool anyway?

The idea of it zipped around her head and bumped into things she was trying to do. Zppt. Zppt. Zppt. And the silence she emitted cloyed at her like a sheet of Saran wrap. Was she acting like a modern-day Suzie Wong? A low-profile Mata Hari? What next, bound feet? Was this not the nineties? What would her girls think if they knew? What if they suspected, after all the talk about inner beauty and strength—about the importance of the voice—that some bully was stalking her in the name of Filipino History—what up with dat? Millie was right in a left-field way. This was not good form.

She marched into the Community Center, knowing that on Senior Sunday the elders would come together and Ferdi would be there, nursing them. Mahjong tiles clicked. Poker chips rattled like bowls of uncooked rice. She made mano to several of the elders as she walked through the space, lifting hands up to her forehead one at a time, kissing the soft cheeks of little old ladies. She scanned the center, armed, ready to get into it. He was nowhere. He was late.

She sat down on a couch. She waited. Lola Espie wheeled her chair up next to her, ran her hands through Isa's long hair.

"Naku!" the old woman said. "When I was a girl like you, before the war, my hair was like this. Blacker, even."

"Really, Lola? How old were you?"

"Maybe fifteen."

"How old were you when you came to America?"

"Almost thirty. I arrived with five children ages ano—five to ten years—and I got to my darling beloved's address where he sent us the money from and do you know what I found?" She leaned in and whispered the next part. "Another missus—another lady in my house with two children. Can you imagine? 'What's dis?' I said. 'This isn't China—it's America. One wife only.'"

Isabel shook her head. "What did you do? What happened? How did you do it?"

"He was handsome but lazy, anyway," she said. "I left him. I took our children and I moved from San Francisco to Virginia Beach."

Somebody yelled, "Pong!" and then the sound of tiles mixing rattled the air. "You going to play mahjong?" Lola Espie asked. "Marunong ka?"

Lola Espie's eyebrows were penciled in like giant question marks. She smelled of rose water. "I don't know how to play, Lola."

"Ay. Wait for Ferdi. He's so good with you kids. He will teach you."

"I'm sure, Lola," Isa said, patting her hand.

It was then that the tenor of the room changed as the kids came lumbering into the Center, approaching all the lolas and lolos, placing the tips of their fingers to the tops of old heads. Miguel, Angel, Derek, Maya and some of the others in their baggy old pants and spiky hairdos blessed themselves as they entered the room. Ferdi shepherded them in, calling, "Halloooo, halloooo lolas, lolos. Halloooo. Nandito kami!"

The kids scattered like dandelion puffs among the tables and couches, joining the elders in a game of mahjong, poker or dominoes. They rolled out coins and bet five centavos here, twenty centavos there. Several of them kissed Isa hello, or patted her on the shoulder. They filled the glasses with ice-cold lemonade, and Edison pulled out his guitar while Ria and Lourdes sang love songs in the mother tongue.

234

"Naku," Lola Espie cried, "here is our Magkasama. Saan si JoJo?"

"Sa bahay, Lola," Ferdi answered. "May sakit ang ina niya."

"Mabait si JoJo," Lola Espie said. "Talaga. He takes care of his family so good after his daddy passed away."

Isa smiled at Lola Espie, nodding her head like she understood the old woman. She thought the words sounded like chimes teetering in the wind like stars; the syllables sang in familiar rhythms now, not so foreign, but still she was clueless. Rising, she excused herself in search of Ferdi. She found him pouring glasses from a pitcher of lemonade. She found him wiping his brow as if he'd been at it all day long. And just as she was about to give it to him, to say what she had kept inside for so long, she heard an old man's voice, crying.

"Okay," Ferdi was saying as he poured the juice. "Okay, Lolo."

The old man rattled a story in words that ran together like rain. Something sad and gray washed the old man's voice. Isabel saw the look on his face, and the way his eyes came together like a heavy sigh. Ferdi put the pitcher down and reached for the lolo, patting his back and rubbing the old one's tired arm.

Isa stood there, watching. Pissed off that he could be so compassionate and at the same time crazed. This couldn't go on anymore. She couldn't let it. She smiled tersely at Ferdi when he looked her way, then she marched back out of the Center—blocking out the scene, making up her mind. He would have to stop.

This Ferdi guy had the whole community fooled, and that wasn't such a big deal. But the phone calls made her feel powerless, and the sight of his compassion scared her. Maybe he was too much of a zealot. That's all it was, but it had given her bruises, and worse than that, his messages haunted her. Ghosts were easier to live with than this.

Her natural tendency was to stay quiet, was to dream that her silence would wish him away. Her natural tendency was not to draw attention to herself, for fear of humiliating her family in front of the community.

When Isa lost her baby, she was afraid to tell her father and mother, because telling them would mean admitting that she and Mark were having sex. And admitting that would mean she was disgracing the family. And disgracing the family would put them in jeopardy. At least in their tiny community. So she held it like a child holding her breath and she turned blue. Nearly expired from keeping it lodged inside her with nowhere to go.

Millie said she was stupid for caring about what other people thought. Didn't mother say it all the time—who cares? But Isa knew her mother cared. Her father cared. Isa cared. Someone was always watching. How could you not care?

Had she spoken up, she might have had support, maybe even the sympathy of some of the women in her community. And she saw herself doing it again. If she brought Ferdi up on charges, then everyone would know that he had attacked her and that she let him.

Would anyone believe her? She doubted it. She stood at her car door, fumbling with her keys when she heard him walking up behind her.

"One of the aunties is very concerned, Isa. She's upset cuz she says you're telling the kids our Filipinas are all hookers and maids. Her daughter came home wigged out cuz her aunties abroad are supposedly in trouble. You better watch it, Isabel Manalo."

"That is not what I said." She took a step toward him. "It's more complicated than that."

He grinned at her, his nostrils flaring out with every breath he took. He was so sure of himself, so cocky. "What are you doing, anyways?"

And that was all it took. Isabel's heart contracted so tight she could not breathe and she remembered the point of her visit. She drove down to the police station and invited Macmillan and Smith out for donuts. She wanted to do this discreetly. Behind a counter of coffee and a dusting of sugar, she shared the event and asked them what to do. "The community will hate me," she said.

"You could file charges," Macmillan said. "He could go to trial."

"File a restraining order," Smith said. "That's like a last warning."

Isa nodded her head. That's it, she thought. He'll get a last warning, not just from me, but from the city as well. And he would understand, once and for all, that she meant business. Stay away. Leave me alone. Let me live my life.

EIGHTEEN

The crate they built nearly filled up the alcove. They painted the wood purple. They stenciled mermaids spinning in circles, floating and dreaming along the sides of the dalaga boat. Each girl signed the box with black lettering, and the Alibata sign for Pinay was carved into the wood. A layer of shellac was washed over the paint so that the crate shined. Inside, they layered the whole thing in plastic to keep the water out. Over the plastic, the girls pasted daisy wallpaper. Pictures of Denzel Washington, Bruce Lee, and Jackie Chan hung on tiny hooks, along with framed pages from Flip zines: the Pinay band from San Fran, a crazy Flip comic who joked on manongs, lumpia and the Pilipino way, and a black and white drawing of Gabriela Silang, Ilocano warrior.

"Kuya JoJo says she's the shit," Maya said. "When her old man went down, Gabriela led the troops against the oppressors."

"Just like we gonna roll against the oppressors," Lourdes sang.

They planted an old rug onto the floor and Angel piled throw pillows in a corner. To get in, the girls had to climb.

"We should have made a door," Ria said. "We should have made a roof."

"What we gonna do here?" Marilena asked.

"Jam."

"Hang with the boyz."

"Tell the world to fuck off."

"Sail to the Pinas," Lourdes said.

"This is dope," Marilena said. She leaned into a mirror, and coated her lips in red lip shine. "Damn, dis is hellacool."

Isa couldn't breathe. The night of the pageant finally arrived. She slipped off her shoes and tucked them behind the fence of her backyard. The sand felt cool and damp against her feet, slid smooth between her toes. She strolled in and out of the water's edge, through pockets of brine. Her toes dug into the sand. She longed to stay there all night, walking along the shore, contemplating the tumult of the sea. Tonight, under the white moon, the water was black as a starless sky. She heard the caw of sea birds circling overhead, and she thought about how the pageant had bullied its way into her life, filling up her days in ways she never expected. This better be the answer, she thought. She'd become initiated into the Fil-Am community of Tidewater by pushing sequins and crowns at her students, hoping to get in, closer to the girls, trusted by their parents. But she felt distant as the moon. Unsure. A sellout.

The night before, she'd dreamed a beauty contest in which beauty was incidental, and who you knew got you crowns and popularity. The event took place in a boxing ring, Lourdes in her ball gown, laced up in puffy white fighting gloves, and Ria in a low-back evening gown, punching and jabbing, darting at air. The house rooted with their fists aloft, encouraging the girls to knock themselves out.

The image of the girls in the ring reminded Isa again that inside every dalaga were three girls—the one the world saw, the one they wanted her to be, and the one she was. Isabel wanted to invite the real dalaga out, wanted her to stand on two feet and say her name out loud. But she knew it would never happen unless they trusted her, thought she was one of them. This battle was something she was still in the midst of.

At the Cultural Center, the girls scurried about backstage, oiling their teeth with petroleum jelly.

"To help with the smiling," Tita Nita had explained in rehearsal. "Otherwise everything sticks to the mouth."

When Isabel walked through the stage door, Tita Nita grabbed her by the arm and dragged her to a vanity, its mirror all lit up, and with tubes of lipstick, brushes, and foundation cluttering its surface. "Thanks God we got you, hija," she said, sitting Isa in front of the dresser. "The make-up artist is sick. So you gotta do it."

"Do what?"

"Make-up, on the girls. You know how, di ba?"

Isa grabbed her water bottle from her purse and took a long gulp. "I can't do this, Tita."

"But you have to—we need you."

"The thing is, I don't think the girls need all this to show their beauty. I just don't feel right." She crossed her arms and looked down at her shoes.

"Naku! Whoever heard of a beauty pageant without make-up? Anyhow, dis is not about you, it's about the dalagas and how you promised to help. Why you always gotta contradict?"

In the looking glass, Isa gazed at the image of Tita Nita. Her eyebrows, drawn big and black, rose up like threats. She blinked, and shiny blue and silver eyelids winked warnings at Isabel. She wore huge caterpillar lashes, and when she fluttered her eyes they drew like curtains on her face. "I don't have time for your kontrabida ways. You gotta help us out. Just look at how I put this on," she said. She picked up a tin of foundation and spread it over Isa's cheeks. "Ganito," she said. "Make sure you cover up the face completely. Tapos, you take this powder, ganon." She sprinkled it on and patted Isa with a giant cotton ball. "Then the blush—make sure there's plenty because the lights are gonna wash out the color." She picked a brush and dabbed at Isa's face, powdered it, lined it, colored in between the lines. Isa wanted to sneeze, wanted to scratch the gook off her face. "Naku!" said Tita Nita. "You are a natural, anak. You could be a contestant too."

She left Isa sitting in a high-back chair, a clown in make-up. Isabel saw a monster in a horror flick. Her eyes popped at her like the undead's. She erased her image with a bottle of cold cream. In the bathroom, she ran hot water over her face, and took a long moment to rub it dry with a thick white towel. At the make-up chair, she pulled her hair back into a ponytail, her face now clean and soft. Then, rolling up her sleeves, she stood and looked around. "Ria," she said. "You first. Comere."

She held a thin brush up to Ria's eyelid, painted a black line, thin and crooked.

"Sit still," Isa whispered. "I might poke you in the eye."

"You're really bad at this," Ria told her.

"Thanks. Maybe if you stopped blinking we'd get somewhere."

"Were you in a pageant?" Ria smelled like strawberry bubblegum.

"Nope."

"They didn't have them in Illinois?"

"Oh yes, they did, but I never got into it."

"Your parents didn't make you?"

Isabel took a step away from Ria. "Look at me. I gotta make sure you're even." The two gazed into one another's eyes and Isa saw her reflection shining in Ria's pupils. Of course her parents didn't make her do anything. They suggested a million things, but they were not the kind that forced her or her siblings to do anything. Ria's eye began to twitch, and then the right lashes flickered and spotted her cheeks with black mascara. "Ria!" Isa took hold of her chin and tilted it to the light. "Look what you've done!"

In between the segments, little girls ran out on stage to hula in a circle, or dance with candles burning in their bandanas. They were wannabe contestants, itching for the stage.

Isa painted her girls, dotted them in pinks and blues using black sable brushes. She streaked rouge across their cheeks and then softened the lines with powder puffs that lightened their brown skin, making them sallow and dry. She made them up like giant dollies in a factory, pasting fake eyelashes on their lids and coloring their eyebrows dark. She did it for the lights; she did it so that out there they would appear beautiful from far away, natural beauties with round eyes—not almond, not squinty, not half-closed but wide-eyed like white girls with big hair.

Tita Nita, wrapped in red sequins and matching feather boa, stood on stage and chatted at the audience. Her voice filled the auditorium and reverberated in Isa's head like a fly buzzing in the night.

Isa focused on each face, looked into the eyes and saw light. From a distance, the girls were cool and polished. Their hair had been sprayed so thick with aerosol that nothing moved. Little spikes of hair pricked their skin like rose thorns. Up close, she felt them breathing on her. The breath was shallow, fast, irregular. Hands trembled. There was a lot of twitching going on, a little tremor of the heart emanating from the make-up chair. Isa tried to calm them, told them not to think about winning or being beautiful. "You've already won," she said. "You've been beautiful since birth. This is just pretend."

"Pretend what?"

"Pretend life. None of this is real."

They rolled their eyes at her, they giggled. They didn't act tough at all. Their walls tumbled down around their evening gowns. "Do I look okay?" they wanted to know.

Lourdes wouldn't talk to her—and guilt rose to the surface, in the heat, in the look of the eye, in the silence. Isabel held Lourdes's face in one hand and examined her flawless skin in the light. She bent down low to retouch the lipstick. The mouth quivered. The lips bled paint at the corners.

"Hold still," Isa said.

"Fuck you." Lourdes pulled away from her.

"What?"

"Never mind," Lourdes said, grabbing the lipstick and brush from Isa's hands. She leapt off the director's chair and, stomping away, said, "I'll do it myself."

Isabel closed her eyes and focused on her breath. She saw herself, a teenager, screaming at the top of her lungs, her hands folded into fists, pounding at her father's desk. "You say you love me, then you walk away! You say you hear me, but you don't stop long enough to listen! You say you know how I feel and then you embarrass me!" Her father got up and walked out of the room, leaving her there to calm down, to breathe, to focus all by herself.

During the promenade, Tita Nita told the girls to "come forward and give the audience and judges a chance to view you." The homegirls wore their hair teased up and pulled back out of their eyes, perhaps thrown into a faux bun, coifed in wild anticipation of that crown. Though Isabel hated to admit it, they were all beautiful. Even reluctant Maya shimmered. Their bodies slinked around in bright Las Vegas gowns, the kind with slits that traveled from the ankle to the hip, and miniature rhinestones crisscrossed their backs. Despite the weeks of grousing and feet-dragging, the beauties graced the stage, professional in their attitude, smiling.

They faced the audience, quivering as if they were about to cry. "Turn," commanded Tita Nita. The line turned one quarter away from the audience, revealing the homegirls' profiles.

Something inside Isa—a worm, a stone, a rotten apple—upset her stomach. She covered her eyes with her long fingers. I can't watch, she told herself. She felt as if she'd sold her soul and Tita Nita was the devil's mistress. And the girls? What else but fallen angels? Of course there'd been reason to rebel.

They stood there for maybe ten seconds, which was a long time when you were being studied for your nose, your posture, the shape of you—a long time when others were judging the shell your spirit lived in. She wanted the girls to run off stage, flip the judges the bird. Then Tita Nita told them, "Turn," and they did, this time with their bums to the audience. The hall was silent, the audience checking out each ass on stage, marking cards, grading their daughters' beauty.

Behind her, she smelled JoJo's sandalwood and musk. She felt her face flush. She felt him moving closer.

"You better be right," she told him. "This better not be a mistake."

"Hell, yeah," he said. "You're closer to the girls, di ba?"

"It's not right. I feel like shit."

When Tita Nita asked them to turn one last time to give their other profile, Lourdes, who was standing at the end of the line, skinny and sixteen years old, lost her balance, slipped and fell into the girl who stood next to her. The audience gasped.

Backstage, JoJo's warm hands slipped around Isabel's tummy, explored the skin just underneath the hem of her baby-T. She held her breath and whispered, "Stop it."

"Really?"

"Yeah," she said, sighing, "someone's going to see."

"So what? Who cares?"

She hated that he could make her do almost anything. He was so cocky, and still he had this way about him. Didn't he suggest she work on this pageant? She disappointed her parents when she refused to don an evening gown and croon songs with her gut-string guitar. She said it was objectification. She said it was sexist. She said it was archaic. And somehow JoJo talked her into being the assistant director. She felt like such a hypocrite. He had kissed her once when no one was looking, and now he was copping feels backstage and all she could do was sigh. She peeked around the black curtain, searching for Elliot, like finding him would set her straight. Keep her out of mischief. He was leaning on the back wall of the auditorium, watching the show.

She moved away from JoJo. "Does it mean anything at all?" she said. "I'm seeing someone."

"Sure it matters," JoJo said. "Just like it matters that when I kissed you the other day, you kissed me back."

She shooed him away when the girls ran back for costume changes. They ran around the small room, pulling off their dresses, stepping out of stockings and flinging them up in the air. The room filled up with shouts delivered in hisses and grunts. Nerves were taut. Pulling her hair out of its long bun, Angel snuck by Isabel and kissed her on the cheek. "Oh shit, Ate," she whispered, "I can't find my shoes!" Isabel turned in a circle, reached under a dressing table and pulled out a pair of spiked sandals. "Ay salamat!" Angel shrieked, kissing her again.

Isa's hands were never still. She pulled hair. She sprayed it. She powdered the shine. She zipped countless dresses. And each act brought a hug, a squeeze of the hand, a kiss. She moved so fast she couldn't think, but she felt all the energy around her swirling and sending her closer to them. She moved among them as if in a dance, leaning over them, walking around them, reaching out a ribbon, a hair clip, a ruby lipstick.

On stage, Ria's sultry voice belted out an old Aretha Franklin tune. "Betta think," she sang as she kicked around on stage in her little black dress. She had the raspy timbre of a smoker. She played the whole stage, marching back and forth, calling out to the dark. Her arms swept across her body and gestured to the crowd. "FREEDOM!" She was bent at the waist, singing to the floor, "FREEDOM!" She stretched her free hand out to God and called out, "FREEDOM!"

Everyone on the right side of the auditorium hooted, hollered, yelled, "Ree-ah! Ree-ah!"

"FREEDOM!" She kicked her leg out, pointed right into the lights, her voice rising up to Isabel, "THINK!"

Isabel's heart swelled big—she had to admit that Ria's voice kicked. She couldn't help feeling proud of her. She scanned the one side of the room where the arms flailed up and waved. The other side remained completely docile.

In the wings, the other contestants jumped up and down, cheering their sista on. On the opposite side of the stage, Lourdes and her mother stood just out of the black curtains, waving their hands at one another, tossing looks of anger to and fro. Lourdes stormed away and her mother raised both hands to the sky and stomped both feet into the stage, the bang of it lost in all the applause. Lourdes turned slowly around and then, walking to the edge of the stage, she waited for the sons of the Filipina American Auxiliary of Hampton Roads to wheel a baby grand piano onto the stage, prop up the lid and exit.

Lourdes strolled out, a curtain of black chiffon trailing her. She bowed to the audience and turned to her mother, who was standing offstage, blowing kisses. A wild smile, stiff and automatic, grew from the corners of Lourdes's mouth. The Ilocanos chanted, "Lou—des Starr! Lou—des Starr! Lou—des Starr!" Lourdes sat on the piano bench, placed her hands on the keys, took a breath and, bowing, attacked the keys with full force.

Her hands chased one another in a fast game of tag. Her fingers trilled notes high like a battery of words. She stopped. Silence. She breathed. She pressed each note slowly, deliberately. Her fingers worked through the trill. A little faster. Stopped. A little faster. Again. "Come on," Isa whispered, "you can do it, you can do it."

Lourdes's fingers rattled back and forth, trying desperately to move the music forward. Finally, she leaned into the microphone and whispered, "Shit, ya'll know I was going to play you this piece an I just can't do it." She grabbed the mic and stood up, stepping away from the piano.

Isa searched for Tita Nita, who was on the other side of the stage, furiously waving her arms at Lourdes.

"But I wanna do something," Lourdes announced. "I wanna do something for you. This is a rhyme that my brothers Arturo and Miguel once wrote."

Tita Nita hissed at her daughter, calling her to stop, but Desa only waved her away with her free hand. Kissing the mic, she began to rap: "Pintig is the beat of the Filipino heart." Her free hand thumped on her sequined chest. "Pintig. Pintig. Pintig." She reached over and tossed a rose from her hair out to the audience. "It's the beat of my Filipina heart." The teens rose to their feet and hurled their hands to the skies. Desa leaned over the mic and gestured with her free hand, her dress glittering under the hot lights. She smiled and revealed a deep dimple.

"Go, Desa!" They chanted. "Go, Desa!"

"It's da primal bang of bamboo rappin' to the off-tune strings of my daddy's mandolin. It's da clap-clap-clappin' of the lolas when we dance."

From the hall, a slow beat rose as the youth pounded their feet and then drummed their fists on thighs. They thumped on their chests, made their heartbeats the backdrop for her slow-moving rhyme.

"It's da bee-bop-boppin' of homies when we rap—It's da pukpukin kita of Nanay's slipper when we bad. It's da magbabarílan poppin' when the crew has all gone mad."

Isabel scanned the audience, held her breath. The parents sat perfectly still as if they too were listening.

"Pintig," Desa sang. "Pintig. Pintig. Can you hear my heart?"

The crowd roared. The parents clapped.

"Filipina heart. Pinay on da beach heart. Homeless unanswered heart."

Desa raised the roof, pumping her hands to the ceiling. Bowing, she ran from the stage. Behind the black curtains her mother was on her, beating her with words, hammering her with accusations. Lourdes faced her mother, looked her in the eye. Didn't budge.

Isabel felt so overwhelmed—exhausted, too, as if she had just been in a battle. She sighed, and when Lourdes walked past, she placed an arm around the girl's shoulders. But Lourdes pushed her away.

Maya stood before Isa, pointing at her own face. "Do you think they'll see my scars?" she asked. "Maybe you should put extra shit on it an shit."

"Not from far away. And anyway, what do you care? These are tiny scars—not as big and beautiful as your heart, sweetie."

"That's nice, Ate Isa, but seriously, I'm not playing around. Coat my face with that shit so you can't see it, okay?"

From behind the curtain, a bare foot peeked out at the crowd, tapping to the rhythm of the mountain bells. Slowly, the curtain revealed a mountain princess dressed in traditional Muslim costume. Maya curled her fingers out, wide like a fan. From the ends of her hand extended a set of long iron fingernails, curling up and out in tiny swirls. She crossed the stage, her head held up and her gaze cast away from the audience. Unlike the others who deferred to the crowds, Maya danced in spite of them. She moved slowly, her arms held away from her body. She was draped in luscious linen—fuchsia and purple, green and blue—all laced with gold fibers. The energy inside her radiated from her limbs. Her curves rolled out like the waves of the sea. She cast away the tsismis that had followed her all this year, the comments from the aunties who felt it necessary to announce to her and everyone around her, "Naku! You're gaining weight." The grace of her steps erased the injuries inflicted by girl crews who scarred their enemies with painted nails. On this night, on this stage, under the ocean's full moon, Maya took on the role of a beautiful Muslim princess, a strong woman, a woman who danced for herself.

The winner would serve as the Filipino-American Ambassador of Tidewater. "What a thrill!" Tita Nita announced, sashaying across the stage. She flipped a red feather boa over her shoulder and winked her false eyelashes at the crowd. "What a moment!"

The finalists trailed back onto stage, holding hands and glancing back and forth at one another. From behind a black curtain, the reigning Miss Virginia Beach waddled onto stage, dragging a four-foot trophy made of green glass, her back a little swayed from the pregnancy.

At center stage, Tita Nita waltzed with her microphone. "Miss Congeniality 1996, winner of selling the most tickets for tonight's raffle," Tita Nita sang, "Lourdes Starr! Way to go, hija!"

Lourdes stepped forward, breaking away from the line of girls. She smiled and waved, her hand stiff and automatic. Miss Virginia Beach-Philippines 1995 placed the trophy at Lourdes's feet, and, taking a sash from around her waist, she draped it over Lourdes. One of the hula dancers brought out a bouquet of red roses and a crown on a velvet pillow. The queen cradled the flowers and handed them to Lourdes, then took the crown and placed it on Lourdes's head.

"And the second runner-up for Miss Virginia Beach-Philippines of

1996 is . . . Marilena Vincente!"

Marilena smiled, but her eyes shut tight and tears began to flow. The pregnant beauty queen pulled a trophy from behind the curtain and placed it at Marilena's feet. Then she hung a silk sash, with a giant number two embroidered near the breasts, around the weepy girl's neck. She placed a tiny tiara on Marilena's head. The crowd cheered in a very distracted way. They were more interested in first runner-up and, of course, the winner.

Isa felt sad for Marilena so she clapped wildly. She put her fingers to her mouth and she whistled. She didn't know what had gotten into her, but she wanted Marilena to hear her, to know she was there.

Finally, Tita Nita called out, "And the first runner-up for Miss Virginia Beach-Philippines 1996 is . . . Ria Pagtama!"

The Bicolanos on the right side of the auditorium booed. Unwilling to accept the call, they stood from their chairs and hissed. Knowing what this meant, the Ilocanos on the other side of the auditorium whistled at the stage. They leapt from their seats, throwing their fists in the air as though someone had pushed a button and ejected everyone on the left side of the hall out of their seats.

Ria stepped into the light and threw her hand up to her face, a fake smile curling at the edge of her lips. "Thank you!" she mouthed to the audience. "Thank you!"

From behind the curtain, Miss Virginia Beach-Philippines 1995 dragged another trophy out, taller than the last, shinier too. Ria's body heaved up and down, a flush of tears smearing mascara across her face. The former beauty queen sashed and crowned her in a perfunctory way.

The three girls stood in a row with Lourdes at center stage. The glass statues surrounded the contestants' feet like a garden of hardware. Bundles of long-stemmed roses spilled from the arms of each girl, a gluttony of red. Miss Virginia Beach-Philippines 1995 slipped a silver sash over Lourdes's head. She threw her arms around the new queen, kissing her on each cheek. "Oh my gosh!" yelled Tita Nita into the microphone. "Oh my gosh! You won, hija! My daughter won! I'm so proud, hija." When the little girl brought the tallest beaded crown out, she curtsied to Lourdes. The ex-queen snapped the beauty queen's second tiara over the first one. Lourdes wobbled a little bit, her head thrown off from the weight of the two crowns. She had to hold her hand up to keep them from falling off.

The girls rushed in a circle around Lourdes, all of them reaching out to pet her or to kiss her. Maya made her way to the reigning queen of the beach, wrapped her heavy arms around Lourdes and held her tight.

Offstage, Isabel closed her eyes. Lourdes looked so uncomfortable weighed down by two crowns, her sashes slipping off her shoulder like bra straps. She was a lopsided queen. It was only when Maya embraced her that Lourdes trembled and tears streaked her flawless skin. Isa heard the boo-hiss-cheer of the crowd. She'd been so busy winning everyone's approval she'd lost of sight of who the girls really were. Las Dalagas were not beauty queens. They were not dangerous gangstas either, and they were not little girls. In that moment, Isa realized she was wrong. She indulged their tantrums, and at the same time she held them down, pinning crowns to their heads and coating them in war paint. She expected things from them they could not deliver.

Caught up in the moment, Isa ran on stage and held out her arms. The beauties embraced her, one and all. They stood under the hot lights, balloons floating everywhere, cameras flashing like a galaxy of stars.

NINETEEN

For six weeks in the heat of summer, Isa continued to teach creative drama during day camp. The kids pantomimed, re-enacted, improvised and delivered new versions of history to one another. One day, she asked them if they knew why Cory Aquino became President of the Philippines and nobody knew. So she pulled out yellow ribbons from her kit, and taught them how to gesture with their hands, how to raise their voices, how to chant, "Laban!"

"What they fighting for?" asked one kid. He twisted the end of his T-shirt and cocked his head to the side like he was challenging her.

"Let me show you," Isa answered and she gathered them on the grass. "Okay!" she yelled to her actors on the playground. "Ready, and action!"

A flight of bikes descended upon the gravel parking lot. Dust flew in giant clouds. Tires slammed into rock. Skidded. Crashed. Pop-a-wheelies rose like horses on their hind legs. A makeshift airplane flew from America to Manila. Cargo? Presidential hopeful, formerly exiled Benigno Aquino. Riders shielded their eyes with sunglasses too big for their cheeky faces. From the center of the cavalcade, a thin boy with curly black hair dismounted and winged open his kickstand. The crowd cheered. He waved at them. He wound his way through bicycles, pushing aside horn-like handlebars and wire baskets with bells. Five boys in dark T-shirts covered him. Bodyguards. Rumor was that Ninoy was so good his presence threatened Marcos.

Across the grass, four girls with toothpick arms and legs bowed, waved big banners reading, "Welcome Home, Ninoy!" and "Justice come Home!" Several of the children chanted, "Ninoy! Ninoy! Ninoy! Ninoy!" In all the confusion of bikes, in the waving of the Philippine flag, nobody saw the bully pulling out his finger-gun, holding it gently to Ninoy's head. Pah-POW-POW! Cory Aquino's husband, Ninoy, spun in circles, grunted, died.

Isabel draped her nephew over her shoulders as she marched her family through a cluster of picnic tables, booths, and stages at Princess Anne Park. She turned occasionally to make sure everyone was keeping up— her mother, her father, brother, sister, Rachel and the kids. She led them around like a mother duck, her head raised up high.

"Where's the stage, Tita Isa?" Kevin asked her. He used his hand to block the sun as he scanned the crowd.

"Sit still," Isa told him. "Stop squirming and I'll take you there."

The fourth of July picnic was payback for all those hours rehearsing beauty, putting it on stage, competing for it. Isa's high school kids were going to perform their rendition of the Spanish-American War. She knew their Independence Day drama might lead to controversy, but wasn't that her job? To open up their minds? To empower the youth with knowledge of their history? Last month, when she sat the kids down and they read alternative versions of the war, the crew got so excited they wanted to start their own revolution.

"Man," Miguel said, waving his hands in the air. "You spose all history is like dis?"

"Like what?" Isabel asked.

"All one-sided and white-sided. How come we never heard this before?"

She shrugged her shoulders and watched their faces move through moods of confusion, light and anger. "Don't just take the answers from one book," she told them. "Ask questions, look for other versions, ask your parents what they know."

Most of the time their dramas were committed in private, their questioning contained and harmless. But today they were going up on stage, and all of Virginia Beach was going to see a new version of the Spanish-American War and she wasn't sure they were ready for it.

The Manalos weaved in and out of the crowd. Two-thousand

Filipino Americans had threaded banners, flags and crêpe paper throughout the trees, clustering into regions and provinces from the Philippines. They gathered picnic tables and benches, loosely forming seven-thousand islands. Provinces marked their territories, hanging yellow signs with magic marker names.

"Damn," her brother said. "Have you ever seen so many Filipinos in one spot?"

"Maybe in the Philippines," her mother answered.

"I wonder if I have town mates here," her father said.

The elders held court at their tables, lolas and lolos, manongs and manangs, waving everyone to eat seven-thousand variations of pansit and adobo. Over spits of hot coal, they roasted lechon, chicken and beef skewered on long poles. The smoke rose to the sky, hot and fragrant.

At the beach, people crowded in a half-moon, each peeking over the next person to catch a glimpse of a ship from the Navy floating out in the bay. A smaller boat carried a crew of men clad in khaki.

"Look," Frank called out to his grandkids. "See that man out there? Why, that's Douglas MacArthur!"

"Who's that?" Lucy asked.

"You don't know anything," Max said. "Does she, Tita Isa?"

"She knows some things."

Isa watched a tall figure in uniform walk to shore. Several soldiers waited their turn, climbing out of the boat and following him. Alongside of the American soldiers were two or three brown men, smaller than the others, smiling widely. Filipinos. Moving through the shallow end of the bay, the general took long cool strides, swinging his arms casually at his side. Every now and then he stopped, put his hand to his hips and huffed on his pipe. Isa recognized the gait of him, the way he sauntered through the water, trying to be tough. At one point, he stepped on a piece of driftwood, slippery with algae. And just as he neared the shore, he slipped. The crowd took a collective breath. The general caught himself before he was completely drenched. He smiled, still chewing on his pipe. Several major news cameras taping the event, dashed off to their stations to broadcast the moment.

"Did he really trip like that?" Max wanted to know.

"Course not, hijo," Camila said. "That was just an accident."

"Well, now," Isabel said, "you never know. MacArthur was human."

"That is so like you," Frankie Boy said. "You always have to start trouble."

"What are you talking about? I'm just saying that it's altogether possible that MacArthur, like you or me or any human, can slip and fall. What's the big deal?"

"That's what I mean," Frankie Boy said. "You're always questioning everything. Can't you just let it alone?"

"What kind of talk is that?" their father said. "What kind of example? You're adults now, remember?"

The family continued to slip through the crowd with their father trailing at the end, camcorder to his eye. Isabel dropped them off at a cluster of tables they called the island of Luzon. "I have to make sure the kids are okay," she told her mom. "I'll see you at the stage."

She made her way to the center of the park, behind the giant gazebo, to the members of Magkasama. Across from them, another stage had been raised. Hemp fans sprawled against the walls, and a tier of mahogany carved thrones awaited the royal court: Miss Virginia Beach-Philippines, Mrs. Virginia Beach-Philippines, Lola Virginia Beach-Philippines, and Little Miss Philippines. Isabel glanced over her shoulder at the empty chairs and felt a pang deep in her belly. Lourdes was not appearing in their show. She had been too busy to attend rehearsals. It seemed royalty had busy schedules, and her agent, Tita Nita, didn't think this gig was a priority. Isabel wondered how Lourdes was doing.

The girls were jumping up and down, tying scarves around their heads, waving their arms in the air like butterflies. The boys paced in circles, grunting. When they saw Isa they all ran to her and gave her kisses on the cheek.

"Sup, Ate?" Elvie mumbled nervously.

"Where were you, Ate?" Mercedes wanted to know.

"Remember," Ria told them. "She got her crew in from Chicago."

"I do. But I'm here now." Isa turned Maya toward her and pulled her chiffon scarf up and around Maya's body. "Did I cut this too short?" she asked. "This should be thrown over your shoulder like Angel's. See?"

"Maya's just more taba than before," Edison said.

252

"Hey," Isa answered, swatting him. "What kind of talk is that?"

"It's all good," Edison said, kissing Maya on the cheek. "Homegirl knows it's nothing but isang mahal."

Isabel shrugged her shoulders at him.

"One love, Ate. One love. Nothing but."

"Right, well, one love and still don't talk like that. It's mean. You guys ready?"

Miguel raised his arms in the air and shouted. "Let's do it!"

She pulled them to her and they draped their arms about one another and bowed their heads. She closed her eyes and let the silence fall over them, felt their bodies slowly rising and falling to the same breath. Together they asked for grace, for gifts, for ways to tell the story with new eyes.

A series of gongs, bells, and cylinders chimed. Edison and Derek strutted the stage, their foreheads wrapped in red bandanas, their torsos bare beneath tropical-print vests. Royal as two Muslim princes, the boys seated themselves before the Kulintang. They held their sticks high above their heads, and began the battle cry. In unison, they stroked the copper drums. And suddenly, the sticks flew and fluttered up and down the gongs like birds scattering among the brush.

Offstage, Isa's heart kept to the beat of the gongs as she watched the faces in the crowd light up. Meanwhile, the other students climbed the stage, their faces white, red or brown. White to indicate U.S. soldiers, red for Spanish church officials, and brown to show the revolutionaries of the Katipunan. Indigenous spirits haunted the drama, slipping on and off the stage, dancing. One of the spirits held a photo of Arturo, dancing it about the stage, holding it up to the hot sun. These ephemeral anitos of the jungle, draped in green and blue chiffon, pointed at minor actions like stolen kisses between foreigners, transactions under church altars, the cry of a dispossessed dancer.

U.S. soldiers marched about, unable to catch the rhythm of the Kulintang. Their black boots smashed against the stage, disrupting the song of the beautiful chimes. They weaved around Spanish friars who were waltzing with Filipino revolutionaries. The red and brown couples spun a passionate tango. In a beat, the priests joined with the Filipino warriors, tightening their grip as they turned, dipped, and dragged the revolutionaries across the sun-drenched stage. Every partner danced cheek to cheek. One Spanish friar danced alone, wielding a gold crucifix stapled to a bamboo stick.

The soldiers tapped the priests on the back. After all, it's a dance, isn't it? They wanted to cut in, but the priests would not relinquish. Here, both friars and soldiers turned to the audience and winked.

Isa scanned the crowd, looking for a reaction, but they seemed too dazed to process all the movements on stage. She looked to the other side of the wings and saw a figure like General MacArthur, sucking on a corncob pipe, rocking on his heels. His uniform was still damp from walking to shore. Elliot hid behind the aviator sunglasses so she couldn't see his eyes, couldn't tell if he was smiling at her or impervious. Since they had broken up weeks ago, he'd sent her notes and little packages of gifts, but she had ignored them all. Couldn't he see she was moving on? She grabbed JoJo's hand as if to show Elliot, see? No turning back. Elliot blew smoke from the pipe.

On stage, a fight ensued, revolutionaries pulling away from friars. Behind the backs of the revolutionaries, soldiers waved madly to the friars, allies smiling big fake smiles. The U.S. soldiers pretended to help the brown brothers, played like they were punching priests into submission. Breaking free from the dance, the revolutionaries threw their fists in the air, pointed to the priests who had fallen onto the stage, their legs and arms still struggling. The battle won, revolutionaries shook hands with soldiers, threw their arms around each other like drunks coming home from a night of brawling.

Sitting at the foot of the stage, the fairy anitos covered their eyes, cried big dramatic tears. They held their hands up to the audience, palms flat against the wind. They shook their fingers no, no, no. Shook their heads no, no, no. Shook their feet in terror. The anito carrying Arturo's image whispered something into the photo, held it to her heart and cried.

The friars rolled to a back corner of the stage, a fist of green bills spilling from their pockets. They squatted behind the dancers, quietly counting their paper bills, stuffing their shirts, their pants, stuffing their socks full of American blood money.

At center stage, revolutionaries danced independently, bending their knees to the gongs, flicking their palms to the sky like birds. They maneuvered their way around the white soldiers, who still marched systematically. Slowly, the soldiers raised their swords, their free hand stretching out, reaching. Then suddenly the soldiers snatched the revolutionaries' wrists, capturing them once and for all. And then the music stopped.

MacArthur strolled onto stage, the brim of his hat low on his forehead. Turning to the crowd, he waved wildly. He saluted the actors, and the dancers, all the red, white and brown masks and fairy nymphs. JoJo pushed her from the other side of the curtains so that she met MacArthur center stage.

He smiled, "I have returned."

"Yes, sir, General. I knew you would," she said. Laughter pealed throughout the grounds.

Back stage, Isabel and JoJo high-fived the members of the cast. Her brother stood next to her, the kids clinging to his knees. Above the craziness she heard him say, "No, Max, I have no idea what that had to do with the fourth of July." Rubbing Max on the forehead, she glanced at the stage across from them, at the court of beauty queens displayed like an exhibit of tropical butterflies. The beauties waved to the audience. Baby Beauty fluttered fake lashes, silver eye shadow glittering and melting at noon. Lourdes waved her thin arms at the crowd, seemed so small. She was drowning in her gown, a traditional Maria Clara woven of pineapple threads, embroidered with delicate sampaguita flowers. Next to her, Wife Beauty bowed to her people, her curves flaring out, sagging heavy with motherhood. Finally, the old grandmother— Matriarch Beauty—posed, a fan flickering fast about her painted wrinkles. Mechanical as dolls, Isabel thought. She caught Lourdes's eye and smiled. She waved. Lourdes looked away, slipped on a pair of dark sunglasses. The contrast between the glasses and the dress displaced her, a bride deserting her groom.

When Tita Nita called for Miss Virginia Beach-Philippines 1996 to step forward, Lourdes rose to her feet and delicately climbed a pedestal adorned with white roses. She looked like a doll popping out of a child's jewelry box. The pedestal rotated as she waved. Plastic doll. The kids turned their heads for a second. Glanced at the teen queen. Then they waved her away.

"Bye bye, Queen a All Dat."

"See ya, Miss Too Good for Crew."

"How come she Miss Philippines when she half white?"

Someone put an arm round Ria, consoled her with, "That could have been you—an thank you no thank you cuz now you have us and the Queen stands alone. Know what I'm sayin'?"

The teens drifted past the royal court, their voices fading as they dismissed Her Royal Highness. Maya trailed behind the crews, holding onto a Pinoy Isabel had never seen before. He was tall and lean, and his hair had been shaved close to his head, which seemed to draw attention to his brown eyes, to his heavy eyebrows. Oversized pants fell loose and lazy down his backside, and Isabel could see his white boxer shorts rising up above them. He must have been three feet taller than Maya. His long limbs were wrapped around her curves like he was holding her together. Isabel wondered who he was and why she'd never seen the two of them like that, why Maya had never mentioned him. Just as she approached the couple, her parents came darting through the crowds.

"Hija, that was beautiful!" her mother said.

"Bravo!" her father said. They embraced her at once and Isabel closed her eyes like she was ten and it was the end of her spring recital. The nephews and nieces yelled at her feet and threw their arms around her too.

Then that voice began to speak. Loud and shrill. The voice worked its way through the many arms and legs that enveloped her. Pried them loose from her. Singled her out. And Tita Nita was there, painted red lips and all. A line of sweat seeped through her beige powder.

"Isabel, dis must be your mom and dad?"

Isabel introduced them quickly to one another; hands were offered to shake and cheeks to kiss. Tita Nita nodded at them like she was the queen.

"We are really delighted to have Isabel with us," Tita Nita sang.

"This is some opportunity," Frank said. "We really are glad for her."

Tita Nita's nose was flared out and wide like the snout of a bull.

"I must apologize for Isabel's show. I know how embarrassing it must be for you. I sympathize."

"Didn't you like it?" Isabel asked. The sun was so hot.

"Too radical," she said. "What will Americans think?"

"We are Americans," Frank said. He took a step toward Tita Nita, his legs thrown in a wide stance.

"Yes, yes, but I mean the other Americans. The real Americans. We should be respectful. Show the beautiful side—not that what-you-call-it."

"But that was beautiful," Camila said. She wore a big smile on her face. It looked painful to Isabel. "All that pageantry, and the magic of the forest spirits guarding the battle."

"Naku, don't you see what the kids are doing there?" Tita Nita hissed. She leaned in and whispered loudly. "Di ba scandalous yan? And on the fourth of July pa!"

"Mrs. Starr," Frank said, "don't you know what today is?"

"Oo nga," Tita Nita agreed. "But you know she is always so kontrabida and sometimes, naku! What is she teaching these kids? What are Americans going to think?"

Her father placed a hand on Tita Nita's shoulder. "My wife and I are very proud of our daughter. When all that trouble happened with the shooting, we wanted her to come home, but she was loyal to you and your kids. You know, every night my wife prays for her. We're worried over there in Chicago, but today she demonstrated how important it is for her to be here. You must be proud too?"

Isa could not believe what she was hearing. Tita Nita's eyebrows collapsed into a straight line. And the more her parents spoke, the taller they appeared. Isa felt her heart expanding, filling up her whole chest, aching with the growth of it all. She had not expected this. Frankie Boy clapped his hands and the children jumped up and down.

Rachel flung her red locks out of her face, picked up Lucy and said. "I'm a 'real' American and I think it's cool."

Tita Nita ran from them then, indignant and scared. No one ever talked to her that way. No one. How dare they.

"Thanks, you guys," Isa said, kissing her parents.

"For what?" Camila said. "We were only speaking the truth."

Later, walking the grounds with her nephews and niece, Isa spied Lourdes backstage, her hair still bundled up into her crown, but the gown gone and replaced with a T-shirt and jeans. Her friends, Marilena and Mercedes, sauntered by and Lourdes called out to them. They sashayed past like she was a ghost. Since the pageant, since all her duties, since her mother made her, she had abandoned her friends. She was too busy being the queen, and Las Dalagas had had enough. Isa wanted to smooth things out for the girls, make everything right, but she knew they had to work it out on their own. So she watched from afar, pulling her nephew up and straddling his legs across her shoulders, pretending not to see.

At dusk, Isa crawled into Frankie Boy's fifteen-passenger van and closed her eyes. She felt her bones settling back into the cushions, each one whispering a sigh of exhaustion. She was so tired and burnt from the sun, she might have fallen asleep despite the noise and the smell of dirtied diapers.

The rest of the Manalos piled in, folding up their arms, legs, and torsos so they could fit into three rows. The children kicked their bare feet at the backs of their seats. They smelled of the sun, of salt and wind, of barbecue and lumpia. Isabel took a long sip from her water bottle and tried to freeze this moment. The day felt like something from her childhood, an afternoon of playing with her siblings, of eating too much food, and watching her parents play the role of superheroes. Would she remember today in another week, she wondered.

Her brother drove through a sea of people, her father seated next to him like the captain advising his son. "Careful, careful, huh? Careful." Six-year-old Max recounted the day like a CNN reporter while his younger siblings were fighting for space. He was trying to talk louder than the adults, who were also all speaking at once. Isabel had to tap her brother on the shoulder when they got on the streets. This was how she directed him to the beach. They were on their way to the Dairy Queen on 22nd Street. One tap meant right, two meant left, pounding on the shoulder meant, "I said turn, I said turn." The music from the speakers added another heartbeat.

Isa leaned forward in her seat, her knees to her chest. On either side of her were her mother and her sister-in-law. Millie was sitting in back with the kids.

"So," Rachel said, "you're dating that guy JoJo now?"

"He's so greasy," Millie said.

"You mean," Isabel said, "he's so not a yuppie."

"I think he's handsome," her mother said.

"I liked Elliot," Millie said. "I like how he played the general today."

"I'm glad you were able to make it, Ma," Isabel said, tapping at Frankie's shoulder.

On the street before them, red and blue flashed down Pacific Avenue. Hot lights flooded against a beat-up Chevy and a man with his legs straddled apart, his hands on the trunk. Two police barked at the man.

"Isn't that—?" Millie said. "That car. That guy." Frankie slowed down and what they saw was Ferdi spread-eagled.

"Slow down, slow down," Isabel said. She tapped her brother on the shoulder. "I said stop."

"What?" he said. "You crazy?"

"STOP."

She crawled over her mom and leapt out of the van, heard nothing but the cop radio spitting orders, destinations, calls for back-up. It was Smith and Macmillan.

"What's going on?" she asked them, looking over her shoulder. She saw her family's faces pressed up against the windows, straining to hear against the rush of the wind and the beating of the tide. Frankie came up behind her, his hands in his pockets.

"Hey, Ms. Manalo," said Smith.

"What are you doing?" she asked.

"There was a robbery. Guy came into the 7-11 and stabbed the clerk."

"He wouldn't do that."

"Well, he fits the description," said Macmillan.

"What?"

"Five-seven, dark-skinned, about 180 pounds," Macmillan said.

"It's okay," Ferdi said. "Just another example of racist America on the fourth of July."

Ferdi hung his head down between his shoulders, and Isa knew that this was the revenge she had been dreaming of. But he looked so pathetic. He was guilty of trying too hard, of pushing himself onto people, but she knew he'd never rob a convenience store. What for? She called Macmillan to her, away from the lights and the car, away from her brother and Ferdi. Why would he do this, she wanted to know. He's a caretaker, she reminded him, a geriatric nurse.

"Didn't he hurt you?" Macmillan asked.

"Oh come on," Isa said, pleading. "That was different."

"How exactly is that different?" Macmillan wanted to know.

"The circumstances."

Smith shoved Ferdi's legs farther apart.

The lights on the street created a false daylight. She felt like she was in a house of mirrors, of distortions. Cars on the boulevard honked as they passed. Teens walked by in clusters, screaming, "Get him, man, book him!" She could hear her nephews and nieces calling her name.

"This guy's an asshole, and out of control most of the time, but come on," she said. She saw Ferdi looking up from between his raised arms, wiping his face on the sleeve of his jacket. He appeared small and broken against the trunk of the car and the flashes of red and blue assaulting his fat body. "Besides, you know JoJo will bail him out in a half-hour and then he'll be all over your ass." She looked into the cop's eyes, blue in daylight, black under this sky of fireworks.

Macmillan walked her back to the van, calling out to his partner, "Come on man, let's go." To Ferdi he yelled, "Watch yourself, man. You just better watch yourself." He turned the lights off, the chase of colors still echoing against the buildings.

That night Isabel sat with her father on the back porch, listening to the sea. The skies held no clouds—dangled stars and a slice of moon. She closed her eyes, took a breath. She smelled the salt of the ocean and her dad's cigar. She was feeling dreamy.

"Some performance today, hija," Frank said.

"Wasn't it?" she answered, eyes still shut. She pictured the dancers in slow motion, moving to the bells and gongs. "We were a little nervous."

"I can see why," he said.

She heard him sink lower into the rocker, the cushions expelling air, the wicker creaking like the bones of an old man. In the dark, under this partial moon, his face lost age. The lines filled out, relaxed.

"Thanks for sticking up for me."

"Oh—you mean that lady—she's crazy." He waved his hand. "That was something else."

"I feel so sorry for her daughter," she told him. "She's so beautiful and so angry at the whole world. It's amazing."

"Which one is the daughter? The beauty queen?" he asked, nodding. "Sayang naman."

"I can't even imagine Mom acting like that."

She got up from the steps and sat next to him. The wind pushed the chimes on the porch so that they zinged bright as tiny stars.

He told her he saw himself in her today, the little bit of spark that was his youth. He was always speaking up, he said, always trying to make the people around him see. "I know your life here hasn't been easy."

"That's an understatement," she told him, leaning her head on his shoulder.

"So, was that the guy?" He took a long slow drag of the cigar, expelling the smoke in rings. "With the police. Is he the one who assaulted you?"

She looked at her dad, at the way the silver in his hair shimmered. It got lighter and lighter every time she saw him. She looked away, afraid he might grow older still. She thought of him as a young man. That's how she saw him in her dreams at night, how she remembered him during the day. A young man. It hurt her to think they were all growing older, farther apart. She'd rather spare him the details of Ferdi Mamaril. She knew he was wondering why she stuck up for Ferdi. She'd tell him if she knew why.

"I thought the enemy was going to be—" she started to say.

"The Caucasians?"

She nodded.

"You could have turned him in, hija."

"I already filed the restraining order."

"I know. That was good. Very good. You know how to take care of yourself. That's good."

Isabel reached down and began to play with a bucket full of little shells. She always pictured her dad working late at the hospital in a gown and mask, saving all kinds of people. She grew up assuming everyone appreciated him and thought of him like she did—a hero.

Maybe, he told her, life in America was not what he expected. He learned the hard way that the people who lived in houses on tree-lined streets, who worked in supermarkets and gas stations, who came to his hospitals with broken hearts and tangled arteries were not Frank Sinatra, John Wayne or Dean Martin. Happy endings were easier to come by on the silver screen. Maybe, but who said he and Camila weren't happy?

As a boy, he sat in the town's theater, while America rolled out of tin reels, glamorous as Esther Williams rising from her Hollywood swimming pool. The movies taught him the American way. In films, Rita Hayworth, Betty Grable, and Ginger Rogers inhabited small farms and high-rise metropolis buildings. They were typical American women. In black and white, he learned of freedom, democracy, and the wild Wild West. Here's your American dream—a house and job and the right to start as poor immigrants. You are here, pointed the movie map—Ellis Island, just outside of New York City. Your destination? Hollywood. In school he learned America was a melting pot of immigrants, and this was how he fell in love with the United States of America. Come to find out, he was only in love with the dream. With Hollywood.

"You know, hija," her father said. "These hard times really help, it's true what they say. They make us better people."

"It's unfair," she said.

"Never mind, hija." Smiling, he winked at her. He told her that "to fix the heart, I have to wound the patient. I must take a saw and rip open the chest, and then I have to make my way through various skin, muscle, tissue and so much blood to get to the heart. So much pain," he told her, "just to get to the heart of the matter."

"That's gross, Dad."

"You have to do all that in order to fix it." The process scared and somehow humbled him. "And sometimes the patient dies. But if you don't even try, the patient could die anyway. So you try."

She nodded. "I see what you mean, Dad. I get it."

"You don't just give up. That patient cannot give up."

Get-Together with Foreign Doctors from Morgantown, Blowing Rock, NC. 4th of July, 1967
Photo by Frank Manalo's Automatic Timer

The skies are so blue, this high in the sky. The green mountains surround them like the waves of a capped ocean, and the wind blows everyone's hair up on end. Frank squints his left eye shut and looks through the viewfinder. His hands fly over his head as he motions the group to move together. They are too busy telling jokes to notice his arms. The faces represent the world—China, India, Turkey, Norway, Canada. Most of them work in Morgantown, where the state mental institute cannot seem to keep up with demand. High stress, high turnover, high numbers of Americans going insane. At least the foreign medical team in Morgantown has one another. At Watuaga Memorial it's just Frank and Benson, and they treat Benson like he's American. So really, it's just Frank. The lone foreigner.

"Make room! Here I come!" The group bunches up tight, like they're afraid of falling to their deaths. "Make room, make room!" Frank says, and, laughing, they inch left. Frank is running when the high-pitched beep beep beep goes off. Then a collective groan arises as everyone from China, from India, from Turkey, Norway and Canada realizes that the man from the islands did not make it into the shot.

Sitting on her porch, Isa and her dad listened to the water, to the hush, hush, hush of the tide. Her mind wandered between the past and present, slipped back and forth like the water on the shore. In the distance, a fin flipped in the sea; fish flew in the night. "Tell me about Boone," Isabel said, sipping her beer. "How did we come to leave?"

His face softened. Isabel saw it in his eyes.

He began with the silences. There were so many silences. He found them in crowds at the grocery store and at church. He met silence in the hallways at the hospital and in the doctors' lounge. Silence grew, blossomed like bougainvillea in the springtime—hot-pink petals weighing branches down so low they nearly hit the sidewalks. This was what he noticed first. Everything, he told her, was divided. Colored and White sections in the cafeteria, at the gas stations. "There was a chair for Whites," he said, "and one for Colored. Everything divided, black and white."

"Where did we fit in?" Isabel asked him.

"We didn't." He placed the cigar between his teeth, biting down on its end. "But that didn't matter. Boone was not our life. It was what they call a pit stop. You know what a pit stop is, ha?" She nodded. Opened another beer and offered one to her dad.

"Well, anyhow, for some reason, in the Philippines foreigners are revered—locals want to be like the Spanish, the Americans the Chinese— whoever. Here, they call foreigners stupid, savages. No matter what their education, no matter how badly the community needs them. Stupid," he told her. "And my superior would not believe anything but that."

Standing up to Moorland at the State Medical Society was not the problem. In the end, they reprimanded her father because his accent was too strong. Because he dressed too much like an islander in his pineapple fiber shirts, embroidered white and blue. "The patients cannot understand him," argued Moorland. "They don't trust him and he is too abrupt with them. They think him rude."

"I'm surprised you and Mom didn't go back home," Isabel told him. "Don't you hate this country?"

"Because of Moorland and his cronies?" her father asked.

A white bird cawed, dipping between the stars, looking for his flock. He circled the sky and flew directly at the moon.

"I always dreamed of being a surgeon. I've always known. No son-of-a-gun was gonna take that from me."

Anticipating the trouble with Moorland, he had written one of his teachers in Chicago and that doctor wrote back. "Sponsored us," Frank said. "Brought us back to the town where your mother and I met and gave us a new start. We left the Boonies just as Moorland came down on us."

"Man, you guys were bold," she said. She thought about her own life, how different the world seemed, how much it felt the same. "And when I miscarried, Dad. How did that make you and Mom feel?"

"Of course we were disappointed, but you know, what can you do?" He puffed on his cigar and the smoke spewed out like wild animals set free.

"Every time I tried to talk about it, you guys would stop me—like you were embarrassed."

"Not embarrassed, hija. Protective."

"Of our reputation?"

"You're so sensitive, you know. You always think it's about other people, but we were worried about your feelings, anak. Why still talk about it? Bad enough you had to go through it. My gosh."

She gazed at her dad for a long time. Sometimes, on certain nights, when everything was lined up just so, and there was a moment designated for miracles, a person could make connections and the hue of the world would be altered forever.

"What is it?" her father asked. "Did you see a shooting star?"

"Something like that."

Isa and her dad waited for the others to trail onto the porch one at a time. Even JoJo joined them. The children ran laps along the beach, pointing at the sky, at the explosions of red, of white, of blue. Four-year-old Lucy held her ears with two small palms. Hands the color of sand protected her from the sound of firecrackers, a sound that startled her like gunfire. In the distance, car speakers shouted hip-hop to the sky. Isabel knew the kids were having a party. She hoped everyone would be safe, that guns would not let fly.

"Sometimes," she told her dad, "I think Arturo comes to see me."

"Like a ghost?" Rachel asked.

"Like an angel."

"Ghosts?" Max yelled. "Oh no!" He spread his arms wide and chased Lucy in circles till she tumbled on the sand.

"I said angels!" Isa shouted.

She sat with her siblings on the front porch, counting memories for their mom and dad, finding new ways to show their independence. Every now and then, fireworks burst as words, as revised histories and old wounds between brother, sister, mother and child. JoJo nodded when they tossed their words at one another like a child's game of hot potato.

"What?" she asked him.

"Nothing," he said. "Sounds like home."

She smiled at him. And then he told her, "You know my brother Jay, he had the finest voice. He had lungs and he could sing."

"Yeah?"

"Yeah. I got this picture of him in my head, standing on the roof of his car, calling out to God, and his voice is so sweet that God took him right then. Snatched him off the hood of that car."

She leaned over and kissed JoJo, whispered in his ear, something so small the breath tickled her mouth.

And Isa knew that this holiday was just an excuse, a reason to pull everyone together, to feed them, to count the heads and bless each one of them. Seven-thousand islands were purchased for less than the cost of a brand-new car. Somewhere in the ocean swam her baby's spirit—a little fishtail waiting to be. They were all tied to one another and to this place, this country, this America where everything was black and white. Red and blue. Stars and stripes. Forever.

TWENTY

The LDs scattered among the rocks, while thunder rolled above them. Now and then, shards of light cracked against a starless sky. Half a dozen candles flickered against the crate, shimmering purple and gold like some pagan altar. The wind teased each flame, threatened to make everything black. Lourdes flicked ashes from her cigarette. She exhaled deeply and released a long trail of smoke up into the night. The salt from the sea was so thick, she could taste it on her lips. She wanted them to forgive her. She wanted to ride right out of this world, through a tunnel, long and narrow. How far could it shoot her soul? So far she never had to return, she hoped.

"That far?" Ria leaned on her elbows, reached out to Angel, who handed her another stick. "That bad?"

"I'm telling you," Lourdes said, sucking on her smoke. "It's shit." She wasn't looking at her girls, but she felt them all around her like an energy field, all tensed up and ready for a fight. She felt them looking at her, watching her move, waiting. She knew she had let them down. She knew she was losing respect. She held her breath then let it go. The rocks felt jagged and poked her skinny bottom. She savored the tobacco, the way it invaded her body.

Mercedes studied lipstick prints running round the rim of her cigarette, pink and round. And then she said, "Yeah, well you the one abandoned us." She squinted one eye shut. "Queen a All Dat."

Lourdes took another drag, held it there inside of her, breathed. "Like my mother hasn't tortured you?" She threw Mercedes a long look out of the corner of her eye. "Like you don't know?"

The rain began just off shore and hit the ocean like a smattering of applause. Marilena buried her head into her lap, closed her eyes. Now the air smelled of rain and sea, of water.

Above them, the sky rumbled like a hungry belly. Maya threw down her cigarette and crushed it with her shoe. "Cut the sista slack. Nobody wants to be Queen a All Dat, not even her." And not looking up, she waved at them and walked away.

Anita Starr crawled onto her husband's belly. Kissed Louie softly again and again until his lashes flickered and he shooed her away. Like she was an itch. His face was wide, and the pores on his nose were the size of pinheads. He had long lashes for a man.

"Not now, baby," he muttered. "Let me sleep."

She ran her fingers through his tangled hair. She sniffed his neck and smelled last night's beer. Smoke in the hair. Stale perfume. Not hers. She trembled, but not enough so he would know. She kissed him again, and this time he roared, "Can't a guy sleep in his own goddamn house?"

They'd been together for almost twenty years. He courted her while he was stationed at Clark Air Base in Angeles. A beautiful man with long curly locks, he reminded her of young Tony Curtis—smooth-skinned and smelling of aftershave cologne. He had a dimple in his chin, and blue eyes the color of stained-glass windows. They had met at the palengke where she worked with her mother selling sampaguita flowers. "Parang movie star," her mother told her. "Baka mayaman yan." Someone that tall and guapo had to be rich too. Even though his hands were rough and even though his body was so big and covered in so much hair, she found a way to love him, to charm him, to make him hers. He brought her luck, a new house for her family in Angeles, and a ticket to America. She would never want for anything again. She'd hold her head up high and be respected.

But that was twenty years ago. He was so fat now, his white skin pouring out in rolls in front of her, his body still covered in a carpet of curly black hair. He used to love to hear her speak. "That accent," he'd tell her. "It's so cute—talk a little bit more."

She had laughed at him and said, "English is too heavy on my tongue. You know like I cannot chew the words so good." But now he wouldn't listen to anything she said. He wouldn't listen and neither would their daughter. With all the work she put into raising that daughter, Lourdes seemed to be following Louie's lead, not hers.

Anita Starr blamed it on that Manalo girl. Ever since, she thought, Lourdes is kontrabida; the Manalo girl makes the kids so unruly. Lourdes was growing up so wild, so American. The point of bringing in that teacher was to discipline the kids, not teach them to rebel. Ano ba yan, she thought. She couldn't imagine ignoring her mother the way Lourdes ignored her. If she had, she'd never have gone out with Louie in the first place. He was handsome, yes, but he frightened her.

"Anak," her mother had scolded her. "How do you want to live your life? You can't be Sampaguita Girl forever. Walang gana yan." She remembered how her mother called him over, "Hello, American Joe. You wanna buy a little flower?" He strolled his way around the baskets of vegetables and crates of fish, smiling all the while, his G.I. Joe hands stuffed in pockets lined with gold.

This is how it is, she told herself, as she slipped on her terry-cloth slippers and snuck out of their bedroom. The mother sees the whole life before the daughter and she guides her to the better way. Di ba, she thought. Isn't it the way? And her daughter was not following the natural law of life, stubborn-headed and kontrabida all the time. If she had not pushed, Lourdes would not have won the beauty contest. She would be gallivanting the beach with those girls all summer long. No telling kung anong klaseng trouble she'd be in now. Pero now, she thought, look at her so regal, so beautiful. She is a queen.

When Nita Starr reached the bottom of the stairs, she gazed around her living room and sighed. Naku, she thought, if I had been stubborn like her, I wouldn't have all this. She shuffled her slippers across the rubber runners she'd placed to protect her carpet, and, reaching for the drapes, she let the sun filter in. Big white sofas filled the room, wrapped in plastic. She'd covered the walls with glass tiles so visitors could see themselves from every angle, like a dressing room at a department store. Frames filled with portraits of family and of her reigning queen sprouted up from credenzas and side tables. She thought they filled the house like a garden full of beautiful blossoms.

In a corner of the living room, Nita Starr got down on her hands and knees before a full-size statue of the Blessed Virgin Mary and, digging in her duster, she pulled out a glass-beaded rosary and prayed. There were many things to attend to. She begged Mama Mary to intercede. Why was her daughter so mean, she wanted to know. Why was her husband always like that? He was just like their daughter. And then she thought about the other day, that Manalo girl and all the trouble she made. "Naku," she whispered to the Virgin, "can you imagine? She embarrasses us like that. Bad influence naman. They say she teaches the children to move like prostitutes, to shoot guns, to rebel. What kind of teaching is that? She doesn't listen to authority, and even the parents! Naku! No wonder she is so kontrabida. What do you think, Mama Mary? Maybe she has to go?"

Nita Starr began each morning by listing all her blessings and then all her burdens. Lately it seemed that the burdens outnumbered the blessings, and as she rattled away at her Hail Marys and Glory Bes the problems clustered together like a growth on her heart, and all that pain merged like a shooting star bursting into a million rays of pain. She collapsed in the middle of her Glorious Mysteries, her body folding up like a child's. She couldn't understand why she worked so hard to please her family and to make her community something to be proud of, and sometimes it felt like walang galang, no respect, not from any of them! When she was a girl, living in the provinces, sometimes there was nothing in the house to eat but rice and bagoong, salty shrimp that had been crushed to a paste. No meat, no vegetables, nothing but rice and fish eggs. She and her mother spent long evenings stringing sampaguita blossoms together like little prayer beads, and then long hot days standing at the palengke or in front of the church after services, peddling strings of white blossoms. Lucky for her family, suffering people needed sampaguitas to dress the statues of Mama Mary, of St. Joseph and the Christ Child. They'd drape their hands and necks and even their feet in rings of pretty flowers, hoping God would grant them some serenity. The day that Louie Starr proposed to her, she knew her old life was over and she'd never want for anything again. She knew her mother would be so proud. But twenty years later, pain seized her body and her stomach fell right out of her. Her only solace was in the mornings: before the sun or anybody rose, she'd talk to Mama Mary. And Mama Mary would answer her, lifting some of the pressure from her chest, picking up one burden and laying it aside until, little bit by little, Nita found her way to a seated position, and then to standing. Then, wiping her eyes, she'd turn and start the day.

Lourdes ran down the stairs, her hands trailing on the walls of the staircase. Nita heard her daughter wandering the kitchen, her movements sleepy and cumbersome, heard her knocking over plastic cups and bowls as she felt her way through the cupboard.

"Anak," Nita called as she stood up. She made the sign of the cross, kissing the rosary's crucifix, rolling her eyes at Mama Mary. "After breakfast I want you to dust the living room and vacuum the house before you dress for the luncheon." She heard Lourdes opening drawers and sifting through the silverware. "What do you want for breakfast— you want fried eggs and rice? You want longanisa?" She turned and walked into the kitchen. Lourdes had her head buried in the refrigerator, her bottom sticking out, round and perfect. She was wearing a pair of her dad's plaid boxer shorts, and on her feet she wore white socks scrunched down at the ankles. She pulled a chocolate cheesecake from the top shelf. She peeled the Saran wrap away and began attacking it with a fork.

"Naku, what kind of breakfast is dat, naman? You're gonna get fat if you don't stop!" Nita reached over and pulled Lourdes's face to her chest and kissed her several times. "Who is gonna want to see a fat beauty queen?" Lourdes yanked her body free, turned her back to Nita. "I know those girls are calling here again, anak. You are too busy to gallivant, huh? Today you have that luncheon with the Rotary Club and then you have to give away flyers at the conference for the poor." She ran cold water into the coffee pot and began making breakfast, all the while enumerating Lourdes's schedule. She loved seeing her daughter up on stage in her pretty crown. It was so hard to believe she was already a young lady with a figure and everything. When Nita was a dalaga in Angeles, all her dresses were worn rags from her relatives in Manila. She didn't even get a pair of shoes until she was fifteen. The only make-up she had was a lipstick she had inherited from her Ate Rosalie, a call girl at the base. But now, in America, Lourdes had everything. She had a hairstylist and a make-up artist, she had the nicest clothes and a closet full of shoes. "You know, anak," Nita called to her, "you are so lucky.

At least you have a mother who remembers where she came from and knows how to respect the community, and this brings you many things— Naku! Just this morning I'm thinking about that crazy Isabel Manalo girl and her parents— can you believe they talk to me like that? Walang hiya! No wonder that girl is so negative all the time, always criticizing our community and making bola with her drama. Good thing I got you out of there, anak, don't you think?" She waited a moment, hoping to hear some response. "Anak, don't you think? Anak?"

"WHAT!" Lourdes shouted from the living room. "I'm trying to watch TV."

"I said . . ." Nita walked into the living room where Lourdes had turned on MTV and peeled off the plastic from the white couch. She was snuggling into the cushions, one leg crossing the other and dangling in the air, her cheesecake balancing on a fork. "If you spill chocolate on that sofa you gonna get it, hija. Why are you so disrespectful all the time? I can't even imagine what you gonna do if you are still gallivanting with those girls and with that Isabel Manalo. Since when do you act like dis? Get your feet off the couch. Get outta there."

Lourdes finally looked at her mother for the first time that morning. The girl's long hair stood up on its ends and fell around her face and shoulders like a veil. Her eyes glowed cobalt-blue as she glared at Nita. "Why you always got to be talking down on everything? You got what you want. You got my life. I am da Queen. I ain't got my crew cuz of you, and I ain't got a life cuz of you. What else you want? Why you in Ms. Manalo's shit anyway? Ain't she doing what you guys want? Teachin' da youth. Keepin' em off the streets. Least they gots each other. Whatta I got? You. Always talking at me, givin' me no peace. Not even after this. Shit, ma. Leave me alone."

Lourdes bounced words off the living room mirrors, ricocheted angry looks from one wall to the next, looks that bled into infinity. Her head swayed as she spoke and her image filled the room. No matter where Nita looked, she saw her daughter bursting through walls, loud and mean and full of rage.

TWENTY-ONE

All the lights were out. The gymnasium echoed with tennis shoes scuffing hard wood and with the whispering of small voices. A structure of discarded boxes taken from stoves, refrigerators and other household appliances loomed big in the dark. The children stacked the boxes. They cut out arches for windows, rectangular flaps for doors, and holes on the roof for stacks of construction-paper chimneys.

In the darkness, the children carried flashlights and rioted around the brown castle of cartons. They came from the other side of the room, marching across a bridge made of wooden blocks. It was the bridge of Mendiola, the last gateway before the palace entrance. They shook their fists. They stormed the palace. They woke the guards—two sleepyheads with bad fake snores—who ran away in terror. Behind the castle, Marcos and his family climbed aboard four metal folding stools—a helicopter with blades made of tissue paper and silk scarves. The Marcoses escaped in the middle of the night as Imelda's shoes flew out of cardboard windows, off rooftops, through flimsy castle doors. A sandal, a pump, a high-top tennis shoe. A clog, a platform, a ladies' bedroom slipper. A flip-flop, a boot, an open-toed high heel. Shoes everywhere. The people, barefoot and angry, tagged brown cardboard boxes with giant brushes of yellow tempera paint. They held their hands up and pointed their fingers into giant L's. The people's fight was Cory's fight, and everyone shouted, "Laban!"

Isa and JoJo stood behind the black curtains of the Philippine Cultural Center stage, kissing. She could hear the rumble of five-hundred youth on the other side of the drapes. They squirmed on metal folding chairs, they shouted out, they stomped their feet.

"Can you believe this turnout?" said JoJo. He brushed the hair from her face and kissed her cheek.

"I know." After the 4th of July picnic they decided to make fireworks too. They wanted to shoot words into the dark sky, let them pop and shine, illuminate the hearts of everyone around them. "The whole point behind the dramas," she told the crew, "is to get some dialogue going, and that doesn't mean just spouting, it means listening too." If they could learn to hear each other, she argued, maybe they could unite and begin a dialogue with parents too. JoJo thought the idea was whacked—who'd show up, who'd give out secrets?

"Where you gonna find that kinda trust?" he wanted to know. But she was certain that once it began, like it was starting to in the dramas, they'd feel it too.

"Tha'd be dope," Derek said.

"Could we also have a dance?" Mercedes suggested. "Tha'd be the bomb."

"Yup," Elvie said. "I'd go."

"You'd talk?" JoJo asked.

"Hell, jus gimme a mic, bro, and I'll talk."

When they opened the doors of the Center and the kids began coming in, JoJo grabbed Isa by the arm and dragged her backstage. "Ain't nothing we can't do," he said, kissing her again.

They filed in, some with shaved heads and gold earrings, some with spiky blond and red hair, some in heavy black hooded sweatshirts, some in sleeveless white T-shirts. Jeans, khaki, baggy and falling-off-the-butt kinds of pants hung loose and dragged as the kids seated themselves. There was a heat in the room, the voices low and mumbling, waiting for the presentation to start.

The energy ran through Isa, out her fingertips, into kisses she planted on JoJo's smooth face. She could hardly stand it. "Let's do it!" she told him. "Let's go!" They pushed aside the heavy drapes and climbed down the stage.

Isa loaded up her camera and shot the night away. She wanted to get the youth in action, but every time she held the lens up they instinctively leaned, flashing hand signals, posturing like warriors and queens.

The kids sat in the very same folding chairs their parents placed their bottoms on, week after week, during council meetings, officer elections, novena prayer meetings and unity planning strategies. Their parents—who dressed in wool pants and cotton shirts, who wore tsinelas made of straw and suit coats made by Yves Saint Laurent—came to this very building in the heat of prayer or anger or hope to meet with their kumares and kumpares. Their fathers were doctors, and lawyers, and navy men and cooks. Their mothers sewed dresses for rich white women, wrapped lumpia in bulk, baked pan de sal and sold them at their storefront shops along the ocean boardwalk. Their grandparents stamped luggage at the airport, served paper cups of coke, and hot dogs wrapped in wax. They cleaned bathrooms, windows, factories. Their kids were here now, five-hundred of them, waiting.

Back in Evanston, the Filipinos were all medical. Her dad was a leader in a medical society numbering a hundred others from his class at the University of Santo Tomás. And if the husband wasn't a doctor, it was the wife. And if the wife wasn't a doctor, than maybe she was a nurse. And if the wife was neither a doctor nor a nurse, then maybe the husband was the nurse. But in Virginia, the Filipino community had infiltrated Tidewater. They were people from all classes and fields. They were people from all regions of the archipelago. She watched the night unfold like a dream.

Along the edges of the room, the college boys from Old Dominion University, Norfolk State and Tidewater Community College guarded the doors. Their broad backs were pressed against the wall, their arms crossed in front of them, their jaws set. They stood ready to tackle anything. Something serious was going down tonight.

Somehow, Ferdi had made it into the youth dialogue and was wandering the room like one of the brothers, slapping homeboys on the back, raising the roof with his hands sprawled out to the ceiling. Isa caught his eye and nodded.

She listened to the kids buzzing in their seats and she imagined all the words they were longing to say, so deep inside they didn't know how to realize them. She was certain that her own experience with her parents, her misunderstanding their understanding, was not an isolated incident. For nights after her family left Virginia, she'd imagine their confrontation with Tita Nita. She saw them standing over the former beauty queen of queens, and her little baby spirit floating over their shoulders. She realized they had always been on the same side.

Members of Magkasama scanned the floors, handing out flyers and greeting people. They scattered themselves among the seated, waving and smiling like good hosts. Above the shift of voices hovered a loud and rhythmic guitar riff, a bongo beating, popping out of big black speakers. Isa and the girls sat on the stage, looking out into the audience. By the east door, Isa saw one lone girl figure, thin as a thumbnail-moon, hesitating. Her hair was piled high on her head, and in the dimly lit room her face was indiscernible, but Isa knew—and before Isa could articulate it, Mercedes ran down an aisle, her fingers scratching at the air. "Hey girl," she cried, "Desa! Desa! Desa!" Angel, Maya, Marilena and Elvie waited onstage for Lourdes to strut down the aisle, and when she got to them they pulled her in, lost her in an accumulation of arms and faces, of brothers and sisters. Isa sighed, felt her chest welling up. Finally, she thought, she's come back. She wondered why Tita Nita let her out of the house.

The lights glowed red on the dalagas' faces and the camera framed their expressions up close. Eyes shut. Mouths wide open. Arms circling necks. The shutter snapped. The lens blurred. At the fringe of the circle, Isa shot as she waited to welcome Desa back. She smiled through the crooks of elbows and in between the shoulders, caught a glimpse of the girl wrapped in the arms of one of her sisters. Breaking free for a moment, Lourdes found her way to Isa, sighed as they embraced.

"Hey, long time no see," said Isabel.

"You know, lotta speaking gigs, dinners, shit like that."

In her arms, Lourdes felt like a silk purse full of needles, soft and jagged at once. Isabel stepped away so she could get a better look. She could see that Lourdes's eyes were wet, as if she'd been crying.

"Do you like being queen?"

"It's a job," Lourdes said. "Someone's gotta do it."

The lights dimmed, and the music started to fade into the walls. A light from above hit the stage, pulled their attention to the front of the room.

"PEACE AN BLESSINGS, PEACE AN BLESSINGS, TAKE A SEAT MY BROTHAS AND SISTAS, TAKE A SEAT," said JoJo into the house mic. He jumped up and down, roamed the stage left and right. He threw up a fist at the crowd and shouted, "CAN I GET ME SOME LOVE, SOME LOVE, SOME LOVE? CAN I GET ME SOME LOVE OR WHAT?"

The voices from the floor rumbled, started low like a distant train, gathered speed and power, barreled through a tunnel and burst out in response. Someone pulled Lourdes away, and everyone scattered to the edges of the room. Derek, Miguel and Edison stood behind JoJo, each with a microphone in his hand, each chanting, "UNITY IS POWER!"

"ISANG MAHAL, ISANG MAHAL."

"CUZ UNITY IS POWER."

"ONE LOVE, ONE LOVE."

"UNITY IS POWER!"

"ISANG MAHAL, ONE LOVE."

JoJo ran across the stage, speaking fast, as if he were afraid they might run away. "We brought you here tonight, we brought you here—"

"To dance!" called a voice from the audience.

"Yeah, man," JoJo said. "Yeah, to dance. But first we need to have a word. We need to discuss what's up on the street these days. Young brothers and sisters having it out. What's up with that shit?"

The boys in the folding chairs growled, the girls screamed.

"UNITY IS POWER!"

"So rather than taking it out on the streets, man, let's talk tonight. Let's have some words. Let's stop the violence."

"ISANG MAHAL, ISANG MAHAL!"

"Me and the young brothers," JoJo said, indicating the boys who were chanting behind him. The girls squealed loud, one voice rising high. "We're gonna give up the mics—"

"CUZ UNITY IS POWER!"

"We're gonna give the floor to you so you can rap with us, tell us WASSUP?"

More screaming, more groaning, more wild sounds from the floor. A whirling energy grabbed hold of Isa and she screamed along with the girls. She held up her fists too. "ONE LOVE!" she shouted. "ONE TRIBE!" She watched JoJo move on the stage, a natural, a superstar of sorts. She knew what Elvis fans must have felt like, all melty and swooning at the sight of the King on stage, as he sang what they never dreamed of singing, as he moved in ways that were forbidden. She had a hard time imagining that this was the same guy who sat quietly on her porch, nuzzling her ear like a bear cub.

"Okay," JoJo yelled, "who wants to go first?"

The rest of the crowd started to chant along with the boys, "ONE LOVE, ONE LOVE!"

"UNITY IS POWER."

Nobody stepped up. JoJo moved to the edge of the stage and tried to hand the mic off to someone, a kid in a bandana. But the kid shook his head and pushed the mic away. "You!" JoJo said. "How 'bout you?" Another one pushed the mic away. Isa felt her heart beating. She grabbed her water bottle and drank. She worried nobody would stand up, and then what? No, she thought, this is too good, someone's got to.

Miguel, who was dressed in baggy windbreaker pants and T-shirt, stepped forward, his free hand pointing to his chest in time to the chanting, his other hand holding his own mic. He had on a dark pair of sunglasses. His skin shined like newly mined coal. "ISANG MAHAL!" he shouted. "Lemme start. I'll start, Kuya!"

"MEE—GELS!" chanted the crowd. "MEE—GELS!"

"I wanna know wassup with young brothers and sisters fighting, jumping each other, pulling each other down. CRAB MENTALITY!"

Screams.

"Is that a disease? Have we gone and caught it from our mommies and daddies? CRAB MENTALITY? Pulling each other down, never helping one another up and up and up. Making it harder to make it. Making it hard. Each one trying to find a way out of the pot, don't care who you step on to get there—that ain't us, is it now?" He threw his fist up to the sky, offered the mic to the crowd.

Derek ran up behind Miguel, tossing an arm around his brother. With his free hand, he held his mic to his mouth and whispered, "Hell no. That's the grown-ups, man, that's the ninety-four organizations round the Tidewater area, ninety-four Pilipino clubs and not one of them's friends. Wassup wit that? That ain't us. Thas our moms and pops."

Isabel walked the aisles of the Cultural Center, shooting the faces of the listening youth, who leaned on the edges of their metal seats, cheered with their fists. They ignored her lens. Last time they were together like this was for a dance. Back then she felt so small, so insignificant. Tonight she walked the auditorium as if she owned it.

"Dunno, brotha, dunno," said Miguel. "Tsismis had it brothas in Nor-fuk are messin' with the crews from the Beach. Rumor had it they ain't the only ones." He sat on the edge of the stage and hissed, "Ain't that true? Didn't you hear that too?"

Ferdi scrambled onto the stage in his patent-leather shoes and his light-blue golf jacket, reaching for Derek's mic.

"I'll tell you what the problem is," Ferdi yelled. "Do you know who you are? Do you know you're Filipino-American? Do you know what that means? What's it mean to be Filipino? To be American?" When Ferdi spoke he put one hand in his pocket and strolled down the stage, pointing his brown finger at the audience. He lectured. "All those manongs sing their allegiance to the Philippine flag and then they wonder why they don't get treated like the Caucasians."

Derek leaned on Miguel, craned his neck toward Miguel's mic and said, "But Kuya, you gotta know where you come from so you can go forward."

"Yeah," Miguel said, "you gotta study all history, man, not just your favorite one. Then you got the power to represent. Y'all wanna represent now, don't you?"

"Was dis gotta do with dancing?" yelled someone from the floor. "Let's have us some music."

"Ms. Manalo!" Ferdi motioned to Isabel to come up on stage. She shook her head at him, waved him away. "Come on up here, Ms. Manalo, tell these young people."

"No offense," she yelled, cupping her hands over her mouth, "but this is a youth dialog. It's about the youth. Give the mic back, Kuya Ferdi!"

Someone beat a drum and the girls all shouted, "ATE ISA! ATE ISA! ATE ISA! ATE ISA!"

Their chanting filled her body up, ran through her limbs and made her heart race. Her name repeated over and over like the beating of her heart thrilled her because she knew that finally she was in, one of them. Trusted.

A small line had begun to form at the bottom of the stage, and slowly the kids climbed the steps and hung onto the mic. Each in his or her own voice spoke words into the system, filled the auditorium with sound.

"My kuya got hit by the crew on the beach," said a fifteen-year-old boy. "Don't know why, either, cuz we're not in any gangs. We just came up from Kentucky. Ain't no Filipinos in Kentucky, hardly any. We're all happy to be here, round so many brothers and sisters. Y'all shouldn't be fightin', should be proud."

More screaming.

JoJo climbed the stage and, taking the mic, he told the kids, "Wassup? It's me, your Kuya JoJo!"

The kids hooted. Raised their fists. Chanted.

"Some of you knew my little brother. He went down in a drive-by." He thumped his chest with his hand. "Broke me, you know? And thas why I'm here—right? For you! For Jay!"

Isa felt her heart swell. What made him stand up like that, she wondered. He never talked about that boy. And there he was.

"Some of you," said a girl. "Some of you are jokin' on some of us that don't look like you." She stood with her hand in her back pocket, her feet crossed so that she swayed when she talked. "Just cuz we're only half, or we have a bigger nose, or lighter hair, just cuz our skin's the color of your milk, think you're all better than us. Ain't right. I'm Pinay too."

Cheering.

"You got that!" screamed Lourdes.

"Yeah, yeah, Miss Virginia Beach Pinas knows what I'm sayin'."

"Hard nuff, dealing with the man at the mall. Everyone thinking you're a troublemaker cuz you wit your friends, cuz you wear baggy pants and a Nike tee. Cuz you shave your beautiful round head, smooth as a TASE-TEE CO-CO NUT!"

The audience said, "Oooo." The audience said, "Ahhh."

A boy, maybe seventeen years of age, heavy and wide, gestured with his fat fingers. "It's crazy fighting other brown brothers, crazy when we got nuff to do. First our parents, now us? Why?"

"Eddy! Eddy!"

"For true," said Marilena. "Talaga naman, grown-ups and their Bayanihan this, or their Women's Auxiliary that—tsismis flyin' off the walls, makin' us do this, do dat cuz if we don't, WALANG HIYA— shame on them, I say. What kind of example's dat? Talking down an auntie cuz she comes from Visayas instead of Luzon—Davao instead of Quezon. Wassup wit dat? We're in America now. We need each other. Pushin' your girls into pageants an shit, makin' em lose friends on account of some regional pride—Ilocano this, Bicolano that."

Silence. A metal chair creaked and crashed to the floor. Lourdes rushed out of the room, her footsteps clicking on the hard floor. By the time Isa was able to weave her way to the door, Lourdes was in her car, her taillights red and flashing, moving quickly out of the parking lot. Isa decided to check in with her in the morning. The good thing was, she was here tonight. It was something.

When Isa walked back into the Cultural Center, she heard voices like the mewing of lost kittens. A boy was whispering, his voice echoing in the stairwell, "Ain't no big thing, baby." And then came the sighing of tears drawn deep from the belly. Isa snuck around the stairwell and peeked up onto the landing, where she saw Maya rolled up like a ball of yarn, her hair falling into her eyes, hiding her cheeky face. The long lean boy she had seen from the Fourth of July held Maya on his lap, rocked her back and forth. They didn't see her, didn't feel her breathing from the bottom of the stairs. He sang to her, promised her ain't-no-big-thing again and again, his voice shaky and low. He had his eyes closed, so Isa couldn't make out the beauty of them. But his face was wet with his own tears, and she swore there was a light coming from his face. "Aw baby," he cried, "no worries, no worries, ain't no big thing."

Isa left them on the landing. Whatever the problem, she knew it was something between them. Maya would come to her, she knew, would speak to her when she was ready. Since Ferdi had jumped Isabel, Maya watched over her, followed her around the house like a second kitty.

Back in the hall, they circled the mic Oprah-style for almost two hours. Spoke from the heart. Called it like they saw it. And the beautiful thing was that nobody disagreed with them. Nobody said, "Be quiet" or "Not true." Nobody said the words didn't count. Isa saw the kids breaking down walls, she felt their energy releasing into the night, voices calling out and tears shooting from the moon. At the end of the evening, Magkasama partied down in a flash of red light. DJs scratching beats and young rappers freestyling, and Isa and JoJo in the middle of the mix.

Isa was hung over the next morning, intoxicated with the breakthrough she and JoJo had made with the kids. She woke before the sun came up and hid away in her darkroom, soaking film, mixing chemicals, conjuring up the night all over again. It didn't matter that her eyes were red and itchy from lack of sleep. She wanted to keep last night's momentum going. Finally, her work was coming together for her: she could see how the move had changed not only her outlook on life, but the way she saw herself. All her life, she had been a one and only in her school. She remembered that everyone's parents were easygoing and free, unlike her own strict Old World clan. She had no one to talk to, so she collected feelings and let them pile up inside, take up room that should have been devoted to growing and healing. And later on, after she graduated, her circle of friends worked Chicago's Loop as traders and buyers, legal assistants and consultants. Her work with children was seen as cute, or fun. Last night was neither cute nor fun; it was exhilarating.

Her sister Millie saw the world in a different light. Millie entered school with the same set of kids she graduated with. By the time she had made it through twelve grades, she'd taken on the role of white Midwestern girl, cornfed and all. Unlike Isa—who was the new girl in school, the outsider—Millie was always in, so even in those moments when their parents cracked down on curfews and dating and careers, Millie just flowed. But Isa was always running into obstacles, feeling out of place, alone. She knew that so many of her dalagas had the same experience, and she knew that they believed no one understood. Last night was a coup because their stories made it clear that no one was alone.

When the phone rang at eight in the morning, she had already developed a set of five-by-seven black and white photos. She caught the kids with their mouths wide open, their arms raised up to God. The images moved, like black shadows dancing on a wall. She got them clustered together, gesturing with their arms, their hands moving as fast as their rapper lines. She hung the photos to dry like Christmas lights strung from one side of the room to the next. When she picked up the phone, she expected to hear JoJo, sleepy-drunk with the night before. But it was Dr. Andrea Calhoun, calling to say that the parents were livid, that Anita Starr had screamed at her in the middle of the night and filed accusations of bad conduct on the part of the kids, on the part of the teachers.

"She says the other parents want to know what you are teaching. That the children are restless and angry, and that last night you organized some kind of rebellion. Is this true?" Calhoun's voice was high-pitched and irritated, cracking.

"No, of course that's not true." Isa told her. "It's just the opposite. They've opened up. Wait till you hear."

But Calhoun didn't want to hear. Instead she told Isa that she was suspended. "I hate to do this to you," she said, "because I think you're on to something. But these parents are angry. Several of them complained that you're teaching lies and pagan rituals, that you encouraged the girls to act in provocative ways."

"Those are the dramas," Isabel answered. "Those are the reenactments of things that happened in history."

The executive committee would review the case, Calhoun told her, and in the end they'd decide whether or not to renew her contract. "Of course there shouldn't be a problem. The parents just need time to cool down. But until then, I don't want you meeting with the kids."

"But what do you mean?" Isa shouted. "This is what the parents wanted! They wanted to stop the kids from hurting each other—they wanted them to remember where they came from."

Calhoun told her not to get hysterical. The words sounded crazy to Isabel. She gazed at the photos swinging in the breeze from her electric fan.

"Don't meet with them."

"But—"

"Not after hours, not on the beach, and not with your boyfriend. It's too dangerous. Too volatile."

"But what do I tell the kids?"

"They'll understand. If anything else happens, you'll never get to work with them again, dear. Just listen to me."

"Lose my job?"

"Or lose the programs all together."

What she feared most was losing their trust. She feared the teens would think she had abandoned them.

I JUST WANNA THANK YOU FOR HELPING ME OUT THERE. I KNOW YOU DIDN'T HAVE TO DO THAT. AND I'M SORRY ABOUT THE THING AT THE GROCERY STORE, BUT SOMETIMES I GET SO WORKED UP WHEN I'M BEING IGNORED. MAYBE WE CAN START AGAIN? ANYWAYS, ISABEL, I WAS JUST THINKING— HOW IS IT THAT FILIPINO AMERICANS ARE THE HIGHEST GROWING POPULATION IN ASIA AMERICA, BUT WE DON'T GET NO PLAY. YET HERE WE ARE CONTRIBUTING LIKE GOOD CITIZENS, AND NOBODY CALLS IT LIKE IT IS. IN CASE YOU DIDN'T KNOW, WE HAVE NOTABLE FILIPINO AMERICANS CONTRIBUTING TO ART, TO POLITICS, TO THE BETTERMENT OF THE UNITED STATES OF AMERICA. WHO ARE THE FAMOUS PINOYS? I THOUGHT YOU'D NEVER ASK. EVERYBODY KNOWS THE ARTIST FORMERLY KNOWN AS PRINCE HAS A FILIPINA LOLA—AND JOCELYN ENRIQUEZ, THE QUEEN OF FREESTYLE? SHE'S FROM THE BAY AREA, GIRL. THERE'S BROADWAY STAR LEA SALONGA—THE ORIGINAL MISS SAIGON IS ONE OF US. TIA CARRERA, THE MOVIE ACTRESS AND SINGER—SHE IS ONE OF US TOO. SO ARE ACTORS NIA PEEPLES AND LOU DIAMOND PHILLIPS. SO IS THAT CRAZY COMEDIAN ROB SCHNEIDER. MAN, HE KILLS ME. IN GOVERNMENT, MARIA LUISA MABILANGAN HALEY IS CLINTON'S HIGHEST-RANKING FILIPINO-AMERICAN OFFICIAL. DON'T FORGET U.S. ICE SKATERS ELIZABETH PUNSALAN AND TAI BABILONIA. IN THE MILITARY, EDWARD SORIANO WAS A FIRST LIKE YOU, ISABEL. HE WAS THE FIRST PHILIPPINE-BORN SOLDIER TO BECOME A GENERAL IN THE U.S. ARMED FORCES, AND EDISON TAGUBA WAS THE SECOND PHILIPPINE-BORN SOLDIER TO BECOME A

GENERAL IN THE U.S. ARMED FORCES. THERE WAS THE LABOR
LEADER, PHILIP VERA CRUZ, AND THE FOREMOST FILIPINO-
AMERICAN POET JOSE GARCIA VILLA. AND LAST BUT BY NO
MEANS LEAST, THERE'S OUR GREATEST BOXING CHAMPION
OF ALL TIME—MISTER PANCHO VILLA HISSELF. ARE YOU
GETTING THE PICTURE? ARE YOU CATCHING MY DRIFT? WE
ARE A FORCE IN AMERICA. WE ARE FILIPINO AMERICA.
PLEASE ACCEPT MY APOLOGIES. PLEASE. LET'S HAVE SOME
COKE AND LUMPIA, OKAY?

When Isa knocked on the door, Louie Starr answered, wearing a pink
polo shirt and blue golf pants. "How ya doing?" he asked.

She said she was there to see Lourdes—was she around? But
Lourdes was getting ready to go to a barrio festival. "She's sashaying
God knows where today. Why don't you come in?"

Through a white hallway of marble and glass, Isabel could see the
living room.

"Honey—will you get Lulu?" Louie Starr yelled out into
the house.

The sound of slippers shuffling and bracelets banging announced
Tita Nita's entrance. "Why, who is it?" she said.

Here was a sight Isa didn't count on. Tita Nita stripped of all her
make-up. Plain-faced and, to Isa's surprise, beautiful.

"Naku, anak, you have some nerve showing up here! Your
boyfriend is riling those kids up." Tita Nita pulled Isabel into the white
living room and sat her down. The plastic stretched and squeaked against
her skin. Her image filled the mirrors endlessly. "You guys are suppose
to be peacemakers. But you know you are doing the opposite. I'm willing
to forgive and forget that thing at the picnic, but this is getting too
dangerous. You gotta help me here."

Isa took a deep breath. Her throat was sticky, her mouth dry. "No
disrespect, Tita. But why did you make that phone call?"

"Anak, listen to me, I'm saying this for the kids."

"Tita, the kids need that forum. That youth dialogue was meant to
get them to talk and open up about their feelings, about their problems."

Tita Nita arched her brow. Her face turned rosy. "Naku. What problems? There are no problems except that you are teaching them to be kontrabida, how to talk back, to question. Ano ba yan, you're supposed to teach them how to have respect." Her voice was getting louder now. Two veins in her neck were rising blue and angry.

Louie came into the room. "Leave the girl alone, Anita. She's only doing what she thinks is right."

"You see that. Just like an American."

"Tita Nita, I came today because Lourdes was really upset last night. I wanted to see what was the matter, if she wanted to talk."

"You are so stupid sometimes, anak. I sent her there to spy on you. So she could confirm what we suspect, that you are up to no good!"

"Mah," Lourdes cried. She stood in the foyer, a silver crown shining in the dark. "Don't talk to her like that."

"It's okay. We're just trying to—" Isa began. But as quickly as Tita Nita had pulled her down, she yanked her up off the couch and escorted her to the door.

"You better think about it, anak," she said as she pushed Isa away.

Outside, Isa sat in her station wagon, running the morning through her mind over and over again. What did Tita Nita mean—she sent Lourdes to spy on her? Then why was Lourdes so emotional? She recognized the panic in Lourdes's eyes, the way the girl had felt soft and fairylike in her arms. Lourdes was disappearing, her voice breaking out of her and escaping like rain showers, her body shaking like lightning. And now that Isabel understood this world, she was being told to take a step away from it, to hold back, to pretend she hadn't seen a thing. How was she supposed to do that?

TWENTY-TWO

Las Dalagas swam undersea because they figured that was one place nobody would find them. Down there was too deep for their moms and pops. They'd never bother to look below the coral reefs, to seek them mingling with the starfish, hot flashes of glitter-light twinkling in the black sea. LDs knew that in the Philippines, nobody swam past the shallow end. You get too dark if you stay out that long. Their moms and pops could wade as far as their knees, maybe their armpits, but they'd never venture farther than that. So the mergirls shot their fine-finned bodies deep into the bottomless sea, floated effortlessly far away. Life on land was painful, like someone setting fire to skin, or carving beauty along a stretch of the back, or ramming a truck right into your bones. If LDs could survive that kind of pain, they knew they'd be sistas for life. So they went through it all together, even tested one another and then they let it go at the deepest end of the sea. They swam at midnight, water ballerinas in an Esther Williams movie, holding hands underwater, blowing bubbles at each other, sprouting up like a chorus of silver flying fish. Sometimes they sang at the top of their lungs, "So we come to the end of the road . . ." and they held each other up, their limbs floating to the surface like ocean fairies. "And I can't let go . . ." The night sky absorbed the pain, and sea salt calmed them little by little. Only the strongest could be a Dalaga, a deep-sea swimmer, a tropical finned lady, a sista.

Today they were recording their victories. They waited against the rocks as Maya held the camera up and shot them one by one. Angel posed with her arms up above her head, her face turned away from the lens. The T-shirt rising up her back revealed a terrain of muscles and—just left of the spine, below the hip-hugger jeans—the Alibata ideograph for Pinay, dancing there, rippling like a mirage in the middle of a brown desert. Maya zoomed in. Clicked.

She shot a medium close-up of Ria's left arm, and the array of scratches rising up from her smooth skin. Her body over-healed, bumpy, marred and discolored. It was a sort of Braille.

Next, Maya zoomed in on Marilena's right eye, at the corner, where the knife nicked her, tore a little flesh right off her. The cut was not so deep, but so close to the eye, and it bled fast and furious, made her think she had gone blind. Now the heavy liner and the shadows—the lavender, the pink, the magenta powders—made the scar a wild exotic flower. "Shut your eye," Maya told her. And when Marilena's lashes fell against her skin like thick black petals, Maya captured the frame.

Maya clicked, rewound, clicked. Moved closer with each sister, caught the movement of skin, as they held themselves in the light. Beyond them, the pelicans charged the ocean floor for fish. When she focused on the scars—on the eruption of skin, disfigured forever—memories of the nights her sistas were jumped usurped the lens, came back in flashes. She could hear the sista screaming and it was loud, vibrating as the cry ricocheted inside her like a bullet.

"Don't be scared," she whispered, peeling the fabric of Mercedes's shirt open. She focused on Mercedes's right breast. Not the whole breast, just the crest that peeked over the top of her Miracle Bra. The sun cast a shadow on the valley that sloped up and over the top of the fabric. The breast, a beautiful globe of brown skin, was perfect save for the wound. The stitches haunted the flesh, faint as ghosts.

When Maya got to Lourdes, the beauty queen spread her thighs apart and revealed teeth marks, a circle of little mountains rising just above the knee. The lens picked up the cris-cross texture of the skin around the mark. The fine pores, the depth of the scar, a little uneven, a little off.

They chose to be mermaids and not fish girls because there was that other part of them that wanted to be on land, beautiful girls with phat boyfriends and families they would die for. As much as they hated the world, they could not forget it or their peeps. They were brown girls,

Pinay, one of the tribe. Ocean life twenty-four-seven meant they'd be alone forever. "And I can't let go . . ." they'd sing to each other in the deepest part of the bay, their arms wide open to the sky, ready to embrace anything. The circle of teeth buried in Lourdes's skin was so dark and deep that Maya felt like running her fingers along the rim of those teeth, erasing them with a dabble of spit. Is this worth it, she wondered. Is this cool as all that? She was losing faith.

Maya handed the camera to Lourdes and, facing the sun, she wiped the tears that had begun to blur her vision.

"What are you crying for?" Lourdes said. "You should be proud."

"Yeah," Angel said. "Dis gonna be hellacool."

"That's right," Ria said. "Las Dalagas, forever."

Lourdes zoomed in, said, "I see the red in your eyes. Do you want that to show?"

"Doesn't matter. Just make sure it's in focus."

Lourdes squinted into the viewfinder, searching Maya's face. She trembled and Maya saw understanding color Lourdes's cheeks. Lourdes could see what Maya knew. It was all bullshit—the beatings, the tattoos, the swimming with the fishes.

"Hold your breath," Maya told her. "And focus."

Lourdes darted the camera around, tracked the grooves that ran the length of Maya's face: four scabs, long and thick, brown as mud, running parallel to one another, even as rows in a field of rice. Clouds floated across the sky and hid the bright sun, made the air feel cool as rain.

Isa was surprised. Even though it was the end of summer, Tidewater seemed gray to her. Gray tunnels, gray highways. Clouds crowded the sky like smudges on a winter windshield. Old wrappers and swatches of garbage washed up on the beach, and everything looked the color of grime. Used condoms rushed in with the tide and she was never sure if it was the bubbles from sea foam, or another see-through jellyfish, or simply that—a discarded condom. She stepped around the foreign objects.

The dolphins were swimming south again, and some nights when the seas were heavy with changing winds, she heard them cawing to one another, leading one another by their beautiful beaks, a herd of flippers and fins gliding their way to the mouth of the sea. Once she saw a documentary on dolphins suffocating in shallow waters just south of Florida. Only a few were sick, really. One or two calves. But the reporter revealed that dolphins were loyal creatures and that their devotion to the herd made it nearly impossible for them to leave each another, especially if one of them was dying or caught in between the tides. They'd rather perish together, the expert said.

Sometimes, when she and JoJo waded in the ocean, the tides riding higher than a navy ship, she caught them out of the corner of her eye, sleek torpedoes zipping past, leaping into the air just one-hundred feet away. "I want to swim next to them," she whispered into JoJo's sandy ear. "I want to run my hands along their skin. Maybe hold onto their fins and let them take me south."

"Yeah," he told her. "They're cute, huh?"

These days, gray days, she waited for school to begin, felt odd when she saw the dalagas on the beach, or the boys wandering the parks. She wanted to go to them—say, "Wassup?"—but she knew she was not supposed to.

"You can if you want," JoJo told her. They lay in low tide, bodies wrapped around one another, sand seeping between them as if through a sieve.

"No, I can't."

"I don't see how you let them run you like that."

She pinched his ear and told him not to make it harder for her. "If they see me with the kids, that's it—I'm dead," she told him.

"Scared of Mother Whitie," he said, brushing hair off her forehead. With his finger, he painted wet sand on her belly. A shadow floated over them, masked the sun from them.

"You think I'm selling out." Sometimes she woke in the middle of the night and he was gone, his blankets thrown wide open like he was a thief coming clean. The rumors made their way 'round town, and since everything was a secret, there was no telling what was true, what false. "You make me feel like an outsider," she said.

When she drove around the town, the only colors she saw were gang letters on walls and tunnels. Spray-paint art. Tagging. Fat fins of mermaids swept across the bridges on 264 and 464. Mermaid hair, long and loose as hula skirts, sailed from under the bridge into the bay. The mermaids had almond eyes, brown bellies, wide lips. Erratic markings like chicken scratching, edgy as an urban subway, tagged streets and storefront windows. She wasn't sure—were they there before? Was it new? They marked their boundaries like cats.

At the hairdresser's she heard old aunties talking about the sound of guns. "Woke me up out of my sleep," an auntie in blue curlers said. "From a good dream too. Then I'm up all night, worrying about my apo. Where was he? Asleep in his bed? I got up and called my daughter. Woke her up. The rest of the house too. Anak, I say, where's my grandson. In bed, she told me. Then she goes to check. He's not there, he's gallivanting. Sus! Pagud na pagud na ako!"

"You should get some sleep, manang," said the hairdresser. "Then you won't be so tired."

In church the father asked them to pray for the owners of the small Asian market on the beach: "Pray for their safety, and their goods." A fire devoured their store; its charcoal foundation faced the sky like burnt offerings. "It's like they assume it's the kids," Isabel told her mother, "but maybe it's not gang-related at all. Maybe it's some white arsonist or maybe he's black, or not even a he. Maybe he's a woman and she's crazy or something. But why do they assume it's the kids?"

She heard the rumors, like everyone else, and felt helpless. She worked on her photography—that was how she stayed close to the kids. Dark tones gathered in the corners of the eyes, in the lines of worry between the brows. She memorized the mouths, the shape of the hair, the curve of the cheek. White streaks at the bone, in the contrast of the eye and its cornea. She locked herself up in her darkroom, developing print after print. She organized her life into giant photo albums, starting with her parents' lives in the Pinas and making her way to Virginia Beach.

Dalagas at the Beach. Chick's Beach, VA. April 1995.
Photo by Isa Manalo

She catches them right after they break the pose, the one where they stretch their bodies long and lean like Charlie's Angels—limbs flared akimbo, hips cocked like they've got lives of their own. She catches them relaxing, their bodies softening, looping their arms around their shoulders. Maya's infectious laugh starts everyone up. She rolls her head back and her cackling fills the air. Angel and Ria do the bump, click hip to hip like bony castanets. Mercedes makes a face, gesturing with her hands. She is a bird. She is a cat. She is a catbird. Whatever, says, Marilena, reaching for her beeper. You is whacked, she mutters. And Lourdes breaks into a smile, her wide mouth stretching the breadth of her small face. Behind them, the tide climbs the sky in a big white streak, sprays them suddenly so they all scream. Isa clicks just as the water hits the lens.

She started meeting Ferdi for lumpia and coke, forgiving him and toasting their new friendship with colas on ice stuffed into tiny Styrofoam cups. "It's not that I disagree with you," she told him at last. "It's just the way you go about it. You have to give people a chance to respond. You have to give them space."

He nodded slowly, sipped the soda till there was only ice, and then he chewed what was left. "I hear that, sister. I hear that."

On television the reporter said that security guards at the mall were coming down harder on gangs. She saw Migs on the six o'clock news, his face wide and dark against the screen, his mole shiny as a film star's beauty mark. He said, "We just shopping, me and my friends, and they haul us in like criminals. Just cuz we together don't mean we gang-bangers or nothing. In America, we suppose to be innocent till proven guilty. Know what I'm sayin'?"

The camera panned the dark mall, and the faces of a thousand teen tribes loomed past the lens, jeering, winking, tossing looks. The camera shot down an escalator where clusters of teens floated up, spiraled toward the heavens, past Banana Republic and the Gap, past Eddie Bauer and the giant neon Food Court. The video cut back to Miguel, who was looking at the mall and pointing to himself, to his friends. He knocked on his chest with the palm of his hand. "We used to kick it with our kuya till they took that away. I'm hoping we get it together. Once school starts, know what I'm sayin'?"

It was as if the whole town had gone to sleep long enough for the world to change. One night Isa went to bed in her own house; the next day she woke up and everything looked the same, but felt different.

She felt so alone, she found herself wandering the little chapel bookstore, searching for a set of prayer beads. She fingered the silver ones, the see-through glass beads, the mother of pearl. The prayers had been set one after another in little rows no bigger than babies' teeth. She was still unsure of the whole rosary ritual, but she liked the uniformity of the beads, the way the prayers whispered back and forth across the church like waves in the ocean. She liked the idea that maybe someone other than herself could carry this burden, intercede.

She knew the kids were losing their light. They looked so angry; they looked dark. She wanted to wrap her skinny limbs around them and hold them until they quieted. She wanted to sit next to them and let them choose to confess their lives. She wanted to hold a hand or rub a back. She wanted to nod her head, to listen. She worried nobody else was doing it. She knew from the way they looked, from the gestures they made in the malls or the way they screamed on the beach. She recognized all of it. It was Frankie Boy at 16, it was Millie at 17, it was herself on any day. But if she ever wished to work with them again, she would have to heed the warnings of her superiors: stay away, keep a low profile, make no trouble.

She settled on a rosary of wooden beads. Each prayer was carved from soft sandalwood and resembled a rosebud in the midst of bloom. She bought herself a little prayer book with a picture of Our Lady of Fatima floating on a cloud, three peasant children underneath her.

Isabel began at the church, bowed before the Virgin, posing like the girl on her prayer book. She hissed her prayers at the feet of Mary, convinced that she could learn to believe everything the Creed declared: One God. Maker of heaven and earth. Jesus Christ. Holy Spirit. At first she felt like a fraud, desperate and willing to try anything at all. She was looking for angels. She was looking for her spirit baby to attend to her. She was looking for God. And then something happened. Everything inside her grew quiet. The wish wish wish of her Hail Marys and her Our Fathers washed over her and then it didn't matter that she was alone. She had found a way to quiet her nerves.

She carried her wooden roses everywhere. She fingered her beads in the car. She counted out prayers and sent them off while waiting in the doctor's office. She'd wake up and her stomach would be full of panic and she'd reach past JoJo and grab the beads from under the nightstand lamp and she'd parcel out intentions like she was the ocean itself, rising and ebbing, "Hail Mary Full of Grace, Hail Mary Full of Grace, Hail Mary Full of Grace the Lord be with thee."

She didn't know what else to do, she didn't know if God was getting the message, but she prayed and she called on the children of Fatima as if her words were rising up and being heard.

At dinner JoJo begged, "I'm going to see the kids tonight. Come with me." Almost every night, he brought it up, this and her worry. "Calhoun doesn't have to find out."

"Don't you think I'm dying to?"

"So why can't you come?"

"You know why." She looked at him—the messy hair and sandalwood smell of him—and asked. "They hate me, huh?"

"I explain it. They know."

But she knew they were mad at her anyway. Once she saw them at the mall—maybe six or seven of them. Lourdes and Angel and Derek and Ria and Edison. She couldn't remember who else. They were walking toward McDonald's, coming out of an arcade. They sauntered, cool as a music video. She sighed at the beauty of their movements. The sight of them all together made her want to run up to them, give them a hug. She remembered waving at them, shouting out. And the girls looked right through her, mumbling. No smiles, no waves. Nothing. Just a look.

"I want to know what's going on with them," she told JoJo. But he didn't answer and the tension which had been growing now for weeks gave way to a tiny hurricane, right there in the middle of the room. In between the chicken adobo and rice, right before the bowls of ice cream, a wind spat out hot energy and spun them as if they were not on the same side, as if they didn't share the same bed.

"You don't make this easy!" she yelled.

"Not the point. You're not in an easy place."

"Well, if it's that tough, you know you don't have to be here. Go."

"Maybe I will."

"Maybe you should."

"All right then."

"All right."

And the house grew silent, and the wind died down, and the last

294

of the hurricane sputtered when JoJo took his windbreaker from the floor, walked out the door. Left her.

Christmas. Evanston, IL. 1993.
Photo by Auntie Isa Manalo

She finds the three of them bubbling in a tub of bath water, splashing. Max's using soapsuds to make bunny ears on Lucy. Isa yells over the echoes in the bathroom. The three scream into her lens. Lucy turns onto her belly, sticking her feet up in the air so her bottom peeks out from a mountain of bubbles. Kevin lathers soap all over his face—makes a mask of white and yells, "Ho! Ho! Ho!" She crowds them into the shot and they splash at her just as she clicks the picture. Someday, maybe for Christmas, she wants three whole babies, like them.

Later that night, she drowned in linen, legs kicking at the cotton sheet, the blanket, the comforter. Too many pillows made her sleep lumpy and uneven. Flounder sat on her chest, made it hard for her to breathe. She cried herself to sleep, waiting for him to return, but nothing. No phone calls, no cars in the driveway. He left her alone with the cat. She called her mother and father, who told her to calm down, be patient. Wait, they told her, wait. She almost called Elliot, she was feeling that alone.

She thought about the night she broke up with Elliot. There was no fight. No fights. Did they ever fight? She couldn't think. He had made her a dinner and set the table with candles and sloppy bunches of wild flowers stuffed in pints of water. She should have been charmed. She should have been swept off her feet. She was bored. And when he pulled her close for a kiss and a toast to the work she had done on the pageant, she sat very still.

"What's the matter, baby?" he whispered. "You should be happy."

"I am."

"Naw, something's wrong."

Her heart raced. She knew she had to do this, and do it fast. He was so clueless.

"I'm just not into it," she said.

"Don't you feel well?"

His eyes were wide with concern. Reaching over, he cupped her chin in the palm of two hands and lifted her face to the light, as if he were a doctor, looking for symptoms. He pressed his lips onto her forehead, as if he would find the answer there. "You aren't feverish. What's wrong?"

"I mean—you must have sensed that things are different—I'm not into this anymore—you and me. That."

He didn't believe her. He looked around the room, as if searching for another person, maybe the Isabel he loved. How could this be? "Is it someone else?" he asked her.

"Not really. I mean there is someone, but that's not why. You and I—too opposite. Too different."

"Who is it? JoJo, right?"

She didn't answer him, peeling his cupped hands from her face. She leaned over him and the scent of his cologne saddened her. She kissed his cheek and whispered, "I'm sorry, really I am."

Too opposite. She was too opposite of JoJo too. And he made her angry in a way Elliot never could. When her father was going through all that mess, when Moorland had called her mother and asked her to persuade Frank to back down, stop publishing that newsletter, Camila told Moorland to drop dead. She told him she supported her husband and his every move. Isabel wondered why she and JoJo didn't act like this—a team. She considered Elliot, and he was the same. She would always be in this alone. Isa lang. One only. Only Isa.

She grabbed her rosary from a shelf and ran her fingers over each rose, felt the carving go deep inside the wood of each bud. She closed her eyes and, rolling onto her tummy, she clutched a palm to her breast while the other ran through the Sorrowful Mysteries. It was Saturday and she should have been praying the Glorious Mysteries: she should have been dreaming about rising from the dead, flying off to heaven—Jesus first, then Mary and maybe herself. She should have been contemplating tongues of fire dashing the tops of their heads, and crowned jewels for everyone, but she couldn't go there. She didn't feel like it. She wanted to feel the sadness. She wanted the tumult mixing up her insides. This way she knew they meant something to her. Those kids and that JoJo. The more it hurt, the more she knew she was a part of them.

And then she finally closed her eyes, and the tears made her sleepy enough to drift away, to float into a restless sleep. She dreamed the teens to her home. She dreamed their music beating like the heart: pintig, pintig, pintig, pintig. She could even smell their cologne. The boys drowned themselves in that cheap stuff, then donned gold chains around their necks. Sometimes the gel they greased their hair in was more fragrant than their aftershave. The girls wore different scents of flowers. They blossomed with lavender, lilac, lemon grass.

All she wanted since she'd arrived was this: to be part of that mix, to understand them and learn from them, this experience of Pinoy. What Lourdes said was right: the books won't teach you what they lived day in, day out. It wasn't that she was not Pinay. It wasn't that she didn't know who she was, just that their experience was so new to her, so empowering. "What does it mean to be Pinoy?" called the voice of Ferdi Mamaril.

"Many things," she whispered, "many things."

"Oh yeah," he said. "Tell that to Will, Mister Red White and Blue." On his left was the TV actor who played the young Republican.

"Is it okay if I call you Rock?" she asked him and all his super-white teeth.

In her dream, she sat them down at a coffee shop, and she set them straight, not with anger, not with righteousness, but with pictures of her family. "Here we are in Boone at my father's hospital. Here we are in Evanston, painting the walls with seven-thousand islands. My family," she said, gesturing to the Fourth of July picnic at Princess Anne Park. She showed them pictures of her students, the dramas, the uncles and aunties around the mahjong tables. She showed them the pageant's royal court. "This too," she said, a little embarrassed. Lourdes's crown was so heavy with fake rhinestones that it slid from her head. "Pinoy," she told them. The community meeting, all the fighting, very Pinoy. "Grabe!" said Ferdi, amazed at all the yelling. "Why can't they get along?" She showed them a night during Arturo's novenas. "His funeral week," she said, pointing to the rosaries woven through the fingers of elders and mothers alike. She showed them a photo of Ferdi attacking her. In the dream Ferdi said, "What makes you so sure this was Pinoy?"

"Well, it's not America," said Will. "That's for damn sure. Whatever it is, it's not my America."

"Hell it's not," Isabel said.

The beating of the heart got louder about here. Turned hot. Made her clench her fist and then she woke, the voices growing louder than the dream. She woke. And JoJo was still not in her bed. But the voices, low and steady, like the sound of conspiracy, drifted into her bedroom from an open window.

She slipped out of bed, her feet sliding across hardwood floors. She thought about how she needed to sweep. In the morning, she told herself. The cat leapt just footsteps ahead of her. Together, they discovered this:

Magkasama sat on her porch. A gathering of spirits whispering. Their bodies threw long shadows on the beach. The moon spilled silver on their faces, beautiful faces—she counted Maya, Angel, Mercedes, Edison, Derek, Miguel, and Lourdes. At JoJo's feet sat Marilena. They were complete. She wanted to step out there, be part of the secret. She held her breath, watching, hoping they wouldn't see her. Hoping she could just be a part of this moment without disturbing them. Flounder leapt from the window and ran circles among their legs, around their bodies. They looked toward her.

"Who's there?" she asked. "Who is it?"

"Come on out, if you want," JoJo told her. "I brought them to see you."

"Hey, Ate Isabel," said Lourdes. And the others called out, voices soft as wind chimes blowing at midnight, as children waking from sleep.

Third-Graders Making Burial Jars. Independence Elementary. Virginia Beach, VA. October 1996.
Photo by Isa Manalo

The children are covered in paint and glitter like someone has decorated them. Grinning, they hold up their milk bottles, their cartons, their empty jelly jars. They've painted them blue and red and hot pink. They've glued them with sticks and shells and comic strips. They've placed in them all the things their ancestors will need on the other side—keys to their houses, lip balm for dry skin, sticks of chewing gum and little handfuls of rice. They stand before large tubs of water, ready to sail the jars home. They are learning that life never ends, just circles around.

She gazed at the crew from her bedroom window. Mostly, they looked tired and small. The sea had tousled them, and when she kissed them she tasted salt on their skin.

"We do awright," Derek said.

"A little hungry, though," Edison said, laughing.

"We gots a new dance," Miguel told her.

"Subversive," Lourdes said. "You up for it?"

Isa nodded her head and the boys ran off the porch to fetch long bamboo poles, a boom box and tape.

Together, they strolled onto the beach, just as the sky lost its veil of darkness and the stars began to shut down. The crew posed still as statues, waiting for the music with the sea as their backdrop. Isa grabbed onto JoJo's arm, her hands weak and trembling.

The mandolin announced the traditional dance. Bamboo poles slid together like two hands clapping. A waltz began. Boys stepped quickly and stiffly through a bamboo canal, the girls flitting in and out of the poles, waving their hands up high like beautiful fans. There were no smiles on the faces, only stoic expressions, expressions of indifference.

Isa held her breath and conjured up indigenous people in the fields, making sugar cane for Spanish guards, serving priests as maids, as cooks and concubines.

"Autoridad—the man—el conquistador—called our peeps barbaric. Uncivilized!" Elvie shouted. "Didn't know we was on to dem and subversive."

Elvie spread his arms out and surveyed the land. "Homies didn't go down without a fight. Tinikling was a dance to train the tribe to beat the switch of conquistador's reed, the sharp whack of bamboo at our feet! Resistance always in our blood!"

When the last measure of the mandolin played out, Puff Daddy's rap hit the air. The kids nodded their heads, swayed their torsos, pumped their shoulders to the beat.

The dancers slipped into new roles, became the New People's Army, guerrillas hiding out in the mountains, fighting Marcos and the presence of U.S. military bases. They crawled on their bellies and whispered, "Isa, dalawa, tatlo. Ayaw ko! Isa, dalawa, tatlo. Ayaw ko!"

Isa turned to JoJo, whispering, "One, two, three, I don't want it?"

He kissed her on the cheek, a little smile on his lips. "Now you walk the walk and talk the talk."

"They did this?" she said, moving her body to the beat too.

"You got that."

The crew slid the poles, grooved like snakes to the hip-hop beat of Puff Daddy and Tupac. They raised bamboo high. The guerrillas weaved their way in and out of the bamboo sky. "Ayaw ko!" The rhythm was slow, the beat sinking heavy in their hips and in the step of their walk. Down, down, up. Down, down, up. Down, down, up. Ay-aw-ko! Down, down, up. Ay-aw-ko! Resistance was always part of their ancestry, their blood.

Isa closed her eyes, swayed to the beat, feeling it hit all her joints, popping her body into place. She went deep inside to the darkest part of the night and found the New People's Army chanting in the chambers of her heart. She leapt up from her seat and joined them on the beach, darting her small frame in and out of bamboo cages, kicking sand up as she moved to the boom-boom-pop/boom-boom-pop/boom-boom-pop of Tupac, Puff Daddy, and her crew.

For breakfast, Isa cooked chicken adobo. She steamed a fresh pot of rice. They waited on the porch, where Derek strummed his guitar and they played crazy eights. Maya came in with her.

"I've really missed you guys," Isa told her. "Especially you." Maya's face was swollen, her hair falling in giant strands across her face.

"We're makin' it. Don't worry." She fished in the drawers for silverware and napkins. She had grown broad in the back.

"Have you been shooting any photos?" Isa asked. She stirred the chicken and a waft of vinegar, soy sauce, ginger and garlic curled out of the pot.

Maya turned toward her and threw a packet of photos on the table. "Look," she said. "Your copy."

At Ate Isa's
Homegirls from da pageant pile on Ate Isa's sofa, reading brain books and eating bowls of pansit. Ate Isa in the middle, holding our man Flounder—a.k.a. HOMES. He's one crazy cat.

On da Beach
These are my homies asses all lined up and walkin on the shore at Chick's Beach. Edison's jeans fit six of Derek. Check out Miguel's shirt. Comes down past his knees like a nightie. These are my brothas. The sky is all full of clouds like its gonna rain. They walk in a line, shoulders drooping to the ground like they know its gonna rain.

Elvie at the Mall
In the background the boyz stand with arms out, their faces all squished up like worried mothas. Elvie's facin off with our man the security guard. The guard much bigger than Elvie fills half da frame. Elvie looks over his shoulder. Grins a shit grin.

The Crew as En Vogue
My girls pose pretty—made up like funky high fashion models on the cover of a zine.

And then there was a series of wounds, of markings carved crudely in their skin. Extreme close-ups captured the texture of scars, how they disrupted the beautiful flow of fine skin, how they rose from the landscape of the body in ugly little volcanoes.

"What's this?" Isa asked. She flipped through the photos, and when Maya saw she grabbed at the stack.

"Not those. Those aren't yours."

"Too late." Isa shuffled through them. In some of the photos the girls were partially nude. Scars were everywhere—on the melon of a breast, on the inner thigh, on the small of the back. There was a close-up of a belly, pouting. Fat with someone just becoming. "Is this you?"

Maya's pitcher of water shook in her hand. She nodded.

"How many months?"

"I dunno. Six, maybe. Seven. I dunno."

"Has JoJo seen these?"

Maya put the pitcher on the table and water spilled everywhere.

TWENTY-THREE

Outside the wind moaned like a mother grieving. Palm trees swayed violently, bending low to the oceanfront. Debris—plastic cups, newspapers, grocery bags—sailed across the street as Lourdes and the girls cruised Pacific Boulevard.

Hurricane season hit Tidewater with great rage, and every few days the skies grew black. Sand, cast by angry winds, assaulted their bodies. The cold numbed their bones. The rest of the world ran into their houses, marking windows with giant tape marks shaped like the letter "X," taking all the jugs of water from the grocery stores, the plastic bags and candles, stealing matches from bars and local restaurants, withdrawing hundreds of dollars out of cash machines—hurricane money. Las Dalagas carried on, undaunted by the threats of Hurricanes Amanda, Beatrice, Carly and Daphne. Every time the radio called them, the world went crazy, but the hurricanes never came. "They on Flip time?" Angel joked.

"Doubt it," Marilena answered. Now Tidewater waited for Emilia.

"Where's Maya?" Lourdes asked.

The girls looked at one another, shrugged their shoulders.

"Whatever," Ria said, "let's cruise."

The speakers in Lourdes's hatchback pumped hip-hop. The whole car vibrated. Las Dalagas nodded and moaned, spoke every little word and sighed. Despite the lack of sun, each girl wore dark glasses—looked onto streets shaded for disaster. Hurricanes bored them. Where were the boys?

Maya put the pitcher on the table and water spilled everywhere. Ice tumbled to the floor, iridescent pellets of hail hitting the linoleum. The sting of the water dripping down her pant leg scared her. She jumped, knocking the pitcher across the table. This shattered too. She collapsed on the floor, soaked her tired body in a puddle of ice and wept.

Ate Isa embraced her, hushed her, but Maya only cried all the harder. The more Ate Isa told her everything was going to be okay, the more the tears came. Maya was so mad at herself. "Fuck this," she said.

"What happened?" Isa asked her.

"Nothing," Maya answered. For months Maya followed Ate Isa around, hoping she would notice something was wrong. Didn't she see Maya was gaining weight? Couldn't she tell she wasn't eating so good? How about all the times she was dizzy with fatigue? The night of the youth dialogue, when she was nestling in Kenny's arms, she caught Ate Isa's shadow at the bottom of the stairs. She had moaned long and low, hoping it would make her come running, demand she tell her everything. But instead, Ate Isa slipped away. Like she didn't give a fuck. Like she didn't care.

"Tell me everything," Ate Isa said.

"Why should I?" But Maya wanted to, and now she didn't know how. She wanted to tell someone, but who she gonna tell? Homegirls would have her ass if they knew Kenny got her pregnant. She wasn't supposed to go near him, especially after what happened with Arturo. Her parents would die. She had hoped to tell Ate Isa, but the longer it took, the harder it became.

Kenny and Maya had fallen for each other. The most unlikely pair, he tall and slender with a moon face and she short and curvy—rolling flesh at the hips, in the breasts, where the waist should have been. But they were drawn together and there was nothing anyone could say. Kenny wooed her, put his arms under her two-moon ass and floated her away. That homeboy was Norfolk. He was blood, but from a different baranggay. Maya was ordered to stay away from him, to keep to herself. First it was her own homegirls who warned her, sister mermaids trash-talking Kenny about his peeps, his territory. And when tsismis hit the air,

Inday Romero and her Norfolk crew couldn't handle it. They stalked her and Kenny, shouting out, "Don't you fuck with our boy!" So Arturo, who was like her brother, all sweet and fresh, tried talking to them, make it cool with them. Even flirted just a little bit with them so everybody would chill. "Let's get along cuz we still blood," he sang to Inday's crew. But the Filomafia wouldn't have it, couldn't stand it. They pictured Arturo with their homegirls and it made them crazy with hate.

They shot him down when his hands were up in the air, raising the roof, breaking it down. His eyes were shut and his head was tilted to a red light, and he was smiling like he had been kissed by an angel. He never saw it coming. They shot him down like it was an accident. Like oops, the bullet gone through the window and shot you down. Guess you can't mess with our girls now, homeboy. She saw Filomafia riding off in their souped-up cars, arms sailing from the back seat windows, shaking their heads like, Whatever . . .

Maya's heart soaked up all that blood. She had all kinds of crazy nightmares, and even though she knew it was because of her and Kenny, it was Kenny she ran to. She'd fall asleep weeping in his arms, the two of them wrapped like kittens, curled up with their arms and legs overlapping. Arturo would speak to her in the middle of the night, say, "Ain't no big thing. If it's love, let it happen. Don't let them take you down."

Maya and Kenny tried to split, but it was no good. They snuck around like shadows, tucked away in alcoves by the beach. Still they got found out. And after Inday's crew jumped her, scraped the skin off her face and maimed her, they tried to split again. She stopped returning his pages, but he kept on paging her twenty-four-seven. They got hungrier and fat with all that sadness. All that hate drew them together, made them want to hold onto each other, kissing all over just so they wouldn't have to be alone.

Maya told Ate Isa how hungry she had been. "I just kept eating and eating so's when I got a little taba, I said whatever. Di ba, they call me Taba? But then I stopped my period. Then I started tossing all the food. Then nothin' looked good. And I say, that's not me. All food looks good to me. Twenty-four-seven. Know what I mean?"

The aunties called her Taba. Maya learned to laugh every time they said it, covered up the hurt pinching at her heart. She knew they made tsismis at parties, at churches, at grocery stores. Good thing she understood only a little bit. Ang taba! Kita mo, ng pwet! Naku! Laki ng tiyan. Di ba? Taba! Parang buntis si Maya. Then the aunties squeezed her face, her arms, even slapped her on the rump. Sayang, they lamented. Too bad. And she laughed and kissed them just in case they really were just joking around.

"Oh, Maya!" Ate Isa said, pulling Maya's hair back into a ponytail. She began braiding it. She told Maya that tsismis drove her out of the Midwest—the sensation that everywhere you went people were looking at you, whispering. It drove her crazy.

"No shit," Maya said. "I know that."

When she suspected the worst, Maya locked herself up in her girl-teen bathroom, lined with the black and white photographs she had shot and blown up into wallpaper. She pulled out the box, reading the tiny print on how to take the test. The popsicle stick turned pink. Pink like the sun rising, pink like rose petals, pink like pregnancy.

"What did that feel like?" Ate Isa asked her. "When you found out you were pregnant?"

"What do you think?"

Nobody guessed she was pregnant. Kenny was clueless. He loved her body. Maya said he loved how large she was, how he could spend hours holding onto her, exploring her, feeding her love. She wanted to die.

She went to the ocean on the full moon and she undressed. She examined her body under the golden light. It was so round, circles of fat looping everywhere. It was so smooth. She stepped into the water and felt her skin prickle up from the cold. She waded in until her breasts came bobbing up with all that seawater. She swam in circles, let her belly float up above the surface of the water. The moon kissed her, calmed her. The water made her body so shiny and soft. The salt teased her, made her thirsty. She swam for hours, trying to figure out what to do. Who to tell? Where to go? She spied on Ate Isa, living all alone, a strong ate. She waited. "But you didn't even notice."

"I did. I noticed." Ate Isa frowned, like she was uncertain here. "I knew something was wrong. I saw you at the picnic too. You and Kenny.

But I didn't want to pry. I didn't want to push." Now Ate wept too. "It's so hard to know how to handle you guys. I figured you'd come to me if you needed me."

"I did." Maya closed her eyes, felt herself bursting wide open, spilling everywhere. Her whole body shook and all the worries trembled right out of her, leaving her hiccupping and worn out like the time she had been jumped and all the fists finally stopped beating down on her. It was that kind of relief.

"It's too deep," Maya said. "Too fucked up. We sneaking around cuz people too stupid to mind their business. Ain't no one's call who you love, ain't that right? But look what they did to Arturo. What they gonna do when they hear this?"

Ate Isa promised it would get easier now. "You're not alone anymore," she said.

Maya didn't want her parents to know. She threw her fists down on her thighs when Ate Isa suggested it. She accused her of abandonment. "But sweetheart," Ate Isa told her, "they have to know. You need help. You need medical attention. The baby will."

She promised to go with Maya. She promised the girl she wouldn't be alone. When Ate Isa was pregnant, she was scared shitless. In fact she waited until it was over, until the baby had given up, like it knew she was embarrassed and decided to leave her. They had to guess. They had to guess because her face went gaunt and all the color drained from her life. Her skin had a blue tint. Garish black streaks circled her eyes. She wore black and black and black. They guessed something had happened. Something went wrong, and even then—even when they guessed—she was reluctant. Ate Isa said she should have spilled the news from the start. Now she saw how they understood; then she knew only fear. And even after the miscarriage, she believed she had shamed them. That the world would look at the Manalos and say, "Anak nila? Walang hiya." No respect. Shameless.

Maya held her camera out the car window and peered through the viewfinder like this would help, like seeing the world in thirty-five millimeters would somehow comfort her. Through the lens she saw a blur of color, the world zipping by at sixty miles per hour, running together and swirling. They had rolled the windows down, cranked the radio and let the bass blast them right past Mount Trashmore. Wind filled the cab, made it difficult to talk.

"I'm glad you're doing this," Ate Isa yelled over the boom-ba-boom of the radio.

Maya felt her gaze, felt her tugging at her sleeve, but she continued to shoot out the window. She knew she was wasting film. Everything would come out just like she felt, out of focus and spilling off the page.

"I told you about the time I was pregnant—remember? The hardest thing was telling my parents, but that's because, well . . ." Maya glared at her. "Never mind," Ate Isa said. "I'm just glad you're finally going home."

Maya's baby stretched her tummy like a crescent moon rising. She circled her hand over her stomach, let it run the course of her body—all curvy and full.

"It's okay," Ate Isa told her. "It's all right. You wouldn't believe how amazing love is, how forgiving." But Maya was afraid. Other girls who got pregnant got sent away. Some of them gave the babies up for adoption. Some of them raised the baby as one of their siblings. Hardly anyone married a boy. Who married a boy when you were sixteen? "Right, but did anyone stop loving the girl with the baby? Probably not," Ate Isa said. "Maybe they got angry. Maybe there were fights. But I can almost bet my life, the loving was still there."

Maya imagined her parents raging around their tiny house. Maybe her mother would clutch her chest, fall into the sofa with a broken heart. Maybe her father would stop seeing her, go blind. Maybe the sistas would walk out on her. Maybe Kenny would forget he loved her. She thought she saw a flash of something out of the corner of her eye. She held the camera up again. She clicked at the breeze, at a cloud. She imagined Arturo sitting in the back seat, leaning over to her and saying, "It's all good, Maya."

"Maya!" Isa yelled. "Maya?" She turned down the radio and rolled up the windows. "Maya," she said quietly.

Maya looked at her, wiping away the tears stinging her eyes.

"How long has it been since I moved here—almost a year, right?" Maya nodded. "Do you know what I've learned in a year that I should have always known?"

Maya bowed her head. Ran her fingers round her stomach. "You're Pinay?"

"Funny. I learned to trust my tribe."

"You mean the crew?"

"I mean the family."

"Calhoun or Tita Nita find out you hanging with me, they gonna kick you out."

"Doesn't matter," Ate Isa told her. "If they aren't going to let me do my job, then they might as well kick me out."

Shoot dang, Maya thought. Thas deep.

When they got to the house, Maya's mother welcomed them in. She opened the door and wrapped her arms around her daughter. Maya cried and cried. They sat at the kitchen table where Mommy fed them cassava cake and coke. Egg rolls and rice. Kare kare and pan de sal. A mix of salty and sweet, of bitter and tart. They waited for Papa to come home, and when he joined them at the table, Ate Isa held Maya's hand. Maya's tears grew into words, fell from her mouth and washed over her family. That night, the secrets that had been filling up inside her—obstructing her breath, making painful pockets of air—left her body and she felt lighter than she had in a long time. Her father tossed about the room, his voice hitting the walls, making curtains fly, shaking the lamps. Ate Isa squeezed her hand tight. Tears rained down her mother's face. "I don't care what you say," she told her husband. "Anak ko yan. No matter what. Hija mo rin. Think, mahal." She got up and wrapped her arms around Maya and they waited for Papa to calm down. And when the storm had passed, Maya watched Ate Isa get in her car and make her way home.

TWENTY-FOUR

Ten in the morning and the skies were darker than after sunset. The wind chimed like the death knell of a child, sweeping the earth with long arms and leaving a battery of dirt whirling in its wake. The sea churned, unsettled by giant gusts of wind. Schools of fish scattered. Fingers of algae rooted themselves to rock and coral spun to freedom. A girl tribe of sirens gathered, moaned the blues, rattled scat, and breathed the wind.

The sun refused to lift its heavy head. Clouds crowded its mind like a migraine, made the act of rising too unbearable.

Residents at the beach lined up in their cars. They piled their mini-vans with all their precious cargo. The children. The dog. The cats and parakeets. A child filled a plastic bag with water and two goldfish. A convoy of vans, like Noah's Ark, headed for higher ground.

Climbing the roof at the Cultural Center, JoJo, Ferdi and the boys unwound fat rolls of masking tape, making giant X's on the glass like targets. The wind bullied them, made their weight shift. Made their hair fly all over the place. It was hard to see anything. It was so dark, and the debris flew everywhere. They almost lost Elvie to the wind.

Across town, Tita Chic Chic stocked gallons of bottled water on her basement shelves. She reached with her whole body to make room for all of it. Next to her, Uncle Oscar stacked cans of Spam. He filled up three flashlights with six C batteries. "Anak," he yelled to the girl upstairs, "bring down the candles. Make sure you put them in plastic. The matches too."

Far from the ocean, Lola Espie reached for the fixtures. She shifted her body, leaned out of her wheelchair, nearly falling against the big white tub. With one hand she held herself; with the other she turned the knob. Cold water rose to the top, echoing and splashing as the tub filled. So, just in case, she'd have fresh water. Okay. Gritting her teeth, she pushed her body up with two hands. The wheels rolled a little bit away from her, and she nearly fell out of the chair again. Perspiration dotted her brow like dew on petals. She made the sign of the cross. Kissed her beads. Began reciting the rosary.

Macmillan and Smith cruised the streets. The main roads were stopped. Everybody was trying to get out. The side streets were empty. Like ghost towns in the west. No tumbleweeds, though. Only empty plastic bags billowed, ballooned like something beautiful. The cops pulled into a bank and waited behind other cars at the cash machine. Hurricane money.

The wailing was so loud, it transcended the wind and all the angels of rain. The lights flickered, and when Maya reached her mother, she put her arms around her and held her, as if to still the crying. "Anak, anak," her mother cried. "Anak." No longer able to bear the suffering, Maya left her there, sneaking out of the house, windbreaker in hand.

Isa had never really been through the rituals of pending hurricanes. She didn't know that when the news anchors warned them to move away from the shore, they meant it. She poured herself another cup of coffee. She flipped through photos, burned the images in her mind. Flounder paced along the windows, spun in little circles. Meowed at the wind. Isa was too distracted to care. "It's only rain," she told the cat.

*

Last night, there was no sleeping. Every time Isa closed her eyes, she saw Maya standing with her arms stretched out, her belly sagging like she had swallowed the moon. Isa heard Maya sobbing, saw the girl's whole body weeping, and yet Isa would walk right past her. The whole time Maya was hanging in Isa's home, she had been mourning Arturo's death, feeling responsible and unable to say it. No wonder he lived in the walls of the house. No wonder he was there with Isa now.

"I should let you go," she whispered. "Send you off at last."

She knew that if she had been a little smarter, maybe asked the right questions, she would have spared Maya this pain. She wondered how often Maya had brought Kenny into the house when she was in school. How often she had lent them this moment to make a baby.

"Aw, Isa," JoJo said, "how would you know?"

"Did you know?" She looked him in the eye, at the way his eyelashes curled back and revealed the pupils—dark and shiny and naked. "Don't you feel responsible?" she asked him. "You knew. At least I didn't know."

"Course not." He reasoned with her by pulling up her shirt and running his hand round her belly. "There's only so much you can do."

"That's crazy," she said, and rose to pace her bungalow.

JoJo followed her out of bed, like a shadow, but noisy and relentless. He wanted to know what was so crazy about that. "Talk to me," he begged. He smelled of sandalwood and toothpaste. Picking up Maya's photos, Isa shuffled them like tarot cards. She piled them into stacks. Past. Present. Future. What is the circumstance? What is the action? What is the outcome? What is tribe? Everything was her fault. Then she worked herself up, thinking about that crazy Tita Nita. Grabbing her hands before she could shuffle the pictures again, JoJo kissed her. "What are you talking 'bout?"

She danced around him, reluctant to explain. "She said she was waiting for me to ask her what's the matter," she said.

"She knew you were cool," he said. "She could have offered it up."

"You don't understand. This whole time I've been saying that my parents never heard me, didn't listen, and wouldn't let me talk about my problems. And I go and do the same thing."

"But you said they cared. So what's the matter?"

"They do, but I didn't know that. And this whole time I'm hanging back because I think the kids don't want to be pushed. Look at Lourdes. Man, I bet she's got problems."

They walked the shore. The air felt heavy, like it wanted to cry. Rising high under a full moon, the tide had created bridges of sandbars and shimmering pools of ocean. More signs of the impending storm.

"Look, stop feeling sorry for yourself. It sucks. You fucked up, but you figured it out. Maya's cool now." His teeth were so big and white.

"Yeah, but I'm not going to hold back anymore. Did you see those pictures? Do you see what they're doing to themselves?"

He led her up a hill so they could see the sea rolling in, and the moon reflecting light everywhere. "Close your eyes," he told her. "Close your eyes and listen." She heard the water shifting back and forth, regular as breathing. She fingered the rosary in her pocket, rattled the beads in her hand. Whispering, the wind blew sighs, scattering issues in her head like particles of sand. It was getting harder to tell who was the enemy. Is there an enemy? The wind whistled. Shush, shush, shush, said the water. Holy Mary, said her heart, Mother of God. Pray for us. The tide chanted, steady as a tribal drum. She thought she heard Las Dalagas swimming in the current, giggling like dolphins, cooing like sirens, splashing at one another with their hands, their fins fat and glittery with scales. "Sometimes those girls are so much like I was," she told him. "And sometimes they are little aliens." She was thinking about Maya and the baby. She was thinking about Desa—her long hair, wild as seaweed, and her jaws, clenched and ready for battle. This job was more than Isabel had imagined. A storm broke out inside of her, and she began to rain.

The water washed over the land as if to say, Be still, don't worry, somehow you will find your way. Let the water calm you, let the water quiet you. Things will be okay. JoJo let her weep, let her speak all her stories. He cried with her and kissed her gently, made it so there'd be no sleep. No worry. No sleep. No rest. Only dreaming and the sea.

*

This morning she gazed out the window, running her hand down Flounder's back. His gray was so deep it was almost blue. He was blue as midnight, silver like stars. Spoiled kitty. She yanked on his tail. "Yeah," she whispered, "you like that, don't you?"

Debris flew past her windowpane—twigs and paper and leaves, feathers and branches. She thought she saw a bird batting its wings, resisting the current of wind. She thought she saw a vapor of smoke, like a ghost, like a dream, like a boy she once knew. She thought she saw his face, a face she had not dreamed of in a long while. His Alibata tattoo scarring the black sky like a letter from God. Flounder leapt from her arms, scared of her racing heart. Meowed at her, angry that she had disrupted his love moment.

She picked up the packet of photos and grabbed her purse and keys.

Outside it began to rain. The water fell like sadness. The wind rocked her wagon as she flew down 264. She felt like that lady from *The Wizard of Oz*, the one who rode her bike in the middle of the storm.

If she could help, she would. If the girls needed someone to talk to, she'd be the one. She didn't care about the job. Fuck the job, she thought. Maybe they were waiting for her the way Maya had been waiting. Maybe they weren't waiting for her but for anyone, anyone who would hear them.

She pulled into Tita Nita's driveway and ran up the walk, holding her hand before her like a shield. Pounding the door, she stood in the porch, where the motion light shined on her and on the black morning. The rain fell in sheets. Maybe they couldn't hear her. Maybe the storm was too loud. She rang the doorbell, and when Tita Nita opened the door the older woman's eyes got wide. "Go home, anak," she said, shutting Isabel out.

Isa clutched the stack of pictures—the evidence—under her shirt so they wouldn't be rained on. She knocked again. Rang the doorbell. No answer now. She leaned her head back and opened her mouth, took a drink of rain. Then she noticed the garage door, its mouth wide open and two cars parked underneath the eaves along with bicycles and lawnmowers, grills and lost bamboo poles. Yes, she thought, making a dash for the garage. At the kitchen door, Lourdes's little sister Lila welcomed her in. Kissed her on the cheek.

Las Dalagas stowed their backpacks, their bundles of clothing, and their snacks into the purple crate. Marilena took her windbreaker and wrapped it around her waist and, leaning over, she pushed with all her strength. "Come on, you guys," she called to them. Lourdes ran to the front of the crate and pulled. "Maya, Ria, up here," she told them. The wind tossed sand at their skin, felt like an army of ants biting at their faces, their necks, their bare arms. The girls answered the wind, howling as they pushed and pulled the crate, now loaded with their belongings, across the sand.

A used condom hit Mercedes in the forehead. "Fuck," she said, holding it in her fingers. She tossed it back to the wind and rolled her feet into the sand, kicking off her shoes. She felt the earth conform below her, the sand shifting with each step. She continued dragging the crate toward the water. Their voices were lost now, trailing out to sea without being heard. Their hair flew across their faces. "Sure this is a good thing?" Mercedes cried out to Lourdes.

But Lourdes couldn't hear her. She was focused on the task. Peeking over her shoulder, she yanked at the planks of wood. Her hand slipped, a nail broke, a sliver of wood needled its way into her skin. She figured the water was only another few hundred feet away.

Maya leaned into her ear and hollered, "Dis is dangerous!" She thought about her baby swimming laps in her belly, all wet and slippery as a fish.

"I bet we sail with dolphins!" Lourdes called back. "I hear them out there!" The sky swirled, angry as the historic battle between sky and sea, and Lourdes considered how the islands of the Philippines were born. She wondered what Ate Isa would say when she heard how brave they'd been.

The house hummed, all its electricity intact. It glowed gold because all the lights were on, resisting the dark skies, the heaviness of air.

"Thanks, Lila," Isa said. "Where's your mommy?"

Lila pointed to the bathroom. "Just wait." She handed Isabel a towel to dry herself.

"Where's your ate?" Isa asked. "I need to talk to her."

Lila shrugged. "Beats me. Out."

When Tita Nita opened the door and saw Isa at her kitchen table, she yelled. "Do you want me to call the police?"

"I just want to talk to you. I want to show you." She extended her arm, offering the manila envelope, but Tita Nita swung at it.

"Why can't you understand, you are embarrassing us when you do these things." The envelope sailed across the room and the photos

316

fluttered from its mouth like a million dollar bills. Isa watched the girls in mid-air, and for a moment she imagined them frozen in space, pissed off and proud, their wounds exposed. Isa stretched out her arms as if to catch the pictures, but the images scattered across Tita Nita's kitchen floor, bled under the light of her yellow lamp. Maya's pregnant belly filled an entire page like a globe of the world.

"We have to pay attention," Isa said. "We have to hear them out. Can you see what they're doing?"

She gathered the photos one by one and held them up. Tita Nita could not help herself. She took the pictures in her hands and ran her fingers over the scars, over the faces of her Lourdes, the dalagas, the boys. The children had a world of their own, a language of their own. Isa watched Tita's face open up wide like a child's entering the world for the first time. She felt Tita walking in the spaces of the photographs, circling the teens, who were frozen in time. She was like a tourist in a gallery of waxed figures. She was looking for the first time, and she was seeing them—Isa could tell from the way Tita's body moved in shifts and starts of horror.

"This is a secret they keep," Isa said.

Tita Nita flipped through the images. Over and over. "Oh my gosh," she whispered. "Oh my God."

Miss Virginia Beach-Philippines 1996. Chick's Beach, VA. August 1995.
Photo by Maya Antaran

She sits on a rock with knees pointed in two directions, a hand resting on her skinny thigh. Blue jeans so tight, even Miss Thing's rolling fat in little waves round her middle. Mascara trails the corners of her eyes like the end of a nightmare. The howling wind scares her crazy hair up high to the sky. Puffing on Virginia Slims, she picks sand from her nails. Waits for the sun to rise. Blows smoke the shape of silver bracelets. Her crown has fallen to the sand like an empty soda can, its rhinestones shining like cheap glitter. Hanging loose around her flat chest, she still wears that sash all crumpled and stained. "You look like shit," Maya yells over the roar of the sea. She racks the lens, snaps the focus against a sea of fog and captures the reigning queen of the beach, holding her hand up, giving everyone the finger.

Isa was waiting, and when Tita Nita lifted her gaze, she knew it wasn't good. "I don't know where you got these," Tita Nita said, "but you better never show them again. I'm telling you now, they do these things because you are bad influence. You teach them to talk back, to be wild.

You are too American and this is affecting the kids. You stop now, okay. Just stop."

It was pointless. Grabbing the pictures from Tita Nita, Isa slid them back into the envelope. "Okay," she said. "It would be better if you helped. It would make it easier for Lourdes, but I can do this alone."

She walked out into the storm, the rain falling everywhere, drenching her. The hurricane spat cool water onto her hot skin, washed away all the agony.

On the highway, wipers thump, thump, thumped across the glass. They went fast, but they couldn't wash away the blur of the storm. She couldn't see beyond the hood of the station wagon. Something tickled her leg. The rain had found a way inside.

She heard her dad, telling her this was about opportunity. She nodded, as if he were there next to her. She said, "Yes." She resolved to act on this. To move beyond the elders. To hell with tsismis and hiya. The tires slipped and the station wagon swerved out of line. She let the wheel turn, and gently pulled it back the other way.

The water streaked before her in sheets. In shapes. Water fell like a flock of butterflies beating at her windshield. She couldn't see what was in front of her, and the water showering down her car made it hard for her to hear anything but rain. She leaned over the steering wheel and squinted at the road, letting her foot weigh down the accelerator. The car was lost in a cloud of water, and still she moved through the storm, tires whirring down sleek streets, brake lights blinking red, wipers whipping back and forth steady as the heart.

Her car was the only one on the road, slipping toward home like a fish out of water. She flipped on the radio, sang to the B-52's, and her voice filled the cab of the car and echoed. She was a retro rock star with a beehive, false lashes, and vinyl go-go boots. She got lost in the bass, in the boom chick-a-boom of it all. The rain was seeping in now from a crack in her window— the dashboard, too. She took a long breath and sighed. She blinked and then it happened.

The rain was coming from inside her too. The world spun like a load of wash, everything colliding, wet and indiscernible. And in the windshield she saw visions of Arturo and Maya and Lourdes and Kenny tumbling about. She saw them in parts—two lean legs, silver fish, brown arms cut and tattooed, a pair of breasts scarred and beautiful, seaweed for hair. She saw the globe of Kenny's bald head rising, and then the smile of an infant. She saw the lacy wrinkled skin of Lola Espie hanging like a curtain over the windshield. She felt Ferdi's breath fogging up her vision. Still squinting, she leaned over and wiped the windshield with the palm of her hand. When she had cleared a little patch of window, Tita Nita's greasy red lip prints smeared across the windshield. This time she used a tissue to clear the lens before her. Even Flounder's wide whiskers flashed like crazy window wipers. She was not a retro rock star after all. She was Isa Manalo and they were all in front of her, floating like astronauts, reaching for everything and nothing. Her spirit baby, webbed feet and all, danced among the tumbling images of teens, mermaids, community leaders. Baby raised the roof, hip-hopped to bamboo poles and candlelight. And in that moment, Isa made a vow to herself. There was an image of her in that rainwater, a Midwestern Pinay in her thirties, chilling with the crew, listening to them, sharing her own story. Isa had a memory of what it was like and what it could be. She could see it. Finally.

Water fell in heavy sheets, soaking their clothing tight to the skin. Ria shook her head at Lourdes. "I don't want to do this!" she yelled. Her skin was riddled with tiny goosebumps. Her lips felt blue and swollen.

But Lourdes only smiled, opened her mouth and drank the rain. "How dope is this," Lourdes said. "How fuckin' dope!" Their feet slipped into the sea. Wet sand stuck to their skin, dirtied the cuffs of their rolled-up jeans. "Get in!" she told them. Ria shook her head no. "Don't be a baby," Lourdes said. "Get in, Dalagas. Do it now!" She climbed into the crate and told the others to push. Maya locked eyes with her and for a moment there was stillness between them. "I don't think so," Maya said.

"What the fuck? Are you checkin' out?"

"This is messed up!" Maya shouted. But Lourdes stared her down, so Maya pulled her body up. But she couldn't lift high enough. The rain weighed her down. Her body resisted. She didn't know why she was going. It was stupid.

"Again, again!" Lourdes commanded.

Maya pulled her body up again. Her arms quivered underneath her weight as she tried to flip herself into the crate. The ends of her hair stung her face like a thousand miniature whips. The wind carried her backward into the white foam. For a moment she disappeared and the water rushed down her throat and filled her up. Everything tasted salty and raw. When she opened her eyes underwater, she saw everything. It was as if God had set free a herd of pissed-off elephants, all of them trumpeting, rampaging and roaring, pounding at the bottom of the sea. She opened her mouth wide as if to scream, but the ocean swallowed her up. She worried her baby was drowning in salt. She worried he would not be strong enough to swim against an angry ocean.

Mercedes, Ria and Angel waved their hands and plunged into the tide after her. She could feel their hands on her body and her body kept slipping away. Long fingernails grazed her skin, and she thought about the day she had been jumped, at the way the Norfolk girls clawed at her skin. Her face had bled for hours. When she emerged from the water, she was weeping, thrashing her arms and legs, pushing them away. "Forget it," she said. She waved them away.

Marilena shivered, felt her lips go numb. "Whatever. Let me push the crate a little deeper," she said. "Hold on. Mercedes, help me! Angel!" Together the girls shoved the homemade balikbayan box further out to sea. Mercedes and Marilena crawled into the crate effortlessly. They called to Angel, who only shook her head at them, wrapped her arms around her skinny body.

"I can't!" she screamed. "My parents will kill me!"

Everything went black. The waves tossed them like a sailboat in a child's bath. Lourdes saw the tunnel, narrow and spinning east toward the Pacific, toward the islands. She tasted salt. She understood that freedom was near. Maya was stupid to give up so easily. The fearless boat weaved its way up and down the white caps, in and out of rain, and Lourdes felt strong. She reached her hands up to the sky and stretched her body. *Pintig is the beat of the Filipino heart.* She loved the sea in tumult. Looking back, she saw Angel, Maya and Ria, three little pins against the expansive beach. Smiling, she raised her brown fist to the sky. *Pintig. Pintig. Pintig.* The sky rained down warm water, tasted sweet on the tongue. Not far from them, a family of dolphins rose out of the sea and guided them through the turbulent waters. The girls released a battle cry so loud and so shrill, even sea sirens covered their ears. Las Dalagas egged Hurricane Emilia on. Defied her. The craft spun like a ride at a carnival, and just as Lourdes imagined, the angry hurricane lifted them up and catapulted them to the sky.

photo by Diane Yokes

M. Evelina Galang was born in Harrisburg, Pennsylvania and lived in seven different cities before settling down and growing up in Brookfield, Wisconsin. The author of *Her Wild American Self*, a collection of short stories, and the editor of *Screaming Monkeys: Critiques of Asian American Images*, Galang is the recipient of numerous awards, among them the 2004 Gustavus Myers Outstanding Book Award sponsored by the Gustavus Myers Center for the Study of Bigotry and Human Rights and the 2004 AWP Award Series in the Novel, for this book, *One Tribe*. She is currently writing *Lolas' House: Women Living With War*, personal histories of surviving Filipina comfort women of World War II. Galang teaches in the MFA Creative Writing Program at the University of Miami.